THE
OTHER
YOU

ALSO BY CARYS GREEN

Always on My Mind

THE OTHER YOU

CARYS GREEN

HARVILL

1 3 5 7 9 10 8 6 4 2

Harvill, an imprint of Vintage, is part of the Penguin Random House group of companies

Vintage, Penguin Random House UK, One Embassy Gardens,
8 Viaduct Gardens, London SW11 7BW

penguin.co.uk/vintage
global.penguinrandomhouse.com

First published by Harvill in 2026

Copyright © Carys Green 2026

The moral right of the author has been asserted

Penguin Random House values and supports copyright. Copyright fuels creativity, encourages diverse voices, promotes freedom of expression and supports a vibrant culture. Thank you for purchasing an authorised edition of this book and for respecting intellectual property laws by not reproducing, scanning or distributing any part of it by any means without permission. You are supporting authors and enabling Penguin Random House to continue to publish books for everyone. No part of this book may be used or reproduced in any manner for the purpose of training artificial intelligence technologies or systems. In accordance with Article 4(3) of the DSM Directive 2019/790, Penguin Random House expressly reserves this work from the text and data mining exception.

Typeset in 13.2/16pt Garamond Premier Pro by Six Red Marbles UK, Thetford, Norfolk
Printed and bound in Great Britain by Clays Ltd, Elcograf S.p.A.

The authorised representative in the EEA is Penguin Random House
Ireland, Morrison Chambers, 32 Nassau Street, Dublin D02 YH68

A CIP catalogue record for this book is available from the British Library

HB ISBN 9781787304598
TPB ISBN 9781787304604

Penguin Random House is committed to a sustainable future
for our business, our readers and our planet. This book is made
from Forest Stewardship Council® certified paper.

For anyone who has ever felt like they weren't enough

Be yourself. Everyone else is already taken.

Anon.

I do not wish [women] to have power over men; but over themselves.

Mary Wollstonecraft

Be You . . . but More!

At More You, we promise more than just an organic clone of yourself. We promise you a better life!

Tired? Overworked? Wrung out?

Find out why thousands have already signed up for the More You programme. Our units are just as unique as you are – they come fully functional and ready to integrate into your life.

They say two hands are better than one; here at More You, we believe that two of you are better than one! Why not come by today for a consultation? See for yourself our outstanding work and bring this flyer for an introductory offer of 10 per cent off a base model.

Discover just how great you can be at More You.

From: POP@outward.co.uk
To: Full Mailing List
Subject: Yesterday

Our banners may be tattered, our throats sore, but our spirit will not be diminished. They can lock us away in cages all they want but still we will rise. It is not us that should be in prison cells but THEM. Until humanity is protected, preserved, we will never cease. We will not stand idly by while this injustice reigns, while we are replaced. Know that we are stronger than ever in our defiance. That we will not stop. Not now, not ever. Not until every last one of them is silenced.

.1

This wasn't how she'd pictured it. Any of it. She wasn't supposed to be teetering upon the edge of exhaustion, the air around her soured with the tang of fresh vomit. Elena Roberts stood upon the soft beige carpet in her bedroom and looked into the mirror atop her dressing table, giving herself a long, hard stare.

It was a mistake. The woman reflected back at her was a stranger. Blonde hair darkened with grease, drawn back in an unflattering top bun that couldn't hide the shadows beneath Elena's usually bright brown eyes. When she'd met Stu her gaze had been bright; now, like the rest of her, it had dulled. Elena dipped her chin, leading her stare south, to the squishy mound of flesh that now counted as a stomach. Still the fresh ribbon of a wound across it burned. Elena winced on cue.

A murmur from the small bundle clutched tightly to her breast.

'Come on.' Elena commenced bouncing gently on the spot, voice soft yet strained. 'You can't be done yet. Come on.'

The little bundle withdrew from her, face pink, mouth widening.

'No, no.' Elena bounced with more urgency. The screaming, she wasn't ready for the screaming. The way it would cut through her, seemingly to the bone. 'Please, Olive, honey, just drink a bit more, okay? Just a bit, for Mummy.'

A mere three weeks old, Olive took a sharp intake of breath before sound exploded through the room.

Elena kept bouncing. Too tired to cry. Almost too tired to stand.

'Come on, please.' Elena closed her eyes as though that might somehow stop the sound from creeping in.

It wasn't supposed to be like this.

Her own mother had spun tales of golden moments with a baby swaddled to her bosom, soothed and content.

'Best thing that ever happened to me,' she'd always tell Elena before kissing her forehead. Elena's mother had been the epitome of pride. Their family home a place where love seemed to pour out of every corner.

Now something other than her scar stung. Loss. It was a knife that would for ever twist in her side.

'Olive, baby, please.' Elena leaned down to whisper against her newborn's head; the sparse scalp was spotted with what looked like the start of cradle cap. Saying the name still stung.

'It's a way of honouring your mother.' Stu had smiled when they'd settled upon it. 'I like it.'

'Won't it seem strange, though,' Elena had pondered in her darker moments, 'giving her name to someone else? *Using* it with someone else?'

'But it's not someone else. It's our daughter.'

Our daughter.

Back when her stomach was swollen, when little kicks were delivered through the night, Elena felt buoyant with excitement. She was going to be a mother. Have a baby. All the love she'd shared with her own parents was about to be handed down, extended. As she lay on the operating table, a blue paper curtain hiding her own body from her, Elena had braced herself for the moment. The magic of it. She was about to lay eyes upon her child for the *first time*. Nauseous, weak with fatigue, she pushed through that to smile at the little collection of arms and legs that was being wrapped in a blanket and carefully placed by her head. Gently, Elena raised a hand, a cannula strapped tight to the back of it. 'Hi, little one,' she rasped. 'Hi, Olive.' Blue eyes squinted at her from a face streaked with white gunk. A stranger's face. Elena didn't see herself. Or Stuart. Or any of the members of her family who had come before her. This new face was small, shrivelled, unfamiliar. Something caught in her throat.

'Okay, Mummy.' A midwife was swiftly lifting Olive back up. 'You can hold her in the next room once we've stitched you back up. Until then, Daddy can have a hold.' The midwife eyed Stu expectantly.

Stuart Roberts, who always knew what to say to anyone. At any time.

'Cocksure,' her mother had commented when she first met him. When Elena's husband walked into a room he filled any remaining space. He wasn't afraid to be loud, confrontational. They'd met when he'd bumped into her outside an English lecture, knocking over the stack of papers she'd been holding. Her first words to him were 'You utter prick.' But he'd won her over. As he usually did most people.

'I hope she has your sense of humour,' she'd told him.

'I hope she has your smile.'

They'd gone on like this throughout her pregnancy, noting parts and attributes like a shopping list, slowly forming their perfect child.

Olive Roberts.

And after a thirty-two-hour unsuccessful labour she'd ended up having an emergency caesarean section.

'It's her age,' Elena had overheard Stu's mother remarking over the phone when he called her with an update. 'I always told you not to leave it so late, she's thirty-six, remember. A geriatric mum.

In my day, we had them young. None of this waiting-around business.'

If Elena hadn't been strapped to a monitor filling the room with the sound of her baby's heartbeat she would have sprung from the bed and snatched the phone out of her husband's hand and screamed '*Bitch!*' into it. Even though she knew Stu would just blame her hormones and try to smooth things over, forever desperate to keep his overbearing cunt of a mother happy.

But she hated that there was truth in the comment. Too much of it. If Elena hadn't waited, her own mother might still have been around to meet her first grandchild. Tears stung her eyes as she looked at the ceiling.

She'd wanted to travel. See the world. Progress in her career. She loved being a surveyor and when she became managing director at her company it felt like everything was falling into place.

Above her fireplace there was a framed photo of her and Stu atop Everest. At twenty-eight she had climbed to the summit. It remained her proudest achievement.

'I've climbed fucking mountains.' Elena locked eyes with the pale woman in the mirror. 'Mountains. I can do this.'

In her arms, Olive continued to howl. A screeching, mewling sound.

'Okay, okay.' Elena moved the baby to rest against her shoulder and began gently tapping her back. 'Here, come on, now. Shhh.'

Mountains.

She could still recall the icy bite of the air, the way her lungs throbbed with the effort of being in the death zone. But it had been worth it. Elena had looked around her, at snowy peaks that pierced through clouds. It felt like she was in another world. No traffic. No emails. No madness. Just the azure stretch of sky, the blinding white of the snow. If heaven did exist, Elena reasoned it would be something like that. Something perfect. Untouched. When Stu reached for her hand to guide her towards the descent, a part of her had wanted to stay.

'We did it,' he'd breathily told her. Elena could barely see his face; he was hidden behind goggles and mouth guards. But his words landed all the same.

'Yes, we did it.'

'Together, we can do anything.'

Elena felt full. Of life, love. All the trite sentiments she usually hated. Things had turned out pretty well between her and the twatty guy who'd knocked all her papers to the floor and then carelessly stomped over them.

When they'd reached base camp and the gap between life and death had rescinded enough to let them start to look ahead, talk turned to babies.

'Are we ready?' Stu had asked.

'Nearly,' Elena mused. 'But first, K2 and Annapurna.'

'You don't want much,' Stu teased, a dimple forming in his cheek.

'I want to do all the impossible things with you.' Elena kissed him.

'You'll kill yourself with this desire to touch the stars,' her mother had wept before each expedition. 'Why do you do this to me, Elena? You are my *world*, baby girl. My whole world.'

'It's the feeling, Mum. Of being infinite. Of connecting with something.'

'Mmm.' Her mother wasn't convinced. 'One day, you'll have children of your own and you'll understand. *Years* this is all taking off my life. You understand? *Years*.'

Her mother had died while Elena was summiting K2.

*

Elena blinked woozily at the mirror, realising that her mind had drifted, that for a few snatched seconds she had possibly been asleep. Still she rhythmically patted Olive's back while the infant continued to scream.

'It's not meant to be like this,' Elena told herself, a single tear escaping from her red raw eye and sliding down her cheek.

.2

Catherine Roberts had waited patiently for the call. She had resisted the urge to just appear on her son's doorstep, knowing her daughter-in-law would disapprove. And the resistance irked her, didn't feel right. Ever since she'd learned, via text, that her granddaughter had been born – her first and only grandchild – she had waited anxiously beside her mobile phone, willing it to ring, incapable of doing anything, even making a simple trip to the shops.

She needed this.

Granted, the announcement arriving via text was less than ideal. She imagined how her own late mother would have responded to such an impersonal delivery of grand news. Catherine had known full well what was expected of her, what wouldn't be accepted. When she'd had Stuey, she'd gone to her mother's house on the way home from hospital. Straight there. No dawdling. With her innards still burning, she'd plastered on a smile for her mother and let her hold her little Stuey, gazing at him with adoration. Because that was the role of the grandmother: to adore and to preen herself over the baby. The role of mother was to work. To feed the baby, breast only, of course, and to keep up with the housework. Catherine had been a *good* mother to both her boys, giving them everything – and a good wife, too. She remembered how tired she'd be when she'd pull herself from a deep sleep, feed Stuey and then tiptoe to the bathroom to carefully apply her lipstick, her mascara, bringing her features from ghostly to passable. All while her husband slept.

Catherine had known her role. Had played it to perfection. She'd known what was expected of her. And now she was to be grandmother. As she waited for her son's call, she paced her grand home, felt the emptiness of each vast room, imagined how they would soon echo with the patter of little feet.

And a girl.

Catherine pressed a jewel-laden hand to her chest as a sigh of elation left her rouge-painted lips.

How she had longed for a girl. She imagined taking her to ballet class, curling her hair, teaching her to pout as she carefully applied lipstick. All these moments that had eluded her were now so tantalisingly close.

Now she was almost seventy; it had been five years since Catherine became a widow. Her husband had dropped down dead on the golf course. A lifetime of whisky and steak had finally caught up with him. But he was not the first man she had loved and lost.

It had been her eldest son, Clive, who first broke her heart. Stolen from her. A motorbike, a slick rain-soaked road. He became the subject of the horror stories other mothers would pass down to their little boys. Mothers who were more careful than she. More lucky.

And then her Stuey, her beloved Stuey, he kept climbing those mountains. One after another. He'd text flippantly about an avalanche here, a storm there. Catherine was convinced that the men in her life were sent to test her. But she wouldn't lose Stuey, she couldn't. He was her everything. And now her Stuey had given her a granddaughter. The greatest gift a son could bestow upon a mother. Catherine's chest swelled at the mere thought of it all. How wondrous it was going to be. She just needed to be called. Summoned.

'Can't I come to the hospital?' she'd asked Stuey when she'd phoned him. Three attempts it had taken before he picked up; on each ring her heart ached with the belief that he was surely ignoring her. Stuey was never far from his beloved phone.

'Mum, no.' She heard the weariness in his voice.

'Let me come, I can help.'

'Elena's exhausted, she just wants to rest.'

'I know, but—'

'I'll call you back.'

Only, he didn't. He rarely had, even as a child. No calls to be picked up from school. No request for a bedtime story. A hug. And now there was nothing: Catherine was alone in the grand home her husband had made for her. For their family. Now she only had her cat, Felix, for company. His loud purr would rattle through the emptiness, soothing her. But it wasn't enough.

She stared at her mobile phone. It suddenly buzzed. Not a call, but a message.

Catherine didn't understand why people didn't *phone* one another any more. She preferred to hear someone's voice, to hold an actual conversation.

Finally, he was reaching out.

Finally, she was needed.

She pushed out her chest, eager to fulfil her duty as matriarch. Yes, things were different than in her day, but grandmothers were still the beating heart of any family; she would prove as much to Elena.

New Mommas WhatsApp group

Elena: She is finally here. Meet Olive Peony Roberts. Sorry for the radio silence this week, been a long few days in hospital ending with emergency C-section. Hope you're both okay, meet up soon! Xxx

Leanne: Oh wow, she is absolutely gorgeous! So pleased for you and Stu. But more importantly, how are you? You doing okay? C-sections are brutal, please shout if you need anything xxx

Margot: BEAUTIFUL! You make gorgeous baby! Not like mine, he came out like potato. Make sure you rest and we see you soon! Xxxx

Leanne: Baby dates soon, definitely! Xxx

Protectors of Purity

POP

Mission Statement

We do not recognise More Yous as human. They are an abomination. Clones. Created in a lab, away from God, fused without a soul. Empty replicas of what came before them. We do not want them among us, deceiving us. They are not our equals. We seek to protect the purity of the human race!

.3

Elena was in the kitchen, Olive curled against her chest, kettle wheezing, when her phone pinged with a message that made bile creep up her throat:

I'm stuck working late so sending my mum over to help xx

'Oh, fuck no,' Elena told the cluttered surfaces, eyeing the stack of plates in the sink, the assortment of pans, slick with days-old grime, forming a haphazard tower on the draining board. The breast pump left beneath the window, sagging and forlorn. The last thing she needed was the judgemental gaze of Catherine Roberts sweeping over her home. 'Dammit,' Elena muttered through clenched teeth as she lifted her phone in one hand, balancing Olive in the crook of her other arm. Awkwardly, she tried to tap out a response. She was aiming for something along the lines of:

Over my dead body is she coming here!

But it was too late. The doorbell chimed sweetly from the hallway. Of course Stu had messaged with seconds to spare, leaving her no space to back out, to complain. To run. Elena hastily considered her options while her mother-in-law loitered on the front step. She could bundle Olive into her pram, take her out the back, through the side gate, and hope to avoid Catherine as she powered down the street. But that risked waking Olive, who was currently content against her chest, small face squished and red, eyes firmly closed. Exhaling loudly Elena thought about running upstairs, closing the curtains and pretending she was asleep. But that meant crossing the hallway, the mottled shape of Catherine looming behind the glass of the front door. *Why hadn't they got a solid door, like normal people?*

'For the light,' Stuart had said. 'It will fill the space with gorgeous, natural light.'

And he was right, it did. The surveyor in her approved of the choice. But it also prevented any stealthy advances up the staircase when someone was at the front door.

A click.

Elena heard it over the grumble of the kettle, the breathy whispers of Olive as she slept. Catherine had put a key in the lock.

Shit.

Was there time to put on the chain? Baby in arms, Elena paced towards the hallway, blood curdling. By the time she padded onto the walnut floor the front door was being nudged open, revealing the overly made-up face of Catherine Roberts.

'Ah, there you are.' Her thin lips drew into a smile, lipstick cracking. 'I wasn't sure if you'd be resting, dear.'

'No, no, I was just—' Elena's gaze strayed to the key in Catherine's hand, clasped between thin fingers and long, polished nails. It looked shiny. New.

'Don't be mad at Stuey,' Catherine said in that nauseatingly soft tone of hers. She never raised her voice, ever. Always spoke as if they were in the back of some cinema. Apparently it was *unladylike* to raise one's voice. 'He thought you'd need some help, didn't want you to be alone.'

Elena's face felt like it had been welded with steel. It was so, so deathly hard to give the woman a kind smile. But somehow she managed it.

'After all, it's a mother's job to be there for her grandchild, isn't it?' She briskly brushed past Elena, sweeping towards the kitchen, taking a cloying cloud of dense perfume with her. Elena stood in the pool of sunlight cast upon the floor from the front door and pushed back tears.

'Tell me what you need, dear,' Catherine called over her shoulder.

Yes, it was a mother's job to be there for her grandchild. And *her* mother should have been there. Her mother, who was kind. Warm. Elena whimpered at the hammer blow of loss in her chest. It had been striking with increased regularity and force since Olive's arrival.

'Oh, my.' Catherine was in the kitchen. She'd put her leather handbag upon the kitchen table and was now pivoting in the centre of the room as though addressing a congregation. 'Too tired to clean, dear?'

'I'm . . .' Elena's exhaustion, raw and gnawing, shredded any veneer of politeness. 'I'm fucking tired, Catherine. Yes. I have a newborn baby.'

She felt a swell of satisfaction when her mother-in-law's pale, pinched eyes widened for a moment in horror. 'No need to speak like a sailor, dear,' Catherine whispered, lips puckering as she took Elena in. Elena knew she must be a sight to behold – she was wearing joggers and a jumper, both were perhaps pyjamas; she wasn't sure any more. It had been days since she had showered or changed. Against her chest, Olive stirred.

Catherine, in contrast, wore a pale blouse, tucked into high-waisted denim jeans. Her flaxen hair, a shade between grey and pale blonde, hung neatly to her shoulders. As always, Catherine wore a full face of make-up, though that did little to hide the lines forged by too many holidays spent in the south of France. 'You should really consider my offer of paying for some help.'

Catherine turned away and began opening cupboards, busying herself with the task of finding a clean cup and saucer.

Not a mug.

Queen Catherine only ever drank from a cup and saucer.

'I sent Stuey some recommendations of wonderful au pairs. Let me pay for one, dear. Let me *help*.'

Anger coursed through Elena, hot and potent. But she had to stay calm. Already Olive was stretching out her tiny hands, eyelids fluttering.

'I don't need help.'

That was a lie and Elena knew it. But she was determined to scoop up what remained of her dwindling pride.

'Stuey had a nanny,' Catherine remarked as she opened yet another cupboard.

'*Stu* and I don't wish to use a stranger to raise our baby.'

'Oh, it's perfectly natural,' Catherine insisted tightly. 'Babies don't even know what's going on until they are at least two.'

'Really, I'm fine, I just—'

'Like I said, I'm more than happy to hire someone for you.' Catherine rounded the far side of the kitchen, cupboards slapping open and closed with abandon, the sound smacking through the room, reaching Olive's delicate ears. 'Even just a cleaner, dear.' The old woman's nose crinkled with distaste as she looked at the cluttered countertops. 'Someone to *help*.'

'That won't be necessary,' Elena told her icily, lingering near the doorway. She thought of her own mother, her fortitude. How she had done it all. The cooking, the cleaning. Raising her. Always with a smile, seemingly effortless. Elena could do that, couldn't she? Follow her mother's example? Be as good as her.

'Where is . . . I used to keep that bone china cup and saucer here, the one with the forget-me-nots on . . .' Catherine's whisper reached Elena, who couldn't suppress a smirk.

'Oh, I don't know.'

She knew. After one particularly tense visit from her mother-in-law Elena had taken great pleasure in removing the china from the cupboard and tossing it straight onto the tiled floor, watching as it smashed into pieces, the little blue flowers torn asunder.

'What the hell?' Stu had run in, face contorted with surprise and then anger. 'Elena, what are you doing?'

'I hate that cup,' Elena told him coolly, studying the debris. 'Almost as much as I hate your mother.'

'She's a lot, but she means well.'

Elena narrowed her eyes.

'Besides, we need all the support we can get. Family is important.'

Elena wiped her sleeve across her nose, refusing to cry. She, an only child, a veritable orphan at thirty. Stu kept his mother close, too close for Elena's liking. She understood how losing Clive, his older brother, had made them all more vulnerable but that had been so long ago. Before Elena even met him. If she and Stu were ever to make a family of their own, it would need to be on their terms. Away from Catherine's influence.

As Elena's stomach swelled, the sadness within her expanded too. Instead of sharing every burgeoning moment with her own mum, it was Catherine who would bear witness to it all. Catherine who would be sole grandparent. There was something terribly cruel about that.

'Anyway' – Catherine was striding over, cupboards left open in her wake, her quest for the cup abandoned – 'how is my favourite girl?' The bracelets she wore on her spindly wrists clattered loudly as she raised her arms. 'I have been so utterly desperate to see her.'

'I'm tired,' Elena told her tightly, knowing full well that she wasn't the girl Catherine referred to.

'Ooh.' Catherine came too close, pressing a single finger against Olive's button nose, causing the baby to stir. 'Isn't she just precious? Let me—'

She tried to dig a hand into Elena's side, to form a wedge between mother and baby, but Elena quickly stepped back. 'She's sleeping.'

'She'll wake up for Nana, won't you baby girl? Yes, come see Nana.'

'Catherine, she's sleeping.'

Only now she wasn't. Olive's eyes were slicing open and her startled gaze was flitting around the room.

'Dammit.' Elena repositioned the baby to rest against her shoulder, gently patting her back.

'You shouldn't teach her to be so clingy,' Catherine chided.

'She's a baby; she's allowed to be clingy,' Elena snapped.

'You're smothering her.'

'What do you know?' Elena felt the heat of her anger on her tongue. 'You had *boys*, not a girl. And you didn't even raise them. You had a nanny, remember?'

If Catherine was hurt, she didn't show it. Well versed in masking her emotions, she kept her weathered face still. 'You're tired, *dear*. It's making you cruel.'

'I'm exhausted,' Elena admitted as Olive began to kick and squirm against her. Soon her baby would scream. Then she would need to feed, which meant an hour of her hard gums suckling against Elena's tender breast until her nipple bled.

'Then let me help.'

'Help?' Elena nearly choked on the word. 'Since you got here all you've done is tell me what a dump the place is and try to make yourself a cup of tea.'

'Well, you certainly weren't hurrying to make me one and welcome me into your home.' Catherine peered down her nose at Elena. 'And I *am* here to help. Let me hire someone for you. I know people. Cleaners. Nannies. Whatever you need.'

'I don't need anyone.'

'Elena, you're drowning. Anyone can see it.'

Against her chest, Olive began to whimper.

'I need to feed Olive,' Elena declared wearily, too tired to fight.

'Hire someone, dear. Please. It will do you and Stuey the world of good.'

'I can do this.' Elena summoned up all her remaining energy. 'My mum managed all on her own. So can I.'

'With all due respect, dear, don't mistake being poor for being proud. If your mother could have afforded help, she would have taken it. Any sane person would.'

That was it. The line that Catherine always loved to cross. Stuart was from a rich family, went to *good* schools. Elena had fought her way into university to pursue a degree in chemistry. She'd studied until her eyes ached, poured herself into her coursework and every extracurricular activity she could access. Her family name carried no weight, held no history. And still Stuart had loved her. Still he'd married her. Elena knew the worst part of it all for Catherine was that her late husband only ever saw her as a cash cow, had never loved her. In their warped world, status was king. Elena loved how she'd unbalanced it all, just by existing.

'I need to feed Olive and you need to go,' Elena stated tightly.

'There are *options*.' Catherine was already picking up her handbag and making for the hallway, clearly losing her appetite for waging war, perhaps having felt she'd already won. 'If not a nanny, then get a More You unit.'

Elena's face hardened into a scowl.

'With my position on the board I could make it happen very quickly for you.'

With a snort, Elena narrowed her eyes. 'You've got a key, you can let yourself out.' She turned towards the lounge, desperate to sit down for a bit.

'At least *think* about it,' Catherine implored, voice as loud as she would ever permit it to be. 'You might not trust someone else with your baby, but you'd trust *yourself*, wouldn't you?'

It was dark in the lounge, the curtains sealed tightly shut. Elena couldn't remember when she'd last opened them. From the glow of the hallway Catherine peered in at her, soft hair almost a halo around her head. 'It doesn't have to be like this, dear. You don't have to be this unhappy.'

'I'm fine.' Elena struggled to cough out the lie.

'Promise me you'll think about it. I've told Stuey I'm more than happy to pay. You two, like it or not, you need help.'

Elena leaned back and lifted up her jumper, resting her head against the sofa cushion as Olive's wet mouth clamped around her nipple. When she heard the front door closing she permitted herself to relax a little, lingering on the cusp of consciousness, her body desperate for sleep.

Protectors Of Purity

POP

Do you wish to live in a world where you are replaceable?

Where you are not unique?

Of course not. You want to live in a world where you are special, loved. Original. If More You is allowed to continue their production of units we risk living in a world overrun by clones. We won't let this happen! Stand with us! Find your local POP contact. Together, we can make a difference, we can save humanity before it is too late!

.4

Catherine sensed she'd got it wrong. Again. She was merely pointing out the necessity for help, that was all. With Elena she always seemed to be making mistakes. As she hovered on the doorstep, the new key pressed against her palm, she steeled herself and blinked back tears.

I'm trying. I'm really trying.

She was doing as Stuey had asked. Showing up for his exhausted wife. Being there. And still she had not held the baby.

Olive.

She'd felt that pinch when he'd told her his daughter's name. That slight. Named for Elena's dead mother. And here was a living, breathing, loving grandmother being rushed out of the house. Turned away.

Didn't even offer me a cup of tea.

This was not how things were done. How people were treated. Catherine had never particularly liked her own mother-in-law, but she respected her. When the old battleaxe turned up, always unannounced, she would drop everything to prepare a fresh pot of tea, to make the woman welcome. If Catherine dared to show up at her son's house unannounced she knew she would find no welcome. She'd probably be barred from entering. Especially if Stuey was at work. She blamed Elena's upbringing, the lack of propriety with it. No manners. All bluster and vulgarity.

And the *language* she used.

Catherine winced.

She began a genteel walk to her car, ensuring her shoulders were square, chin held high. Always a lady. Even when she was spurned. Such a fleeting glance she had caught of her granddaughter.

I should have waited until Stuey was there.

Then things would have been different. Then her visit would have been heralded with open arms, hot tea, smiles. But he had called her for help. And a mother never ignores a call like that. Stuey needed her.

As she got to her car, Catherine paused to take in her son's house. All the curtains drawn tight across the windows. Elena was so keen to keep the world out. To lock herself away. Motherhood would change her, surely. Soften her. How could it not?

And if it didn't...

Things had always been tricky between them. Catherine had never understood her son's devotion to the girl with the northern accent, but she'd humoured him, hoping the romance would run its course. And now he and Elena had a baby.

With Olive there was the chance for a fresh start. Shame the same couldn't be said for Elena.

Catherine tucked the newly cut key for Stuey's front door into her purse.

More You.

She'd raised the suggestion. Lightly. Casually. Just like Stuey had asked. When his father originally became an investor in the company her son had been so sceptical.

'It's not ethical, Mum, for him to be getting involved in something like that.' Stuey, had, of course, not felt like he could approach his father directly on the matter.

'He's passionate about it, Stuey. You know how he gets when he's set his mind on something.'

'There's going to be backlash. A lot of it.'

'There always is with change.' She said this as someone who was seasoned in watching the world implode with each passing phase, each passing decade.

Catherine thought again of the message her son had sent her that morning:

> Mum, can you pop in and check on Elena later? Use that key I gave you if you need to. And maybe float the idea of More You. She refuses to get anyone in to help but that would be, you know, her. So surely it'd be fine? X

Elena and her pride. Refusing help when she so clearly needed it. Catherine drew in a long, satisfied breath. She had done her job. Her duty. Sadly, she had not yet held her beautiful new granddaughter. But that would come. Catherine studied the curtained windows, imagining her daughter-in-law scowling behind them.

She can't keep me locked out for ever.

Leanne: Elena, just checking in to see how you're doing. These first few weeks feel like you've been hit by a bloody train. Be kind to yourself xxxx

Margot: Is Olive sleeping? Are you sleeping? If not, put some whisky on the dummy. Never fails xxx

Leanne: Marg, not sure she should be doing that xxx

Margot: Trust me on this

Leanne: Let us know how you are, okay? Else we will just turn up unannounced xxx

Leanne: I'm obviously joking, would literally never commit such a heinous act. But seriously, would love to hear from you. Or I'll come round. You've been warned.

Leanne: I'm only half joking. Love you xxx

.5

Bleary-eyed and exhausted, Elena stared at the screen in front of her. Olive had not slept. Which meant she had not slept. Time had started to lose all meaning after midnight had crept by. Elena felt like she was just endlessly fumbling through the darkness while the rest of the world rested. She hadn't even had the energy to shower that morning; she'd just let Stu bundle her and Olive into the car and drive them over to More You.

After Catherine had planted the seed of the idea, it had germinated. When Elena had casually mentioned a More You unit to Stu, he had lit up, grabbing his phone and insisting they make a consultation appointment right away.

'This will be so good for us,' he kept saying.

Elena didn't like that it had come from Catherine, but she also couldn't deny how tired she was. How utterly wrung out.

'And besides,' Stu told her cheerily, 'it's not like we'd be letting a stranger in our home. It'd be *you*.'

It'd be you.

Elena listened to podcasts, visited the More You website so many times she heard their welcome music in her sleep. A clone, of her as she was right now. In this moment. Many people raved about them.

Many people feared them.

Elena felt twisted with indecision. The only thing she knew

for certain was that something had to change. She was drowning as a new mother. And Elena didn't fail. When she slipped, she dug in deeper. Held on tighter.

And Stu . . . there were fresh flashes of grey at his temple. The light in his eyes had dimmed.

He needs me to do this.

The burden of being a wife. A mother. It dug into Elena's shoulders, a pack she could never put down.

It'd be you.

The date for the consultation was set.

'Are you sure we should be doing this?' In the More You car park, Elena turned to her husband. His hands were still on the wheel, a reflex rather than a necessity since the car drove itself.

'We're just going in to ask, get some information. That's all. There's no pressure to—'

He was cut off by a high-pitched whine erupting from the baby seat. Without the motion of the vehicle to lull her to sleep, Olive had awoken, With a groan, Elena clicked off her seat belt and climbed out to retrieve her daughter. It was then that she heard the voices. The chanting. It sent a cold sensation shooting down her spine.

'Stu?' She threw her husband a worried glance. He was looking towards the building, having heard it too.

'Urgh,' he groaned. 'Looks like a damn POP protest.'

'What?' Elena instinctively curled her body over the car seat, shielding her daughter. 'Are you serious?' She peered towards the source of the chants. The front entrance was obscured by a small crowd, clutching placards and banners. Elena squinted to read them.

Crime against God
Ban More You

One You, the Only You
No More Clones

'I don't like this,' Elena told her husband.

'What's to like?' Stu dragged a hand through his hair, studying the crowd. 'My mum says they're here most days now.'

'Really?' Elena rubbed her temple. Had it been in the news? If it had it could easily have slipped her attention as most things did these days.

'No more More You! End to More You!'

With a start, she realised that members of the crowd were looking at their car, directing their chants at them.

'We need to leave.'

'No.' Stu placed a hand on her shoulder. 'We need to just carry on and go inside. Just ignore them, okay?'

Elena looked at the banners, the angry words held aloft. 'I'm not sure—'

He squeezed her shoulder. 'You can do this.'

For a second she almost felt the scratch of snow upon her cheeks. How many times had he urged her on? Ever higher? Always pushing, always reaching. Always wanting more.

She blew air out of her cheeks. 'I can do this.'

A consultation. That was it. Elena squared her shoulders, climbed out and attached Olive's car seat to the pram that Stu had produced from the boot. She tugged the hood as far down as it would go, and began to walk in, Stu's arm wrapped tightly around her. The chanting reached fever pitch as they came towards the doors.

'Don't do it!' someone cried.

'Think of your baby!'

'Come on.' Stu kept his head low, shouldered his way through, and then they were inside, free.

Everything inside the More You building was sleek. Smooth.

Soulless. Elena stared at her pale, crumpled reflection in countless mirrored walls, hating the gaunt woman who peered back at her.

'It's going to be fine,' Stu kept telling her as they walked in step. Olive sucked contentedly on her fist.

They were met at reception by a slender woman with jet black hair and startlingly bright blue eyes. She greeted them as if they were old friends.

'Mr and Mrs Roberts, I'm so very sorry about the disturbance outside.'

'Can't the police move them on?' Stu asked.

'Here at More You, we respect the public's right to express their opinions,' she told him.

Stu gave a tight, uncertain nod.

'Follow me, right this way.'

From reception they were ushered into a lift that played gentle piano music as they ascended sixteen floors. And then they were in a darkened cinema room, sitting in plush recliners. Elena lifted Olive to rest in her arms and for a brief moment she felt content, relaxed. Her little family, finally calm and collected in one space. The velvet of the chair was so soft, so welcoming, that as the screen before them flickered to life and began to play, Elena feared she might drift off.

'Any questions at all, I'll be waiting just outside after the presentation video.' Their guide, who they'd learned was called Aria, gave them another wide smile before stepping out of the room.

'You don't suppose she's . . .' Stu was pushed from his train of thought as the film began.

Elena blinked to keep herself focused and marginally engaged, although she soon realised that most of what was in the film she already knew.

'Welcome to More You,' the voiceover began. 'Where you can be you. And more.'

There was a panning shot of a beach and a couple walking hand in hand towards a salmon sunset.

Elena, like most people, had been aware of More You for some time. It was a commercial cloning company. The most successful of the few that had cropped up over the past five years since human cloning had been made legal. It had been a messy business to get to that point. Protests in the street. Questions over human rights. Ethics. There was a time when Elena proactively followed the ramifications of the swiftly developing science, back when she and Stu had the energy to passionately debate it come the evening.

The scientist in her understood.

It was about advancement: practical, helpful uses such as organ donations. But it was also hard to sever the link between heart and mind. The question that was asked in their household and countless others:

But are they still human?

In her arms, Olive curled against Elena's chest, eyes closing.

'Here at More You, we believe in enabling our clients to live their best lives. Already we work with world leaders and many famous entertainers whose demanding careers mean extra intervention is often needed.

'We can develop a clone of your current self, grown right here in our onsite laboratories. A perfect replication right down to the smallest detail, even with matching fingerprints and distinguishing marks. Once in your home, they will assimilate to your lifestyle, mannerisms, and you'll start to wonder how you ever coped without them.'

Now on the screen were two grinning brunette women, one holding a baby, another reading a tablet on the sofa, both identical. Elena strained to differentiate them. A passing glance would cast them as twins. Only—

'See.' Stu pointed at the screen. 'Help in the home, that's what we need.'

'Sure.' Elena glanced down at her sleeping baby, gently stroking her rosy cheek, which was buttery soft to the touch. She imagined someone else holding her. Someone who looked like her but wasn't her. Someone who Olive would think *was* her mother. A feeling, primal and uncomfortable, began to work through her. 'I don't know.' She shook her head first at her husband and then at the screen, no longer bothering to whisper. 'I mean, what if something goes wrong, you know? With it.'

'I've heard you bring them back here,' Stu said, flicking his gaze between his wife and the screen, 'for decommissioning and rehabilitation.'

'What does that actually mean?'

On the screen the first couple were once again walking along the beach as the camera panned away from them, towards an ocean that glistened golden beneath the setting sun.

'All models come fitted with state-of-the-art tracking chips so that you can experience complete peace of mind and know where your More You is at all times.

'Efficient. Energetic. Engaged.

'With More You the possibilities are endless. Our proven safety measures mean that you are always in the best of hands. Your own. Secure your appointment today. Begin your new life. Be More You.'

The lights slowly came up and Elena winced at the brightness.

'I really think we should consider this.' Stu turned to her, eyes holding the shadows from his own struggle to sleep the previous night.

'Let me help,' he always mumbled sleepily from the bed as

Elena kicked off the duvet and stumbled towards the Moses basket containing their wailing daughter.

'She needs me.' Elena's words were always a whip, cutting between them.

'Would it, I mean, me, the . . . the thing.' Elena fumbled, unsure which term she felt comfortable with. 'Could it feed her?'

'I guess.' Stu scratched at his jawline; he'd failed to shave that morning. 'They said it's a clone of your *current* self. So . . . milky tits and all.'

'Thanks.'

'You know what I mean.'

'I'm just—'

The door to the theatre opened and Aria swept in, elegant in a silver jumpsuit. Like everything else in the More You building, she was polished to perfection. Only now she wasn't alone. Beside her was what appeared to be her identical twin. Both women were smiling warmly as Aria spoke. 'So, what did we think? Any questions?'

Elena's mouth fell open as Stu muttered, 'My God.'

'Wait.' Elena gestured between the two women. 'Is she . . . Are you?'

'This is my More You.' The woman beside Aria spoke. 'As you can see, she's more than competent in her abilities. The differences between us are . . .'

'Non-existent,' Aria finished with a grin. 'We work seamlessly side by side here at the facility.'

'I don't . . .' Elena looked between them, openly scrutinising them. Same height, same smile, same shimmering outfit.

'It's extremely impressive.' Stu rose up from his chair. 'May I?'

'Of course.' The first woman stepped away from her More You to enable Stu to come closer.

'Remarkable,' Stu muttered as he stood between them. Elena

remained where she was, feeling no compulsion to get closer. If anything, a sense of betrayal burned in her chest. Which one was actually Aria? The blurred line of it all was unsettling.

'The video.' Elena shifted Olive into her other arm as she was starting to grow numb. 'It doesn't explain what happened once you are' – she nervously averted her gaze from Aria's More You – 'done with your . . . other self.'

'Of course.' Aria's voice lost none of its warmth at the question. 'At More You, we offer a swift and caring decommissioning service where units are relieved of their current duties and rehabilitated.' Both women were looking at her, expressions welcoming.

'Right.' Elena felt the heat of her baby against her chest, the feather-light beat of her tiny heart. 'But what does that really mean?'

'Because at the end of the day, they're people, right?' Stu added, a little uneasily. 'You're' – he looked nervously between the women and retreated back to the sofa – 'people?'

'Right. And, as such, we treat units that have fulfilled their duties with the utmost dignity and care. Here at More You we retain retired units within our employ.'

'What if they don't want that?' Elena was frowning, attention flitting between the two women.

'In all honesty, units are rarely returned.' Aria's smile widened as she locked eyes with Elena. 'But when they are, they are always happy to return to the fold and continue to assist with the work we do here.'

'I see,' Elena replied flatly.

'We adhere to all current cloning laws.' The first woman was speaking now, her tone bright and chipper. 'As mentioned in the video, many world leaders use us and enjoy the benefit of having multiple More Yous in service.'

'Do they age?' Elena asked. The technology was still so new;

five years was such a short space of time for clones to be integrated within society. On the news, they were constantly rehashing arguments for and against, politicians spouting the rhetoric that change takes time, that in fifty, a hundred years' time, clones would be the norm and every household would have multiples of them.

'Yes, they age,' Aria confirmed. 'Same as you.'

'Same as me,' Elena repeated. She gently stroked her daughter's cheek. 'I'm . . . I'm breastfeeding right now.' She smiled gently at her baby and then looked directly at Aria. 'So, would my . . . my More You be able to breastfeed too?' The question made her stomach clench. She didn't want that. But she wanted to know. Olive was always so very hungry, and Elena . . . she was giving all she had. Still it never felt enough. If the More You could possibly express milk, that would help, wouldn't it? The feeling in her stomach tightened and Elena felt heat in her face. Fresh unease burned through her.

'She will be an exact replica of you as you are right now.' Aria gave her a broad, bright smile. 'So yes, she will be able to produce breast milk and assist with feeding as necessary.'

'So can they have babies?' Stu asked.

A shake of Aria's head. 'All More Yous are sterilised before they leave the facility.'

'I see. I guess that makes sense.'

Elena glanced at her husband, tightened her grip upon Olive. 'What if they get sick?' she found herself asking. 'If they age like . . . like their original. Do they also risk getting sick? Or hurt?'

'They do. When such issues arise, we encourage patrons to return their models to More You.'

'What about . . . memories?' Elena absently lifted a hand to her temple as she spoke, thinking about all the thousands of moments that made her . . . her. 'Will it have my memories?'

'Presently our More Yous don't share their originals' memories, but they are, of course, keen to develop their own!'

'Presently?'

Stu interrupted. 'So it would look like Elena, talk like her, but not have her history?'

'Not her history, but she'd be made from the blueprint that is Elena.'

Blueprint.

The term made Elena think of houses. Of work. Of the developments she'd assisted with, poring over designs for homes that were duplicated again and again. One identical building after another. Was that what she was doing here? Creating a soulless version of herself?

'Do they dream?' she blurted, unable to stop herself.

Aria's More You responded. 'My brain processes the events of the day when I sleep, just the same as yours.'

'The video mentioned proven safety measures?'

'Yes.' Aria clasped her hands together. 'As I mentioned, we adhere to all current cloning laws. We also go above and beyond in that we aim to suppress any disruptive behaviours in the genetic code of our models while enhancing nurturing qualities.'

'You tamper with their DNA?' There was a slight rise in Stu's voice.

'We *suppress*,' Aria smoothly corrected him. 'It ensures all our units are always compliant.'

'That sounds . . .'

'Ethically ambiguous,' Elena concluded for her husband.

'We always operate within the parameters of the law and we are at the forefront of cloning technology. I assure you, our More You models are developed only to enhance your life, never to cause distress.'

'You've definitely given us a lot to think about.' Stu wrapped a protective arm around Elena's shoulders.

'If you want to secure your appointment, please do not hesitate to get in touch.' Aria continued to smile at them.

'Thank you.'

'We get many new mothers in,' she continued, eyeing Olive, 'all of them looking at getting the extra help we can offer. Think of it like hiring a nanny. Only one you can truly trust, as it's you.'

'But a nanny has . . . life experience,' Elena cradled her baby to her chest. 'A clone would be . . . completely new.'

'Assimilation happens surprisingly quickly,' the other Aria explained smoothly. 'Our rapid growth technology means that complete brain development only takes a month in our growing pods.'

'A month?' Stu looked up at both women.

'Four weeks, that's it.' Aria grinned at him. 'Barely any time at all. We are the fastest in our field,' she said with more than a hint of pride. 'I sincerely hope we hear from you again soon.'

Elena was rising to her feet, returning Olive to her car seat, clicking in the buckle. She felt so weary, her movements so wooden.

Hand on her back, Stu guided Elena towards the door that Aria and her More You were now standing beside. 'Thanks so much.' He returned their smiles. 'We'll be in touch.'

'Will we?' Elena asked once they were alone in the lift, silver doors sliding shut.

'I think . . . I think it's definitely worth considering. Don't you?'

'I don't . . .' Elena sighed, closed her eyes. 'What does it cost?'

'My mum will handle it.'

'What does it *cost*?' she repeated, growing irritable. 'I refuse to be beholden to that woman.'

'Well it's not cheap.' Stu ruffled his hair and then stooped to smile at Olive. 'But you get results. Ethel Collins has three, I heard.'

'The prime minister has three?'

'It would be just like you.' Stu continued. 'I don't see how that's a bad thing.'

'Because it's not me. It would be a neutered, docile me. That's not natural.'

'People used to view IVF as unnatural,' Stu countered. 'Things change. They advance.'

'I don't know.'

'You saw those two women in there. It was . . . uncanny.' Stu sounded impressed.

'Uncanny valley,' Elena muttered tersely.

'Then let's hire a nanny, or let my mum help more.'

'Can we talk about this when we get home?' Elena's mouth widened into a yawn. 'I'm tired.' And the thought of navigating her way once more through the POP protest only added to her exhaustion.

'Things need to change, sweetheart. That's why we're here.'

'Hmm.' Elena gave a grunt of acknowledgment as the lift doors opened on the reception. She pushed the pram across gleaming tiles towards the exit, head low, temple throbbing, the chants from outside leaking into the serenity of the lobby.

From: Unknown
To: POP@outward.co.uk
Subject: More You Centre

Positioning ourselves outside the main facility has been most helpful. We have seen countless individuals going inside who have hopefully been deterred and, through us, have had the chance to see sense. The most troubling of these is people with babies. We remain sickened by the prospect of babies being exposed to these abominations. Or, worse, babes cloned themselves. All further evidence that More You must be stopped. We will not rest until they have ceased production. Clearly, our protests are no longer enough. More must be done. We can see now how widespread the disease is – no longer just a failure of the rich and famous. Regular people now frequent the facility. The disease must be cut out. It is time to make a stand!

.6

'I don't know.'

Elena must have uttered those three words over a hundred times throughout the rest of the day. Stu was incessant in his questioning.

So what do you think?
Are you happy to do it?
Should we book an appointment for DNA data collection?

Elena simply *didn't know*. Exhaustion. It felt like a chain around her, closing tight, compressing even her thoughts until they became a jumbled, indecipherable mess. And through it all Olive cried. Her nappy leaked, twice. In a trance, Elena went through the motions of changing her daughter, turning on the washing machine, clutching the small infant to her shoulder to burp her while her breast pump sucked anything left within her into a waiting bottle.

She hoped come the evening they would at least sleep. But it didn't take long for Olive's screams to split the night apart. Elena jolted awake, wrenched out of a dream and instantly feeling sick.

'Urgh.' She scrambled from the warm cocoon of the duvet, her body protesting every step.

'Are you all right?' Stu mumbled groggily.

'Fine, I'm fine, I've got her. Sleep.'

She knew that one of them needed to sleep. She couldn't keep sending Stu into the office like a zombie. It was going to start taking its toll on his work. And only the previous week she'd returned to the room, Olive fed and changed in her arms, to find him crouched in the centre of their bed, curled over something, rocking back and forth.

'Don't worry, I've got her, she's fine.'

Elena blinked away her fatigue to notice her husband was clutching a pillow to his chest.

'Shh,' he continued, 'it's fine, she's fine.'

'Stu?' Elena slowly approached him, touched one hand to his shoulder. 'What are you doing?'

'Looking after Olive. She was crying.'

'No, honey, she's here. With me.'

Stu made a sound she'd not heard come from him before. Something between a whimper and a sigh.

'Go to sleep,' Elena urged, guiding him towards his own pillow. The second he was horizontal his eyes closed and his breathing slowed. Elena studied her baby, then her husband, the house so still around them.

The next day she learned from a brisk online search that Stu's hallucination was completely normal.

Brought on by severe exhaustion.

The term stuck in her mind.

Severe exhaustion.

Their time climbing mountains had taught Stu and Elena the dangers of being so dangerously tired. The cognitive implications. An inability to make decisions, assess risk. In the dead zone, there was no margin for error. Exhaustion could kill.

Olive was struggling to settle after feeding.

'Come on,' Elena whispered over and over. She felt detached from the moment, distant. As though in some sort of dream. 'Come on, sweetheart, Mummy needs to go back to bed.'

For Elena, paradise no longer looked like the pristine peak of a mountaintop. It was a bed. In a hotel room. Where she could rest undisturbed for forty-eight hours. No crying. No screaming. Just sleep. Blissful sleep. As she moved past the refrigerator, she caught the spectre of her reflection in its smooth surface.

Against her chest Olive kept squirming, crying. It was going to be a long night.

'Right.' Elena hoisted the baby into a different position and opened a cupboard. With some difficulty she fumbled around and eventually pulled out a pan, placing it on the hob. Next she returned to the refrigerator for some milk. Again, the simple task was greatly hindered by the baby in her arms. 'Come . . . on.' With a grunt Elena balanced the milk in her free hand, shuffled over to the pan and poured some in. As she fought a second time with the fridge door she considered that a second pair of hands would be greatly useful.

And they'd be my hands.

She slammed the door closed and looked at her free hand. At the mole close to her thumb. Would a clone also have that? Perhaps. But not the scar across her knuckles from a bicycle crash when she was six.

Not my hands.

As she paced around the kitchen while her milk warmed, she ran over all the questions she still had. The points that truly troubled her involved the decommissioning of a clone. The rehabilitation. Did she really want a version of herself working over at More You indefinitely? Was that truly what happened to retired units? Was their entire business run by returned models? And what about Olive? Would she be fooled by a new version of Elena? And could she trust her with her baby?

Elena's head felt heavy. As she did countless times, she wished her mother was there. She'd have known what to do. Better yet, she'd have already stepped in to help and Elena would have trusted her, welcomed her into her home to hold her granddaughter, to be a part of her life.

Upon the counter, her phone chirped. More messages from her friends Margot and Leanne.

> **Margot:** Today I go shopping and I look at ALL the pink stuff! We must go shopping for your princess! Send more pictures! Xxx

> **Leanne:** Yes, pictures please, Elena! Or just, you know, any sign of life! We miss you! Xxx

She really needed to find time to reply.

Elena was warming milk for a hot chocolate in an attempt to comfort herself. It was something her mum would always do. Failed an exam? Boy broke your heart? Crashed into another bike and torn open your knuckles? Hot chocolate was the fix. Warm and consoling, with a sprinkle of marshmallows and a dollop of whipped cream. Elena needed the sweetness of both the drink and the memory.

The stars were still bright outside. She walked into the lounge, put down her drink, settled on the sofa, Olive warm against her chest. As the television quietly played, her daughter stilled, content. And then, just for a moment, she allowed herself to close her eyes. To find some release.

.7

Her name. It was a foghorn blaring, booming into her thoughts. Intrusive and alarming.

'Elena. Elena! ELENA!'

With a shudder she awoke. Blinked.

'Christ, Elena!'

Another sound. Sharper than her husband yelling, pealing in the background. Groggily, Elena looked around the lounge, waiting for the shape of the armchair to solidify into focus. The lights were on but everywhere felt dim. Dusty. Olive was still in her arms, slowly unfurling like a daisy in sunlight. Then she noticed the smell. Acrid and sour. Heavy in her nostrils, her lungs.

Burning.

The sharp sound.

Elena bolted to her feet, panic suddenly gripping her.

Something was burning. The fire alarm was shrieking. And now she could see it. Taste it. The smoke that laced through her home, gathering thickly.

'Get in the garden,' Stu ordered tersely, thrusting open the French doors and letting in the sweet night air, instantly cold against Elena's hands and cheeks. She protectively swaddled Olive closer to her.

'What's happening?'

Stu followed her into the garden, haggard and angry, muscles thick beneath his tight-fitting T-shirt.

'The pan. The fucking pan, Elena.'

'The . . . the pan?'

'I woke up to the sodding alarms going off, scared me half to death. I ran down and there was smoke everywhere, billowing out from the fucking pan you'd left on the hob. And now we have to wait for the fire brigade to turn up.'

'What? Really?' Elena's face grew hot from shame. 'Is that . . . necessary?'

'It's the fail-safe, remember?' Stu growled tightly. 'The fire alarm goes, a call is automatically put in to the services. Same for the burglar alarm.'

'Right.'

All those safety features they'd added to their home now seemed to be betraying them. Olive's eyes fluttered open and her mouth puckered. 'Shh, it's okay honey,' Elena whispered soothingly to her daughter, feeling a sick sensation in the back of her throat. The combination of the waking suddenly and the adrenalin now coursing through her veins made for a heady mix.

'They're here.' Stu checked his phone and then stalked back inside, leaving Elena in the darkness, out on the damp grass, watching the smoke unfurl from their home in delicate tendrils and drift up towards a clear night sky.

A ruined pan was the main casualty of the event. Elena could barely look at its gaping base as the woman in uniform standing in her kitchen briskly addressed her. Words like *caution* and *unattended* were thrown at her. Elena found no sympathy beneath the woman's weary, steely stare.

'I'm so embarrassed.' Elena wilted over the kitchen island when her house was finally empty, the French doors and windows thrust open to let the last of the smoke leave.

'Come on.' Stu's anger had thawed and he now hovered at her

side, one hand on her back. 'It's easily done. You're just . . . you're exhausted. We both are.'

'But it could have been worse,' Elena exclaimed, her voice close to breaking. 'What if . . . what if I'd caused an actual fire and just slept through it? What if—' She bowed her head towards Olive, still in her arms, letting her lips graze the baby's soft head, breathing in her newborn scent.

'Hey, it's *okay*. We're fine. Everything is fine.'

'Is everything fine?' Elena challenged tearfully, striding towards the obliterated saucepan and holding it high with her free hand. 'Does this look *fine*?'

'You know what we need to do.' Stu held her in a steady gaze.

'No.' Elena smacked the remains of the pan down with unnecessary force, the jolt racing up her arm. 'We're not there, Stu.'

'We've literally just had the fire brigade round in the middle of the night.'

'It was a mistake. An accident. I'll be more careful.'

'Elena—'

'I'm just *tired*. I just . . . I need to catch up. That's all. I can do this.' She tasted the salt of her tears as she looked down at her baby.

'What if it had been a real fire?' Stu asked quietly, as though he were her conscience upon her shoulder.

'Don't.'

'It could have been. I know it was an accident. I know you'll be more careful. I'm just saying that with us both so shattered, standards slip. I think we need to—'

'Don't!'

'I'm not going to pretend this didn't happen,' Stu said in a warning tone, 'and I'm also not going to pretend that it didn't scare the shit out of me.'

Elena turned away from him, feeling fresh shame.

'We need help,' he continued. 'Real, actual help.'

She wanted to protest. To tell him no. That she was fine, she could *do* this. Elena was fearless. Driven. But as she bounced Olive in her arms her resolve was weakening. She imagined not smoke, but flames curling through her home. Finding her slumbering on the sofa, circling her. Licking their way up the sofa, towards her baby. Her delicate, innocent baby.

Then she pictured Aria beside her clone at More You. How immaculate they both were. How perfect. Aria mirrored seamlessly, the two of them working together in sync. Like having a twin.

'Fine.' Her shoulders fell as she voiced her consent. 'Let's do it.'

'Really?' Stu didn't mask the surprise he felt as he approached his wife and gently placed a hand on her shoulder.

'Really,' Elena sighed. Together they craned their necks to look at the little baby they had made together. 'I can't . . . I can't risk anything happening to her. She deserves more than this. She deserves a mother who isn't falling apart at the seams.'

'And it will only be temporary,' Stu assured her.

'It will only be temporary.' Elena nodded in agreement. 'Until we're sleeping more, feeling more stable.'

Stu leaned in to kiss her cheek. 'This is going to be good for us.' His breath was warm against her face. 'I just know it.'

Elena smiled thinly, still tasting the smoke in the air.

.8

Catherine heard about the fire. Or rather, the 'close call', as Stuey put it. But in her mind there was no doubt – the house could easily have fallen in flames. She was about to tell her son as much, drawing in a righteous breath, when he uttered the words she had been hoping to hear.

'She's agreed, to More You. This . . . this made her see sense.'
A jolt of joy shot down her spine.
The newness.
The possibilities.
The *fresh start*.
'Oh.' A hand upon her chest, a smile on her face. 'Oh, Stuey, that's such good news.'
Two Elenas.
The new Elena would be a blank slate, a new person for Catherine to impress herself upon. To not make mistakes. This new Elena would have no memory of the deceased mother Catherine knew she was always being weighed up against.

Weighed up and proven wanting. At least in Elena's eyes.

And even if those memories did eventually surface, as they could in newer models, Catherine would have already claimed her space as mother-in-law. Matriarch. It would be within her shadow all others would exist.

'Let me get everything arranged,' Catherine was saying as she practically skipped into the golden light of her conservatory.

'Really, Mum, you don't need to—'

'No, no,' she cut him off. 'I want to help, Stuey. Give you the very best.'

'I know, but—'

'They've come on so much. The More Yous.'

'We saw one, at the centre. She was . . . impressive.'

'The technology, the advances, I can see why your father was so enamoured with it all.'

'Dad just liked the colour of money.'

'But it could be more than that, couldn't it?' Catherine caught sight of her reflection in the glass that overlooked her large garden. She liked to think she was still elegant, still beautiful in her senior years. Still *enough*.

'We just need some help, that's all. And Olive . . . she's so clingy. She only wants Elena.'

Only wants Elena.

Catherine clenched her jaw. There was a time when her sons only wanted her. Even over the nanny. Mummy's cuddles were always best, only Mummy could kiss away the pain of a grazed knee. Now she had one son, who was grown.

Who only wants Elena.

She scowled at the old woman in the glass. How swiftly time had placed her in a supporting role when she had once been the leading lady.

'Whatever you want, darling,' she told her son. 'For you, I'd do anything.'

'Thanks, Mum.' He hung up abruptly. No 'goodbye', no 'love you'. Returning to this new life he had forged with his wife. His daughter. Catherine slowly lowered her mobile phone and pressed her palm against the glass. How grand and glorious her garden was in the sunlight, a stretch of emerald lawn dotted with daisies and buttercups. Just waiting for a little girl to sit out there and make delicate chains. Catherine imagined calling little Olive in for sandwiches she had made, how the girl's face would light up with gratitude.

'Thanks, Nana.'

Her home would be filled with love again.

With a sigh, Catherine looked again to her phone and pulled up her contact at More You. Only the best for her darling Stuey.

.9

It was cold. That was the first thing that crossed Elena's mind as she stood in the replication chamber. At points, it was the only thing she could think about. The way her breath caught in the air, how her skin prickled. She wore only a hospital gown, thin as paper, as she stood in a glass tube. Around her lights pulsed and whispered. Taking her in.

She closed her eyes, thinking of what her friends would say. She'd finally fired off a message to them that morning.

> **Elena:** Sorry both, it's been a lot. I'm just so tired x

> **Margot:** Get the help! Too much for one woman! Xxx

> **Leanne:** So lovely to hear from you! It is a lot! Rest when you can. You've made a human, it's huge! Please let us know when we can come and assess the chaos! I've still not unpacked my hospital bag . . . from when I had the twins! Lol xxx

> **Margot:** See, this is why ppl need help! Xxx

> **Leanne:** Margot! X

They said 'get help', but *this*? Would they judge her? Or would they understand?

Initially when they'd arrived at the More You centre, Elena had been afraid, unwilling.

First, there had been a blood test. Standard and simple. Then she was taken to a changing area, handed the neatly folded gown as though it were a mere letter. As she unfurled it and slipped out of her clothes, pan pipes played through an overhead sound system. Elena was alone as she placed her clothes into a locker, slid on the gown. Stu was in the waiting area with Olive, who Elena prayed was still sleeping in her pram. Gown on, she gently ran her hands down it, feeling each brittle fibre and, beneath it, her skin. Her bones. Herself. The last time she'd worn something similar she'd been sliced open. Sometimes she could still taste the copper in the air as Olive was pulled from her.

'Here it comes,' the surgeon had declared from behind his plastic face guard, 'the best moment of your life.' Elena had peered up at him through tear-filled eyes as she lay open and bloodied on the table beneath him.

Elena had been told to place her items in a locker then follow the curve of the changing room towards a door marked with a golden infinity symbol. Slowly she moved her bare feet along the warm tiles on the floor, feeling her heart rate growing stronger, surging in her chest, echoing in her ears.

You can do this.

The walls of the changing area were pine, reminding her of a woodland lodge. She headed down a small corridor and there it was, the golden symbol. Elena swallowed, throat dry.

Can I do this?

She stretched out her arms, studying them. Each mole. Each strand of pale hair. There was a sound of air being sucked out and the door ahead of her slipped up into the ceiling. Elena looked ahead into a darkened space, ringed with monitors that burned bright like the moon. And in the centre of the space, a single, glass pod. Large enough for one person to stand within.

'Ah, Mrs Roberts.' A short man in a white lab coat emerged, extending his hand to her. 'Are you ready?'

Elena said nothing, just stared at the glass pod.

'It is all nominally invasive,' the man assured her, stepping away and tapping on one of the nearest monitors. 'What we are doing now is mapping a blueprint to attach your DNA to. All very simple, really. It can be a little chilly in the pod, I'm afraid, but other than that you'll be completely comfortable. All in all, the whole process will take around ten minutes. I can have some of your favourite music streamed into the pod for you, if you like?'

Elena nodded slowly. She knew all of this, had gone over the steps with Stu the past few days. Over and over. They'd watched videos, read reviews. Delved as deep as they possibly could into More You.

'And I see you're having the platinum package, which comes with express replication. Good choice.' The man turned from the monitor to briefly flash her a smile, chestnut hair falling into his eyes. He looked young, even with his face framed by thick glasses. 'That means your model should be ready for collection in seven days. This express service is only offered to our most *prestigious* clients.'

'When we had our consultation, they said it would take a month.'

'It usually does, but like I said, you're getting our express service. And a newer model. Top of the line. The best that we can offer.'

'Seven days,' she managed nervously, giving another nod of her head.

'No time at all.' The man beamed, and she saw on his lab coat an ID badge bearing his name, Dr A. Schmitt. 'We are always improving our service. We are exceptionally proud to be able to produce a More You in just a week.'

One week.

Elena exhaled uneasily. It felt too soon. Too fast.

Of course, the platinum package had been Catherine's idea. How she'd cooed with approval when she came round the previous Sunday while Elena silently seethed in an armchair, nursing Olive.

'Wonderful, Stuey, just wonderful,' she gushed, clasping her wrinkled hands together, baked to a shade of bronze that was both unflattering and unnatural. 'I think this will make such a huge difference to you both. I only wish they'd had it when I had you.'

'But that was such a long time ago,' Elena offered bitterly. 'The technology has really come on since then.'

'Hmm.' Catherine pursed her thin lips and kept her focus on her son. 'Anyway, it is wonderful news, and I, of course, am more than happy to pay.' She threw a preening glance at her daughter-in-law. 'Stuey' – she was again staring at her beloved boy – 'I looked over everything and I think we simply have to get the platinum package. It has the swiftest delivery time.'

'Do you think?' Stu openly wondered at the suggestion.

'Why wait?' Catherine smiled vapidly, as though they were discussing purchasing another sofa. 'It will make things *so* much better for you both. And you'll have the most advanced model available. Just think' – now she held Elena in an icy stare – 'two of you. It's almost too much to bear.'

'I assure you, you won't feel anything.' Dr Schmitt pressed a button and the pod opened up, steam creeping out from it across the floor. Elena continued to hesitate, thinking of the old science fiction horror films she used to watch as a teenager, giddy on the thrills of watching people in peril.

'The worst bit is over,' Dr Schmitt continued, misinterpreting her fear. 'This part is so simple. Trust me.'

'I just . . .' Elena nervously stepped into the room and the door promptly slid shut behind her, sealing her in. 'It's a lot. Making another . . .' She gestured to herself.

'It is all completely organic.' Dr Schmitt guided her towards the pod. 'And it is you. Through and through. You know yourself.'

'Yes but . . .' A chill already running through her, Elena entered the pod. She stood at its base, noticed the flicker of lights on its edges, beginning to glisten with more fervour.

'It's fine, this is fine,' Elena breathed to herself, thinking of all the things the machine couldn't capture.

The moment she learned to ride a bike and thought she could fly.

Tasting strawberries for the first time, in her grandmother's garden on a sun-baked July morning.

Laughing with her mother until she cried over some old television show, sharing a bowl of popcorn while snuggling under a blanket.

Her first kiss with Stu.

Finding out she was pregnant.

Reaching the peak of Everest. Of K2. Tasting that icy, pure air. Feeling like she could touch heaven.

All these moments that had made her. Elena was more than hair, skin and bones. She knew that. She was a tapestry of so many moments, so many instances. Her behaviour, her sense of self, it was all learned and finely tuned over three decades. How could she be replicated in a mere week?

Elena leapt out of the chamber, breathing hard, skin glistening with sweat.

'Is . . . is everything all right?' Dr Schmitt was at her side, concerned.

'I . . . I just . . .' She felt dizzy. Hot. Was she having a panic attack? The doctor led her towards a small metal chair, advised her to place her head between her knees, to breathe.

'It will be okay,' he told her.

'Stu.' Elena rasped. 'I need Stu.'

She'd never scaled a mountain alone. Stu had always been beside her, her rock, her constant. Her support. She needed him now, just to look in his eyes and know she was doing the right thing.

'Hey, *hey*.' Stu wrapped his arms around her as he entered the room, Olive just beyond the door, sleeping in her pram. Never far from them. 'What's going on, baby?'

'I can't . . .' Elena was shaking her head, nuzzling into him, crying. 'I can't do this. It's too much.'

'You can do this.' Stu stroked her damp cheeks. 'You're the toughest person I know. Look, how about I do it all too? Go through it together?' His hands knitted in hers.

Elena sniffed, remembering the blast of snow in her face, the roar of his voice over the wind.

'It's just one foot in front of the other, baby. You've got this. I'll be right here. *Right here*.'

Always united. Always a team.

'I mean, if that's all right.' Stu threw a glance towards the loitering Dr Schmitt, who frowned in displeasure.

'No, not really. We are all set up for—'

'You know who my mother is, right?'

Elena blanched beside her husband. She hated when he did this, mirrored Catherine in ways that made her skin crawl.

Dr Schmitt scratched his jaw nervously. 'I suppose I can make an exception this time.'

'I literally just want to show her that it doesn't hurt, that it's simple enough to be scanned, okay?'

'Okay,' Dr Schmitt agreed with a sigh of resignation.

'Stu,' Elena hissed in warning.

'This is for you,' he whispered to her, 'for Olive. To prove there's nothing to fear.'

'Great, thanks,' he called to the doctor, shedding his clothes and making for the chamber. 'Just you see, it'll all be fine,' he called to his wife, who managed to force a smile of gratitude, unable to explain that it wasn't the procedure that scared her, but what came after.

'How will it know?' Elena had asked insistently in the days leading up to their appointment, Olive nuzzled at her breast. 'To feed her, to change her? How will it know?'

'They come with functioning brains,' Stu reminded her, 'fully formed, adult ones. Yes, it might take time for her to adapt, but she will be more than capable of all those things. Like the brochure says, she will need several days to acclimatise and then will begin functioning adequately.'

With Stu it was always *her*. While for Elena it was *it*. What would they even call it? Elena Two? No, that would be ridiculous.

'We could just call her Lena,' Stu had suggested.

'No.'

That was too close. Elena. Lena. It needed to be something different. Separate. *Other*.

Stu was looking on his phone as he spoke. 'What about Nellie? Apparently it's a nickname for Elena.'

'Like Nellie the elephant?'

'I like it.'

'Fine,' she sighed, too exhausted to argue, already imagining the way Margot would laugh at the name while Leanne suppressed a smirk. That's *when* she finally saw them, stopped hiding in the whirlwind of early motherhood.

They'll understand. They're your friends.

'Nellie.' Elena tried the name in her mouth, not liking how it felt.

And now it was too late to back out. As Stu exited the chamber, beaming, proclaiming how it all felt absolutely *fine*, it was Elena's turn to step inside. Shivering while the lights in the pod shimmered. Catherine had eagerly completed the purchase, almost giggling with delight as the money left her bank account. That had surprised Elena. Surely it was Catherine's worst nightmare to have two sullen daughters-in-law? Perhaps she hoped she could mould this new one to her will. Or, most likely, she just couldn't see past the point of helping Stu. If her beloved *Stuey* was happy, then so was she. Bugger the expense.

'You're doing great,' Dr Schmitt's voice was suddenly inside the pod, transmitted through speakers beside Elena's head. 'We're almost done.'

She forced herself to smile. Would *it* feel nervous? Feel fear? Trepidation? Anything?

Elena closed her eyes and tipped her chin up, trying to picture her daughter and husband, waiting for her. Then she thought of them both engulfed in flames, their skin becoming twisted and charred. *Yes.* It was the right thing to do. To give Elena peace of mind, safety. Who better to leave her daughter with than herself?

Only it wouldn't be her, would it? Not truly.

And then there was Stu . . .

'I mean, it's win-win for me,' he'd joked. 'I get two of you.'

Elena's face had been like thunder.

'I'm . . . Babe. You know I'm teasing.'

Still the hardness didn't leave her face.

'You're *you*.' He came to her, placed his warm hands upon her cheeks, tilted her face to look up at him, into that ocean of blue eyes. 'You're more than your body. More than your hair, your arse. Though they are good.'

Elena broke free of his grip and stalked away from him.

'I love *you*,' he called after her, 'and that isn't something that can be replicated, or transferred. I hope you know that.'

'I do,' Elena sighed, fear twisting in her gut, small and sincere. Like a seed that would germinate and grow. She *knew* her husband. That he loved her. But those moments when his eyes strayed to her arse, or her tits, when she saw a longing in his stare, would he really be able to contain that for just her? Would he have thoughts over . . . over *it*? In a way, how could he not?

And Olive.

Elena's breath caught. Her daughter would surely have no way of telling them apart. What if she liked *it* better?

'And we're all done,' Dr Schmitt announced as the pod eased open, lights dimming. 'That really wasn't so bad now, was it?'

From: POP@outward.co.uk
To: Full Mailing List
Subject: Vigilance

Given the apparent rise in More You models being bought, we must be extra vigilant when out and about in our communities. Please inform us, via this email address, of any suspected More You models that are sighted. It is only through our network that we can remain informed about how these models are infiltrating our society. They can and will be stopped. Information on our next protest will be sent out soon. We urge as many of you to attend as possible.

Remember, they could be among you right now. Check everyone, vet everyone. Don't accept the explanation that someone has a twin. Check the facts.

There is also a planned protest outside Downing Street, since those in power are compliant with all this technology, using it themselves to further devalue the sanctity of our government. We cannot let ourselves be ruled by clones. Stand with us. Stand against the onslaught of fakery.

The clones are getting smarter, making it easier to fool the average person.

We will not be fooled.

.10

There was no sleep while they waited. While it formed. The minutiae of night feeds, soiled sleepsuits and endless nappy changes were a tide that pulled Elena through each day. But behind that there was the drumming on her nerves, pounding and relentless, growing loudest in the snatched rare quiet moments she had. When her head hit the pillow, when she stole a second to use the toilet, she pictured it. Her. Her other self. Soon to be in her home.

Things were happening so quickly, a tidal wave pulling Elena along. Drowning her.

She missed her friends.

Her sense of self.

> **Elena:** I miss you guys. I'm sorry for being shit xxx

> **Leanne:** Don't apologise, babe! Just lovely to hear from you. Can we come round soon? We miss you too! Xxx

> **Margot:** You have been shit. But it okay. We forgive xxx

> **Leanne:** Margot!

> **Margot:** You need your town now you have baby xxx

> **Leanne:** You mean village.

> **Margot:** No . . . town.

> **Elena:** Soon! Things will be better for me soon. I promise. Then I'll stop being such a ghost! Xxx

> **Margot:** You did look pale last time I saw you x

> **Leanne:** Jesus, Margot! Xx

It was raining softly when they went to collect Nellie, making everything appear dusted with fresh dew. Elena was silent in the car ride over, her forehead pressed to the glass, body tightly coiled with tension. She felt each bump and twist in the road, as though in giving away her blueprint, she'd diminished herself. Made herself lesser.

'You okay?' Stu asked over and over as he drove, stealing quick, anxious glances at his wife.

'Fine,' was all Elena could mutter in response. 'I'm fine.'

Dr Schmitt was waiting for them in the lobby, a bright smile on his young face. 'Collection day is here,' he declared as they walked in. Elena was pushing Olive's pram, Stu at her side, his hand on her lower back.

A united front. A team. A family.

The smile Elena offered the doctor was uneven. Was she ready for this? Should they even be doing this?

They were led to a waiting room filled with plush cream sofas and faceless concrete walls. A central table was overflowing with fruit and pastries. 'Help yourselves,' Dr Schmitt instructed as he eased out of the doorway, 'I'll be right back.'

'We're calling her Nellie,' Stu quickly shouted after him.

The doctor gave a brisk nod. 'Nellie. Got it.'

'This all looks great,' Stu declared as he scanned the table, reaching for a cinnamon roll.

'How can you eat?' Elena muttered as her own stomach churned. Was Nellie feeling the same way? Consumed with nerves? Or was anxiety a feeling she'd yet to learn? How much would she know? Feel? Elena had spent too many nights falling down online rabbit holes about clones. Reading dark stories about people who had been attacked by theirs. Then lighter moments where people claimed a clone had saved their life.

> They're just like me.
> Trust them with my life.
> He turned on me with a knife.

It was so difficult to tell where the truth tapered off and hysteria kicked in. More You models assimilated with their hosts over a number of weeks. Becoming more and more like them.

Elena watched the news, studied the prime minister when she gave press conferences as Stu had mentioned she had a unit who stood in for her. Possibly many. She seemed fine. More than fine. She seemed normal.

But Nellie . . . she would *be* Elena. At least all the parts that made her. And Elena trusted herself. Didn't she?

Then there was the safety measure. In online forums they called it the 'do-no-harm gene'. The way the company ensured all models were safe. Subdued. But was that even possible? Was it *right*?

Seven days didn't feel like long enough to consider it all, to grow a human, but seven days was all she had.

'The doctor is just collecting your new you.' A slim woman with white blonde hair came in, ethereal in a silver suit that caught the light as she moved. 'While you wait, here are some of the instruction manuals we highly recommend you go over. These have also been sent to you electronically but we believe in the importance of physical copies within the home.' She set down a hefty maroon binder on the sofa beside Elena. 'There is a lot to go over, including the acclimatisation period, how best to utilise this time.'

'It said about three to four weeks,' Stu said between mouthfuls, 'and best practice is to keep mirroring the . . .' He gestured at Elena. 'The host?'

Elena grimaced. 'Host' made it sound like she had incubated some awful virus. Surely she was just the 'original'.

I'm not ready.

'Here she is.' Dr Schmitt's voice was suddenly loud from the hallway. Elena wanted to be sick. 'Mr and Mrs Roberts, meet Nellie.' He returned to the room with a slim figure walking softly in his wake. Head bowed, her golden hair was drawn back in a bun. She wore white trousers and a white T-shirt, hands clasped at her waist. She entered the room and slowly raised her head to look at Elena and Stu.

'Hello,' she greeted them, eyes crinkling in a smile.

Elena instantly felt hot and dizzy. Speechless, she slowly rose to her feet; behind her she could hear Stu muttering things like, 'amazing', and 'remarkable'. Elena approached Nellie, drawn to her by something primal, something beyond her conscious thinking. She stood before Nellie and took her in. The curve of her nose, the plump space of her lips, the darkness in the centre of her eyes that stared back at her.

'Jesus Christ,' Elena whispered, tears misting her vision. She lifted a hand and touched Nellie's cheek. So soft. It was like looking in a mirror. Only not. It was more than that. Nellie's hair wasn't thick with grease, there were no shadows in her face. She was fresh. Alert.

Alive.

Cupping a hand to her mouth, Elena staggered back, turned away from Nellie.

'Is she all right?' a voice, hers but not her own, was asking the doctor.

'It's a big adjustment,' Dr Schmitt replied smoothly. 'She just needs time.'

As Elena scurried towards a corner Stu rose to take in their latest purchase. 'I can't . . . it's uncanny. She . . . My God. Nellie, hi.' Then he was pumping Nellie's hand, voice high and enthusiastic. 'I'm Stu and the person quivering in the corner is my wife, Elena. We're thrilled to meet you.'

'I am thrilled to meet you,' Nellie replied brightly.

Fuck.

Elena's head was pounding. What had she done?

'She seems so . . . so compos mentis.' Stu was talking to the doctor in more strained tones now. 'How long until she could . . . could handle the baby?'

'Take her home, study the manual,' Dr Schmitt advised. 'She has a fully formed adult brain, with speech and thought capabilities like your wife's. What she lacks is *experience*. But that will come. We always say that the assimilation period should be between three to four weeks.'

'Right, yes.'

With her head pressed to the wall, Elena felt thick, hot tears falling down her face. It was too much. All of it. She jumped when a hand rested upon her shoulder, turning to see her own face peering back at her, brow pinched with concern.

Is this how I look when I'm worried?

'I want to help,' Nellie told her earnestly.

'I . . .'

'Please.' Nellie kept her hand on her shoulder, connecting them. 'I want to learn from you. To learn how to help. That's why I'm here, isn't it? To make things better?'

Elena blinked, unable to respond, not quite believing that Nellie was there at all. That it was real. She stared at her other self, shaking slightly, recalling what she had read in the More You manual. The way the model's genetic make-up might be 'slightly' altered.

Enhanced nurturing.

Suppressed aggression.

'Aren't they just playing God?' she'd asked her husband, handing him her tablet, the screen glowing gently. Stu scanned the page, shrugged nonchalantly.

'I'm sure the same questions were thrown about when people began scanning their DNA for inherited illnesses. Testing for birth defects during pregnancy. It's just progress, Elena. You don't need to fear it.'

'But what if I do . . . fear *it*?' she asked as her stomach knotted. And she did fear it; all of it. The prospect of More You, of a clone in her home. Of another . . . her. 'I've read stories . . . of people being attacked by their More Yous . . .' She was talking fast, face growing hot.

Stu put down the tablet, leaned towards his wife, cupped her chin in his hands. 'Sweetheart, those are just stories, I promise. Made up by people looking to take down the company, to stall change.'

'But—'

'There's never any weight to them. Any evidence. Trust me.' He placed a kiss upon her lips, forcing her silence. 'Besides, I would always protect you.'

Elena looked into his eyes. He kissed her again.

'I'd do anything to protect you and Olive. Anything. You know that.'

She gave a nod of acceptance, knowing that he would. Her gaze drifted to the tablet, to the words glowing upon it.

Enhanced nurturing.

Suppressed aggression.

The knot in her stomach became tighter.

'It will be all right,' Nellie assured her with startling confidence. 'I'm here to make things better. You'll see.'

.11

Elena hugged Olive to her chest, the house before them.

'I guess, welcome home.' Stu smiled awkwardly at Nellie, who was climbing out of the car.

'Wow.' Nellie smiled enthusiastically, showing all her teeth. 'What a beautiful house.'

'Thank you.' Stu opened the front door and Nellie followed him inside while Elena hesitated, looking upon her white-bricked end terrace with fresh eyes: the bay windows, front-door steps, the slip of wrought-iron fencing and the tuft of hedge. Two storeys, though many of her neighbours in Whitstable had converted their loft space, giving them sky lights and that most sought after commodity – extra space. A climbing rose twisted up the wall between their door and the next house. To Elena it was all decidedly ordinary. Very nice, but nothing spectacular. Yet Nellie had beamed like they'd just parted the gates to Windsor Castle. Was that what it was like to be so . . . so new? Would Nellie be in awe of everything?

On the car ride home Nellie had been silent, staring out of the window, taking it all in. This world. It struck Elena that all Nellie had known until that morning was the lab, its slick sterilised spaces. Now there was a sky, blue and vast, smells, people.

'You coming?' Stu hissed a little tersely from where he'd reappeared in the doorway.

'Y-yes, sorry.' Elena hurried towards him, into the tiled hallway off which rose their staircase. The door to the right led to the kitchen, and if you followed the length of the hallway you reached the lounge and the patio doors, which opened onto the garden. This was where Elena found Nellie, peering out at the grass, eyes aglow.

'This is all so wonderful,' she muttered, the tip of her nose touching the glass doors.

'This is our garden,' Elena explained, feeling awkward.

'Garden.' Nellie repeated the word and gave a tight nod.

'Do you . . . do you want to go outside?'

As though not hearing her, Nellie stepped back from the doors and gazed up, at the light fitting above, then she walked towards the fireplace, now idle and cold, shadows clustered within.

'This is all so . . . so lovely.'

'Thank you.' Elena rocked Olive gently in her arms. She assumed taste was something Nellie had yet to acquire. Perhaps at this moment she really did savour the nautical theme of the lounge, the cream of the sofa, the blue stripes of the cushions.

'Is this you?' Nellie spotted the photograph of Stu and Elena atop Everest, their exhausted but elated expressions. 'What is this?' Nellie jabbed the picture with a finger and Elena gritted her teeth, hoping it wouldn't get knocked from its perch atop the hearth.

'It's . . . Stu and I climbed a mountain once. Many years ago. It was . . . it is, the highest point on earth.'

'Wow.' Nellie spun to look at her, apparently genuinely amazed. 'That is . . . incredible.'

'Thank you.' Elena's cheeks grew warm. She'd forgotten how it felt to tell someone she'd done something so few had done. To inspire awe.

'So' – Stu strode in, glancing between his wife and Nellie – 'cups of tea all round?'

'Sure.' As Elena nodded she realised how dry her mouth was. 'Nellie?'

Nellie wasn't looking at Stu, but at Elena. 'How should I . . . Do I like tea?'

'Yes.' Elena smiled nervously. 'You like tea.'

'She likes it strong and sweet, like her men.' Stu winked at Elena. 'Shall I make yours the same?'

'Yes.' Nellie kept watching Elena as she answered. 'Yes, please.'

Elena was relieved when Olive began to fuss and she had to excuse herself to the kitchen while she instructed Nellie to sit on the sofa watching television. 'What are we doing?' Elena fretted as she began preparing the breast pump for the inevitable moment when Olive had decided she'd had enough. Already the baby was clamped to her nipple and suckling furiously but Elena sensed it wouldn't last long.

'Her vocabulary is way better than I was expecting,' Stu commented thoughtfully as he stood beside the boiling kettle.

'Agreed.'

'And she can walk, talk, take things in,' he continued, peering quickly over Elena's head to ensure they were still alone. 'It did say in the manual that she'd come with a fully formed brain, exactly how you were, what, a week ago.'

'Right.'

'So language, speech, cognitive capabilities, are all there.'

'Sure.'

'It's just . . .' His voice trailed away, brow furrowed.

'Memories.' Elena considered. 'She has none. She's like this fresh, empty vessel.'

'So happy.' Stu laughed drily. 'Like, *so* happy. Do you think we would be like that if life hadn't knocked it out of us? Made us jaded?'

'Maybe.' Elena's arms began to ache from clutching Olive to her breast; soon she'd have to return to the lounge and surround herself with cushions for support. 'She's like a new puppy.'

'Well let's hope she doesn't piss all over the carpet.'
'Stu.'
'Maybe I need to take her to puppy training,' he jested.
'Is this weird for you?'

He blinked. Inhaled. 'Is this weird for *you*?' he said, rallying the question back to her, eyes wide with concern.

'Yes, very,' Elena admitted, voice now a whisper.

'Same.' Stu glanced again towards the door that led to the lounge. 'But we needed this, we needed the help. And she seems . . . fine. She seems fine.'

Once Olive was fed and sleeping in a sling, Elena began showing Nellie around. 'If you have any questions, please just ask,' Elena insisted. But Nellie just kept following her around, exclaiming how wonderful and amazing everything was.

'The bathroom.'

'Washing machine.'

'This is our room.'

'This will be Olive's room when she's old enough to not sleep with us.'

'And this is your room.' Elena swallowed as she held open the door to the spare bedroom, which was now fitted out with a single bed beneath the window, a white wooden dresser and side table. Not that Nellie had any belongings other than the simple clothes they had bought for her and placed inside the wardrobe.

'So this is where I sleep?' Nellie enquired, drifting towards the bed and then the window, a smile pulling on her lips when she saw the garden below.

'Yes, this is where you sleep.'

And dream.

Elena gently stroked Olive's head, wondering if Nellie would dream. *Could* dream. If dreams were the subconscious replaying events, worries, would she just drop into dark, empty slumber?

'Such a beautiful room,' Nellie gushed. Again, Elena felt the burn of discomfort run through her. The room was far from beautiful, it was basic. 'And I'm just across from you,' Nellie noted, pointing to the door left ajar across the landing, revealing the corner of Elena's bed. 'That's good, since I'll need to come in during the night to help with the baby and—'

'Let's not get ahead of ourselves.' Elena cut her off sharply. 'What I mean is' – she took a steadying breath, wondering if she'd ever looked as hopeful, as filled with wonder, as Nellie currently did – 'let's let you settle in for a few days, okay? Give you time to get a feel for the place.'

'I do like it here.' Nellie's eyes crinkled in the corner as she smiled. 'It feels like home.'

'Wonderful.' Elena was already backing out of the room, the comment leaving her cold.

It feels like home.

Only it wasn't Nellie's home. It was Elena's. Clicking the door shut behind her, she went to her own bedroom, protectively clasping her hands against her sleeping daughter.

'Will she sleep?'

It was dark outside. Elena was sitting up in bed beside Stu, Olive sleeping in the cot at her side.

'Of course she will sleep,' he mumbled as he turned a page in the hefty manual he'd bought up with them. 'She's a clone, not a robot.'

Elena strained to listen for any sound from the landing beyond. It had been just over half an hour since they had all retired to bed. Nellie had dutifully gone to her room, closed the door, and switched off the light.

And then done what?

Elena had anxiously offered her a few old paperbacks to read. All of which Nellie had brightly declined.

'I like to just sit and be quiet, taking it all in,' she explained.

'It says her taste in food, drink, will be similar to yours,' Stu said as he studied the manual. 'But other things, like taste in music, will develop differently. As those come about through environment and experience.'

Elena looked at her husband and then scowled in despair. 'Can you put something on?'

'What?' Stu's face crinkled sadly. 'I always sleep in just my boxers.'

'I know, but . . .' Elena took in her husband's torso, the dark hair on his arms, his chest, the ropes of muscles on display. Stu had always been in good shape and he remained committed to his fitness regime. Elena was accustomed to the odd appreciative glance following her husband when they were out. It didn't bother her. But the thought of him colliding, barely dressed, with Nellie during the night, stirred a tempest of jealousy within her. 'Just put on a T-shirt or something. Please.'

'Fine,' Stu grumbled as he flicked back the duvet and climbed out of bed. 'But you know this is ridiculous, right? That we need to get used to her being here.'

'This is just the first night.'

'I know' Stu pulled on a navy top. 'But you've not even let her hold Olive yet.'

'It's the first night,' Elena repeated with more steel.

'I *know*.' Stu rolled his eyes and got back into bed. 'But please try to remember why she's here. Okay?'

'Okay.' Elena sagged back against her pillow. She intended to lie awake agonising over it all, listening for any sound of their guest, but instead exhaustion crept up to meet her. She drifted off within minutes, heart rate slowing, while across the landing she hoped Nellie was doing the same.

.12

Catherine studied every word of the message her son had sent her.

She's great, Mum. Everything is fine.

She itched to go round, to see her latest purchase in the flesh. All these years of being connected to More You but she'd never really seen it before, not first-hand. Yes, there were More Yous in the office when she visited. But she didn't *know* them. Or, at least, their original. She *knew* Elena. Could recall their icy first meeting when they went out for dinner and Elena used the incorrect cutlery.

'It's the other one,' she'd told the young woman through clenched teeth, hoping no one at a neighbouring table had noticed the faux pas. 'Didn't your mother teach you about table etiquette?' She'd merely been enquiring about Elena's upbringing but Stu made a sound of warning in his throat. Elena stared rigidly at the correct knife she was now holding and Catherine half expected her to lunge across the table and plunge it into her chest, so stormy was her gaze.

'She's not like the others,' Catherine had later told her son, thinking of the well-bred young women who'd hung on his arm in the past.

'I know,' he told his mother, his gaze hard. 'That's why I like her so much.'

It was unfathomable to Catherine why her son loved this girl, with her rough edges and lack of charm. And manners. And despite Catherine's attempts at polite conversation, throughout that first meal Elena's face never thawed from a scowl.

'Think of it as the perfect blank slate,' another member of the board told her. 'Imagine how you'd be if you hadn't had all your experiences, if life hadn't ground you down.'

Catherine didn't want to imagine it. She wanted to think only of Elena, of her More You.

Of this blank slate.

This potential new start.

She hoped Stuey would now be getting some much needed rest. How she hated thinking of him burned out, exhausted. Fathers weren't supposed to be getting up in the night, changing nappies. Eric would have balked at the idea. It was why he was so happy to pay for additional help. And Catherine was happy to accept it.

'Men should be men,' she'd told Stuey when he originally told her how much he planned to pitch in. He'd rolled his eyes at her in that way of his which suggested she both bored and annoyed him.

'Mum, times have changed. A baby has two parents, you know.'

Catherine did know. And she knew that each parent had a place, a role to play. For decades she'd played hers so dutifully.

Perched upon a wicker chair in her conservatory Catherine read the message from Stuey again.

> She's great, Mum. Everything is fine. It's definitely a bit strange . . . like another Elena. Sometimes . . . sometimes

I can't tell them apart. Just to look at of course. But she's good.

She's great, Mum.

Everything is fine.

At some point she would need to relay all this back to the board. First she was going to focus on being a mother, so she carefully typed out her response, hating how long it took. With a sigh she pressed send, then decided she needed a glass of wine. Her footsteps echoed through the empty rooms of her home.

.13

The morning light was pale, the sky the colour of turned milk. In the kitchen Elena waited by the toaster, knife in hand, Olive in a sling against her chest. She still felt curdled from too little rest; eyes sore, skin dry. When she ran her tongue around her mouth she felt the telltale curve of an emerging ulcer.

'What do you like for breakfast?' she turned stiffly to ask.

Nellie was perched atop a stool at the island, glancing towards the window, letting the soft sun warm her skin, which held a glow Elena was quite certain hers never had.

'I . . . um.' Nellie touched a hand to her neck, delicate and unsure. 'I don't know.' She wore the same clothes she'd had on the day before.

'There's stuff in the wardrobe you can wear,' Elena told her, thinking of the items she'd grabbed in a supermarket the previous week. Items she herself would never wear.

'She could share your clothes,' Stu had said unhelpfully when they were pushing a trolley through the chilled aisles, Elena watching a sleeping Olive in the car seat perched above their shopping like she was a bomb about to go off. 'I don't think so,' she'd snapped at her husband.

Those are mine.

'What . . . what should I have for breakfast?' In the kitchen Nellie seemed wide-eyed and vulnerable despite being a grown woman.

'I usually have porridge, with a dash of honey. And some toast,' Elena suggested with a half-smile.

'Sounds wonderful.' Nellie briefly returned the grin and then resumed gazing out the far window. Elena frowned as she slathered butter upon a freshly popped piece of toast. There was nothing remarkable about their street – a slip of sky, houses clenched too tightly together and cars wedged like dominoes in any slice of space. Elena felt it, the tightness of it all. She missed the open mountain air. The freshness. The freedom.

Olive released a single, mournful howl.

'Someone is hungry,' Nellie commented.

'Yep.' Elena passed over a plate of toast towards the island and began bouncing on her toes. 'Just one minute, okay, baby? Hang on.'

'I could feed her.' Nellie stood, expression open and hopeful.

'What? No. It's fine, really. Besides, she's—'

That's when she saw the dark patches forming upon Nellie's chest, spreading through the white top she wore. 'You're . . .' Elena could only point, mouth growing dry.

'Yes.' Nellie beamed, cupping her breasts with her hands. 'They were aching so much all night. Could I please use the, um,' she made a pumping gesture, 'that way she can still have it.'

'You want to use the—'

'Here.' Stu walked in from the hallway, swiftly reached for the breast pump cluttering up the countertop and tossed it onto the island. 'Have at it,' he told Nellie. 'Saves any milk going to waste.'

'I—' Elena froze, stunned, as her husband came and kissed her cheek. He was freshly showered and carried the oaky aroma of his favourite cologne.

'Have a great day at work,' Nellie gushed at him, 'and thanks so much for this.'

'If you need me, call me,' he told Elena, voice low and firm.

'Great. Thanks. I will.'
'Love you.'
'Love you.'

Elena didn't want to admit how nervous she felt being left with Nellie. With herself. She listed chores to do around the house to keep Nellie occupied. Hoovering. Tidying out cupboards. Scouring the showers. Anything to keep those new hands busy and away from Elena, who set up camp on the sofa, Olive tight against her. Really, she should get out. Get some fresh air. But as always she'd awoken exhausted and defeated before the sun had even slipped above the horizon. The thought of setting up the pram, pulling on some semi-decent clothes and actually going somewhere felt impossible. Elena listened to footsteps passing overhead, to the swill of water whenever Nellie used the toilet. Every nerve in Elena's body was too tight, too attuned to what was happening. It felt like there was an alien in her home.

'Anything else I can do?' When Nellie appeared in the doorway to the lounge she was flushed and smiling, still in her soiled T-shirt.

'Can you prepare dinner?'

'Sure.' For a second, the smile fell. 'What do you like to eat for dinner?'

'Lasagne. From scratch.'

'Great.'

'That includes the pasta and the sauce.'

'Great.'

Elena watched Nellie disappear towards the kitchen, guilt tickling the edge of her thoughts. She never made anything from scratch, preferring ease. As Nellie cooked, Elena stole away upstairs, found a bottle of freshly pumped milk on her bedside table, waiting for her. For Olive. Elena picked it up and promptly flushed it down the sink in the nearest bathroom, watching the soiled water spiral around the plughole.

'I could get used to this,' Stu declared as he folded himself into bed that night.

'Course you could,' Elena replied sourly, readjusting her posture so that Olive could feed more easily, her left arm already growing numb. 'The house is clean, your shirts are all pressed and you came home to a freshly cooked meal.'

'You say all of that like it's a bad thing.'

'It's just . . .' Elena shrank against the pillows, nervously glancing at their closed bedroom door. She half imagined Nellie crouched behind it, ear pressed to the wood, focusing on their every word. But given the way she'd worked her all day, she was fairly confident that Nellie would have passed out the moment she lay down in bed. She was relatively human, after all. 'It all makes me so nervous,' Elena admitted.

'I know.'

'The thought of her being with Olive. *Feeding* Olive.' She looked down at her little baby, pink-faced and suckling, content. Elena's chin trembled. 'What if she's . . .' The house was cleaner than it had been in months. Stu had exclaimed that dinner was one of the best meals he'd had in years. Both facts wedged like thorns in her side, catching each time she drew in a breath. 'What if she's better than me?'

'That's ridiculous.'

'You said yourself how much you loved dinner, how clean everywhere is.'

'Yes, but—'

'And what if Olive prefers her?' The thought was almost too unbearable to say out loud. Elena's voice cracked as she buried her head close to her daughter's.

'Sweetheart, she won't.' Stu began rubbing her back, his touch warm and gentle. 'That's not how this works. Nellie *isn't* you. She's not some replacement, she's an addition. You need to see it that way. Like a live-in nanny.'

'I'm just struggling with it.'

'I know.'

'What if she does something while I'm asleep? Like, takes Olive?'

'Firstly, I don't believe she would; secondly, we'd find her instantly because of the chip.'

Elena blinked and furrowed her brow.

'In her ankle.' Stu expanded. 'It's in the manual, remember? A GPS tracker is in every model, it contains their unique assignment number. So she can never go missing.'

'Okay.' Elena didn't feel the slightest bit consoled by this information.

As Olive withdrew from her breast, Elena pressed the baby to her shoulder and began to gently bounce her, while her hand worked up and down Olive's tiny spine. 'Do you think she dreams?' she asked, nodding at their closed bedroom door.

'Probably.'

'What must it be like, to be a person and be so . . . so fresh? So unblemished by the world?'

'I bet it's pretty good.' Stu reached for Olive and gingerly stroked her plump cheek. 'Like being a baby.'

'Hmm.'

'But' – when he looked into his wife's eyes, his tone was serious – 'it's your experiences that make you. That make us. Maybe she dreams of nothing. Maybe she dreams of everything. I don't care. I only care about you and Olive. About your dreams.'

'Tell me I did the right thing,' Elena whispered, eyes too tired and too dry to even release a single tear.

'You did the right thing.' Stu kissed her cheek again. 'You just can't see it yet. But you will. In time, you'll realise how much easier Nellie will make things.'

Once Olive was content in her side cot Elena lay awake, thinking of Nellie's mind, wondering if it was this great vacuum or if she, too, felt consumed by circling, perilous thoughts.

From: POP@outward.co.uk
To: Full Mailing List
Subject: Be Alert

Our contact at More You has informed us that a new model has been released, without public knowledge. This newer model, though in its testing phase, has more expansive neurological capabilities. The contact said that the company are monitoring this unit closely with a view to rolling out this newer model widely as early as the end of this year.

The issue here, they claim, is that this new model comes with fully formed memories. That the integration is seamless. That ultimately, they think they are the host.

We don't need to highlight here how catastrophic this would be. Currently, More Yous can be controlled to some degree. They are generally docile. Like dogs. This could change everything. We need to find this model swiftly and eradicate it. Be. Alert.

.14

It was dark when Elena opened her eyes. And still. For a moment she lingered on the edge of sleep, lethargic and content, savouring the calm. Sounds began to drift to her: the steady groan of Stu's breathing, the tick of the clock on the far wall. Elena could almost drift off again. Almost. But her chest ached, pressure building behind her nipples. And she really, really needed the toilet. Turning, she pushed herself up, swung her legs out of the bed, knee accidentally tapping against the edge of the bedside cot.

'Shit,' Elena hissed through clenched teeth, then leaning down, tone delicate, 'Sorry, baby girl.'

She expected to see her daughter swaddled in a growbag, cheeks flushed and brow damp. Instead, the cot was empty.

'What the fuck?' Elena wasted no time leaping forward and flicking on her bedside lamp. She heard Stu grumbling behind her but didn't care. 'Olive?' In the golden glow of the light she could clearly see the space where her baby should have been. Gone was the growbag. Gone was her little girl. 'Olive!' The name got strangled in her throat.

'What's going on?' Stu was straining to sit up, voice rough with sleep.

'Olive!' Elena snapped at him, growing more frantic by the second. 'She's not *here*. She's . . . she's . . .' No. She couldn't, wouldn't say it. Her daughter wasn't gone. This had to be a mistake. A nightmare she just needed to wake from. Elena ran from the bed, checked the bathroom, throwing on lights as she went, making the house burning in its radiance. She ran out onto the landing, slapping on more lights, cheeks damp from panicked tears. And then she heard it. So soft, so gentle, it could almost be the stirring of the wind outside.

Humming.

Someone was humming.

It was coming from the spare room.

Nellie's room.

Elena marched towards the door, thrust it open and took in the sight before her. The room was bathed in delicate, ambient light, courtesy of the lamps Elena had placed around the place several months before. Nellie was sitting up in the bed, pillows at her back, chest exposed. Olive suckling at her breast.

Elena wanted to scream. Cry. But all feeling seeped out of her as she stood and stared, eyes wide and raw. Her baby. Her beautiful, pink bundle, in the arms of this . . . this stranger. Stu was behind her just as she turned away, burying herself into his chest and whimpering.

'Make her stop,' she rasped.

'Sorry.' Nellie spoke quietly, carefully. 'Have I done something wrong? Olive was crying and you were so very deep asleep you didn't hear her. I changed her and then gave her a feed.'

Against her husband Elena shook with rage. He smoothly stroked her back as he addressed Nellie. 'No, thank you, Nellie. Elena clearly needed the rest. We appreciate you stepping in.'

Elena was trying to voice her disgust, her anger, as he bundled her out of the room and onto the landing, closing the door to Nellie and Olive behind them. 'What are you doing?' Elena's voice was high and fraught. 'I told you to stop her!'

'She's just feeding Olive,' Stu stated, eyes red with exhaustion. 'You know, the very exact thing we got her for.'

'Yes, but she's—'

'Olive is *fine*.' Stu rubbed her shoulders, offered her a tired smile. 'Everything is *fine*. Okay? She's basically being fed by you. This is what we wanted. Remember?'

'But she's not being fed by me.' Elena threw a desperate look at the closed door. 'I'm her mother. I'm the one supposed to be in there with her. Caring for her.'

'Christ, Elena!' Her name was a dagger unleashed from his mouth. Elena flinched, sank back from her husband as he dragged his hands through his rumpled hair. 'You refuse a nanny, you refuse my mum. I get you a fucking new *you* and still it's not enough!'

'I'm . . . I'm not . . .' She fumbled for her words, surprised by Stu's outrage. His anger.

'I'm doing my bloody best here,' he lamented, staring at her, breathing hard. 'I'm knackered too.'

She looked at him, at his bloodshot eyes, the lines gathered around his mouth. 'You can't do everything.' His voice softened as he reached for her shoulders, gently placed his hands upon them. 'Go back to bed.'

'No.' She pushed herself away from her husband. An ache in her which couldn't be ignored. 'I need to go and fucking express, since Olive won't want *my* milk now.'

'Baby—'

'It's fine. Just . . . just leave me to it.' She was already making for the stairs, shoulders slumped.

'Okay,' she heard him call weakly after her. 'I love you.'

In the kitchen it was cold and Elena liked that. She savoured the chill that snaked up her legs as she walked barefoot on the tiles. It woke her up. Made her alert. She wouldn't let herself sleep so deeply again. Grabbing the breast pump, Elena padded into the lounge, straining to hear any sounds from overhead. She couldn't shake the image of Olive feeding from Nellie from her mind. It was seared there, burning and painful. As she set up the pump, Elena tried to imagine the events before she had woken – Olive crying, Nellie creeping in like some thief in the night. Instead of waking Elena she had chosen to feed the baby herself. Had her shadow crossed over the bed as she stood by the window and stooped low to lift Olive out of her cot? Had she even glanced at the sleeping parents as she stole back into her own room?

Does she feel like she's Olive's mother?

Elena looked up at the ceiling as she attached the pump to her left breast. Soon the room was filled with the sucking sound of her milk being forced from her. Nellie was her DNA clone. Everything Elena had, Nellie had. Size six feet. Brown hair. A 125 IQ. Breast milk. This made Elena feel nauseous, the adrenalin easing within her, leaving a metallic taste in her mouth. Was Nellie going through the same hormonal changes as Elena? She must be experiencing something similar, to produce breast milk. Elena blinked away a tear as she looked again at the ceiling.

She's my baby.

She could just tell Nellie to stop pumping, to let her breasts swell and throb for a day or so and then the milk would stop. But then there would be less for Olive.

She's my baby.

I'm enough. Aren't I?

A fresh tear traced a line down her cheek.

She had no doubt that Stu would have returned to bed, straight back to sleep, untroubled by the events of the night. He didn't understand; how could he? He wasn't the one being usurped.

.15

The morning arrived like a slap, sudden and harsh. Elena blinked into consciousness, limbs still heavy and sinking into the bed. How she longed to close her eyes again and drift back into the nothingness. But something was wrong. Taking in a breath, she listened for Olive, the air around her still, thick with all their curdled dreams from the night before. Turning on her side Elena reached for the cot, tugged it close, saw Olive's bundled form within, eyes closed, long, dark lashes spread atop plump pink cheeks.

Thank God.

With a sigh Elena rolled onto her back, peered up at the ceiling. She sensed that Stu wasn't there, his side of the bed cold and empty. What time was it? Had he already headed off to work? Surely he'd have woken her to say goodbye? That's when Elena noticed the figure at the end of the bed.

'Christ!' With a gasp she quickly sat up, her hand instinctively reaching for the cot once more. 'What the hell are you doing?' she demanded of Nellie who was standing at the far end of the king-sized bed, head bowed, lips pursed in thought, studying her.

'I was waiting for you to wake up,' Nellie explained, face instantly breaking into a bright smile.

'You were . . .' Elena ran her fingers through her tangled hair. 'How long have you been there?'

A light shrug. 'A while.'

Elena went cold. 'You . . . you don't watch people sleep.'
Nellie's expression was blank.
'It's . . . it's fucking weird.'
'What if Olive needed me?' Nellie wondered simply.
'She doesn't,' Elena snapped in response.
'She fed twice in the night.'
'What?' Elena began to feel sick, a roiling sensation in her stomach. Had she slept while Nellie entered her room a second time, took her baby from her cot and fed her? Acted like her mother? She looked across the bed at the mirror image of herself, searching for dark circles beneath her eyes, the telltale look of someone losing sleep. But Nellie was immaculate. Her blonde hair was drawn back in a neat bun; she wore jeans and a crisp pink shirt. A shirt Elena recognised. Bought over a decade ago for an interview for an office job which she'd tanked. She could just imagine Stu passing it to Nellie earlier that week – 'She never even wears it anyway.' As though that mattered. It was still *hers*.

'Look—' Elena began sharply, ready to reclaim some boundaries.

'Did you know you talk in your sleep?' Nellie interjected with a bright urgency to her words.

'What?'

'You keep saying, "Don't fall."'

'I . . .' Elena frowned. 'I don't talk in my sleep.' Stu would have mentioned it, surely, after over a decade of sleeping side by side. Dreaming in unison.

'Were you afraid when you went up those mountains?'

'No,' Elena replied, the sick feeling rising within her again. 'I mean, yes. It can be scary up there. It's dangerous.'

'But you did it anyway?' Nellie was staring at her intently.

'Yes,' Elena confirmed, 'I did it anyway.'

*

It was a day where the sun never shone. As the sky began to darken to evening, Elena rocked Olive in her arms and paced the length of the lounge, one eye keenly turned in the direction of the French doors. In the garden, the distant form of Nellie was crouched in the flower bed near the back fence, plucking out weeds.

'I don't like her,' she told Stu again as he leaned back upon the sofa, his tie freshly loosened around his neck.

'That's kind of like saying you don't like yourself.'

'No, it's not.'

'My mum says it's normal, you know.'

Elena clenched.

'If you look back, there have always been wet nurses, women who constantly breastfeed various babies, not just their own. It's a way of managing the burden within a community. My mum says there's nothing to be upset about.'

'Oh, well, if your mum says that,' Elena stated in a scolding tone.

'Don't be like that.'

'Like what?'

'Mean.' Stu gave her a levelling look. Elena wilted slightly beneath his stare. Was she being overly cruel? Was exhaustion grinding her down to her worst parts?

'It's more than feeding Olive.' With a shake of her head Elena was again focused on Nellie, on how swiftly she plucked a weed by its furled leaves and hauled it up from the ground, roots sprinkling soil upon the grass. 'I caught her watching me sleep this morning.'

'Okay,' Stu conceded, turning to look at their guest, the light outside weakening by the minute. 'That is weird.'

'Right? She just seems . . . so with it. More than I was expecting. She's . . . more together than the unit we saw at More You.'

'I agree that she seems smart.' Stu tilted his head. 'But you're smart as hell, so that's no surprise really.'

'Thanks,' Elena replied flatly, in no mood to receive a compliment.

'Look, we keep her until Olive is sleeping through the night. That's it. And it won't be long.'

'Leanne said her twins didn't sleep through until they were two.'

'Jesus.'

'I know.'

'Well,' Stu stood, came and placed a hand on Elena's shoulder, looked down tenderly at their daughter cradled in her arms, 'let's see how we go. It's definitely helping you to get more rest.'

'She makes me uneasy.'

Stu didn't answer. He was watching Nellie continue to methodically attack the weeds in the flower bed.

'Did you give her that shirt?' Elena asked, nodding at the French doors.

'Huh?' Stu blinked, looked at his wife. 'That pink one?'

'Yeah. Did you give it to her?'

'No.' Stu shook his head. 'She's got the stuff in the spare bedroom that you picked out, but I've not touched any of that.'

Elena kept watching Nellie, on her knees, clearing the flower bed until it was perfect. Until there wasn't a single weed left. The pink shirt now stained with dirt.

'She's not afraid to get her hands dirty,' Stu remarked as Olive began to wake up. With a grin he reached for her, gingerly took her from Elena's arms and smiled into her flushed little face. Elena barely noticed, still staring into the garden.

'No,' she replied absently, 'she's not. But neither am I.'

It was a strange evening. Elena bathed Olive with Stu while Nellie cleaned up the dinner things downstairs. Then, as Stu settled Olive in her cot, Elena crept downstairs, feeling foolish for being nervous in her own home. She found Nellie in the kitchen, wiping down the counters, still in her pink shirt, some hair now broken free from her tight bun, framing her face, making her pretty, even, in the glow of the ceiling spotlights.

'You don't need to do that,' Elena told her, so casual in contrast, in soft joggers and a white T-shirt stained with baby sick.

'I like to help,' Nellie remarked primly.

'We like to be busy.' Elena approached the island, leaning against it. 'We like to have purpose.'

'Do you need me to feed Olive tonight?' Nellie finished cleaning, kept the cloth in her hand and stared at Elena.

'You don't—'

'I'm here to help,' Nellie told her forcefully. 'I *need* to help.'

'Do you . . .' Elena studied her, trying to find the words. To Nellie, the world was new. Though she was not. She wasn't a baby like Olive, who would grow and explore everything in time. She was already grown. An adult. With a fully formed brain. 'Are you okay here?' Elena concluded lamely.

'I'm fine,' Nellie's reply was tight, her gaze never leaving Elena's face.

'Where did you get the shirt?'

'Oh.' For a second Nellie glanced down at herself. 'Don't worry, I'll clean it.'

'I asked where you got it.'

'From Stu.' For a moment Nellie looked wounded.

'Stu?' Elena repeated, incredulous. 'I don't think that—'

'Babe!' Her husband's voice was suddenly loud atop the stairs, drawing the attention of both women. 'We've had a poonami up here, can you help?'

'Coming,' Elena and Nellie replied in unison. Elena gave the other woman a hard look. 'I've got this,' she stated icily.

*

In bed, the windows open wide to air the room, the sounds of the night slipping in, Elena sat up, feeling fraught.

'For something so small, our kid does some nasty shits,' Stu complained from beside her where he was lying down.

'Nellie said you gave her the pink shirt.'

'What?' With a groan her husband joined her in sitting up, rubbing a hand down his tired face. 'She must be confused.'

'She specifically said that *you* gave it her.'

'Well, I didn't,' Stu remarked, a note of annoyance in his words.

'I don't trust her.'

'You're being paranoid.'

'Can you . . . can you show me the thing?' Elena gestured to his phone charging on the nightstand.

'The thing?'

'You know, the chip. You said it locates where she is.'

'Sure.' Stu leaned over, unplugged the device and then opened an app with a golden O on his home screen. 'Here.' He zoomed in on a map of their street, where a golden star was glowing. 'This is the tracker, showing she's here, at the house.'

'But where?' Elena pressed. The grumble of passing cars and late-night bird calls were making it increasingly difficult for her to hear any sounds from downstairs.

'It just says she's at the house.' Stu frowned at her. 'Not which room.'

'Right.' Disappointed, Elena sagged against her soft pillows.

'Tomorrow, why don't you go and meet your mum friends? Leanne and Margaret.'

'Margot,' she softly corrected him.

'Margot, right.' Stu leaned over to kiss her forehead. 'You've barely seen them since Olive was born. Might do you some good to chat with other mums.'

'I'll take Olive with me.'

'Of course.' He yawned and rolled onto his side. 'And set that app up on your phone; that way you'll know what Nellie is doing. Give you some peace of mind.'

'Should I tell Leanne and Margot about her?'

'You haven't already?' This made Stu sit up again, hair tumbling into his eyes. When he was like this, unguarded, he reminded Elena of the boy she'd spent countless nights tangled up with in her single bed at uni. Her lips against his, their breathing slowing as dawn crept over the horizon and they finally succumbed to sleep. The spell of him; she had been lost to it. He made her world brighter, her heart beat faster. 'Why haven't you told them about Nellie?' he gently nudged.

'I guess . . . I guess I'm worried they'll judge me.'

'They're your friends, they won't judge you.'

'You clearly don't know women that well.'

'Okay . . .' Stu's mouth widened in a yawn. 'Well, if they do judge you, that's on them. Doesn't Margot have a live-in au pair?'

'Yeah, from Sweden.'

'Well, there you go. They can't judge you on getting, well, another you, can they?'

'Is that how it feels with Nellie, that she's another me?'

Stu considered the question as he scratched his chin. 'I mean . . . she looks like you.'

'But does she *feel* like me?'

'No,' he answered quickly, 'but how could she? You're *you*. She doesn't laugh like you do, or give me that knowing look when—' He was reaching towards her, bridging the space between them but Elena shrank back, distracted.

'Olive can't seem to tell the difference.' She didn't even bother to hide the hurt that flushed up her neck, her cheeks.

'Olive is a baby.' Stu drew her towards him for an embrace. 'Babies don't know anything other than needing to eat and shit. Don't worry about it.'

'Okay.'

He kissed her firmly on the lips. 'Elena Roberts, you are irreplaceable. You hear me?'

Elena kissed him back, savouring the closeness. A car drove by, windows open, a sad melody leaking out into the night, covering the sound of a creak on the landing, by their door, which Elena could have sworn she had heard. But then the moment had passed and she was in her husband's arms, almost feeling like she was eighteen again, lost in love and lust.

Taken from an Article in the *Herald*

Recent reports suggest that the organisation Protectors of Purity, more commonly known as POP, may have access to firearms.

While the group firmly states this is not the case, there have been suggestions of more violent uprisings in the group's ongoing protest against the growing use of clones, particularly aimed at the company, More You. Some eyewitnesses claim to have seen armed guards at POP meetings.

A spokesperson for More You responded to these reports saying, 'While we permit POP to conduct their peaceful protests outside our offices we will not tolerate any threat of violence or violent acts.'

Previously, POP has staged protests against the clones. Graffiti regarding their stance is evident throughout London. When we reached out to POP for comment, they stated, 'We are only ever looking to protect humanity and adhere to all current laws while doing so.'

The firearms report could be speculation, but authorities have committed to look into it if further eyewitnesses come forward.

.16

They were warned about the rising presence of POP. Repeatedly. Catherine grew tired of finding fresh emails whenever she logged into her computer at home. When she'd last visited the office she had been appalled to find what was basically a mob surrounding the front entrance.

'Can't you call the police?' she asked the pale one – what was her name? Aria? The young woman arched a single eyebrow and looked at Catherine as though it were the most ludicrous suggestion.

'Of course not,' she'd told her in a feathery voice. 'It's their right to protest.'

Young people. They thought it was their right to do every damn thing they pleased. As she'd barged her way past banners, ears ringing with their asinine chants, Catherine found herself missing Eric. His decisiveness. He was a man not to be trifled with and he certainly would not have tolerated the kind of spectacle that soiled the street beyond More You. Catherine had hoped that Stuey would be cast in his father's mould, and he had been once. Before Elena softened him. Now he talked to Catherine about organic food and being 'sensitive to others'. When had she ever *not* been sensitive? Catherine gave to charity at least one a month. She *cared*.

But to the young, unless they saw a bleeding heart they thought you a monster. Catherine envied their energy to always have a cause, a reason to hoist themselves up onto a soapbox and cry out. They'd learn. Life would harden them as it hardened all who lived long enough.

She didn't like that POP seemed to be everywhere. When she came away from her computer they were on the television, being blamed for blocking the M1 or spray-painting a chain of stores that hired More Yous. But Catherine only ever saw them as an irritant, a nuisance. Flies buzzing too close. She didn't think that they had poisoned stingers. That they could ever actually hurt anyone. What a fool she was.

.17

The antenatal classes had been Stu's idea, by way of his mother, pitched to Elena as a chance to make friends with other mums-to-be. Elena suspected the suggestion was born out of Catherine's belief that she had no idea what she was doing. Elena had gone along, begrudgingly, expecting to find a room full of jobsworth women, overly keen and already refusing to eat anything that wasn't organic. Instead, she found Margot and Leanne.

Margot had swanned in late, carrying a large takeaway cup from Starbucks. She was impossibly slim except for her middle, which bulged like an alien growth from her willowy frame. Her jet black hair was cropped to her shoulders and her lips were a slash of fierce red. When the instructor frowned in disapproval at her cup, Margot narrowed her blue eyes icily. 'Trust me, I need this. I will literally die without it.' Then she took an overly dramatic sip from the cup, leaving a lipstick stain upon the plastic top. No one could ever place Margot's accent. When asked where she was from, she'd wearily reply, 'Everywhere,' as though she had seen so much of the world she was tired of it. Elena envied her, envied all the places she must have seen. She continued to yearn for travel, even as the baby within her grew and she knew her chances to explore the world would soon diminish.

Leanne had already been at the class when Elena arrived, a double pushchair wedged behind her containing two identical sleeping toddlers, both white-blonde and cherub-cheeked. 'I only come here to get my parking approved,' she whispered to Elena as Elena struggled to sit on the floor beside her, 'then I head into the centre to do some shopping.' She nodded in the direction of the pushchair without turning her head. 'Got to make the most of nap time,' she added with a smirk. Leanne was short, the shortest of the three of them, and had hazel eyes which always shone with mischief. She was from Lancashire and would start stories with caveats like, 'between you, me and the gate post'. Elena instantly liked both Margot and Leanne and it wasn't long before they were meeting for coffee – never decaf for Margot – after classes.

Margot's baby arrived first, a week before her due date. A boy with hair as dark as hers and tiny hands that seemed to permanently make fists. 'Already so angry,' Margot had cooed with pride, 'just like his daddy.'

Leanne's baby was next; a third boy for her brood. He was a week late, flame-haired and lethargic. 'They had to shake him to get him to scream,' Leanne later recalled to her friends, laughing slightly. 'Going to be a lazy one, I can tell.'

Finally, Olive came. Though there was no pushing, no clinging to gas and air as Elena lay spreadeagled on a bed and gave it her all. With her delivery there were IVs as she was induced, a hook to break her water, doctors and consultants shining lights into her core and exchanging worried glances. Until the decision was made for an emergency C-section. Elena remembered seeing the colour drain from Stu's face as he was told to quickly get in scrubs while she was wheeled down to theatre, needles hastily forced into her spine. The world upside down. The surgeon over her wore a face shield that got spattered with Elena's blood. Dark and dripping. And then she was being cut open, Olive pulled from her, so tiny and curled into a ball. From the table Elena watched her baby get passed from midwife to doctor, to Stu. Waiting for her chance to meet her daughter, to have her moment.

Her recovery felt long. It would take six weeks to fully heal. But there was no rest. Each night Elena had to drag herself out of bed to feed Olive, work against the pinch of her stitches. How she ached. How her body burned in protest with every single movement. She shied away from Margot and Leanne, ashamed of how she had struggled while they'd handled their new babies with relative ease. And while Olive awoke every forty-five minutes without fail, screaming and hungry, their babies slept for four, five hours at a time. It was hard to be around them when their days weren't tarred by sleepless nights. But Stu was right, she did miss them, it would be good to see them. Which was how she found herself that next Tuesday morning in their favourite café, Olive sleeping in the car seat that Elena had wrestled atop the pram, nervously sipping on a cappuccino while her friends absorbed what she had just told them.

'A . . . another *you*?' Margot frowned, red lips plateauing with distaste.

'I mean, I've heard of it.' Leanne nodded with enthusiasm, her newest baby clenched to her chest, feeding contentedly, while she intermittently shoved crackers into the mouths of her toddlers perched either side of her in highchairs like some strange gargoyle adornment. 'Seen the adverts and stuff. Apparently the prime minister has a few. And that, that guy . . . he was in the superhero thing. Dates that girl who had that video leak.'

'Robert Penderson?' Elena ventured nervously.

Leanne clicked her fingers. 'That's the one. I read that he uses his so much that he started sending it in on set to do his takes and no one could tell.'

Elena put down her cup, the frothy milk tasting sour. 'Oh, really?'

'Not natural,' Margot declared loudly in a sour tone. 'Baby should be with mother.'

'First' – Leanne raised her eyebrows at her friend, accent thickening, as it often did when she was angered – 'you're one to talk, Lady Muck, with your live-in help. And second, Olive *is* with her mother. Sort of.'

'So she's like you? Totally?' Margot asked brusquely, staring at Elena, squinting as if checking it really was her.

'I mean.' Elena squirmed in her chair. 'She looks exactly like me. But she's . . . I don't know. Calmer. Purer.'

Leanne laughed drily. 'I can imagine. She's yet to be fucked by the world.'

'Mouth!' Margot exclaimed in faux horror, gesturing to the toddlers.

'Please.' Leanne rolled her eyes. 'They have no bloody idea what I'm saying. Let me enjoy my dirty mouth while I still can.'

'How is she with the baby?' Margot glanced at Olive, who was still sleeping.

'She's . . .' Elena inhaled, looked at her friends. She didn't want to burden them with her turmoil, she wanted this to be a carefree, happy catch-up. And yet a tear slid down her cheek. 'The other night I caught her feeding Olive and I . . . I hated it.'

'Okay' – Leanne was instantly fishing in her massive bag for a tissue, which she thrust towards Elena like a white flag – 'I get it, babe. That must be tough. But you do need to rest. It sounds like getting another you will help. You and Stu can finally get some proper sleep. You're no good to Olive exhausted, you know that, else you wouldn't have got the . . . the other one made.'

'Does he like it?' Margot leaned across the table, chin resting atop her gathered hands, long nails painted sky blue. 'Because Simon, he would love it. I can only imagine what he'd be thinking.'

'I know what Jack would be thinking,' Leanne chortled. 'Someone else to cook his dinners, wash his clothes. Bloody pampered thing, he is.'

'I've been making her do jobs. Clean, cook. I kind of . . . I don't know what else to do with her. I want to keep her busy.'

'That's why she's there.' Margot gave an approving nod. 'To work. To help.'

'Yes but . . .' Elena glanced at Olive, then down at the table, feeling weighed down. 'If she really is, you know, like me, won't she want more? What if . . .' She chewed her lip, unsure what she was even asking of her friends. Of herself. 'She's a person,' she concluded simply, shamefully.

'She's a clone,' Margot swiftly corrected her.

Leanne pursed her lips. 'I've heard it takes time, but they are wired to completely assimilate with you, copy all your mannerisms.'

'Wired?' Margot remarked. 'Like some robot? But they are flesh and blood, no?'

'Very much so,' Leanne confirmed, 'but there's something in their DNA, I think. Jack did work on a house for a guy who was an executive for More You, said he heard some interesting stuff when he was on conference calls at home. Shouldn't your mother-in-law know?'

'She's just on the board as an investor. She doesn't actually *know* anything,' Elena replied dismissively.

'Mm.' Leanne pursed her lips together. 'Jack said he heard they're getting smarter. More and more like their originals, these days.'

'What if they get *too* much like you?' Elena fretted.

Margot and Leanne shared a look.

'Was this all Stu's idea?' Margot wondered.

'No,' Elena said quickly, too quickly. 'He just . . . he knew I needed help. That's all. And he knew I'd never accept it from his mother.'

'Ha.' Margot slapped her hand against the table, causing all their cups to rattle. 'I hear that. My mother-in-law is monster. Hate her.'

In the corner, Margot's baby, Reuben, began to stir. Margot leaned in close to him and grimaced. 'Oh good, he make shit. Be right back.' She unceremoniously hoisted him up and then scooped up her sleek changing bag, which glimmered with designer beauty.

Leanne passed Elena another tissue. 'Look, it will be all right. Use the clone while you need her, then turn her back in.'

'Turn her back in?'

'That's what happens, isn't it? When a clone has served its purpose, or maybe gone a bit rogue.'

'A bit rogue?' Elena swallowed nervously.

'Jack said he got the impression it happens more than you think,' Leanne shared gravely. 'But there's procedures in place at the factory to deal with it, to decommission them, don't worry. And they all have that chip.'

'That's right,' Elena quietly agreed. 'Did Jack . . . did he happen to hear anything about how they, you know, decommission them?'

Leanne leaned forward, dipped her head low, voice carrying a slight urgency. 'The company is pretty tight-lipped about it, he said they talked about rehabilitation but he felt like there was something more than that going on. Something sinister.'

'Christ.' Elena paled.

'Right. But remember, they're not us, babe. They're, you know. Made. Cloned. Not proper humans.'

'Sure.' Elena felt uneasy about it all. Nellie *was* a proper human. She was real, in her home. Her life.

'I just worry,' she admitted tightly, 'how much she's . . . like me.'

Leanne eyed her thoughtfully. 'How so?'

'Like . . .' Elena squirmed, the thoughts that swirled in her mind at night, her fears, finally able to break free. 'If she's truly like me, if I were her, I'd be, you know, biding my time to take the place of the original.'

Leanne's eyebrows lifted, then she gave a brisk nod. 'I get it, babe. I do. But isn't that the point of the DNA tampering stuff? To stop them wanting your life? To stop them being . . . I don't know . . . complete, I guess. Make them more . . . compliant?'

'I know they do that, I just . . .' Elena sighed, remembering how Stu had already dismissed her fears, telling her she was reading too many horror stories online.

'You worry it can't truly stop it? Because people are people? Human nature can't be tamed?'

'Exactly.' Elena held her friend in a weighted stare.

Human nature.

Her nature.

How long would Nellie tolerate being subdued? Being kept? How long until her true nature broke through?

'But you're not going to keep her long term, are you?' Leanne asked.

'No.' Elena looked towards Olive, who continued to sleep so peacefully. 'No, we're not.'

'Don't worry yourself too much with it all.' Leanne reached for a muslin and wiped furiously at the face of one of her twins, then she switched her nuzzling infant to the other breast. She moved with such confidence, such assurance, making parenting seem easy. 'If she's helping right now, focus on that. Remember this is just a short-term thing.'

'I know.'

'It's scary what they can create these days.' She held Elena in a steely stare. 'You should have said, babe. If you were struggling. Me and Margot, we would have happily stepped in.'

Elena exhaled. 'You've got your hands full as it is.'

'Use her while you need her,' Leanne advised again, 'then turn her back in.'

'Sure.'

'And keep boundaries.' Leanne hastily wiped the mouth of the other twin. 'Don't let her in your bed.'

'What? I'd never—'

'None of us married saints,' Leanne hissed at her. 'He's only human, Elena. Remember that. At the end of the day, that's the problem we all have: that we can and will fail.'

Elena's mouth opened and snapped shut again as Margot rejoined them, a look of disdain on her face. 'For something so small he make big mess.'

'Try having three shitting in nappies at once,' Leanne jested. And just like that, the conversation moved on. Leanne's warning forgotten, or at least seemingly so, as Elena sipped her drink and smiled at all the right moments.

Don't let her in your bed.

Walking home, Elena thought of the pink shirt. How convincing Nellie had sounded when she'd said Stu had given it to her. When it began to rain she welcomed it, placing Olive beneath her waterproof cover while allowing herself to get soaked, savouring the damp chill that gathered against her bones, reminding her that she was alive. That she was herself.

.18

Elena still remembered how it felt to get that call about her mum. That gut punch. Everything had been so wonderful, she'd just scaled another mountain with Stu, was feeling exhausted and elated. They'd made base camp and Elena was looking forward to collapsing in her tent, to enjoying the kind of deep sleep that only comes from a physically drained body and a true sense of accomplishment. Then she checked her phone, knowing she would finally have signal. So many missed calls. So many voicemails. Growing numb, Elena listened to the most recent message, felt the world beginning to tilt and sway around her.

'Mrs Roberts, I'm so sorry to inform you that—'

The miles. She felt every single one of them, separating her from the hospital where the call was coming from, from the bed her mother had died in; they wrapped around her like a chain, trapping her.

I should have been there.

That was the first, hardened thought that pounded in her mind. Later it sharpened as it attached to her psyche, determined to be ever present: *I have failed.* Her mother, the one person on the planet who she utterly, truly adored in a way the love for a partner could never emulate. The person who had raised her, held her when she'd cried, cheered louder than every parent combined when Elena had won all her sports day races. Her mother had sacrificed everything to give her daughter a good life. And while she took her final breaths, Elena had scaled a mountain. Always striving. Always pulling away.

'Are you all right?' Stu had been at her side, had noticed her expression; his own face had begun to pale. Elena couldn't speak; she just handed him her phone by way of explanation and walked off into the snow, leaving heavy footprints behind.

The feeling of failure was clinging to her again as Elena pushed open her front door, propping it open with her back as she hauled the pram up the steps, Olive already waking. Elena dripped rainwater all over the hardwood floor as she pulled the pram inside.

She looked down at her baby and hoped that one day she could tell her stories of the grandmother she'd never know. That together they could take comfort in them. When she pictured these moments she felt hope flutter tentatively within her. More than anything, Elena wanted to be the kind of mother hers had been. She wanted to build a life for Olive filled with love. When she looked down at the tiny human she had made, she felt it: that love, ebbing out of her. While she was already less than she had been, Olive would be more. It would all be for her.

'Oh my goodness, you're drenched,' a voice exclaimed from the far end of the hallway. Her voice.

'I'm . . . just a bit wet,' Elena demurred as she shook off her coat.

'Here, let me help.' Nellie rushed to her, taking the damp garment and hurriedly placing it on a mounted hook upon the wall. 'Do you want some tea? You must be freezing.'

Elena looked at her and struggled not to cry. Nellie with her smooth skin and strong jawline, eyes always bright and alert, keenness radiating off her. Had she been like that once? Or was this who she might have been, if life had not intervened as harshly as it tended to do?

'Tea would be lovely,' she managed as she turned to lift a mewling Olive out of the pram. Gently bouncing the baby in her arms, she followed Nellie towards the kitchen, noticing the clear counters, the way the cooker top shone. And the air. It smelt clean, fresh. Was there something minty in it? For a moment Elena thought of mountain peaks and that pureness you found up there. 'You've been busy,' she told Nellie, shifting to sit on one of the copper stools beside the kitchen island.

'I wanted to help,' Nellie responded smoothly, focused on reaching for mugs in a nearby cupboard. Elena noticed how she already knew her way around the kitchen, not stopping to ask where the teabags were, or the sugar.

Fumbling at her shirt, Elena managed to free her breast and attach Olive to it before the baby could begin to scream.

'You have a beautiful home,' Nellie enthused as the kettle boiled.

Did she? Elena always felt it was simple, small, and she was growing tired of the effusive comments. But this was the only home Nellie had ever seen, so to her eyes, of course it was beautiful. She had no comparison. Olive was the only baby she had encountered.

Stu the only man.

This unsettled Elena. She could still recall the anger that coursed through her the first time she'd met Stu, but also how conflicted she had been by his smile and his charisma, the way he'd diffused the situation with ease. The way she was utterly charmed by him right from the start, though she knew better than to let him sense that. Did Nellie feel the same way? Was her chemical disposition aligned so completely to Elena's that she couldn't help but be attracted to him? *Was* she attracted to him?

'Are you all right?' Nellie asked as she placed a fresh cup of tea in front of Elena. With a start Elena noticed she'd selected her favourite mug, a navy one covered in the New York skyline and a rosy red apple. A generic souvenir, really, but bought on her first holiday with Stu. Why had Nellie chosen that out of a cupboard full of matching cream mugs? The unusual ones were tucked away at the back, so as to not spoil the aesthetic. Stu would tease Elena that she was naturally eclectic and sentimental, that she just liked to hide it. Her mother's house had always felt so cluttered, pictures crammed on every surface, no matching mugs to be found. Everything had a story, a history. Elena hadn't wanted to be like that, she had wanted to be more functional. More proper.

'My New York mug.' Elena turned it in her hands, remembering how cold it had been as she and Stu ducked into a souvenir shop that smelt of stale cigarettes and roasting chestnuts. The tip of his nose ruby red as they scanned the shelves together, laughing at some of the gaudier items. She'd felt it, her love for him, deep and powerful, like being near a whirlpool.

'Love is supposed to feel safe,' her mother always told her, 'safe yet powerful.'

'What made you . . .' Elena was about to ask why Nellie had pulled it from the cupboard but Nellie was already placing an onion upon a chopping board and commencing to dice it. Working with precision, authority. Her limbs so new but already so skilled. So dextrous.

She watched Nellie work as Olive fed. Perhaps Nellie had merely sensed that Elena had a favourite mug. Was that possible? Or did she know? Could some feelings, some memories, have passed between them during the cloning process?

'You seem sad,' Nellie noted, brow gently furrowed, pausing from chopping. The knife glinted against the board, recently sharpened.

'I'm . . .' Elena carefully shrugged, not wanting to disturb Olive. 'I guess I was thinking about my mum.'

'I see.' Nellie continued to stare at her.

'She . . . she died.'

'I'm sorry.'

'Are you?' The question left Elena before she could stop it. 'Sorry.' She gave a regretful shake of her head. 'I just mean, you don't, I'm not sure you could . . . could understand.'

'Because I'm your clone?' Nellie asked, expression blank.

'I guess, yes. Because of that. You don't . . . you don't have a mother.'

'Don't I have your mother?'

Elena bristled. 'No.' Nellie had never even known Elena's mother. Of course she wasn't hers also. Although . . . 'Shit, sorry. I guess, sort of. You do, genetically speaking.'

'Genetically speaking,' Nellie repeated.

'But you never got to meet her.'

'Which is a shame.' Nellie resumed chopping.

'Yes.'

'So now we both get to be sad.' Nellie looked at her, eyes watery. 'You for the mother you lost, me for the mother I never got to meet.'

Elena frowned at her, puzzled. Did Nellie look tearful because of the onion or was she genuinely upset? Either way, she felt unnerved. 'I think I'm going to have my tea in the lounge, watch a bit of TV while Olive feeds.'

'Of course.'

As Elena carried baby and drink into the next room she could hear Nellie behind her, the crisp smack of the knife hitting the chopping board, imprinting upon it.

.19

'Fuck!'

The following morning Stu's rough cry rang through the house. Elena untangled herself from her sheets, glanced down and felt relief rush through her when she saw Olive in her cot, still sleeping. Pressing the heels of her hands against her eyes she tried to orientate herself.

Stu.

Elena left the bedroom and hurried downstairs. Nellie was already in the hallway, looking polished in leggings that clung tightly to her and an oversized pale blue T-shirt.

Stu was by the front door, a look of anger contorting his face. 'My . . . my fucking tyres, Elena. Someone's slashed them. All of them.'

Elena froze as she watched her husband address Nellie instead of her.

'Oh no,' Nellie uttered sympathetically. 'Bastards.'

The curse word sounded so strange coming out of Nellie's mouth, yet also so natural. As though Elena herself had said it. Because that's what *she* would have said.

Bastards.

Elena could feel her pulse in her ears as the word echoed in her thoughts, anger mounting so that her rage level matched her husband's.

'Stu,' she snapped from where she stood by the base of the

stairs, dishevelled in her nightshirt, hair a tangled bird's nest. 'What the hell is going on?'

Her husband glanced between the two women and for a split second Elena saw it: the confusion. She felt her heart fall to her feet. Then he was walking to her, addressing only her.

'Some prick has slashed all my tyres.'

'What?' Elena looked past him, towards the street and the car wedged against the kerb. 'Are you sure?'

'I'm bloody sure,' Stu told her tersely, 'all flat, every single one. And I needed to be in early today. Dammit. Dammit!' Cheeks flushed, he strode into the kitchen, phone in hand, leaving Elena alone with Nellie, the front door hanging open between them.

'That's terrible about the tyres,' Nellie offered.

'Mmm.' Elena walked across and forcefully closed the door. 'Stupid vandals. We'll need to see if the cameras picked anything up.'

She was careful not to swear, fighting her own natural impulse.

'You think someone did it on purpose?' Nellie asked, still smelling of Elena's shampoo, hair slick from the shower.

'I mean . . . yeah.' Elena frowned at her. 'You don't slash someone's tyres by accident.'

'I see.'

Elena kept looking at Nellie, how awake she was. How quickly she had made it into the hallway even though the hour was early. 'What time did you get up?'

Was it Elena's imagination or was Nellie blushing slightly at the question?

'I'm not sure. I woke up, showered. I was just preparing to come down and make breakfast when Stuart shouted. Why?'

Elena tried and failed to picture it: Nellie squatting down beside each tyre, a knife in hand. It made no sense.

'Just wondering,' she told her lightly as Stu blustered back into the hallway.

'I've called the police but they said without decent CCTV footage there's little they can do.'

'Do we have any? Footage?' Elena asked.

Stu gave her a pained look. 'Looks like there was a power cut last night and the cameras failed to come back online. Fucking typical. They're always playing up.'

'How convenient for our vandal,' Elena deadpanned, flashing Nellie a piercing look.

Did she do this?

She pictured Nellie stealing downstairs in the night while they slept, knife in hand. Elena's stomach churned and for a moment she had to turn away from Nellie and her husband for fear of retching all over the floor.

She just wants to help us, not hurt us.

It made no sense; Nellie wouldn't seek to harm them. But still the feeling of uneasiness persisted.

'My mum mentioned there has apparently been increased POP activity in the area.'

This made Elena turn back sharply, eyes wide.

'I'm not saying it *is* that.' Stu came close to her, put his hand upon her shoulder. 'I'm just saying let's be careful.'

They both stole a furtive glance at Nellie.

'Shall I get breakfast ready?' their third wheel politely asked. Elena found herself nodding even though she was far from hungry.

'Yes, Nellie, thanks.'

Quietly Nellie left them and went into the kitchen.

'I mean, maybe it was POP.' Stu was chewing his lip, frowning. 'We've been so careful and—'

'You thought she was me.' Elena blurted. 'When I came downstairs.'

'No I didn't.'

'Yes,' Elena told him forcefully, 'you called her Elena.'

'What?' Her husband shook his head in annoyance. 'Christ, Elena, don't be on me now. I've got enough on my plate.'

Elena nodded, still burned by his mistake. She listened as he prattled on about tyres, cost, the timing of it all. The inconvenience. All the while she kept thinking that the strangest part of the entire exchange when she came downstairs was Nellie's response. How, when Stu had called her Elena, she hadn't corrected him.

.20

There are things you do without even noticing. Things that are intrinsic to you. How you brush your hair, your teeth. How you hold yourself as you walk up a staircase. Things you do automatically, not even thinking about it. Things that Elena did, with a functional ease, until she noticed a figure ever present at the edge of such moments. Nellie at the bathroom door. Nellie at the foot of the stairs. Always watching.

'It's what she's meant to do.' Stu reassured Elena when she bought it up. 'All part of the assimilation process.'

Elena bounced Olive in her arms as she walked around the kitchen, trying to banish the thoughts of Stu's maimed car. One of her favourite songs was playing on the home stereo system. It felt comforting to lose herself to the melody, the familiar chords, a song she had loved as a teenager; listening to it felt like a small portal back to that time when she was younger, bolder. Back when she was able to come home to her mum.

'I like this.'

Nellie was in the doorway, nodding along to the beat with an approving smile on her face. 'Who is it?' She cocked her head at Elena.

'It's . . .' Elena tried to think, assessing how long Nellie had been standing there and why she was no longer doing whatever job she'd been tasked with that morning to keep her busy. 'It's just an old band I used to like.'

'Mmm.' Nellie kept smiling as the song continued to play. 'It makes me think of sunshine.'

'What did you say?' Elena shot the question at Nellie, tightening her grip on Olive, freezing on the spot.

'Blue skies, beaches,' Nellie continued, giving a light shrug. 'It's a nice song.'

Blue skies.

Beaches.

Elena had been fourteen when the song came out; she remembered it being everywhere. One of those songs that everyone seemed to love and was on in every shop, in adverts. They used to play it in the arcade Elena frequented that summer during their annual holiday to Wales. A relic of another time. Elena liked the smell of copper, the flashing lights, the thump of the pinball machine. While her mum was on the beach, laid out on a deckchair reading a book, Elena would steal over to the arcade where it was always quiet, always dark. And most days, the song played. And that's where she'd met Russell Peters, the first boy she'd ever kissed. Cheeks spurned by acne and hair solid with too much gel, he wore oversized jeans and T-shirts from bands she'd never heard of. Together they'd sit on the beach, watch the shoreline, listen to the gulls diving and enjoy that heady intoxication of being too young to know how fleeting things truly were. When he went back home Elena had wept. And then again when he'd failed to email even though he'd sworn that he would.

The song currently playing in her kitchen made her think not of the heartbreak but of those moments on the beach, side by side, hands tentatively touching, the world golden and glorious. Was Nellie feeling that too? Somehow sensing that feeling? That memory? How was that even possible?

'Do you need me to do anything?' Nellie was now by the island, looking at her intently.

'I . . .' Elena's chest was tight. She was thinking of Russell Peters, of a past she could never get back, while in her arms Olive, the future, began to stir. The little baby had it all ahead of her: first visit to the beach, first sunset over the sea, first kiss.

'Need me to change her?' Nellie asked kindly.

Elena looked at her, at the woman who was her carbon copy. Fully grown and yet as unsoiled and pure as Olive.

'Please.' Nellie came closer, arms extended. 'Let me help.'

Elena felt dizzy as she handed her baby over, noticing the stench rising up from Olive's nappy. 'Do you . . .' She blinked hazily at Nellie, then asked in an anxious whisper, 'Do you remember things?'

Nellie looked at her, eyes bright. 'I remember coming here, to your home. This is my whole world.' Then, to Olive, 'Have you filled your nappy, little miss? Shall we go and get you changed?'

This is my whole world.

Elena felt an overwhelming sense of pity as she watched Nellie withdraw from the room with Olive, making for the changing station that had been set up in the far end of the lounge.

That afternoon the rain came. Hard and fast, leaving them all trapped inside. And for the first time ever, Nellie asked to be excused so that she could nap.

'I'm quite tired today,' she explained apologetically, elegant in her leggings and T-shirt.

'Sure.' Elena nodded at her, feeling shabby by comparison in oversized joggers and a hoody bearing the emblem of a concert she went to many years ago. 'I mean, yeah, of course. Take all the time you need.'

'Thank you.' Nellie gave a quick smile and then disappeared off upstairs. Elena heard the closing of doors, flushing of the toilet, and then things were still, the only sound the patter of rain upon the window. Olive was sleeping soundly in her Moses basket, face pink and content. Elena reached for her laptop, which was wedged beside the sofa, and opened it up. Really, she should have taken the opportunity to rest herself, but curiosity stirred within her. She opened up the More You website, biting her lip. She had visited it countless times before. As soon as she was on the page, the welcome video began to play.

> '... where you can be you and more. Here at More You we embrace cutting-edge cloning technology to replicate you at this exact moment. Your language capabilities, physical attributes, all can be mimicked by your other you. Come and visit us today and learn why countless world leaders and famous stars rely on More You to help manage the load of modern living. We can—'

Elena left the page and found herself on a forum of other people who had used More You. She idly scrolled down the comments.

My clone is taller than me, is this normal?

Does anyone else feel like theirs is their sister? I feel like mine is family.

My 'me' is new and we have had him for about a week but lately he's complaining of fatigue. Is this normal?

Elena clicked on the final comment and read the thread.

This also happened to me, is very normal, especially during an intense phase of the assimilation process. It can be exhausting learning and adapting to being someone new.

She left that chat, moved deeper into the forum.

Is it true that there is a DNA fail-safe? I fear my husband is growing too attached to the other me. Is it right that she won't do anything morally wrong, because of something in her genetics?

Intrigued, Elena read more.

> Hi, yes, More You make changes to their DNA structure to remove any murderous/hazardous intent from clones, thus ensuring they are safe to be in our homes. Although, this might not extend to sleeping with your husband, sorry. It is more a 'do no harm to others' type situation.

Elena kept reading as the people on the forum debated this, how there was no real way to stop someone causing harm. Clones were humans. Humans were fallible. That was just a fact of life.

> A clone is capable of anything we are. Without the moral compass that our years of existence have given us. Which, when you think about it, is truly terrifying.

A floorboard creaked upstairs and Elena shut her laptop, tense, feeling like she'd just been caught doing something she shouldn't. When only the rain continued to pepper the window behind her she leaned towards Olive, sleeping contentedly. Elena felt it in her bones; that edge of exhaustion slipping away, enabling her to enjoy this moment of watching her baby sleep. Allowing her to be present. Even happy. Nellie *was* helping. There was no denying that. But that didn't mean she had to stay. Elena thought of the slashed tyres on Stu's car and felt a lingering sense of unease. Were they being watched? Were POP passing by their home? Surveying them?

'What do you want?' Russell Peters had asked her, boyishly handsome, the sky indigo above them.

'I want to see the world,' Elena exclaimed, 'every single inch of it. I want to explore, see things.'

Often, her world with her mother seemed so small. She'd watch contrails from aeroplanes in the sky and then find out on a flight tracker where they were going. Wonder about the people onboard, what kind of lives they must be living to just take off and explore somewhere new.

'That's a big thing, to see the entire world,' Russell replied, considering.

'Sure is.'

'You got big dreams, Elena.'

'Yep.'

And then he kissed her, tasting of fudge and coke.

This is my whole world. That's what Nellie had said. But did she also share snippets of Elena's world? Elena's past? Or was this it for her? And looking round her lounge, with the matching throw cushions, the framed pictures of her and Stu atop mountains, Elena knew it would never be enough, not for someone who wanted to see it all. If Nellie truly was like her, it was just a matter of time until she left them. Until she yearned for more.

.21

Catherine paid for the tyres. Discreetly, of course. As soon as Stuey called she told him she would handle it. She would help.

And though she feared for him, instantly hating whichever rotten scoundrel had targeted her boy's home, it felt so good to be needed. To hear that inflection of panic in Stuey's voice.

'My tyres, Mum, ruined, just like that, while we slept.'

If Catherine closed her eyes she could almost hear the boy he had once been telling her he'd woken from a nightmare and was afraid.

'Don't worry, Stuey, we'll get it all fixed.'

'When I reported it to the police they mentioned POP.'

'Do they know you have one at home, a More You?' Catherine asked, anxious.

'No, course not,' Stuey assured her. 'They just said they'd been made aware of increased POP presence in the area. Trying to pin the tyres on them, I suppose, maybe because I'm your son.'

This made her pause, one hand upon the smooth surface of her kitchen island. She flexed, let her long talon-like nails click against the marble.

'I told you to be careful, Stuey. That they have been more active lately.'

Catherine was thinking of the emails from More You. The concerns over the threats. So often they were classed as idle, nothing to fear. But Catherine had passed by the heated mob outside the entrance, felt the venom in their voices, the sting in their chants.

POP didn't just fear clones. They hated them. And hate could be an extremely potent motivator.

'Stuey, darling, you need to take more care. Keep the other Elena safe and inside, out of sight.'

'Mum, she's called Nellie.'

'Sure, sure.'

She didn't like it, the thought of strangers watching the house, passing judgement, making plans. Even when he was a child, Catherine had warned Stuey of the jealousy of others.

'People will always want what you have and that can make them cruel,' she'd said. It was a lesson she had learned herself many times over. Having money made you more than a target, it made you a punchbag, or a pit for those less fortunate to throw all their bitterness into. Catherine had done her best to shield her son from the ugliness of it all but even the tightest ships spring leaks.

'Did the cameras pick up anything?'

'They were offline,' her son sighed. 'We had a bastard power cut last night too.'

'That's convenient timing.'

'That's what Elena said.'

Catherine arched an eyebrow. 'Well, Elena is right.' She considered that perhaps they could unite on this, their shared fear over the assailant of the tyres. She imagined going over out of concern, Elena, grateful, ushering her inside. The two of them drinking tea and sharing theories.

'Perhaps I should—'

'Can you just send the money?' Stu cut in. 'It'll be about a grand, I reckon, and I really need it sorted today.'

Catherine wilted against the island, nodding.

'Parents are just overgrown piggy banks to their kids,' Eric had remarked with disgust whenever Catherine paid for something for Stuey. She refused to see it that way. She was helping her son in a way any parent would if they could. There was nothing wrong with that.

'Yes, of course, Stuey, I'll sort it and then maybe—'

'Sorry, Mum, I'm late enough for work as it is. Love you.'

Two words. The call ended and still Catherine clung to them. *Love you.*

Her son's love; she'd do anything for it. Suddenly filled with purpose, she left the kitchen and moved upstairs to the room that had once been Eric's study and housed the single desktop computer in her home. Quickly she typed in a search:

POP

Catherine wanted to think it was all just a coincidence, the tyres, the cameras. And though she could be foolish she was no fool. As she read up on the organisation she made a call to her contact at More You.

'I don't care about the right to protest. It's high time we moved those marauders off our doorstep.'

'That'll only anger them,' came the warning from her fellow board member.

Catherine pictured her son, bereft beside his Mercedes as he noted each deflated tyre.

'Then let's anger them.'

.22

Elena had always liked her back garden. It had been one of the things that first attracted her to the property. Her surveyor's eye understood the importance of outdoor space, a garden they could landscape and improve. While Stu had admired the original tiles in the hallway, the large kitchen and its grand island, Elena had drifted towards the lounge, the French doors, which opened onto a small patch of lawn bordered with flower beds. The sun had been shining and for a moment she had been transported somewhere far away, somewhere vibrant and wonderful. The adventurer within her had been thrilled. 'We could put a trellis there,' she told her husband excitedly, pointing back to the house, 'and a pagoda here. Roses and ferns over there, some hydrangeas. It could be our own little bit of a paradise.'

'Look at you with your green thumb.' Stu had smiled warmly at her, the sun filling his face with a handsome glow.

'I just think we could really do something special here.'

She pictured a little bistro set by the far wall, candles flickering elegantly in jars on balmy summer nights.

'I think so too.' Stu laced his fingers through hers as they both looked across the garden. 'But ease off on the enthusiasm a bit when the agent comes over. I want us to get it for a decent price.'

Elena most liked her garden at either end of the day, when the sun was first dipping above the horizon, the grass dew clad and glistening, or when dusk was falling and there was birdsong and the distant smell of barbecues. When Elena awoke that morning it was still dark. Olive was sleeping soundly, as was Stu. She realised with a start that it was the first time there had been such an occurrence since they'd slowly driven home from the hospital, Elena clutching her aching stomach and wincing each time she turned to the back of the car to check her baby was still there. She knew she could roll over, try to enjoy whatever time of rest remained and go back to sleep. But Elena craved a bit of distance. Some solitude. So she slipped on her dressing gown, pushed her feet into her slippers and quietly padded across the landing, pausing briefly at Nellie's closed door, noticing how no sounds came from within. She, too, must be sleeping.

A mist covered the garden like a hangover from the previous day. It rose above the lawn like a haze, tangled in the bushes. Elena surveyed her small scrap of what she'd once hoped would be paradise. There was no trellis, no pagoda. No bistro set. The only addition they'd made to the garden since moving in was a wooden bench that was pushed up beside the French doors, looking out on all they had yet to accomplish. All they had neglected. Their intentions had been good but life always intervened. She and Stu were either too tired from work to do any gardening, or in their free time, away on holiday on a different continent. And then Elena got pregnant.

She looked for signs of Nellie's labours. Nellie who had stepped in where Elena had failed. The flower beds looked tidier, kempt. Some of the bushes had been trimmed back. Elena walked across the lawn, slippers growing damp. She was looking towards the far wall, the dark soil beneath it, noticing how the ground seemed slightly uneven, as though something had perhaps been buried there. Elena was so consumed with her movements that she didn't see a piece of terracotta pot on its side in the grass. She connected with it, ankle rolling, and then she gasped as she felt the unmistakeable burning sting of pain. Of something penetrating her skin.

'Fuck.' She twisted to look down at her foot, seeing the ribbon of crimson already sliding down to her heel from where her ankle had been punctured by the sharp edge of the pot. 'Fuck!' Hopping awkwardly, Elena looked back to the house, knowing she should go inside, clean up her foot. The pain remained raw, sharp, a tang in her mouth. But the lump in the soil. Curiosity got the better of her and she hopped the rest of the way to the back of the garden, spotting blood upon the grass as she went. After all, she'd only be a minute. And Nellie had spent so much time out there, been so diligent in her weeding, Elena was merely checking what had been done.

Perched on one leg Elena pressed her palm to the rough bricks of the far wall to balance herself. Then, with her free hand, she carefully lowered it to flick through the soil. The lump of it. It wasn't long until her fingertips connected with something soft. For a moment Elena baulked but kept dusting the soil away, not caring about her ankle, the fact she was in only a dressing gown and slippers. As she flicked away soil she saw fur. Though dirtied, she could see it was ginger. More dusting and then it was there. A head. A body. A cat. Face turned down into the earth so all Elena could see was a dirtied back. She shot back, the movement sharp and sudden, ankle burning in protest. And then she was screaming.

Twenty minutes later she was beneath the bright spotlights of her kitchen, ankle bandaged, a blanket around her shoulders.

'Why didn't you tell me?' she fired at Nellie, who had been the one to rush out to her, to crouch beside her and reassure her.

'It's fine,' she kept whispering softly to her, 'it's just a cat. I found them by the front of the house, run over.'

Elena had wanted to shake her off, to run from her, but she'd needed help to get back inside, her ankle now alive with pain, flames of it licking the surface, almost crippling her.

'Honey, can we drop this?' Stu pleaded from where he was anxiously pouring them all a cup of tea, Olive in a sling against his broad chest, sucking fervently on a dummy.

'No,' Elena snapped, eyes on Nellie, who was dutifully preparing breakfast as though everything were fine. 'I need to know why she didn't tell me. You don't just bury a dead cat in the garden and not tell anyone.'

'I don't know what you want me to say.' Nellie ceased buttering toast to stare at Elena. 'I found the cat on the road two days ago, already dead. I thought best not to cause alarm, just to bury them quietly. I didn't mean to upset you.'

'That cat belonged to someone!' Elena cried, feeling exhausted and angry. 'Someone will be missing them.'

'Did they at least have a collar on?' Stu asked.

'I can check.' Nellie gave a curt nod.

'Check?' Elena's face crumpled with disgust. 'You want to check the *dead and buried* cat for a collar? Why didn't you just check when you found them?'

'I didn't think to.'

'Christ, well, we need to check for a fucking collar.' Elena held her head in her hands, anticipating the awkward phone call she'd need to make to some forlorn family. How she'd get to kill their hope.

'Okay.' Nellie gave a smile that swiftly died, gaze hard as she put down the knife she'd been holding. 'I'll go and check.'

'And next time you want to bury a dead animal in my garden, fucking tell me,' Elena yelled after her. 'Can you believe her?' she asked her husband, ankle throbbing.

'Hmm.' Stu looked thoughtful as he sipped his tea.

'What?'

'Burying the cat is strange, absolutely.' His gaze flitted fearfully to the door Nellie had just left through. 'But what bothers me more is *how* did she find the cat? She said they were out on the road, right?'

'Right.'

'Well, I didn't think she'd been through the front door since we bought her home. We're trying to be careful.'

Elena considered this, thinking of the slashed car tyres, a pulse striking beneath the bandages around her ankle. 'You're right.'

'I mean, the app says she's here.' Stu was already checking his phone, frowning. 'But it doesn't say exactly *where*. Just . . . here. What if someone has *seen* her?'

'It must have been when I went to see Leanne and Margot.'

'Do you think she was trying to leave?'

'I don't know.' Elena's chest pinched nervously. But she did know, didn't she? Because if that were her, that's exactly what she'd have been doing. Tired of being locked up, tired of being held in one place.

'There was a collar,' Nellie announced bleakly as she returned, soil on her hands. 'Is there perhaps a cardboard box I might place the cat in, in case the owners want them back?'

'Sure.' Stu handed Olive over to Elena, making for the garden, Nellie following. Elena looked down at her baby, gently stroked her cheek, remembering the horrid absurdity of the moment she'd felt softness in the soil. How she'd almost *known* that the cat was there. Sensed it.

.23

Three hours later there was a family on the doorstep, tear-streaked and broken. Two fathers and a son, the lad barely reaching their shoulders, cheeks speckled with freckles. 'I'm so sorry,' Elena kept repeating on a loop, handing over the cardboard box, shuddering at the heavy weight of it. 'Truly sorry. My . . . my friend found him.'

'Albert,' the boy whimpered, turning to burrow into the chest of the tallest man.

'Thank you.' The other man was carefully taking the box from her, eyes glistening, voice close to breaking. 'Thank you for calling us. We had been so . . . so worried.' A choke. A sob. Elena steeled herself in the doorway, her eyes heavy with the desire to cry. Guilt gathered around her like a shadowy cloak. The cat had been buried in *her* garden, found outside *her* home. She felt awfully complicit in its demise through association and was keen to close the front door, place glass and steel between herself and the grieving family. Albert's family.

Now she knew his name.

If only Stu had been there to handle it; he was always better with people than she was, had that easy, affable way that made everyone like him. But he was at the office. He'd offered to stay home, face pale after helping Nellie box up the deceased feline, but Elena saw the telltale tightness in his jaw. Knew that no matter how much he might want to stay home, he was needed elsewhere.

'Go,' she told him, feigning confidence. 'I'll be fine.'

Front door finally closed, Elena sagged wearily against it.

'Are you all right?' Nellie was at the foot of the stairs, holding Olive against her shoulder, rubbing her tiny back. Which meant she had just been feeding her. While Elena had passed the hallway, snatching nervous glances up the street for the arrival of Albert's family, Nellie had been feeding Olive. Elena's stomach churned. 'You look awful,' Nellie noted neutrally.

'I feel awful.' Elena gave a slow nod of confirmation.

'Why don't you go lie down for a bit?'

Elena remained against the front door, unconvinced.

'Olive is due her nap soon anyway,' Nellie persisted. 'I'll settle her in her Moses basket and then you can sleep too.'

Sleep.

Just hearing the word made Elena's limbs grow heavy and expectant at the thought of rest.

'Okay, sure.'

Nellie turned and went back up the stairs, Elena awkwardly hobbling behind her, the wounded ankle hindering her more than she'd anticipated.

'Are you sure you're all right?' Nellie wondered from halfway up, one hand clutching the banister, the other pressed against Olive.

'Yeah . . . fine.' Elena realised she was panting, a sheen of sweat across her forehead. 'I just need a couple of days to heal. That's all.' Then, with a frown, 'How did you find the cat?'

Nellie returned the look and Elena felt a twist in her gut. Her expression was so familiar, so sharp, so judgemental. And then it was gone, Nellie's features smooth, genteel.

'I told you, I found him by the road, just near the front door.'

Was that annoyance creeping into her voice? Elena was so tired, she struggled to assess the woman on the staircase above her more accurately.

'But why were you . . . there. Outside. Out the front.' Elena's temple throbbed and she had to knead it with the tips of her fingers as she spoke.

'Look, you're tired—'

'You don't go out the front, at all. You stay inside. Where it's safe.'

'I was checking the planter' – Nellie's mouth hardened into a line – 'the one by the front door. As I looked at the flowers in it I spotted something on the road. And I . . .'

Elena sighed wearily. 'You wanted to help, I know, you've said so a thousand times.'

'I couldn't leave him there.' Nellie's voice caught for a moment, eyes watery. 'I couldn't *leave him*, Elena.'

'No.' Elena's shoulders fell as the anger left her. 'No, neither could I.'

'Go get some rest,' Nellie urged, and this time Elena listened, both of them continuing up the stairs.

When Elena lay down in bed she didn't have to will sleep to find her. It arrived instantly, dragging her down into a black abyss while outside the sun broke through the clouds, bathing everywhere in a gentle, ethereal glow.

Soil. The earthiness of it. The damp odour. Her nostrils were flooded with it as she dug down, deeper. Felt it lodging beneath her fingernails; she panted as she fought to work faster, with more urgency. It was dark around her but there were still shapes in the shadows. The curve of a nearby bush, the rise of the brick wall. Dusting off her hands, she turned to lift the mound of fur lying in the grass beside her where she crouched by the flower bed. The body still held some warmth. Carefully she lowered it into the fresh hole, whispering words of consolation. Were they for her or the cat? She couldn't be sure. Then suddenly it dropped limply into the hole, rolling slightly. And even though it was dark, she saw it – the open eyes, the torn skull, the exposed pink of something irreplaceable. Blood. It was warm and smooth, like silk, on her hands. Merging with the soil. Her mouth opened to scream, but only a gasp came out. She tasted iron, dampness, the acrid undertone of fresh death. It needed to be buried now. Quickly. Heart racing, she threw the dirt over its ginger fur. Then, over her harried breaths she heard a low, mournful cry. At first it sounded like a baby but it was wilder, more feline. The soil trembled, fell away, and one of those wide-open eyes turned to her, blood seeping into its corner. It looked at her and—

Elena gasped, sitting up as though emerging from the depths of the ocean. Body trembling.

'Fuck.' She took a moment to blink, to survey her surroundings, to register the light pooling beneath the closed curtains. 'Fuck,' she repeated with slightly less fervour, still shaking. The cat. The soil. She shook her head, knowing it couldn't have been real, noticing how the sheets around her were damp with sweat. 'Dammit.' She pressed a hand to her temple and it came away hot. Mouth dry, Elena knew she needed water, to get out of the room. But first she hobbled towards Olive's cot, her ankle uneasy each time she placed any weight on it. Already she could see blood spotting through her bandages. She would need to change them soon.

'Hey, sweetheart, are you sleeping okay? Where's Mummy's little—'

The cot was empty. Elena touched the bottom sheet. Cold.

'Olive!' She dragged her wounded foot behind her as she made for the landing. The door slapped shut behind her and she could hear the gentle murmur of someone singing. Following the sound, she pushed open the door to the spare room. Nellie's room. Nellie was atop her neatly made bed, all the while singing, Olive suckling at her breast. It wasn't just any song. The one that evoked thoughts of summer in Elena. Thoughts of a boy who now existed for her only in memory.

'Hey!' Elena could hear the thunder in her voice. Nellie glanced up, unfazed.

'Don't . . . don't do that. Don't sing that to her. *I* sing that to her.'

'I tried to wake you when she needed a feed but you didn't stir.'

'Well, clearly you didn't try hard enough,' Elena snapped, wincing from the effort of standing up.

'I think you should see a doctor,' Nellie remarked coolly, eyes briefly flicking to Elena's foot.

'What? No. I'm fine.'

'It might be infected,' Nellie continued. 'But don't worry if you need to go on antibiotics. I can keep feeding her.'

'No, I—' Elena helplessly studied the scene before her; her baby contentedly suckling on another woman's breast. She felt impotent and useless. An extra in her own life. But Olive was happy. Olive was well fed. Sleeping well. And wasn't that what mattered? Weren't Elena's own feelings now surplus to everything? Wasn't that what motherhood truly was? Sacrificing yourself?

'Fine,' she said quietly, resigned, 'it's fine. Just bring her down when she's done feeding.' As Elena struggled down the landing towards the staircase, she kept hearing the wail of the cat from her dream. Seeing its bloodied eye. Staring at her.

It was all a nightmare, nothing more. Elena hadn't even been the one to bury him. Her mind was playing tricks on her, taunting her, so that even rest wasn't restful. And all the while her ankle throbbed painfully, outside the sun was at its highest point, the sky now a blanket of blue.

.24

'I mean, do you think it could have been POP?' Margot asked bluntly while Leanne threw her a scathing look from across the table.

'Why would you even say that?' Leanne hissed angrily.

It was the following day, unseasonably bright, so Elena had met her friends in a local park. They were sprawled around a picnic table, muslins, bottles and baby wipes littering the chipped wooden surface. Olive was dozing in her pram beneath the speckled shade of an oak tree while Leanne's toddlers busied themselves diving into piles of leaves, squealing with joy. 'As long as one of them doesn't land on dog shit,' she'd deadpanned when they began playing.

'You said it was a dead cat, yes?' Margot was looking intently at Elena, ignoring Leanne's anger.

'It was . . . yeah. A dead ginger cat. She said she found him outside and buried him.'

For some reason Elena kept the details about her vandalised car close to her chest, fearing she was already provoking her friends enough with this latest story.

'And all I'm saying is, it could have been POP.'

Elena felt cold as they confirmed her fears.

'Margot—' Leanne began to warn through gritted teeth, but one of her twins began wailing unconsolably, which dragged her away from the table. She quickly threw a heated glance over her shoulder before scooping up her red-faced child, their screams pitching to ear-splitting level.

'I read on the news about what they do,' Margot continued, 'these' – she made air quotation marks with her elegant fingers – 'protectors of purity.'

Elena winced, wishing Leanne was still taking part in the conversation, still steering them away from murky territory.

'They look to scare, imitate.'

'Intimidate,' Elena quietly corrected her friend. Everything Margot was saying was true. Protectors of Purity, POP, for short, were a radical group who were against the cloning movement. When they got wind of someone being a clone they often harassed them, leaving graffiti on front doors, slicing a key down the side of their cars, small acts of angry vandalism. Once they had burned the word 'fake' into someone's front lawn. A prominent MP in the next county. Elena had never heard of them actually hurting someone, or killing a pet. But now Margot had suggested it she found herself glancing nervously over her shoulder. Thinking of her damaged car. The slashed tyres. Were they being watched? Did people know about Nellie? Even though she rarely left the house, the neighbours could have easily spotted her when they'd arrived home. It wasn't something they were looking to keep secret. Should they have been more careful?

'POP aren't going about killing cats,' Leanne announced as she rejoined them at the table, her toddler now completely fine and jumping once more in the leaves. 'A car must have got it, that's all. What I find unsettling is how she thought to bury it in the garden without telling you or Stu.'

'This.' Margot pointed at Leanne, her nails painted a rich shade of plum. 'I agree with this.'

'I want to think that she thought she was doing the right thing,' Elena mused, sipping at the seasonal drink she'd bought in a paper cup on her walk over. It tasted too sickly on her tongue. Too sweet. But still she drank it down, needing the sugar, the caffeine, to help her slump home. Even leaning upon the pram for support, it had been an effort to walk the fifteen minutes to the park, her ankle throbbing with every step.

'Still.' Leanne frowned as behind her, her baby began to stir in their pram. Deftly, she turned, scooped them up and placed them upon her breast without even breaking a sweat. Elena prayed that Olive would keep sleeping until she was back home, aware that it was a much more laborious process whenever she had to breastfeed. 'Is it . . .' Leanne paused, chewed her lip, tendrils from her messy bun blowing across her face. 'Is it what you would have done?'

Elena felt the heated gaze of both friends upon her. Now she suddenly wished her baby would stir, offer her some distraction. 'I don't think so,' she offered weakly. 'I'd have thought first to check the collar. Call the owners. Tell Stu about it.'

'Mmm.' Leanne made an unsatisfied sound and looked down at her feeding baby, readjusting her grip on them.

'But she would not know about collar, about vets. She would have . . .' Margot gestured in the air as she searched for the right word. 'Instinct,' she settled upon grandly. 'She found animal, knew to bury it. Nothing more. She doesn't have . . . have experience of world.'

'I suppose that makes sense,' Leanne offered.

'It's just troubled me,' Elena admitted to her friends. Though she failed to tell them about her nightmare, about the feeling of dirt and fur against her skin. Or about how she seemed to just *know* the cat was out there, in the garden. That it had been . . . alive. Her entire body prickled with fear and disgust.

'In the grand schemes of things, it's weird, yes,' Leanne nodded, 'but it isn't particularly troubling. There's nothing sinister at play here.' She eyed Margot as she said this. Bated, Margot arched a sleek eyebrow.

'I just think maybe it could be POP and—'

'Stop scaring her,' Leanne interrupted sharply. 'She's enough to contend with, having a stranger in her home. Don't let her worry about fanatics stalking her house too.'

'You have man there!' Margot declared grandly. 'Stu would always protect you. From the fanatics. The More You.'

'Margot!' Leanne said her friend's name despairingly.

'I'm just saying' – Margot straightened, locked eyes with Elena – 'men always have the capacity to hurt. When they need to. This should make you feel safe, no?'

Elena shifted beneath her friend's gaze. Somehow, it didn't.

'Please let's discuss something else!' Leanne demanded loudly.

'You're right, you're right.' Margot raised her hands in surrender. 'Let us talk about nicer things, no? Anyone baby actually sleep last night?'

The conversation shifted onto pleasanter topics. Snippets of TV shows they'd watched. A story of how Margot had found her husband asleep on the sofa with the baby on his chest and had snuck up on him, carefully taken the baby, and then blown a horn in her husband's ear, cackling with laughter as he shot up, fear-stricken. But Elena was only half listening.

Having a stranger in her home.

That's what Leanne had said. Even though Nellie was Elena's carbon copy, she was still very much a stranger. The walk home began to seem unbearably long; her ankle aching at the thought of it. Discreetly, Elena checked her phone; the app that showed her where Nellie was – the icon flashing over her home upon the digital map. Was she cleaning? Resting? Burying more bodies out the back? Elena felt nauseous. She tossed the last of her drink in a nearby bin and made her excuses to leave. Her friends hugged her tightly, uttering promises to meet up again soon. It was only when she rounded the corner away from the park, when she was completely out of sight, that Elena permitted herself to limp awkwardly behind the pram as she headed home.

From: POP@outward.co.uk
To: Full Mailing List
Subject: Thank You

We have received so many emails lately about your renewed efforts to stand against the More Yous in our community. This pleases us greatly. The more active we become, and the more difficult we make it for them to falsely exist among us, the closer we are to victory.

Remember to always act within the parameters of the law as best you can. We will always do our best to protect anyone acting on POP's behalf but cannot guarantee anything.

That being said, this is an escalating situation and desperate times do indeed call for desperate measures. These More You monsters must be called out and removed from society by any means necessary.

Keep us updated, keep up the good work. Never stop looking for them. Never stop fighting. We can win this war.

.25

The sun continued to shine as Elena hobbled home, leaving her back damp and claggy beneath the sweatshirt and jacket she'd pulled on that morning. Something Margot had whispered in her ear, breath heavy with coffee, stuck in her mind.

'Just keep husband happy.'

Margot, with her pranks and sardonic sense of humour. Nails always freshly painted, hair slick and styled. Elena imagined that beneath the velour tracksuits her friend often favoured she wore lace-trimmed lingerie, elegant and enticing. A package always primed for her husband to open. Elena had met Simon once; he was bald, quiet, with a steely demeanour. But she caught the glances he occasionally threw at his wife, filled with adoration. Wonderment. It was undeniable that Margot was loved, that her marital home was a happy one.

Elena was happy. She loved Stu.

She turned a corner; her home was now in sight, just as shooting pains began to run up her leg from her ankle.

'Come on,' she grunted to herself, shoving harder against the pram. When had she and Stu last had sex? During the final weeks of her pregnancy she'd felt too swollen, too sore, to let him come anywhere near her. Then there was the C-section. It had surely been months. But how many? Elena was squinting into the sunlight when Olive began to shrilly cry.

'Nearly home, baby,' Elena assured her little girl in a shushing voice. 'Just a bit further, okay?' She'd made it to the base of the steps that led to her front door. Coming down them with the pram had been relatively easy; going up them suddenly seemed a much more daunting prospect. Elena looked up, for a moment seeing the twisting ribbon of compacted snow that was the final ascent to the summit of Everest. She remembered her stomach clenching, body turning rigid. A woozy sense of disorientation passing through her. It was too far, too high. She was already so unbearably exhausted, hanging on by the thinnest of threads.

'You can do this.' Stu at her side, confident, assured. Forever smiling, even in the face of the near impossible. 'You can do anything, Elena. I know you can.' She saw her frightened face reflected in the glassy surface of his goggles. 'You can do it,' he told her again, 'just one step at a time.'

Elena's front door creaked open and the mountain was gone. The snow replaced by gleaming white stone steps. She blinked hazily, Olive's mouth open and screeching.

'Need some help?' Nellie asked, already descending towards her, hair tightly swept back in a low ponytail, a chic shirt dress gracefully hanging to her knees. She always seemed to carry herself with ease whilst Elena felt awkward, stiff. Sore. Elena clocked the dress, struggling to recall if she even owned such a garment. It was navy with gold buttons and a brown belt at the waist. 'Here.' Nellie's hands gripped the end of the pram and together they hoisted it up towards the house. They worked easily, in unison, anticipating one another's moves. In the hallway Olive's cries bounced off the walls. 'Aww, little one.' Nellie bowed at the waist, leaning into the pram and scooping the baby out.

'She's going to be a bit fussy.' Elena opened her own arms expectantly. 'She just needs—'

The shirt dress enabled Nellie to swiftly release a breast, pale and blue-lined. Olive eagerly latched on, instantly quiet. 'There we are.' Nellie smiled tenderly at the baby in her arms, then said to Elena, 'Why don't you go and have a rest? I'll fetch you a tea in a bit.' Her gaze flicked down to Elena's ankle, then shot back to her face. 'You look tired.' Humming to herself, the tune of Elena's summer song, Nellie cradled Olive to her chest and walked towards the golden light of the lounge, sun streaming in from the French doors.

In the shadows of the hallway, Elena stood with the empty pram, arms still stretched out. 'She just needs her mother,' she whispered, a lump lodging in her throat. 'She just needs her mother.'

Elena decided not to wait for her tea. Feeling redundant and useless, she hauled herself up the stairs, using the banister to bolster her failing steps. After collapsing onto the bed she sat up and stretched out her leg, wincing. Carefully, she slid up the bottom of her leggings, lowered the pale sock. Her bandages. Already they were soiled, a dark yellow stain curdling in their centre. 'Shit.' Elena peeled them back to reveal angry red skin. A putrid odour rose to greet her. Her ankle was clearly infected. 'Fuck.' Elena ripped the bandages fully away, making a mental note to clean the wound, reapply antiseptic spray. She was studying the array of red and scarlet, the weep of yellow from the centre, when her gaze lifted towards her wardrobe.

The blue shirt dress.

Now she remembered. When had she last worn it? A year ago? More? It was back before she'd gotten pregnant, back before her body had begun to warp and change. She would glide into work in it, cutting an elegant silhouette, smugly aware of the heads that would discreetly turn in her direction as she swept by. Elena pressed a hand to her stomach. Still so soft, so swollen. Stu always liked that dress. When she wore it he'd nuzzle into her neck, hands reaching for her thighs, drifting the fabric higher and higher. 'You're so insanely fuckable in this,' he'd whisper hotly into her ear. 'Do you know that? When I see you in it I just want to hoist it up and bend you over.' Elena drank up the attention, his desire. She loved it.

Just keep husband happy.

Margot's words. Her advice. Or her warning. Elena continued to stare at the wardrobe. Nellie must have entered her room, cracked open the double doors and then riffled through the coat hangers. Passing on this dress, that top. Before settling upon the blue shirt dress. Designer, Elena now recalled. A treat to herself for her thirty-fifth birthday. How soft it had felt upon her skin in the store with the white walls and dim lights. Like silk. What had drawn Nellie to it? It was functional, yes. A decent choice for a hot day. But it was also elegant, sultry. With the loosening of the right buttons, suggestive.

A knock at the door. Elena scrambled to conceal her leg, eyes smarting at the pain. The door opened and Nellie walked in, a milk-drunk Olive in her arms. 'She needs to sleep.' She nodded at the cot by the bed.

'She slept all the time I was out,' Elena protested. 'Really, I'd like to do some tummy time with her and—'

Olive's little mouth gaped wide and open in a long yawn.

'Perhaps she just needs a little nap.' Nellie smiled diplomatically, moving around the bed and placing the baby down with great care. Leaning forward to plant a kiss upon Olive's clammy forehead. Elena noticed that all the buttons on the dress were done up. She hated how that brought her a slither of comfort. 'That's looking really sore.' Nellie pointed at Elena's ankle, still on show despite being wedged beneath her other leg. 'Do you need me to help you put on some fresh bandages?'

'No, I'm fine.' Elena was staring at the midnight blue of the dress, the shine of each gold button. 'But thank you.'

'Oh,' Nellie declared suddenly, sharply. 'Before I forget, someone called while you were out.'

'Someone called?'

Called who? Where? The landline? It was barely ever used, more a formality to ensure a good deal on the internet connection.

'Yes, she said her name was Catherine and that she would be over tomorrow to visit.'

'You spoke to her?' Elena asked, voice shrill.

'Only briefly.' Nellie began to look worried.

'No, it's okay. It's just . . . she's Stu's mother.'

Of *course* Catherine had phoned the house. Of fucking course. Stu had probably casually mentioned that Elena was at the park so the interfering old crow had dialled the number, salivating at the thought of speaking with Nellie. A fresh way to insert her unwanted presence into their lives.

'Do we like her?' Nellie asked plainly.

Elena had to admit that she liked the united front on it. The *we*. Stu obviously did, she was his mother after all and he remained frustratingly blind to her many, many faults.

'No.' Elena looked up at Nellie, a crook of a smile pulling on her lips. '*We* do not.'

.26

For Catherine, worry was an ocean she was usually able to swim across. She had to fight against the current, the tide, but normally she had the energy to remain upon the surface. But these last few days she had felt herself sinking so that now she stood upon the ocean floor, looking up at the distant flickering sunlight that felt a million miles away.

She knew that she needed to do something.

How many days had it been since she'd heard from Stuey? How long since she had *seen* him?

'Boys outgrow their mothers,' a cruelly pragmatic friend had once told her. 'Be prepared for that empty nest when all you have are boys.'

Catherine had batted the remark away, insisted that her Stuey was nothing like that, when in reality he'd been pulling away ever since he became a teenager. Finding friends, finding sport, adventure. And then girls. Elena. He didn't carry the burden of Clive's death with him as Catherine did, had been only eight when he'd lost his brother, too young to be truly marked by it.

Catherine's sandals slapped against the tiles of her kitchen as she walked through to the garden, her face uncharacteristically free of make-up. She kept waiting for her phone to ring. For a text to come through. Long days tumbled into dark nights. The POP presence at More You had eased but she noticed there had been an increase in news stories about activity likely linked to them and felt the sharp press of guilt within her gut.

But no one knows about Nellie.

Catherine had not told anyone. And she knew that Stu and Elena were being careful. Keeping her hidden behind closed doors.

The people at More You know.

This thought curdled Catherine's stomach as a gentle breeze tugged through her hair. She was now on a bench beneath a wisteria-clad pagoda. It was usually one of her favourite spots in the garden, the air flush and floral, yet today she just felt chilly and nauseous even though the sun shone.

'Be proactive,' she scolded herself. That was what she'd always told Stuey when he was young, when he was nervous. And he'd grown up so bold, so accomplished.

She tapped out a message to her son, politely enquiring about Elena's whereabouts. To Catherine's delight, Stuey replied within minutes.

She's out today meeting her mum friends.

Out.

The word danced before Catherine on the screen. If Elena was out that meant that Nellie was home alone. She inhaled, steadying herself, thinking.

All I want is to see my family; there's no harm in that.

She felt it all the time, Elena's desire to shut her out. Catherine deserved more. Just because Elena had lost a mother didn't mean that Stuey should sacrifice his too. Before she could talk herself out of it she was dialling the number she knew by heart. On the third ring someone answered and for a second Catherine froze.

'Elena?' she asked, fearing her son had been mistaken about his wife's whereabouts.

'Can I help you?' came the polite response.

Catherine found herself smiling. 'Yes, I was just calling to say I'll be over tomorrow to visit. It's Catherine.'

'Oh.' The voice on the other end of the line was so gentle, so warm. 'How lovely, I'll look forward to it.'

Catherine liked her already.

Margot: I don't like dead cat.

Leanne: Margot, drop it.

Elena: What's to like?

Margot: It seem strange.

Elena: Because it is strange.

Leanne: Honestly, don't worry about it. She found the cat, misunderstood what you're supposed to do. It's all sorted now anyway xxx

Elena: What if she hurt the cat?

Leanne: She said she found it on the road, right? Already dead?

Elena: Yes. But . . . I don't know.

Leanne: You think she's lying?

Elena: No. Christ, I don't know what I think. Maybe I'm going mad.

Leanne: Stop dwelling on it, okay? Stop worrying xxx

Margot: See! I don't like dead cat.

.27

Elena hated how Catherine Roberts always arrived in a nauseating cloud, every inch of her skin spritzed to saturation with overly priced perfume that glowed the colour of piss within its twisted glass bottle. She entered the hallway, false eyelashes fluttering as she took in the stairs, the floorboards, Elena.

'How are you, dear?'

'I'm good.' Elena's arms were firmly folded to her chest, chin high, body tense, like she was about to do battle.

'You're here!' Heavy footsteps behind her as Stu descended into the hallway, arms extended wide. 'So lovely to see you, Mum.' He wrapped her in an embrace, kissing the top of her head while Elena quickly fired him a heated look. 'But you really need to give us more notice next time,' he hastily added, face flushing slightly.

'Why?' his mother asked, face dropping. 'I'm welcome to come round and see my granddaughter, aren't I?'

The previous night Elena and Stu had bickered about his mother's impending visit until Elena's eyes grew too heavy, her resolve too weak.

'She called Nellie,' she declared, feeling brittle, 'knowing it was a way to worm an invitation out of us.'

'Elena, she's my *mother.* She's entitled to come round sometimes, you know. She's lonely.'

'Lonely?' Elena had scoffed. 'Hasn't she bought herself enough friends at that country club she loves to slink off to? Or she could go and pose on the board at More You.'

'She'll just be here an hour, that's it. She'll see Olive, have some cuddles and be gone.'

The thought of Catherine Roberts cuddling anything seemed so strange to Elena. So surreal. The woman was all stiff angles – pointed elbows, high cheekbones, strained stares. An embrace from her would be like clutching a pincushion to your chest. And Elena didn't want that for her daughter. Thinking of Catherine made her long for her own mother's easy nature, the gentle curves of her short frame, the way she could make everything better with a single, tight embrace. Her mother had been comfort personified. And to Olive she'd forever be a stranger, someone spoken of only in stories. As Elena closed her eyes she felt the warm presence of tears seeping into her pillow. She kept her back to Stu, not wanting him to see, already too worn down from their argument.

A creak behind Elena.

'Ah, there we are.' Catherine shrugged off her coat and passed it towards the newest figure in the hallway.

'Mum.' Stu grabbed the garment, tone objecting. 'Don't treat Nellie like the help.'

'Nellie?'

As Stu hung up his mother's coat, Catherine turned to stare first at her daughter-in-law, and then at her double beside her. 'My God.' Bejewelled fingers reached for the slick red streak that was her mouth. 'It's simply astounding. So uncanny.'

'Catherine, this is Nellie.' Elena awkwardly gestured to the woman at her side.

'My God,' Catherine repeated, brazenly moving to stand before the two women, openly drinking them in, their every blemish, every flaw. 'Stunning.' She reached for Nellie's chin, clutched it in her hand, nails long. 'I mean, I've seen models before. At More You. But not this . . . close. And not this . . .' Her voice trailed off as she continued to assess Nellie.

Elena rolled her eyes, aware that *stunning* was not a word that had ever previously been flung in her direction.

'Well.' Catherine stared deep into Nellie's eyes. 'It's good to see that my money was well spent.'

'Mum,' Stu muttered in a warning tone.

'Now my Stuey has two wives to care for him.' Catherine beamed at Nellie, whose own lips quirked into a tense smile.

'She's here to help with Olive,' Elena snapped.

'And where is my dear grandbaby?' Catherine spun around theatrically, a hand pressed to her chest.

'Upstairs sleeping,' Stu explained, leading his mother into the lounge.

'Can't you just wake her up?'

'No.' Stu threw Elena an apologetic look over his shoulder.

'Well, I can't wait around all day to see her. I've got a back massage scheduled for three.'

Elena drifted into the kitchen, keen to distance herself from her guest. Nellie followed.

'So that's Stu's mother?' she asked as she automatically moved towards the kettle, began reaching for mugs from the cupboards.

'That's Stu's mother,' Elena deadpanned.

'I can see why we don't like her.'

'Yeah.' Elena gave a light laugh. 'She's not great at being a decent human.'

On Elena's wedding day, face flushed, a champagne flute in her hand, a grimy smear of lipstick around its rim, Catherine had found her. Elena had been outside, stealing a moment alone, savouring the cool of the night air, feeling unbearably hot in her gown beneath the flashing lights of the disco. She'd turned when she heard the tottering heels, noticed the sway in Catherine's steps.

'Beautiful day.' Catherine raised her glass while she smiled flatly at the bride.

'It has been, yes.'

'I remember wearing silk. All white. And back then I could, trust me.' She gave Elena a withering look.

'I'm sure it was lovely.' Elena kept the pretence of politeness going, keen for the woman to stumble back to the party, to embarrass herself some more in front of their guests. But instead Catherine kept studying her new daughter-in-law, eyes watery, hand shaky as she sipped more champagne.

'You'll never be good enough for him,' she declared.

Elena snorted, almost welcoming the admission, a sentiment she'd sensed brewing within the older woman ever since their first meeting. 'I see the free bar has really loosened your tongue.'

'Not free for me,' Catherine said, iron in her voice. 'I am, after all, the one paying for it.'

'You're a ray of sunshine as always, Catherine,' Elena sighed. This was her day; she had no desire to enter into a battle of words with her mother-in-law.

'You'd best give me grandchildren.' Catherine glowered at her.

'And you'd best know your place.' Elena straightened, staring at the garish brightness of Catherine's lipstick, the hideous bouffant of her hair. 'I'm his *wife* now. I'm done taking shit from you.' It must have been the champagne she herself had drunk, topped off with wine and several shots from well-meaning guests. Because it wasn't like Elena to be so rude. So direct.

'Wife.' Catherine repeated the word with puckered lips. 'You think that makes you so special? So unique? We are replaceable, dear girl. Mother is the only role that sticks. Remember that.'

Elena watched Catherine saunter away to replenish her glass, wondering if either of them would recall the exchange come the dawn.

'Ah, thank you, Nellie.' Catherine pointedly said Nellie's name as she accepted the offered cup of tea.

'Pleasure.' Nellie smiled and neatly folded herself into an armchair. Elena lingered in the far corner of the room, baby monitor in hand. On the small screen she could see Olive still sleeping soundly, though she wished the baby would stir, give her an excuse to steal away from the room.

'How are you finding things?' Catherine curtly enquired of Nellie. 'I saw on the news last night something most distasteful regarding those POP people and there have been so many emails suggesting that—'

'Mum,' Stu interjected sharply. 'Let's try to keep things positive, okay?'

'It's just those people, those zealots, seem hell-bent on making life miserable for people who just—'

'Nellie doesn't leave the house,' Elena stated coolly from across the room. 'We are keeping our situation private.'

'Sensible.' Catherine eyed her daughter-in-law over her mug of tea and then stiffly drank from it. 'And I hope you're enjoying all the extra time to yourself.' She continued to watch Elena. 'Hope you're planning something special for my Stuey.'

'Sorry?'

'His birthday.' Catherine scowled. 'It's just over a week away. Surely you've not forgotten?'

'Of course not.' Elena smiled tightly.

'Now that there's two of you, I'd expect you to do something extra special for him.' There was something in her tone, something goading that Elena didn't like. But there was no time to dwell on it as Olive's cries began to bleat from the monitor. 'Oh, splendid,' Catherine crowed, 'she must know her nana is here.'

'I'll go tell her that her grandmother is here.' Elena set the monitor down and moved towards the door. 'It feels a more fitting title, don't you think?' She stared down Catherine as she passed her. 'More traditional.' In truth, Elena merely liked that it made Catherine sound like the cold, cruel old crust of a woman she was. A nana sounded kind. Welcoming. That would have been Elena's mother. But she was gone. So the only role left to fill was grandmother and Catherine embodied it with ease.

'What happened to your ankle?' Catherine's nose crinkled as she studied Elena's gait.

'Nothing,' Elena replied dismissively. 'I cut it in the garden.'

'I see.' Catherine kept watching her.

'Let me help.' Nellie stood up, seemingly as keen to escape the room as Elena was.

'No, no, dear. You stay,' Catherine insisted. 'After all' – she threw a sideways look at her son – 'can't go treating you like the help, can we?'

As Elena climbed the stairs she tried to walk off her anger, ankle throbbing.

You'll never be good enough for him.

In truth, she had completely forgotten about Stu's upcoming birthday. Even doubled, she felt like she was still failing in the role of wife. Still coming up short. Elena was dimly aware that she'd need to do something extra special for him, make sure it was a memorable birthday. One he'd never forget.

From: Unknown
To: POP@outward.co.uk
Subject: More You sighting

A young family has been sighted in Whitstable with what appears to be a More You model acting as a nanny of some sort, or a substitute for the mother. While they have clearly tried to keep the nanny indoors she has been sighted several times by our members, both in the windows and on the street. What sickens us is this emergence of More Yous into the domestic space. No longer are they just a dalliance for the wealthy, no, they are on our streets. In our supermarkets. In our kids' schools. Clearly, this has all gone too far. We will be monitoring the house closely. It is only a matter of time before a More You lashes out. They are, after all, not human. Please know we will send updates as and when we have them.

.28

To Elena it felt as though Catherine would never leave, embedding herself against the fabric of the sofa as if she intended to become a part of it. A piece of furniture for ever in their home. Their lives. The sun was dipping low in the sky when Stu finally caught Elena's piercing gaze, understood the levelling of her eyebrows.

'Mum, it's been just wonderful, but shouldn't you be heading off?'

'I suppose.' Catherine puckered her lips, scowled in her daughter-in-law's direction, sensing the origin of her dismissal. 'But how I do love to spend time here. With you,' she cooed towards her son.

'And your granddaughter,' Elena added flatly, aware of how little time the old woman had actually spent with the baby. She had held Olive for perhaps the better part of five minutes. As soon as Olive's nappy had filled, Catherine had wrinkled her nose and passed her back into Elena's outstretched arms, muttering, 'Ooh, a fresh job for Mummy.' How Elena despised the woman. Thankfully she was saved from having to follow Stu and his mother into the hallway when Olive began to bleat and cry.

'Shh, come here now.' Elena bent low over the Moses basket, scooped up the warm bundle, inhaling that delicate, baby soft scent.

'See you again soon, Elena,' Catherine called as she strutted out of the room, not even glancing back.

Elena was so focused on unbuttoning her blouse, pressing Olive against her chest, that she didn't notice the sofa shift beside her and was startled when Nellie suddenly spoke.

'So she's unbearable.'

It was surreal. Elena glanced first at Nellie, then at the door her mother-in-law had just exited through, certain that she had uttered those exact same words upon her original meeting with Catherine.

'Yeah she's . . . she's something.'

'I don't like her.' Nellie folded her arms and leaned back against the sofa, brow furrowed.

'Few do.'

'Why doesn't Stuart . . . say something?' Nellie pondered aloud. A long sigh escaped from Elena.

'I mean, he knows what she's like. But because of what she went through, with his brother . . . It's like he's given her a never-ending free pass to be a cunt.'

'She doesn't *feel* like a grandmother.'

'Nope.'

'Not like . . .' Nellie was trying to catch her eye.

'Yeah.' Elena nodded sadly. 'Mum would have adored every minute of it. Do you . . .' She studied Nellie's face, a mirror of her own, while Olive suckled loudly. She felt foolish for what she was about to ask, since More Yous didn't have their hosts' memories. Yet with Nellie she felt something within her, noticed a look in her eye sometimes. It was impossible and yet . . .

'Do you have memories of her? Of . . . of my mum?'

Nellie gave a wistful smile. 'More like feelings. When you speak of her I feel' – she inhaled deeply, pressing a palm to her chest – 'safe. I guess I feel safe.'

'Yeah, that's how she made me feel. And pretty much everyone she knew. Everyone loved her.'

'And you worry you're not like that?'

Elena bristled. 'What? No, I, um . . .'

'It's okay.' Nellie reached for Elena's hand, cupped it against her own, both of them now holding Olive as she fed. 'I feel that way, so I guessed you did too. Since we are . . .' She was looking right into Elena's eyes, seeing every part of her.

'Connected,' Elena finished for her. 'I don't . . .' She blinked, feeling both uneasy and content in the same moment. 'I don't ask you enough, do I? About how you are? How you're feeling? If you're okay.'

'I'm fine.' Now Nellie was looking down at Olive, face peaceful. 'Whenever I'm around her I feel completely fine. Like I understand things. My purpose.'

'Your purpose?'

'I'm here to help you with her, right?'

'Right.' Elena nodded.

'And that's what makes me happy. Caring for her. It must be innate, that love we both feel for her.'

'Of course.' Elena discreetly tightened her grip around her baby.

'She's such a lucky girl,' Nellie continued, 'getting to have two mummies.'

The sky was black as Elena drew her duvet cover up towards her chest, wondering if she had the energy to read. There was a paperback on her bedside table, spine still stiff. She'd bought it just before Olive arrived, back when she believed that maternity leave would be full of wondrous free time to sit around in coffee shops and read all the books that had caught her eye over the last twelve months. Stu was still pottering around downstairs, so letting out a committed sigh, she reached for the book, peeled back the cover.

'Everyone reads ebooks now,' Stu had told her when she'd come home with the elegant paper bag from an independent bookshop. 'Much simpler.'

'Not me.' Elena opened the bag, removed the book and admired the embossed lettering, the sheen of the cover. 'I like the real thing. There's something about the smell of them. Being able to touch and fold each page.'

'Luddite,' Stu teased with a smile.

'You're the fool who married one,' Elena muttered, not looking up from the book as she studied it, pleased with her purchase.

Elena had barely read the first paragraph when the door to the bedroom burst open and Stu darted inside, face flushed.

'What's wrong?' Closing the book, Elena watched her husband press his back to the door and shakily run his hands through his hair, face red.

'She has to go,' he hissed, voice low.

'What?' Elena felt her chest clench, threw an instinctive glance towards Olive, sleeping in her Moses basket beside her, dark lashes long against her flushed cheeks.

'She has to go.' Stu scrambled over towards the bed, continuing to look back at the door fearfully.

'What's happened?'

'Downstairs I . . .' A groan echoed out of her husband as he dragged his hands down his face. 'I thought it was you. In the kitchen. Tidying the side. I thought I was being playful.'

Despite the soft bedding around her Elena went cold.

'What happened?' she asked again, ice creeping into her voice.

'Nothing, I . . . I went up behind her and put my hands, you know . . .' He spread them in the air, mimicking the way he had clearly grabbed Nellie's hips. Bile inched up the back of Elena's throat. 'I grabbed her, for a second. Less. Came to kiss her neck, I mean, *your* neck. I thought it was *you*!'

'Only it wasn't.' Elena remarked sourly.

'I know, I know.' Stu's head was again in his hands. 'I realised almost immediately and felt like such a fucking idiot.'

Almost immediately.

Elena hated herself for wondering what had happened in that almost. Had her husband grown hard for Nellie? Felt that pull of desire?

'When I realised it wasn't you, I shoved her away,' Stu continued.

'You . . .' Elena's blood ran colder. 'You *shoved* her?' Margot's voice was in her head.

Men always have the capacity to hurt.

'Yeah, I shoved her and came up here.' A twitch in his jawline. Was he telling her the complete truth?

'Stu, you shouldn't be *shoving* her.' She thought of his hands upon Nellie. Full of want, desire. And then . . . something else. Something darker.

'Elena, she's not you,' he told his wife plainly. 'It's not like I was shoving you.'

But you thought it was me. For a moment.

'I never thought.' Stu anxiously raked his hands through his hair. 'I didn't think I'd make that kind of mistake.' He looked at his wife, crestfallen. 'I . . . I . . . it was awful. I'm so embarrassed.'

'What did she do?'

'She just laughed as though it was nothing and said not to worry.'

Nothing.

'She laughed after you shoved her?'

'Look, Elena.' Irritation crept into Stu's voice. 'It was a heat-of-the-moment thing, all right?'

When he spoke of heat, Elena grew only colder.

She returned her book to the bedside table, all thoughts of reading long abandoned. 'Stu—'

'Tomorrow, let's look into returning her, okay? This is all getting a bit . . . a bit weird. My mum said this would happen.'

'She did?' Elena felt the flint in her voice scrape against her tongue. 'Catherine said this would happen? When Catherine was the one who told us to get Nellie? Who fucking paid for her? Who is on the bloody board at More You?'

'Keep your voice down.' Stu looked nervously at the bedroom door. 'My mum just mentioned to me it was a newer model and things might get . . . complicated.'

'Complicated how?' Elena demanded.

Stu gave a harassed sigh. 'I don't want to get into this now.'

'Has something else happened with Nellie, before today?' Her throat grew tight as she assessed her husband.

His pregnant pause told her everything.

'Stuart, what aren't you—?'

'I thought . . . I thought it'd be easier to tell the difference.' He gave her a pained look, a shameful blush spreading across his face. Elena swallowed, throat raw. 'Sometimes . . . she's so like you. The way she speaks, the way she holds herself. Tonight it just . . . it scared me a little. It's the first time it's happened, I swear.' But he glanced down, unable to look her in the eye.

'Did anything else happen downstairs while I put our baby to sleep?' Elena asked, voice rising, not falling.

She thought of the moment in the hallway, when Stu was angry about his tyres, how quickly he had mistaken Nellie for her. And how Nellie hadn't corrected him.

Newer model.

Nellie always seemed so intuitive. Elena eyed her husband suspiciously.

'Are you sure you didn't do something more than touch her downstairs?' she asked quietly, voice flat and firm.

'No, no.' Stu came close, gripped her hands tightly. 'I've told you what happened. It's just . . . it's creeped me out. I'm not going to lie.'

Elena shuddered, feeling violated by his mistake, the sting of betrayal beginning to pass across her skin.

'Your mum told us to get her. Insisted.' Her pulse quickened.

'I know.'

'Nellie doesn't like her either.'

'Who?'

'Your mother.' Elena shook his grip away. 'We can't just . . .' She winced, temple beginning to throb with the promise of a migraine. 'She's not some shoe from a shop.' She was whispering now. 'We can't just send her back, Stuart.'

She's me.

The thought came unbidden, sudden. But Elena felt it, didn't she? That bond between them. The cat in the garden. The dream. Was Nellie more than her mirror image? Were they linked somehow?

Newer model.

'Can't we?' Stu looked at her, pleading.

'Don't you think you're overreacting?'

'I just . . . let's explore our options, okay?'

'Do we even know what truly happens when they are . . . retired?'

'We can find out.'

Connected. That was what Elena had said to Nellie.

'Please, baby.' Stu reached out to stroke her cheek. 'Can we at least look into it? Like, thoroughly. I don't . . .' He looked pained. 'I don't want a repeat of what happened in the kitchen. I love *you*. I belong to *you*.'

And Nellie belongs to us.

'It was just a mistake though, right?'

'One I never thought I'd make.' He looked into her eyes, gaze searching. Appraising.

Is he checking I'm me?

'Sure.' Elena blinked, too tired and too preoccupied with the pounding in her skull to give the conversation further thought. 'Tomorrow. Let's look into it tomorrow.'

She glanced towards the nearby dresser where two solid silver candlesticks stood. Gifts from Catherine that Elena loathed. Not only because she had to dutifully polish them every six months, but because they were heavy and ugly, looking like they belonged in some sort of cathedral, not someone's home.

'These will be heirloom pieces,' Catherine had declared haughtily when she'd handed over the box adorned with a satin silver bow. Elena had wanted to pawn them the second she'd hoisted them out of their plush casing.

'I think they're nice,' Stu had objected, though Elena failed to see how anyone could. 'They're classy.'

Elena had balked at the word but kept them in order to keep the peace. And now they resided in the bedroom, away from the eyes of any visitors. Elena had tried to relegate them to the bathroom but Stu had found them and placed them atop the dresser. And now there they stayed.

Fucking ugly things.

'Tomorrow,' she sleepily muttered. She closed her eyes, hiding the gaudy candlesticks from her sight. She thought she heard a slight creak upon the landing, but sleep was already pulling her down, drawing her away. Dulling her senses.

.29

Catherine was not one for warnings. She had never cared to be cryptic. She did not read her horoscope, certain that she was in control of her destiny. Eric had always been so assured about everything, so confident in his decisions, and that had rubbed off on Catherine.

But so much changed after losing Clive. Catherine felt herself becoming more brittle, less sure. She began focusing on Stuey, throwing herself into his world.

'You hold onto that boy too tight and you risk him pulling away,' her husband warned. Only Catherine didn't listen. She loved her son, devoted herself to him.

Now, with each new email about the mounting pressures from POP, Catherine felt a little bit more uneasy. A little bit more diminished.

I told Stuey to get one.

She thought of her son's damaged car, of some hysterical member of POP shoving a knife deep into rubber, tugging hard. Then doing it again and again until everything was ruined.

But when she'd visited, Elena had insisted that she'd kept Nellie inside. Were they being careful? Did they know how careful they needed to be? Nellie wasn't just a regular More You model; she was special. Catherine had seen that first-hand, the way Nellie had smiled, the way her eyes shone.

She's thinking, Catherine realised. *She's figuring it all out.*

The models at the centre seemed flatter than Nellie. And that was when they were years old. Nellie was developing at an astounding rate and Catherine knew she'd need to report her observations to the board.

When Stuey had walked her out of his house, the night air cool around them, Catherine had felt buoyed by her visit, by the softness of Olive in her arms. And yet she glanced furtively along the length of the street, an edge of fear creeping in.

'Did the police find who slashed your tyres?' she asked.

Stu shoved his hands into his pockets, a sullen throwback to when he was a teenager. 'No, Mum. I told you, without CCTV footage they've got nothing to go on.'

'Right.' Catherine reached for the door handle of her car and then paused. 'How are you finding her? Nellie?'

A light shrug. 'She's . . . great. I mean, yeah. It's really helping Elena.'

'Just . . .' Catherine sucked in her cheeks. 'Be really careful with her. Don't let anyone' – she lowered her voice, looked to the shadows that gathered beyond them, away from the streetlights – '*see* her. She's a newer model.'

'The platinum package, right?' Her son nodded.

Catherine gave arueful shake of her head. 'Newer even than that. No one else has this model.'

'Oh?' Stuey was frowning.

'I wanted you to just have the best, Stuey.'

'Right?' He eyed his mother uneasily.

'But Nellie will . . . develop more quickly than other models. And I can see that already. She's most impressive.'

'What do you mean, develop more quickly?' Now Stuey was folding his arms against his chest.

'She's able to think, develop . . . feelings, I suppose. Soon, she will be more Elena than Elena.'

'Fuck, Mum.' Stuey turned away from her, groaning. 'That's . . . that's not what we wanted.' When he spun back towards her his face was red. 'We wanted some help, not a . . . a replacement.'

'And she is helping.' Catherine forced a bright smile.

Like me. I'm trying to help.

'Can we trust her?' His eyes were on his mother, wide, fearful.

'Do you trust Elena?' Catherine countered coolly.

'Of course!'

'Well, there you go.'

'But it's not the same, is it?'

'She's helping, Stuey, cling to that.' Catherine leaned up to kiss her son's cheek, leaving a red smear behind.

'Tell me about the new model, what it can do.'

'I can't,' Catherine replied truthfully. She only knew the basics, not the science behind it all.

'If she steps out of line, she's gone,' Stuey told her.

'I've no doubt. But she won't, Stuey. She's Elena, remember, she's your wife.'

He scowled at her. 'But that's the problem.' He pushed his hands through his dark hair. 'They're not meant to be *too* similar.'

'She's a clone, Stuey. What did you expect?'

'Sometimes . . .' He gave a shake of his head, gazed sorrowfully down the street. 'Sometimes it's hard to, you know, tell them apart.'

'But you can't tell Elena that?'

'Of course not!'

'You don't need to worry, darling. Nellie will do what she is there to do. All will be well. She's remarkable, truly. I was most impressed by her. You're just tired.' She fondly took in the figure of her son. So handsome. So like his father had once been. 'Get some rest, you'll feel better.'

'Yeah.' Stuey didn't sound convinced. He paced back and forth for a moment, massaging his neck. Then he froze, looked at his mother. 'Is she safe?'

'Yes.' Catherine insisted but from his expression she knew that he could sense the lie. 'Or rather . . . as far as I know.'

'What have you bought into my house?' he growled at her and for a moment Catherine felt disorientated, like she was looking back in time at Eric when he loomed towards her, muscles thick, neck bulging.

'She's helping, isn't she?' Catherine appealed, forcing a smile.

'What can this newer model *do*?' Stuey demanded, voice like gravel.

'Everything,' she told him, exasperated. 'I'm told they can do anything and everything. That's all I know.'

'If it looks to harm Olive. Or Elena. I'll . . .' His hand made a fist at his side.

'I know.' Catherine gently reached for his hand, felt the tension in it. 'You'd do anything to protect your family. Your father was the same.'

'I'm nothing like him,' Stuey countered quickly, while Catherine gave a wistful smile.

'Oh, but you are.'

As Catherine drove away, she checked the road for lingering figures, eyes peeking from behind curtains.

Nellie was supposed to be making things easier for her son. Not making him a target. Not bringing danger to his doorstep. If Nellie did become a threat, she would be gone. Catherine would see to that herself.

.30

Elena awoke in the night, body aflame. Drawing in tight breaths, she rose from the bed, the sheets damp beneath her. Awkwardly, she stood, pain shooting up from her foot. Not daring to place any weight on it, she shuffled through the darkness towards the bathroom, teeth clenched, braced for the telltale whine of Olive being disturbed. But the room behind her remained still. With a relieved sigh, Elena closed the bathroom door, flicked on the light and peered down at her ankle. It bloomed red, the bandages she'd covered her wound with hours earlier already soiled.

'Dammit.'

Hoisting her leg up on the closed toilet seat, Elena studied her ankle beneath the spotlights as she gingerly drew back the bandages, wincing as the sticky edges peeled away from angry skin. The cut was still open, a slice of red. And pus oozed from it.

'Dammit,' Elena repeated, awkwardly dropping her leg to the ground and trying to hop around the bathroom, hating how heavily she landed, how she was sure the sounds of her movements were reverberating throughout the entire house. She searched the small cupboard atop the sink.

Face wash.
Nappy cream.
Soap.
Contact lens solution.
Toothpaste.
Tampons.

Nothing for a weeping wound.

Groaning, Elena eyed the bathroom door. Her entire body felt clammy, ill at ease. Going back to bed was not an option. She knew that downstairs, in the kitchen, there was antiseptic cream. Bandages. All the things she needed to fix her sodding ankle.

As she hobbled through the bedroom she didn't dare to breathe. She could hear her blood pumping in her ears and beneath that, the gentle rise and fall of both her husband and daughter sleeping. Upon the landing she paused, waited. Braced to run back inside and scoop Olive from her cot, to soothe her. On cue, her breasts began to ache, alerted to the potential for an imminent feed. Yet all remained still.

Slowly, gripping the banister with slick hands, Elena went down the stairs. Now she could dare to flick on lights and she illuminated her progress as she went. Finally, breathing heavily, she was in the kitchen. She went to the cupboard that housed the medicine box, strained on her toes to reach it, felt something wet inch down her ankle towards the floor. Once the box was on the island she rifled through it like a racoon, movements harried and careless. She tossed out a packet of bandages. Then a tube of cream.

'It's infected.'

A voice, hers, only not, cut through her movements. Stilled her hands. Elena looked up to see Nellie in the kitchen doorway, backlit by the glow of the hallway. Hair drawn back in a tight bun, white pyjamas smooth against her body. She did not look like someone who had just been disturbed while they slept.

'It's just a bit angry.' Elena shuffled to conceal her wound behind the island, moving to stand further away from the door.

'You need to see a doctor. It's bad.'

'It looks worse than it is,' Elena lied.

'Let me help.' Nellie stepped closer and Elena flinched.

'No, really, it's fine.'

She saw the droop in Nellie's mouth, the disappointment in her usually bright eyes. 'I just want to help,' she explained matter-of-factly, though her words were tinged with sadness. 'When I'm here I' – she gestured around the kitchen – 'I want to be part of things.'

Elena blinked in understanding. It made sense. That was how Elena felt at home; she wanted to help Olive, Stu. An obligation drawing her towards all the mundane household chores.

'I don't like to see you in pain,' Nellie continued, voice small.

'Does it upset you?' Elena asked openly.

Nellie's eyes glistened. 'Yes.'

'Do you . . .' Elena looked at her, a question forming in her mind. 'Do you have feelings for me? For us as a family? Do you care about us?'

She almost said *love* but stopped herself.

'Of course.' Nellie smiled, crinkles forming in the corner of her eyes. She looked both smart and wistful all at once. Is that how Elena looked? Was it one of the expressions she'd regularly worn when Stu was falling in love with her?

'I feel things all the time,' Nellie continued. 'Sometimes I hear a song and feel sunshine on my skin. Other times I see the rain outside and my chest aches.'

'Oh?' Elena pretended to be surprised, recalling all too painfully the first boy who had truly broken her heart. How she'd stood waiting on a railway platform in the pouring rain for him, soaked to the skin, only to see him step off the train with another girl on his arm. He'd glided right by her as though she wasn't even there. For her troubles Elena caught the flu and vowed to never again fall in love. Six months later she met Stu.

'You really need to get that looked at.' Nellie was close enough now to have another clear look at Elena's ankle. 'It must be hurting.'

'It is,' Elena admitted.

'Why don't you go tomorrow?' Nellie suggested brightly. 'I could make the appointment for you and stay here with Olive.'

'No, no, it's okay, I'll—'

'And you could buy Stuart's birthday gift while you're out.'

Elena stared at Nellie. At the openness of her expression.

'I . . .'

'It's his birthday soon, right?' Nellie asked.

'In a few days,' Elena confirmed flatly. 'Did, um . . .' She shifted her weight from foot to foot, ankle continuing to burn. 'Did anything happen with Stu yesterday? Last night?'

'Last night?' Nellie maintained eye contact as she shook her head. 'No, nothing.'

'Nothing . . . strange?' Elena pressed, thinking of Stu's panic-stricken face when he entered their bedroom. She glanced at Nellie's hips, imagining her husband's hands there.

'No, nothing. Why?'

Elena forced herself to shrug. 'He keeps pushing me for clues about his birthday,' she heard herself lying. 'I wondered if perhaps he'd done the same to you.'

'No, nothing,' Nellie said again. 'I could look after Olive on his birthday, if you like? Let you two have some time together.' The offer was delivered with a smile but Elena felt chilled. What was Nellie implying? That Stuart and Elena *needed* time together? That her husband was unsatisfied? Was that why he was putting hands on someone else?

'It's weeping.'

'What?' Elena snapped.

'Your ankle.' Nellie pointed towards it. 'We really need to get that bandaged up for you.' She looked pointedly at Elena.

'Sure.' Elena was too exhausted to fight an offer of assistance. Together they cleaned her wound, applied fresh cream and bandages, working in easy silence. The two of them. For a moment it felt completely natural. 'You sure nothing happened last night?' Elena couldn't help but discolour it all with her distrust. They were standing where it had occurred, where Stu had made a simple mistake.

'Nothing at all.' Nellie began putting the medicine box away. 'Does it feel better?'

Elena was frowning as she watched her. 'Yeah, it does. Thank you.' Beneath her fresh bandages her ankle throbbed while her stomach turned, the awareness that someone was lying to her settling in, souring everything. Tense, she reached for her phone. Needing her friends, some comfort. Some normality.

> **Elena:** I'm worried I'm losing my mind . . .

> **Leanne:** Join the club xxx

> **Margot:** Ha!

> **Leanne:** Seriously, what's wrong? Xxx

> **Elena:** Things at home are just . . . weird. Strange. I don't know xxx

> **Leanne:** Weird how?

> **Margot:** Like dead cat weird?

> **Leanne:** Margot!

> **Elena:** Weird like, with Nellie. And Stu.

Leanne: He likes having her around, right?

Margot: He like her too much?

Leanne: Dammit, Margot!

Elena: He thought she was me. The other day. He grabbed her.

Leanne: Grabbed her how?

Margot: I know! Like a man grab a woman!

Leanne: Really, Margot?!

Elena: Yes, like how a man grabs a bloody woman. Then he realised and he said he shoved her.

Leanne: Okay.

Margot: Big shove?

Elena: I don't know. It's shaken me up tbh.

Leanne: Need us to come round?

Margot: Say the word we are there!

Elena: No, no. I just need sleep. I just don't like it. That he, you know, grabbed her. And that he shoved her.

Leanne: I'm sure it's not as bad as you think.

Margot: It sound bad.

Leanne: Margot! For the love of God! Seriously, if you need us, shout. We're here for you.

Elena: Night guys, thanks xxx

Leanne: It's okay to find all of this confusing. Not just the More You stuff. But being a mum. It's a lot.

Elena: I know. Love you x

Leanne: Love you more xx

Margot: And I love you all MOST but now phone go on silent as my chubby boy finally asleep. YES! Xxxx

.31

'I don't like it.' There was an unease to Stu's voice that helped lift Elena from the thickness of her slumber. Beside him in the bed she stretched, catlike, her bandaged ankle concealed beneath the sheets.

'Don't like what?' she wondered, rubbing her eyes.

'You won't like it either,' Stu continued, his tablet in his hands, the blue screen glowing against his cheeks, revealing the roughness of his unshaven jawline. Elena always liked him like that, when his smoothness, his togetherness, began to slip away. High up on the mountains, away from razors and barbers, Stu couldn't preen like he did at home. His hair became wild, his face coarse. And Elena would kiss him, savouring the sting of his bristles. 'My wild man,' she'd whisper as the wind that howled through base camp shuddered against their tent.

'Won't like what?' Elena was now fully sitting up, staring across at her husband, at the screen he was studying so intently.

'I've been looking into what happens when you return models to More You,' Stu explained, voice dropping.

'Oh?' Elena tightened, ankle stinging. She'd put off her own explorations into the process, though she wasn't sure why. In some ways it felt like a betrayal of Nellie. Did she want her to stay? Did she feel guilty?

'You've been flat out since the alarm went off. Olive too.' Stu glanced over to the side of the bed where sure enough, their baby still slept soundly. It was an occurrence as rare as an eclipse, one Elena longed to savour. Her body was suddenly heavy with the desire to creep back beneath the bed sheets, to close her eyes and curl onto her side, but the wariness in Stu's words kept her alert. Kept her worried. 'And I've just been sitting here reading up on it all.' He stole a glance at the closed bedroom door before continuing. 'It's difficult to get a clear answer. The terms and conditions read like they have been kept deliberately vague.'

'Okay?'

'So I did some digging around, and I can't be sure, but basically, it seems like when they are . . . when they are, you know, returned, they seem to disappear.'

Elena felt her eyebrows lift high. 'What?'

'There's so many rumours swirling around online, so much false information it is hard to sift through it all. But More You always give the line about rehabilitation, having retired models come and work for them. Yet there's no actual evidence of this.'

'Just ask your mum.' Elena's mouth widened in an involuntary yawn. She wondered if she would ever again feel well rested.

'Yeah, I will. I doubt she'll know but still . . .' For a moment his expression was troubled. Distant.

'Stu?'

'I just don't think it's as straightforward as sending her back and she ends up giving tours of the facility. And it's not as if two yous can carry on walking around ad infinitum.'

'Well, they must go *somewhere*. People don't just disappear, Stuart.'

'Sure they do.' His jaw tightened. 'All the time. We know that more than most. How many people go up mountains never to be seen again?'

Beneath the duvet Elena shivered in acknowledgment. With each climb the dangerous reality was always there, snapping at their heels.

'You really think they'd kill her?' she asked, voice small, strained. Fearful.

'No,' Stu replied instantly, then, as she stroked his chin, 'I mean, maybe. Honestly, I don't know. Like I said, it's so hard to find a straight answer on all this.'

'You can't murder a clone,' Elena stated, frowning.

'Exactly. Although, *technically* you can. Legally . . .' He began tapping upon the blue screen he'd been holding, the text shifting.

'Legally they have no rights.' Elena looked at the door, then at her husband.

'Not yet. No. It's all still so new. The technology. The infrastructure. I guess that's why there's so many movements campaigning for rights.'

Elena nodded. She'd seen them on the news, flashed across the screen in the lounge, along holographic banners in town. Groups not dissimilar to POP. They left graffiti, plagued the offices of More You, made countless viral videos, begging for clones to be seen as people. All the while POP campaigned for it all to just end. In the middle of it all, there were the clones. People like Nellie.

'We can't do that to her. Send her back not knowing what will happen to her.'

Stu gave her a look of surprise.

'If and when we . . . you know' – Elena sighed, wishing she could find the right words – 'when we *part ways*, I'd rather she just . . . disappeared. From our lives. Not from' – she patted the bed – 'the world. If the rumours *are* true, she doesn't deserve to be hurt.'

'I know.' Stu gave a gentle nod. 'I was thinking the same thing. She's . . . she's a person.' He looked over at his wife, eyes misty. 'She's a part of you, Elena.'

Same as Olive.

'But still' – there was unease in her husband's voice – 'I don't feel like she can stay. I'll . . . I'll talk to my mum about it. See how much she knows about what happens when models are . . . returned. Suss out if there's any truth to all the bloody speculation online.'

Elena was barely listening, already reaching for her baby before she could cry out, felt the damp weight of her nappy as she drew the infant to her chest. She was thinking of hours earlier, standing in the kitchen, ankle weeping and Nellie being there. Always attentive. Always wanting to help.

'I keep wondering if she wants more of it,' she mumbled as she released a breast from her nightshirt, fought to get Olive to latch on.

'More of what?'

'The world. Life.' Elena peered down at her tiny daughter. Already she imagined so much for her – a world full of adventure, possibility, love. 'I always wanted to see everything. Do everything. There was a restlessness in my blood.'

'And you think she feels that way too?'

'Possibly. When we don't need her help any more we should just set her free.' It was only after she'd said the words that Elena realised how distasteful they were. How they made her shudder. 'Christ, are we awful?' she whispered hoarsely. 'Are we monsters?'

'Of course not.'

'I just . . .' Olive began suckling loudly and Elena sighed as the discomfort in her breast began to ease. 'What happened with her, in the kitchen?' Her thoughts sharpened back to her conversation with Nellie.

'Don't make me relive it.' Stu gave a sad shake of his head, dark hair tumbling into his eyes.

'Was it truly so bad? Bad enough to be considering. . .' With her free hand she tapped the screen, which was showing an online forum discussing what happened to 'obsolete models' at More You.

'It wasn't that bad, no. Of course not.' Stu scratched at his jawline, nails short, clean. 'But it genuinely freaked me out. Like, I don't want something like that happening again.'

'You're happy, right?' Elena wondered cautiously.

'Of course,' Stu enthused.

'And you're happy with me,' she pressed.

'Of course I am, that's a ridiculous question.'

'And you're feeling, you know. Satisfied. Sexually.'

One thing Elena had always loved about Stu was his openness, especially in the bedroom. He was always keen to please her, explore new things, quick to talk about what worked and what did not.

His mouth twitched. A fleeting movement. Quickly replaced by an effusive, 'Oh, sweetheart. You don't need to—'

'I know it's been months,' Elena interrupted. Because it had. They hadn't been intimate since before Olive arrived. Even then, sex had become perfunctory due to her swollen middle. Bent over a bed or desk, Stu struggling to grasp her widened hips, terrified to thrust too deep, too hard. It was all depressingly unsexy. Elena had fantasies of a renewed hunger for one another once the baby was out. Once her figure returned. 'You don't need to pretend it's fine when I know it's not.'

'Elena . . .' He leaned close, kissed her on the lips, awkwardly shifting to reach over Olive. 'Sweetheart, I love you now more than ever. I hope you know that.'

'But how can you be satisfied when we never even do anything?'

'I'm too tired to even think about that stuff.'

'Liar,' Elena remarked as Stu leaned away, climbed out of bed and made for the bathroom.

'Honestly.' He glanced back at her. 'I'm so exhausted at the end of the day it's the last thing on my mind.'

'Well, now I'm insulted.'

'Okay, maybe not the *last* thing.' He fully turned, one hand on the door frame and there it was – that mischievous grin which had won her over all those years ago. Even now Elena felt it, that dip in her stomach. That desperation to feel his lips against hers.

'I'm not satisfied,' she told him, a playful smirk on her face.

'As troubling as that is to hear' – Stu dropped his gaze for a moment – 'I'd feel more comfortable having this conversation if our daughter wasn't attached to your breast.'

'She can't hear what we're saying.'

'Still.' He waved a dismissive hand at her and entered the bathroom, door closing behind him. Elena pictured him entering the shower, blasting the water so hot it made his skin turn pink, standing beneath the flow of it as he recalled easier, more carefree times, both hands clasped around the part of himself she now was a stranger to.

If she was feeling the sting from a dwindling sex life, then Stu most definitely was too. It explained his behaviour in the kitchen, his hands upon Nellie. Closing her eyes she forced the image out of her mind. She was his wife. He was hers. She already knew what her friends would be urging her to do – to inject the fire back into her marriage. With her free hand Elena scrambled for her phone, tapped out a quick message. There was just one day until her husband's birthday and she was determined to bring him fireworks. She could be more than just a mother to Olive, a milking machine. She could be sexy, alluring, a partner. She could do, she could be both. Elena had scaled mountains. Had seen the world. She reminded herself that she could do anything.

From: POP@outward.co.uk
To: Full Mailing list
Subject: More You sighting

We are closely monitoring a family in Whitstable after a source made us aware of a suspected More You in a home. So far we have had several sightings of what may be the More You. We urge any of our members in the area to be extra vigilant. The family has a young baby, which only makes this whole situation more sickening. Babies should not be subjected to the inhumanity of clones. It is clear that we are needed now, more than ever, to preserve the integrity of the human race.

Any and all sightings of this family should be documented and reported. Modest action has already been taken. We will be looking to escalate things over the coming weeks.

.32

'So, birthday is tomorrow?' Margot asked directly, standing comfortably between the racks of lingerie while holograms of elegant models twisted and gyrated above them.

'Yes, tomorrow.' Elena leaned heavily against Olive's pram. It hadn't been a long walk from the car park to the store inside the glossy shopping centre but already she was feeling it; ankle pulsating in her boot, sweat beading on her forehead. She knew she needed to see a doctor, but first she needed to sort Stu's present. Her foot would have to wait.

'And you want to bring the fireworks?' Margot arched an eyebrow, giving her friend a knowing stare.

'Well.' Elena felt her cheeks warming. 'I at least want to try.'

'This is good.' Margot clicked her fingers at her, nails a slick shade of turquoise. 'Happy man, happy marriage.' She turned from Elena and began to glide through the aisles, twisting her swanlike neck up to study the holograms with the scrutiny of a scientist at a telescope. Her hands flicked across lace knickers, silk thongs, lips thoughtfully pursed.

Almost as soon as Elena had sent the message asking for some assistance shopping, Margot's brisk response had pinged back at her.

Yes darling x

She didn't like admitting she needed help. Usually everything between her and Stu had been so organic, effortless. Fancy pants and bras like spaghetti didn't matter because nothing stayed on long enough anyway. There was a hunger between them, a push and pull that Elena savoured. But things were different now. *She* was different. As Margot studied the items Elena cast a wary glance towards the holograms. At their slim hips. Their flat stomachs. Her body had been similar, once. She'd worked it like a machine, toning every muscle, making herself as strong and as lean as she possibly could be.

'This?' Margot was looking at her, holding up a red push-up bra with matching thong. Elena couldn't help but grimace at the thought of thrusting her now more substantial arse into the pants, hoisting her swollen breasts into the softness of the satin.

'I'm not sure it's very me,' Elena admitted.

Margot shrugged. 'Hmm, okay. I would wear.'

Elena had no doubt that beneath her current ensemble of jeans and a cropped leather jacket that Margot concealed something stunning, something that highlighted her narrow frame. It was why she had sought Margot's help, sensing her friend's affinity with high-end lingerie. She knew that Leanne would have dismissed her concerns.

'Bugger his birthday, babes. You've given him a child, isn't that enough? Men, always taking from us until there's nothing left.'

Elena's inner feminist was already fuming at her current life choices without Leanne dousing that fire with yet more petrol.

'Okay, maybe this?' Now Margot held aloft a black bra with holes where the nipples should be. Elena's eyes grew wide. 'Too much?' Margot tipped her head to study the item again. 'Maybe. Let's keep looking.'

Numbly, Elena followed her towards yet more bras. Pants. Thongs. She clocked a display of vibrators, bright and candy-coloured. What was she doing here? Parts of her still ached from childbirth, did she really expect some lingerie to help reset things between her and Stu? And even though she'd had a C-section she was afraid to let him see her. All of her. As she now was. There was the red slice across her middle, and inside, she felt changes too. Even though Olive hadn't been birthed naturally, Elena felt . . . different.

'He said it was like a hot dog down a hallway.' Leanne had previously regaled them with her husband's words after their first encounter since she'd had the twins. 'I just told him to be fucking grateful we were doing it at all.' Elena envied that kind of confidence. She knew she'd had it once, back when she could always return home, to her mother's arms and kind words. However low she got, that was where she went to get built up again. And now with that gone, Elena hated how untethered she felt. Stu was her home. Yes. And she loved him. Truly. But no one loves you like your mother does. That deep, ingrained connection. Forged in blood.

In the pram Olive stirred, eyes briefly opening to peer in horror at her surroundings. 'Shh, it's okay.' Elena began rhythmically thrusting the pram back and forth. Back and forth.

'Here.' Margot strode over to her, presenting a matching set of a grey and pink lace balconette bra and French knickers. Elena had to admit that they were both beautiful and elegant, with just the hint of sensuality she was after. 'This more your style, yes?'

'Y-yes.' Elena nodded. 'Those are beautiful.'

'He will be unable to resist.' Margot draped the lingerie over Olive's pram and then turned, dipping down to pick up something else. 'And these.' She added some matching suspenders to the pile. 'You will need these too.'

Elena tried to picture it – her clad in new lingerie, the lights low, Olive sleeping in Nellie's room. Just for the moment. Just while Elena and Stuart reconnected. And they needed to. Elena longed to feel his hands on her body, to forget about how she had changed, to get lost in him.

'Is this just about birthday?' Margot asked as together they approached the glow of the digital till point.

'Hmm?' Elena mused absently as she fished in her pocket for her phone to pay.

'Everything okay at home?' Margot waited until Elena's items were in a tissue-filled cardboard bag, dangling from the side of the pram. 'You said about the thing with the other you. The grabbing.' They emerged into the bustle of the shopping centre and for a moment Elena didn't want to even attempt an answer. She considered pretending she'd not heard, feigning tiredness and scuttling back to her car, throwing a hasty wave over her shoulder. But that would be unfair to Margot.

'I'm worried about . . . her,' Elena admitted as they walked side by side, pushing their babies. 'And him,' she added quietly.

Beside them an advert sprang to life, a hologram of a brunette woman smiling outside a simple brick house. 'Discover how to be you,' the voiceover urged, as from behind the woman emerged a perfect reproduction of her, both of them beaming, 'and more.' The house behind morphed into a mansion. 'At More You, we help you accomplish your true potential. Come along and discover why thousands of people are already using our service.'

Margot gave the advert a hard stare as they passed it by. 'Does he look to her like he look to you?' she asked as her attention snapped back to Elena.

'No,' Elena quickly replied.
His hands.
Nellie's hips.
He grabbed her.
Shoved her.

And Stu had been distraught about it all. Had even considered having Nellie returned, rehabilitated back at More You.

'Sometimes.' Elena conceded, hating how her instinct had been to lie even when Margot knew the truth.

Margot gave a curt nod. 'He is man.' Her mouth turned down sadly as she reached out to rub Elena's arm. 'Men hardwired differently to us. It why we must have girlfriends. Be good to each other.'

Elena blinked quickly, on the cusp of tears. 'I know . . . I know it was just a mistake,' she rasped, voice weak.

'I'm sure it was.' Margot offered a sympathetic smile. 'Is she home now?'

'Yeah.' Elena took her phone from her pocket, paused to open the app, showing Margot the screen where an icon throbbed over her home on the map. 'I asked her to do some washing while I was out. And maybe help with baking a cake later.'

'And Stu?'

'He's in the office today.'

'Good.' Margot nodded but looked distant.

'I-if she is me. And she is,' Elena explained, the doors to the centre within sight, the car park just beyond. 'She . . . she wouldn't do that. Because I wouldn't do that, right?' She twisted her head to look at her friend who in profile looked to be cast in stone – every angle in her face so sharp, so precise.

'She . . . no.' Margot turned to look at her, ceased walking, long fingers closed tightly around the handle of her pram. 'Especially not if she truly all you. You are good person, Elena. Good woman.'

'Thank you.'

'But he is man.' Margot's eyebrows lifted knowingly. 'And man, they are weaker than woman. We always know this, yes? I love my husband. I do. I work hard to keep the . . . the fires hot. But would I trust him to stop being man?'

Elena felt the heat of her gaze upon her, pushing her to accept this truth. Margot's eyes glowed with the certainty of it all.

'You are wise to do this now.' Margot poked at the bag of lingerie. 'Make those fires so hot they purge it all. That they burn and scald anyone who try to touch.'

'Thank you,' Elena replied uneasily.

'Anyway.' They'd reached the car park. Margot leaned in for a tight embrace, a kiss upon each cheek. 'Have a lovely day celebrating tomorrow and then you call me later in week with all details, yes?'

'Yes.' Elena managed to smile as pain travelled up her leg. Her fucking ankle. She feared the only fire within her was confided to that point. That wound. She watched Margot walk away, hips swaying as she strutted in her high-heeled boots, more model than mother behind her pram. Elena lingered where she was, feeling dowdy. Feeling unsure. In the pram, Olive began to bleat and cry. 'Okay, okay,' Elena whispered soothingly to her daughter, 'let's get you home and have a feed.' She was a mother. There was no time to dwell on her insecurities. Her fears. There was barely any time at all.

At the end of her car park space, on a raised screen, another advert for More You played.

'Just think of what you could accomplish with twice the time. Twice the energy. At More You we promise to enhance all aspects of your life.'

'Fuck off,' Elena muttered between clenched teeth as she reversed out of her spot, Olive wailing in her cat seat, the sound jarring. Though, for the moment, it was at least drowning out Elena's own thoughts and for that she was grateful.

.33

There was a time when Elena didn't like Stu. When he was just the cocky guy at uni who annoyed her. His bravado. His charm. His bloody charisma. The way he was able to win anyone over with a flash of his perfect smile or a well-thought-out compliment. *Everyone* liked him. And that made Elena dislike him.

'You always have to be different,' her mother would tell her with tenderness in her voice. 'My bold, unique girl.'

Each time Elena saw Stu she felt her stomach betray her, giving a dip of joy. But she couldn't, wouldn't be drawn in by him. And now she was beside him in their marital bed, watching his chest rise and fall as he slept, wondering where his mind had drifted to, what he dreamed of. When she could wait no longer, Elena lowered herself towards him and purred into his ear, 'Happy birthday.'

With a deep groan, Stu twisted, stirred, stretched his arms up above his head, eyes slowly opening. 'Mmm.'

Elena kissed him softly.

'Mmm.'

A hand reached for her as she moved to withdraw, grabbing her hip, returning her to him. Elena couldn't help but smile as she kissed him.

Good.

His desire still burned for her. And with the contents of the little paper bag at the end of the bed, stashed in her dressing table, he could have her. Ravish her. They could turn the clock back to when it was just the two of them and their hunger for one another. Back before her body changed, back before—

Elena broke away from him. Olive was crying. 'Sorry,' she mumbled as she crawled to the other side of the bed, reached for their baby. 'Shh, shhh,' she whispered into Olive's small ear as she bounced her against her chest, patting the nappy that she could already tell was full. 'Let Mummy change you.'

'I'll go finish myself off,' Stu said as he slid from the bed and padded towards the bathroom.

'Oh, no, wait just—' The door slapped closed before Elena could finish her sentence. She glanced at her dressing table. She'd planned for her surprise to come later anyway. And he'd surely be replenished by then. Elena was going to watch him blow out the candles on his cake come twilight and then ask Nellie to watch Olive for a bit. That part she was uncomfortable with. But Elena reminded herself that it was the entire point of Nellie – to permit her and Stu to have some semblance of time together. And they sorely needed it. She'd felt him harden against her just then in the bed, and in his arms she felt her insecurities melt away. This was Stu, her Stu. The man who had seen all of her and loved her for over a decade. What would he care about some new scars? Some extra inches on her waistline?

'Come on, little one.' Elena carried Olive to the changing table in the nursery where a white wooden cot was waiting for when the baby was a little older. She undid the poppers on the sleepsuit adorned with pink sheep, pulled back the tabs on the nappy and the smell instantly hit her. 'Christ.' Elena gagged. 'For one so small you do some almighty shits.' This latest one was what Leanne would term 'a good korma'. And it had spread all up Olive's back as Elena lay her down, soiling both baby and sleepsuit. 'Fuck's sake,' Elena muttered, plucking wet wipes from the nearby packet in abundance.

'Would you like me to bath her?'

In the midst of smearing shit onto wipes Elena turned to the door. Nellie was up, dressed, hair loose around her shoulders, wearing a white cable-knit jumper and dark jeans.

'I . . .'

'It's a messy one.' Nellie came and joined her at the changing table, nose crinkling. 'For such a small baby she does some almighty stinkers.'

'That she does,' Elena agreed, briefly recalling some advice her mother had once given her: 'Get either a baby or a man, you need a peg. Not for the washing line.'

'We could really use a peg right now,' Nellie jested. Elena turned to her, awestruck into silence, Olive now naked and half cleaned upon the changing mat, twisting her little hands into fists while her legs kicked the air.

'What did . . . how—'

'Let me bath her.' Nellie leaned forward and carefully lifted Olive up from the beneath her arms, the only part of her that seemed completely clean. 'I'll take care of little lady while you and Stu enjoy a relaxed breakfast together.'

'The . . . peg . . .' It was too early, Elena's mind too foggy. She frowned in frustration as she stared at Nellie, who was preoccupied with making faces at Olive.

'Enjoy a birthday breakfast with Stu,' Nellie instructed in a sing-song voice, walking out of the room towards the main bathroom. Elena looked to the mound of used wet wipes piled where her baby had been. 'And I'll clean up those too, don't worry,' Nellie called from the landing. The click of a door shutting. Then the hum of water being poured. Alone, Elena felt it in her chest, the ache, the longing. She missed her mother. If only she could call her up now, seek her advice. If only she could have called upon her for help all along.

'Marriages are work, motherhood is work,' her mother would

tell her. 'We are burdened with being women, my girl. We will always be working.'

With a jolt of purpose Elena left the nursery and walked along to the bathroom, opening the door to find Olive in her bath seat while bubbles began to swirl around her, Nellie crouched beside the tub.

'Since it's Stu's birthday,' she began, nerves rising though she wasn't sure why, 'could you later, perhaps, after dinner, watch Olive for a while? Please?'

'Of course.' Nellie turned slightly to look up at her, a gentle smile on her face. 'Have you got anything special planned for him?'

Elena pictured it again – Stu's hands on Nellie's hips. It would have been the first time a man had touched her in such a way. Her first sexual contact. Did it arouse something within her as it did in Elena whenever Stu touched her? Did her heart flutter, her lips part, her groin begin to ache? Elena gave a shake of the head, refusing to continue to dwell there, in that moment. 'I've just got a small surprise for him,' she said lightly.

'How wonderful.' Nellie's smile widened. 'I'm sure he will love it.'

.34

'Happy birthday my darling,' Catherine gushed down the phone. 'You know I can still remember how the morning you were born—'

'Not now, Mum,' Stuey cut her off. 'I don't need a trip down memory lane hearing about how Dad was drunk with nerves.'

'But he was!' Catherine almost laughed, recalling it all too well, Eric's flushed cheeks, watery stare, the whisky on his breath as he stooped down to kiss her as she held their new son in her arms. That was how it had been for Catherine, her husband sequestered away in his office, knocking back tumblers of expensive liquor while she grunted beneath bright lights. Only when the messy act of delivery was done did Eric come over to the hospital.

'I shouldn't be there for all that,' he'd told his wife with a pained look, 'all that *indignity*.'

Catherine made sure she'd brushed her hair before her husband's visit, applied a fresh layer of lipstick. She looked far from her best but she was at least presentable. They'd already decided that if they had a second boy, they would name him Stuart. After Eric's grandfather. And Catherine liked the name, it felt modern. Strong.

Upon the hospital bed she'd looked down at the pink bundle in her arms, at his shock of dark hair, a gift already bestowed from his father. Another perfect baby boy. Catherine was sure her heart grew two sizes bigger at the sight of him.

'Welcome to the world, my little Stuey,' she'd whispered to her fresh baby, ignoring the burn in her loins, wanting only to focus on the preciousness of it all. The goodness. 'I'm your mother and I'm going to love you so much.'

It would be another two hours before Eric joined her at the hospital. Not that Catherine cared; she had her baby boy.

'You used to love that story,' Catherine remarked a little sourly, sweeping by the island in the kitchen upon which stood a blue iced cake that she intended to take round to her son's the following day. 'We would always laugh about it.'

'I'm just a bit busy.'

'On your *birthday*?' Catherine was appalled. It was bad enough that she'd been told she needed to wait until the day after the event to see her son. ('Elena and I have plans on the day,' he'd told her coolly.) 'You can't be busy on your birthday, Stuey.'

'Olive has no concept of birthdays; she still needs me just as much today,' Stuart told his mother stiffly.

'Well, I'll be round tomorrow,' Catherine informed him brightly, already excited to see Stuey open the Burberry scarf and jacket she'd bought for him. And the watch she'd had engraved. The assistant in the store assured her it was state of the art, could monitor your heart, blood pressure. Catherine had smiled thinly and reiterated that she just wanted the best for her son, remembering when all a watch needed to do was tell the time.

'Okay, Mum, see you tomorrow.'

She could tell he was trying to rush away from her and her heart sank.

'Have the best day, Stuey, I hope Elena spoils you.'

'Okay, Mum.'

'Love you.'

'Love you.'

Even though the call had ended Catherine kept her phone pressed tightly to her ear, a bittersweet smile drawn upon her lips.

Love you.

How quickly time had spun away from her since that first day in hospital. When Stuey was just a tiny bundle in her arms and she was his entire world. Catherine glanced at the cake, already sweetening the air in the kitchen. It seemed almost impossible that her baby was spending his birthday taking care of a baby of his own. Feeling the day stretching ahead of her, Catherine made for her fridge, needing a glass of Chardonnay to take the edge off.

.35

Candlelight flickered over Stu's face as he leaned low, drew in a deep breath. Elena watched with joy, elated for what felt like the first time in months. It had been a good day. Together they'd enjoyed a relaxed breakfast, then a walk in the park, pushing Olive together, feeling like a real family. As Olive stared up at the boughs of trees, the smattering of clouds above her, a look of wonder on her little face, Elena caught glimpses of all that was yet to come. Of first steps, first words. First family holiday, the Christmases that would all twinkle with newfound joy. They'd done it, hadn't they? The exhaustion, the sleepless nights, they'd forged a way through.

With help.

With Nellie.

Nellie, who had patiently remained home while they went out as a family, had baked a cake to Elena's exacting specifications.

And Stu had even told his mother to come round the next day, rather than on his actual birthday. She could deliver her gifts after the fact and this made Elena feel more than a bit smug. She had wanted her mother-in-law banished from her life ever since their awkward exchange at her wedding, which remained in Elena's mind as she was sure it did in Catherine's.

'It's helped having Nellie around, don't you think?' she'd asked Stu as they wandered through the park, tracing the curve of the path with the wheels of the pram. A clench of his jaw, a steely look into the distance.

'I don't know.'

'You were the one who pushed for her, Stu.'

'I mean, we're less tired, sure.' Stu snatched a sideways glance at his wife. She could tell what was troubling him, the moment in the kitchen. But like all moments, it had passed. And Elena was working to make things right, to make their marriage fresh and real again. To burn them both with fire. 'But what's the long-term plan here?'

Elena considered his question. When she thought of her future, of their family, Nellie most certainly wasn't in the picture. 'I guess, maybe, when Olive is one, perhaps we just . . . let her go.'

'But she's you.' Stu ceased walking, turned his body fully to face her. 'It doesn't work like that, Elena. Nellie isn't an animal we can release into the wild. She's . . . she's chipped. She's a clone. How is she supposed to get a job? A home? She has no real identity beyond you.'

'I just don't like to think of her—'

'You're getting too attached. You're seeing yourself in her too much.'

'That's not true.'

'Are you imagining her yearning for mountaintops? For a horizon without limits?'

Elena's face burned. She knew she'd been caught out. So often she found herself studying Nellie, wondering these very things. Because that was what she had once wanted, so wasn't it natural to assume Nellie wanted those things too?

'She will have to be rehabilitated back at More You.' Stu turned back to the pram as he said this, resumed walking, pace brisk.

'I don't think that—' Elena hurried on her bad ankle to keep up. It had previously been dormant and now fresh pain bloomed through it. She hoped her husband would mistake the tears in her eyes for anguish rather than discomfort.

'There is no other way, Elena. I'm sorry. When it comes to . . . to clones. There are rules, honey. Rules we can't break.'

Elena knew the rules he spoke of. How clones were denied any rights. Any chance of a life of their own. There were fears that without such rules, dangerous egomaniacs with means would pollute the population with countless copies of themselves. The rules were in place to keep people safe, maintain order.

'I just don't like the thought of sending her back.'

'So you want to what? Keep her for ever?' Stu let the question hang between them so Elena could absorb how crazy it sounded.

'No, but . . . she only ever wants to help,' Elena muttered weakly, glad to be well away from home while they had this conversation.

'I know, because she's a good person.' Stu glanced back at her. 'Just like you. But we can't keep her, Elena. Not indefinitely. We just can't. We always said this was just a temporary thing.' He was unusually resolute on the matter and Elena found herself blaming Catherine. This had all been her suggestion, her money, her pushing. And now it was coming between them; the issue of what to do with Nellie. She wondered if that had been Catherine's intention the entire time; a Trojan horse of Elena's own making. Wasn't it only natural that Elena would eventually bond with Nellie? There was a kinship there. Almost a sisterhood.

Elena had expected to only fear her More You. Now she felt drawn to her. Protective.

Since it was Stu's birthday Elena didn't strain the subject further. They moved on to talk about other things, savouring the freedom to just be together, to not have their every moment hounded by exhaustion. Her old self, Elena felt her come fluttering back in fragments and it felt good. It gave her hope.

*

'Did you make a wish?' Elena asked as smoke curled from the blown out candles.

'If I did, it's a secret.' Stu gave her a playful look and Elena's stomach gave a little flip.

Soon.

Her excitement was pushing back her anxiety.

'If you ladies will excuse me' – Stu leaned back from the kitchen island, glancing between Nellie and Elena – 'I need to go and see a man about a dog.'

'Oh?' Nellie asked, bemused, as she flicked on the lights.

'He means take a shit,' Elena explained with a roll of her eyes, bouncing Olive against her chest.

'I see.' Nellie still looked confused.

Elena waited for her husband's footsteps to recede up the nearby staircase and then looked at Nellie, feeling a jolt of adrenalin. 'Are you okay to have Olive for a bit?'

'Oh, of course.' Nellie's arms were already held out for the baby. 'Is it time for his surprise?'

'I think so, yes.' Elena gave a girlish giggle. It was almost seven, early for many but close to being late for those bound by the night-time antics of a young baby. Elena was determined not to waste a single minute. She planted a kiss upon Olive's forehead, leaving a smear of crimson from the lipstick she'd applied that afternoon, and then she crept up the stairs. Elena tried to be as quiet as possible as she entered the bedroom. The radio was playing in the bathroom, which helped conceal her steps as she tiptoed around, shedding the shirt dress she'd been wearing and reaching for the bag in the dressing table drawer. Even the tissue paper within it was velvet soft. Elena gingerly put on first the bra, then the French knickers. She went to the mirror, expecting to hate what she saw.

Margot had chosen well.

The knickers came up high enough to hide the slash of her scar. The bra hoisted her already ample breasts to epic proportions. Elena hastily dragged her fingers through her hair, checked her make-up. Then a spritz of vanilla-scented perfume, dusting her skin. She wanted Stu's hands on her hips, his lips against her ear. She looked at the bathroom door. Still closed. Music still playing.

She glanced towards the hideous silver candlesticks, which could now serve a purpose. Elena rustled in a drawer for a box of matches, struck one and lit the first, slim ivory candle. Then the second. A shivering, golden light danced within the room. Elena moved to flick off the main lamp, letting only the candles offer any kind of glow. The bedroom became moody, charged with an erotic energy. Over the music in the bathroom Elena heard the hiss of a flush. Then the music stopped. She dragged her hands through her hair one last time, pushed up her breasts, pouted. The door opened and Elena felt a feathery breath escape her. She was about to be ravaged.

.36

There was only the candlelight, golden and shifting. It danced across her husband's face as he entered the room and she was reminded of how handsome he was. How he'd only grown more into his features over their years together. Elena felt lucky. Lucky to have Olive, to have a husband she continued to love. She wanted to wrap herself within him, the way she used to. She wanted them to fall into each other's arms, to end up breathless upon the bed. Her body prickled deliciously with the anticipation of it all.

'Stu.' She tried to sound alluring as she said his name. 'Happy birthday.' Elena watched his gaze briefly sweep over her body, taking in the lingerie, the way it hugged her in just the right way. Feeling confident Elena took a step towards him, hungry to feel his lips on hers. She stopped suddenly when his hands pushed against her shoulders.

'What are you doing?' There was a coldness in his voice that stunned her. Elena looked into his eyes, which were narrowed, guarded.

'Stu?'

'I said what the fuck do you think you're doing?'

'What do I think I'm doing?' Elena repeated dramatically, gesturing to her scantily clad body. 'I'm clearly trying to seduce you, you bloody idiot.'

Obviously, it had been some time since they'd been intimate but Elena had not been expecting this level of resistance.

'Honestly, it's fine.' She moved forward again, pressing her body against his. 'I'm feeling much better now. I need you to take me for a test drive.' Elena went on her tiptoes to whisper this final part into his ear, daring even to dip her tongue against it. Stu was just worried about her body, that was all. Worried that she still ached, still didn't feel quite herself. She needed to assure him that all was fine.

'Get off me!'

This time when he pushed her back he shoved her hard. Harder than he'd ever done before. Elena staggered back from him, legs connecting with the bed, almost losing her footing.

'What the hell?' she snapped tersely, all eroticism seeping out of the room. 'I try to make an effort for you on your birthday and this is how you thank me?'

'Get out of my fucking room.' Stu's face was hard as he snapped a finger towards the bedroom door, commanding her like an unruly dog.

'Jesus, Stu.' Elena folded her arms against her chest, beginning to feel ridiculous, exposed. 'There's no need to be such an absolute dick about it. Obviously you don't want to fuck me, message received.'

Stu remained in the doorway of the bathroom, staring at her like she was an intruder. 'I said get out of my room, Nellie. Now.'

'Nellie?' The name slipped from Elena's lips, heavy and unwelcome. 'You think I'm Nellie? For fuck's sake, Stuart. It's me. Your *wife*.'

'Elena wouldn't do this.' He glanced at her lingerie, face twisting with disgust.

She approached him again, keen to move past the unpleasantness. Clearly, she'd veered too far out of her lane, out of character. Perhaps the lingerie was a step too far. She needed to make Stu see how insane he was being. 'It's *me*.' She laced a hand around his neck, reached up to kiss him, so he'd know. Later, she'd feel the sting of being misidentified, but for now all Elena wanted was to mount her husband, to connect with him as they once did. To fuck away all their stress. 'It's me, Stu,' she repeated, finding his lips, pressing a kiss upon them.

He flung her back. This time she landed upon the bed, back aching.

'Elena!' he roared, looking at the door. 'Elena!'

'*I'm* Elena, you moron!' She got to her feet, back and ankle both now throbbing. 'Can you just stop being so over the top and—'

'Not this *again*. I told you last time!'

He grabbed her, fast and sudden, by the wrists, pushing her against the dresser. Elena winced as a brass handle dug deep into her back.

Again.

The word barrelled through Elena like a bullet. Had Nellie tried to seduce Stu? *Slept* with him? The questions were pushed out of her as her husband's weight shoved against her.

'Get off me!' she cried, trying to free her hands in vain.

'Elena!' he shouted again towards the door.

'I'm Elena!' There was rage in her voice, poker hot. Stu twisted to look down at her, face contorted.

'Stop saying her fucking name.'

'I'm Elena!'

'We should never have let you in our fucking house.' He released her wrists and wrapped his hands against her throat. 'This newer fucking model. I should have said no! Sent you back days ago!'

'I'm . . .' The pressure, it was too tight. His thumb was squashing her windpipe, causing her chest to burn. 'Stu . . . St . . . St—'

'I won't let you ruin my family! You think I don't see what you're doing? Trying to replace her? You'll never be her! You're unnatural!' He was leaning close and Elena could smell the champagne and whisky on his breath, drinks they'd previously toasted his birthday with together. Now they curdled in a fume-filled fog before her. Elena tried to breathe. He pushed down harder. Beneath his grip she fought, thrashed her legs, her arms. But Stu was too strong. He pinned her in place as he tried to squeeze the last breath out of her.

'You're a fucking . . . monster,' he grunted, face flushed.

Elena felt light-headed, spots in her vision. She thought of Nellie downstairs with Olive. Nellie who he would now think was her. Would she die here, in this moment, and be discarded as a faulty clone? Never to be missed. Mourned. The spots became bigger. Frantic, Elena fumbled about, flailing. She heard the distant thunk of a candlestick falling. Spluttering, she reached around, eyes bulging, watering. The other candlestick. Her fingertips grazed it, tugged it close.

'You should never have come here.' Stu was standing so close to her, his body so hot, so tight with anger.

Elena claimed the candlestick. Caught in a feral desire to breathe, she hurled it upwards, forwards. Heard the dull smack as it connected with the back of Stu's head. Then his hands were falling away, her throat burning as she dropped to her knees, drinking in air like water, famished and stunned. Elena gulped in air, wheezing, her vision finally stabilising. It was only when she slowly rose to stand, legs shaky as a baby deer's, that she realised she was still holding the candlestick. Then she turned to look at her husband.

.37

'Stu?' His name was suddenly strange in her mouth, awkward. 'Stu?' Elena called again, throat still burning. Her hands reached for her neck, grazing the skin that throbbed to the touch, the candlestick dropping from her grasp and landing with a single, dense thud. 'Stu?'

He was on the floor. Stretched out towards the bed like a tree that had been newly felled.

'Stu?' Elena braced for him to jump up and lunge at her once more.

He thought I was her. He thought I was Nellie.

The pain of it twisted with the pain in her throat, against her neck. A gasp of sorrow burst from her as Elena blinked back tears.

Her husband was still on the floor.

Elena looked down at his slipper-clad feet, at the candlestick that had landed beside them. There was a stain upon its base, glossy and red.

Panic pierced her like an electric jolt. 'Stu!' She was quickly on her knees, at his side, drawing up close to his chest. His head. 'Stu!' Her husband's eyes were open, staring up at the ceiling, but there was a vacancy in his gaze that froze Elena. One hand hovering over his chest, she didn't dare move.

This is just a bad dream, a nightmare. That's all.

'Stu?' She rasped his name as she shuffled closer to his head, peering down to look at the face that was more familiar to her than her own. 'Stu?' She gave his shoulders a brief shake. He lolled back and forth upon the floor like a marionette without strings.

This isn't happening. This isn't happening.

'Stu!'

Elena felt warmth against her knees, her thighs. She looked down and hurriedly clasped a hand to her mouth to stifle a scream. Blood. It was everywhere. A dark river leaking from the back of Stu's head, sinking into their soft carpet, staining her bare legs.

Oh my fucking God.

'Stu!' She screamed his name, shaking him with all her force. His expression never changed, eyes open, unseeing. 'Stuart! Stuart, stop this! Wake up!' She kept shaking him as the world began to spin, as her tears started to flow so freely they almost rendered her blind. Howling like a wounded animal, Elena fell against her husband, clasping his chest as though it were a life raft. How many times had she lain against it, listening to the reassuring thump of his heart? Revelling in the knowledge that he was hers? Now there was nothing. Weeping, Elena curled her body against his. 'Please, baby, please. Wake up. I need you to wake up.'

This isn't real.

'Stu?' She kept calling his name until she lost her voice, until her body went cold and numb. But no response came.

'What's going on? Elena!'

It took her a moment to register that someone was calling her name. The slice of light that crept in from the open door to the landing seared against her. In a daze, Elena shifted off Stu's chest, his body already growing cold.

'What happened?' Nellie was in the doorway, holding Olive, her eyes wide with horror as she looked upon the scene in the bedroom.

'I . . .' Elena awkwardly rose, struggling to speak. 'It . . . it was an accident and . . .' She looked at the woman holding her baby, feeling so raw, so broken.

He thought I was you.

'Elena.' Nellie locked eyes with her. 'Do I call the police? Tell me what to do.'

'He thought I was you,' she rasped, staring at her mirror image, beginning to shake.

'What?' Nellie's eyes widened with fear. Or was it shock?

'He said . . . he said "again".'

'Elena, focus.'

'Again!' Elena forced the word through clenched teeth. 'Did you sleep with my husband? Did you?'

Nellie's hands were on her shoulders, firm. 'Elena.' Her voice was calm, measured. 'Tell me what to do.'

In her bedroom, standing in her husband's blood, Elena felt like she was falling. Like the world around her had become some treacherous mountain peak and a single wrong step could send her plunging to her doom. She breathed in deeply, forcing herself to stamp out her grief. To think.

Think of Olive. She needs you. Focus.

Dammit. Focus.

'Call the police' – Elena gave a nod – 'but not yet.'

Nellie only looked at her, saying nothing.

'Let me . . .' Elena looked down at her body. She was shaking, her skin darkened with dried blood, her new lingerie stained and ruined. 'I need to get cleaned up,' she concluded. 'Then . . . then we will call the police.'

'Okay.' Nellie pursed her lips. 'I'll be downstairs if you need me.' She didn't even glance down at Stu before leaving the room, Olive held tightly to her chest.

*

Beneath the hiss of the shower Elena watched the water curdle pink beneath her.

This isn't happening.

She tried to keep her thoughts menial, practical.

Wash your hair.

Wash off all the blood.

Burn the fucking lingerie out in the garden with some leaves.

It had all just been an accident, an awful, horrific accident. But if the police came, if that was the story they heard, what would become of her? Of Olive?

Would they believe it was self-defence? Would they look at the bruises that must surely be blooming on her neck and understand? But what then? Even if in killing him she'd saved her own life, would they still take her away?

What if I go to prison? What if they take Olive from me?

Olive.

Thinking of her baby made her pulse race, her thoughts become cluttered and irrational.

I can't let them take me away.

I have to be here for my baby.

She needed to remove herself from the situation. Say she entered her bedroom, found Stu upon the floor, beaten.

Beaten.

Turning, Elena vomited into the base of the shower, plug glugging loudly as it drained away yet more of her anguish.

Her DNA was all over the crime scene. The candlestick. There could be no feigning her innocence.

Her DNA . . .

Elena studied her hand in the flow of water. The shape, the structure, even the prints she shared with Nellie.

He thought I was her.

Was it such a great leap to pretend it had been her, all

along? The lingerie, the seduction? Had it all occurred while Elena was downstairs with her baby, being a good, dutiful mother?

Out of the shower, Elena swept the condensation from the mirror and studied her ghastly reflection. She looked tired. Withdrawn. Afraid.

You're in shock.

Her teeth were knocking together, filling her head with their enamel drumbeat.

Stu would want you to be calm, to protect Olive.

Fresh tears came and Elena had to grip the sink so as not to fall to the tiles.

Stu.

Her husband, the man she loved. The man she'd built a life with, had intended to share the rest of her life with. He was gone.

And it was all her fault.

Elena's grip upon the sink tightened, knuckles white.

No.

She wouldn't let this destroy her. She would be strong, she had to be, for Olive.

This was never you, this was Nellie.

A pulsating in her ankle. Elena looked down to see fresh blood seeping from it, the wound forced open by the shower.

Shit.

She'd need to bandage that before she got dressed, before she phoned the police and put on the performance of a lifetime.

.38

Elena wore jeans and a silk shirt. An outfit far fancier than she felt comfortable in but she reminded herself that she needed to look *nice*. As she brushed out her hair, staring at her distraught face in the mirror she went over what she needed to say.

I was downstairs feeding my baby when I heard a commotion. I ran up to the bedroom and found Nellie, naked, standing over my husband, candlestick in hand.

A fresh wave of sobbing trembled through her. Elena bit down on her lip, trying to calm herself. She drew blood.

It was right to blame Nellie, wasn't it? Nellie wasn't a human, not truly. She didn't have rights. But then why did Elena feel so wretched? So conflicted?

I have to be here for Olive.

What other choice did she have?

After one last final glance in the mirror, certain that all her husband's blood had disappeared down the plughole and no longer clung to her person, Elena filled her lungs with a steadying breath and entered the bedroom.

Immediately it felt colder than it had before. And something crunched underfoot. Elena looked down, grateful to be wearing her Ugg slippers as she noticed shards of glass shimmering upon the carpet. Then she saw the curtains billowing, the gash in the window where it had been shattered.

'What the fuck?' she whispered aloud. Stu's body still lay

amid the debris, unmoved. Eyes still open. Elena permitted herself to pick her way towards him, to stare down at his lips, which were now so very pale. She felt it then. The desire to fall apart. To collapse atop her husband and not move. To hold onto him until every ounce of warmth had drained from her too. But she couldn't.

Olive.

Her baby needed her.

When Elena lost her mother, she found that the cruellest part of it all was that the world continued to spin on its axis. The sun rose, set. Everything and everyone carried on. Staying in one place was never an option.

'Baby, baby I'm sorry,' Elena whispered against the wind that whipped into the room.

He would have killed you. You had to.

He thought you were her.

Elena crunched over glass as she hurried from the room, taking care to leave the door open and wide, the way someone in shock might leave it. She found Nellie pacing in the kitchen, Olive asleep in her arms.

'The window?' Elena demanded bluntly, phone in hand, preparing to dial for the police. She couldn't leave it much longer.

'I went and broke it while you were showering,' Nellie explained, tone equally brisk. 'I figured we would need an explanation for what you did.'

Elena's jaw clenched.

What you did.

'I thought if I broke the window, we could say we heard a noise while Stu was up there showering. By the time we ran up, they were already climbing back out. We could say it was a POP-motivated attack.'

We.

Elena stared at her. It was all so methodical. So thought

through. And there had been a spate of POP attacks in recent weeks, though none had been fatal. Yet.

'You didn't think to check with me first?' Elena wondered, moving forward and reaching for her baby. Nellie took a step back, hands forming a protective barrier around Olive.

'I thought it best we act quickly. Did you have a better solution?'

Elena looked at her carbon copy, holding her baby tightly to her chest. Like a shield.

She's protecting herself. Elena mused. *Just like I planned to do.* How alike they clearly were in their drive for self-preservation.

'Pass her to me,' Elena instructed sharply.

'She's fast asleep.'

'She's my baby,' Elena raged, tears pricking her eyes. 'Give her to me.'

Nellie turned away, moving Olive out of reach. 'You're in shock,' she said quietly over her shoulder. 'I'll take her while you call the police. Take a moment to steady yourself.'

Elena hated that she was right. She *was* in shock. A strange numbness was passing through her body and her thoughts felt detached, as though she were walking through a dream. A nightmare. Without further hesitation she dialled for the emergency services on her phone.

'Hello.' Her voice didn't sound like her own. 'My husband has been attacked and he's . . . he's not waking up. Please. Please, somebody help.' Elena wiped away the tears that had fallen during the call with a shaking hand. Nellie had drifted through to the lounge. Elena was alone in the kitchen. She absorbed the silence, knowing it wouldn't be long until the night was torn apart by the peal of sirens.

'So, tell me what happened?' The uniformed officer on her sofa was staring at her, his face open and kind. He was perhaps a decade or so older than she was. Than Stu. Elena blew again into the tissue she'd fisted into a ball in her hands, frightened by her own ability to keep crying even when her eyes felt dry and brittle, her body hollow.

'We heard a loud bang upstairs,' Nellie offered. She was beside Elena, the pair of them like dutiful twins. Olive was sleeping at the far end of the sofa in her Moses basket, oblivious to the hordes of people in her home. First there had been paramedics, rushing up the stairs. Then came the police, who assessed the bedroom and instructed Elena and Nellie to remain in the lounge while they presided over things. As Elena spoke with the two uniformed officers across from her, she imagined Stu being hoisted onto a gurney, a black liner zipped up over his face. She wept anew.

'Who went upstairs to see what had happened?' the officer asked. Elena tried to find her voice through her sobbing but Nellie was too quick.

'I did,' she blurted. 'Elena was down here feeding Olive. I went into the bedroom and found Stuart on the floor, unresponsive, the window smashed.'

Elena made a sound like an animal caught in a trap.

'Have you received any threats from anyone? Any organisations?' the second officer asked.

'A dead cat,' Nellie told them with eerie confidence. 'We found a dead cat upon the doorstep, which we assumed was a threat from POP. And the tyres on the car were slashed just over a week ago.'

'Right.' The first officer was nodding and typing something onto their digital tablet.

'We will need to take a fresh scan of prints,' they added, turning the tablet so that it released a blue beam of light which scanned the tips of Nellie's fingers as she offered them her hand, palm up. 'Thank you.' The officer looked at Elena.

'We will be the same,' Nellie interjected while Elena shook and wept beside her. 'I'm her More You.'

'Of course.' The officer gave a polite smile. 'I'm so sorry for your loss.' The officer was trying to meet her eye but Elena couldn't look up from the floor. 'We will be undergoing a thorough investigation. We will find who attacked your husband, Mrs Roberts.'

'Th-thank you.' Elena shook as though the room were ice cold.

'It's okay, I'm here.' Nellie scooted close to rub her back, making large circles. 'It's going to be all right.'

He thought I was you.

Elena hiccupped over a fresh bout of grief.

It's all your fault.

.39

For Catherine the news arrived as a text, followed by a call from Nellie.

> Something has happened to Stuart. I'm so sorry x

When she saw the words on the screen she almost dropped her phone, felt the cold spike of fear passing through her.
Stuey.
Her precious baby boy.
What could have happened? Her mind reeled off countless possibilities, each worse than the next as her long nails clacked against the screen as she typed out a stream of responses, demanding answers. Details.
Her son was going to be fine. He had to be.
It was only twenty minutes between the text message and Nellie calling her but it felt like a lifetime. Catherine could barely speak when she answered.
'Someone broke into the house,' Nellie explained, 'attacked him. I'm so sorry. There was nothing anyone could do.'
The room felt like it was spinning as Catherine lowered herself onto the sofa, shaking. Upon the wall all the framed moments of her life: Stuey graduating, Stuey on a beach, Clive as a toddler in the garden of their old house. The pictures began to slip out of focus as thick tears clogged Catherine's false lashes.
'It's . . . it was his birthday,' she rasped in disbelief. 'I'm . . . I'm coming over. Later. With gifts.'

'I'm so sorry,' Nellie repeated.

All the apologies, Catherine remembered enduring them when she lost Clive. Everyone was *so sorry* for her loss. Asking if there was anything they could do.

Just bring him back, Catherine wanted to scream at them. That was all she wanted. Her boy back. *Just bring him back.*

But of course, that was impossible.

Catherine hung up on Nellie, tossed her phone to the floor and held her head in her hands, absorbing the news, limbs trembling.

Stuey.

Gone.

Lost.

It just wasn't possible. Catherine remained on the sofa until the sky darkened outside, broken and alone.

.40

The following days all blurred into one disjointed haze. Elena slept fitfully upon the sofa whenever exhaustion overwhelmed her. Sometimes she heard snippets of the news story echoing through the house, from the radio or television, but Nellie was always swift to silence them, to change the channel. Olive seemed to cry more fiercely, for longer, as though she sensed the great loss that now hung over her home. Her life. As Elena shuffled from room to room, feeling more like an apparition than a person, she loathed to admit that she was grateful for Nellie's presence. Nellie, who kept to a schedule, who flicked on the kettle, popped the toaster, shoved food in front of Elena's broken form. Nellie, who changed nappies, rocked Olive to sleep. All the while Elena kept hugging her arms to her chest, feeling so awfully brittle, as though the slightest touch might snap her in half.

The third day, or perhaps the fourth – Elena had lost track – Catherine arrived. A tiny thought lodged in the back of her mind, wondering why she hadn't darkened their doorstep sooner, but she too must surely be lost in the mire of grief. A place where there were no rules, only pain.

'Catherine.' Elena muttered her name, struggling to look at her. The original Mrs Roberts wore a black dress and a pained expression. Lips painted blood red, eyes fringed by flakes of fallen mascara.

'My boy,' she rasped, pushing past Elena to enter the home. 'My boy.' Hand on chest, she paused in the hallway, struggling to breathe. Beside her Elena wondered if they should perhaps embrace, come together in their sorrow. Wasn't that supposed to happen now? Should they hold one another and weep, lament their loss? Instead, Catherine wheezed while Elena watched her, frozen in place. It was Nellie who spoke first, appearing from the kitchen doorway.

'Can I get you a tea, Catherine?' So polite, so formal. As though this were any other visit. Any other day.

Catherine pushed back her shoulders, drew herself to her full height. 'Y-yes, dear. Thank you. A tea would be . . .' Her lips bunched together, her eyes closed.

'Thanks, Nellie.' Elena glanced quickly at the figure in the doorway before leading Catherine into the lounge, where Olive was sleeping, cheeks still red from her latest bout of crying. Catherine rushed to her, drawn to this last physical trace of her son.

'Oh, sweet baby girl.' She pressed a hand to her mouth then dramatically turned away from her granddaughter.

'Catherine, I . . .' Elena had no idea how to begin. What she should say.

I'm sorry.

How are you?

I'm lost. Stu is gone and we are just here and I'm . . . I'm so fucking lost.

'I'm still not over the shock of it.' Catherine neatly lowered herself upon the sofa, one hand resting against the side of the Moses basket, skeletal fingers bejewelled. 'I know I never will be. My boy. My Stuey. He was my light.' She gave a theatrical flutter of her lashes and Elena noticed the cracks in her foundation, the mask applied with not quite enough care.

'I'm just . . . we're all still in shock.' Elena's throat felt forever sore, words rasped out with effort. She wondered if she would ever again feel like herself.

'It's unimaginable,' Catherine sniffed, reaching down to her handbag, releasing the clasp and withdrawing a soft tissue, which she dabbed against her eyes. 'Utterly *unimaginable* to lose a child. To go through it once is unbearable but *twice* . . .' For a moment her grip on the Moses basket tightened.

Nellie arrived with two fresh cups of tea. 'Please, if there is anything we can do to help, let us know.'

'You can start by telling me what happened.' Catherine's gaze suddenly sharpened as she looked between the two other women in the room.

Elena's cup trembled in her hands, a dash of scalding liquid seeping over the rim and singing her fingers. Gritting her teeth against the pain she looked at her mother-in-law. 'Sorry?'

'I need to know *everything*,' Catherine insisted. 'Every single detail.'

'Look, Catherine, I'm not sure—'

'I don't trust the police,' she informed them shrilly. 'They won't do what needs to be done to bring my Stuey's killer to justice. They're stretched too thin. That's why I've hired a private investigator.'

Elena's cup trembled again but this time it slid from her grip, crashing onto the floor, spreading amber tea in a wide arc across the carpet. 'Oh, shit,' she whimpered, moving to kneel upon the floor, hands shaking. 'I . . . I didn't mean to—'

'Let me.' Nellie was crouched beside her, face kind. 'I'll go and get some kitchen towel. Don't worry about it.'

Elena let Nellie help her back onto the sofa, body so weak.

She pictured the investigator in her home, her bedroom, going over all the facts with a fine-toothed comb. Coming up with fresh questions. Ones she couldn't answer.

He'll realise what you did.

An involuntary whimper escaped from her lips.

'You poor thing.' Catherine thrust a fresh tissue towards her. 'You loved him almost as much as I did. Though of course nothing equates to a mother's love.' One hand still attached to the Moses basket. Claiming it. 'But you must be as broken as I am. How could you not be? It was . . . He . . .' She looked at the picture above the fireplace, Elena and Stu atop a mountain. Beaming and proud. 'So I've hired an investigator.' Her voice suddenly dropped, conspiratorial, as within the kitchen they heard the opening and closing of cupboards as Nellie grabbed cleaning tools. 'Because I don't trust it. Any of it. I don't trust *her*.' Her gaze quickly flew to the door that Nellie was about to return through at any moment.

'You . . . you wanted her,' Elena declared tightly. Catherine had been the cash cow that had brought More You into their home.

Stop.

Think.

Elena managed to nod as though piecing things together. 'Sh-she . . . she was the one who found him.'

'Exactly,' Catherine hissed. 'There's something very *off* about it. All of it. So this private detective, Mr Dalton. He'll be coming round soon. With questions. He's assured me he's going to be thorough.'

'I see.'

'I told him I won't rest until there's justice for my boy. My . . . my Stuey.' Catherine whimpered into her tissue just as Olive began to waken. Nellie was bustling back into the room, laden with cleaning wipes and carpet sprays. Already Elena could see that she was too late, the stain seeping down too deep into the fabric.

Olive's cry was like clicking on a button. Elena stood, walked to her daughter, scooped her up, felt her nappy, kissed Olive's forehead, released her breast from her blouse. 'Here, it's okay,' she whispered as she bounced the baby in her arms, gently easing her close so that she could latch. She was so lost to the task she failed to feel Catherine's eyes upon her. It was only when she sat down, baby clamped to her chest, that she noticed the intense stare stalking her every movement. She nervously tugged the collar of her turtleneck higher.

'It's good that you have her,' Catherine declared. 'She will give you purpose.'

'I guess I hadn't . . . thought, really.' Elena looked down at her suckling baby.

You're all that matters now. Nothing else.

'You should come and stay at mine. You will be safer there.' Catherine remarked, still watching them.

'Oh, thank you, but' – Elena's gaze slid to the nearby picture of her and Stu – 'I like being here. Being . . . around him.'

'But are you *safe*?' Catherine pressed, nodding not so discreetly at Nellie, who was upon the floor, scrubbing hard against the beige carpet.

'As safe as we can be.' Elena stroked Olive's soft cheek, so warm. 'The police are monitoring the house.'

'Well, the offer is always there.' Catherine looked hungrily at Olive before reaching for her tea where it perched atop a side table. 'I'd love to have her around more. Be closer to her.'

'Really, we are fine here.'

'And I'll feel better once Mr Dalton swings by. He comes highly recommended.'

'I'm sure he does.'

Elena's pulse was thick behind her ear.

He won't find out what I've done.

He can't.

'I won't stop.' The old woman's eyes shimmered with inner strength, inner pain. 'I'll find his killer, mark my words.'

'Uh-huh.' Elena kept looking at her baby, savouring the warmth, the connection.

'I'd do anything for him.'

Elena swallowed. She understood all too well the lengths a mother would go to for their child. 'I know,' she whispered quietly, eyes on Olive.

I'd do anything for her.

It was late afternoon, at least it seemed to be, going by the shade of the sky, when Elena cracked open her front door and bid Catherine farewell. The old woman eased down the steps accompanied by the distant click and snap of cameras. Across the street Elena spied two news vans; crouched between them were photographers staring through a long lens. Elena withdrew into the shadows of the hallway, Olive sleeping in her arms.

'Vultures,' Catherine sneered.

'They'll lose interest soon enough,' Nellie offered softly as she came to wave goodbye.

'I doubt it.' Catherine's tone darkened. 'This is quite the spectacle for them. The first POP-motivated killing. Though, of course, POP denies any involvement.'

'They do?'

Elena ground her teeth together. She'd failed to check any sort of news, but it made sense for POP to come forward and publicly claim they had no part in Stu's death.

Because they didn't.

She didn't dare look at Nellie for fear that she wore the same panicked expression that she did. Luckily, Catherine didn't pay either of them any attention as she glided down the steps, a tissue pressed to her mouth, posture straight and strong. Elena knew the paparazzi would be a salve for her sorrows. A chance to prance and preen for the public. To be a star. And for that she almost didn't mind their presence, for the old woman deserved some respite from her pain. They all did.

But their long lenses, their relentless clicks. Elena wondered how much they had seen.

'The world is watching,' Nellie whispered tightly as she quickly closed the front door, sealing them inside. 'We must be careful.'

'True.' Elena was still staring in the direction of the street, feeling numb.

'Thankfully they took him away so you didn't have to bury this one in the garden.'

'*What?*' Elena spun around so fast she felt a little dizzy.

'I said I've been scrubbing away at the carpet but I think I'm done.'

'Oh?' Elena blinked slowly.

'Here, let me take her.' Nellie carefully gathered Olive into her own arms. 'You should really have a rest, you're exhausted.'

'I'm . . .' Elena glanced up the stairs, knowing Nellie was right, but knowing she couldn't enter her bedroom. Slowly she wandered towards the lounge, dropping onto the sofa. Before she closed her eyes she saw the pale shape of the large tea stain close by.

'I don't think I'll be able to get it all out,' Nellie explained sorrowfully, walking with Olive over towards the changing mat.

'No . . . no . . . it's fine.' Elena's mouth widened into a yawn. 'It's my fault anyway.'

'Yes,' Nellie agreed sharply from the other side of the room, just as Elena slipped into sleep, 'I know.'

From: Unknown
To: POP@outward.co.uk
Subject: Family in Whitstable

There has been a development with this family and we may have to cease communication for the time being. But, we hope the More You has been forced out of hiding. As always, we act only for the good of humanity. More Yous should never be in the home, with a baby. They are not us. They are not real. They are not true. That family got what was coming to them.

.41

Exactly twenty-four hours after Catherine had learned about her second son's death, she made the call to Mr Dalton. She couldn't stop thinking about what she had learned.

Someone had broken in.

Killed Stuey.

Left.

It didn't make sense.

Catherine kept circling back to all she had heard during the board meetings at More You. How the new units were presented as sleeker, quicker. *Smarter.* Elena would never hurt Stuey, Catherine was fairly certain of that. But Elena was no longer alone with him in that house. There was also Nellie. And women driven to the brink of jealousy can be strange creatures, Catherine knew that from experience. There was a freshness to Nellie, a beauty that Elena could never possess, despite being identical. There was a cruelty to it, Catherine considered, to every day be presented with the best version of yourself, knowing you'd never measure up. It was surely enough to drive even the most sane woman crazy.

Her research into the detective had been subtle, relying on her few contacts at More You.

'It's possible a unit went rogue,' she told them. 'We need someone discreet to look into it.'

The detective was at her house the next morning, smart in a pressed suit, eyes an icy blue.

'So you don't believe your son to have been killed by POP?' he asked her directly.

'No.' Catherine pressed her lips together and folded her hands in her lap as she sat neatly upon the edge of her sofa, eyeing her guest. 'There's a More You unit in his home that I fear may have been involved.'

The detective arched a single eyebrow. 'And what makes you think that? More Yous come with a fail-safe, do they not?' His eyes bored into hers and she knew what he was suggesting, what he was asking.

How much do you know?

She'd explained her situation to him, her connection to the company. But some things couldn't risk being said over the phone.

'This unit is . . . *unique*. More . . . advanced than others.'

Dalton blew out a short breath, brow furrowed. 'I've heard of these newer units. Smarter, they take it all in. The past, the present. Often they end up believing they are the original host.'

Catherine felt her eyes widen.

'And you put one of these *newer* units in your son's home?' His voice was ripe with judgement.

'I wanted to help.' Catherine heard the tremor in her own words. 'I thought . . . I thought the newer unit might be an improvement. Would . . . would help him and his wife.'

'Seems you thought wrong.'

Catherine threw the detective a barbed look. 'That's why you're sitting in my lounge, detective, because I'm aware that things may have . . . escalated. These units can be . . . unstable.'

'In my line of work I see countless models step out of line. The fail-safe doesn't work, but of course the public can never know that.' He glowered at Catherine.

'My connections to the company aside, I'm hiring you to unearth the truth of what happened to my son, that's it.'

'And if the unit is at fault?'

'Then I want it gone,' Catherine declared forcefully, 'decommissioned.'

'It won't like that,' Dalton warned. 'I assume you know what it means to have a unit decommissioned.'

Catherine shifted awkwardly. 'I know enough.'

'Do you?' the detective pressed, a hunger in his eyes. 'Because the rhetoric the company gives about rehabilitation is just bullshit. A line to feed to the public. When units are returned, especially if they are faulty, they are put down. Like dogs.'

This was news to Catherine but she wasn't about to let him know that. Her lips plateaued as she paled.

But someone had killed her Stuey. She'd bet it was his wife. But which version of her? That's why she'd paid a small fortune for Dalton's services. To get answers. Revenge.

Put down.

Like dogs.

It was what they deserved.

She released a shaky breath. All that mattered was Stuey. 'That's why I hired you.' Catherine tightened her grip on her hands, squeezing her fingers tight. 'I was assured that you'd do what needs to be done.'

'I'll find out what happened to your son,' the detective promised, 'and there's no risk of me looking to protect the unit if guilty. Don't worry about that.'

He stood, shook her head, prepared to leave.

'Why do you hate them so?' Catherine asked as she followed him into the hallway.

'I think we're done with the questions.'

'One last thing, detective.'

He turned to her, eyes bright with curiosity.

'I have reason to believe the unit removed its chip.'

He gave a curt nod of his head. 'It's not unheard of.'

'I just thought you should know.'

'Every detail helps,' Dalton told her before stepping out into the afternoon light.

Catherine listened to his car drive away, to the distant click of her heavy gates closing. Then she moved towards her cream phone atop a small console, a bouquet of lilies beside it. She tapped in the number, nails clicking, then waited for her call to be answered.

It didn't take long.

'The unit,' she said, voice firm. 'I need its chip disabled.'

With a roll of her eyes she listened to the excuses on the other end of the line.

'Need I remind you what is at stake here? Disable the chip. I know it can be done remotely.'

A smirk of satisfaction spread across her face as she hung up the phone, feeling like a spider threading its web, closing in on its prey.

.42

The private detective, Dalton, was in Elena's home. It had been roughly two days since Catherine had swept down the front steps, like a raven in her attire. And now here he was, the investigator whose arrival had been promised. Threatened. Elena couldn't decide which. Her temple throbbed and her vision felt blurry. As soon as the doorbell chimed, Nellie had shaken her awake from where she was curled upon the sofa like a cat. Days had passed since she had last showered, changed.

'First, let me say how sorry I am for your loss.'

Dalton wore a crisp white shirt and suit jacket, no tie. He had thick, dark hair and shrewd blue eyes which were studying Elena as she gave a feline stretch and tried to compose herself for her guest, tugging at matted hair and smoothing down her already-creased-beyond-salvation top. Dalton was freshly shaven, which Elena assumed made him seem younger than he actually was. There was probably a time when he would have been considered quite handsome but he had a hardened, jaded appearance which Elena instantly found off-putting. This was not a man like Stu. This was a man who had known cruelty.

'I've spoken at length with Stuart's mother, Catherine. I've also assessed the police reports and followed the investigation online, as I'm sure many people have.'

'Right . . . I'm . . .' Elena was still trying to figure out what time it was, which meal she should be skipping.

Her guilt. Her grief. They were working in tandem to gnaw away at her until there was nothing left.

'Please just let us know what we can do to help.'

Nellie arrived, a tea for their guest in hand, a genial smile on her face.

'Well, thank you.' He accepted the drink curtly. 'Really I need to review the crime scene. And obviously, ask you both questions.'

'Of course.' Nellie smiled again, placing herself on the sofa beside Elena, hands neatly folded in her lap. She both looked and smelled fresh. Hair in a low bun, a cream jumper covering her arms. Elena knew that next to her she must appear hideously bedraggled. A vision of her worst self.

You've lost your husband, what the fuck do they expect?

Still, with Nellie at her side she couldn't shake the uncomfortable feeling that both of her personas were being presented to Dalton. He could simultaneously see her at her worst and her best.

'You found him?' The question was addressed to Nellie, who nodded.

'Yes, Elena was downstairs feeding the baby.'

'Olive,' Elena croaked. 'I was . . . with Olive.'

Where *was* Olive? Elena discreetly peered around the room, heart beginning to tighten in her chest, until she saw the bulge within the Moses basket. Her daughter was sleeping. Hopefully fully fed, cleaned. All thanks to Nellie.

Elena sank deeper into the sofa, feeling the weight of all her lies.

'And can you describe to me what you saw, when you first entered the room?' Dalton prompted, a small recording device now in his hand.

Elena's attention drifted away. She was so very, very tired. Everything ached. Every bone felt too heavy for her body. She turned to look towards the back garden, to the birds flitting from branch to branch in the bushes at the far end. How fast they moved, darting here and there, little flashes of blue and yellow.

Dirt.

Elena could taste it in the back of her mouth. Its earthy, crumbling presence. The way it wetly broke apart, cloying and sour. How it clung to her tongue, wedged between her teeth. She was remembering the morning she found the cat, the moment she—

'Let me get you some water.' Nellie was suddenly furiously patting her back as Elena doubled forward, coughing and heaving.

Fuck.

'Mrs Roberts, are you all right?' Dalton was watching her, face creased with annoyance rather than concern.

'Y-yes,' Elena spluttered. 'I'm just . . .'

A cold glass of water was pressed into her hands and she drank deeply from it.

'She was having a nightmare,' Nellie explained quietly, a protective hand upon Elena's knee. 'With her struggling to sleep this past week she's been dropping off at random moments. She's shouldering such a huge loss.'

There was a shift in Nellie's tone. 'And then you come in here, with your questions. Poking. Prying. She's *grieving.* We both are. But apparently we can't be left in peace to do that.'

Elena blinked but didn't dare turn towards Nellie, let her surprise show. The veneer of politeness had fallen, revealing Nellie's truer nature. And it unnerved her how much she sounded like . . . well . . . her.

'A man is dead, so forgive me for disturbing your *peace*' – Dalton's eyes never left Elena – 'but my job is to uncover the truth, no matter how inconvenient that may be.' With a quick dip of his head he frowned anew. 'What happened to your ankle?'

'My . . . ankle?' Elena swallowed down icy water. Glancing to her foot she saw the smear of red against her sock. Fresh and bright. 'I cut it in the garden the other week. A moment of carelessness.' She tapped her forehead and shrugged.

'Hmm.' Dalton stared at her foot.

'Shall I show you to the bedroom?' Nellie offered quickly, her genial self again.

'Yes, thank you.' He followed her out of the room, but not before turning back to frown at Elena one last time, gaze settling on her wounded ankle, a look of suspicion blooming across his face.

She listened to the wince of floorboards above, imagined the conversation.

Yes, here was where I found him.
The window was smashed open.
Yes, he was already dead.

Would Dalton see through their lies? Would he look upon the debris of the bedroom and make the assessment the police failed to? Would he see the truth? With Stu gone, Elena wasn't sure what remained upon the floor. A stain? A rip in the carpet? She had not felt strong enough to venture into the bedroom. The ground floor of the house had become her world.

What if while Elena wilted against her sofa in exhaustion, Nellie was betraying her, pouring her poisonous truth into the detective's ear?

Now that we're alone, I can tell you what happened. I heard a loud bang and when I ran up here, he was already dead, she was holding a candlestick above him.

It all felt like something out of a grotesque game of Cluedo. Elena leaned forward, bunching herself into a ball, feeling sick.

Nellie wouldn't betray her, would she?

You were prepared to blame her, lay it all at her feet; of course she would do the same. She's you.

'Dammit.' Awkwardly, Elena stood, instantly feeling the fire of pain shoot up her leg. The wound was weeping again, the infection surely worsened by a succession of days of neglect. Hobbling, Elena struggled into the kitchen, rummaging in cupboards for fresh plasters, gauze.

You need to snap out of this.

She'd been in tight spots before, on mountainsides with only the flimsy fabric of a tent to separate her from a freezing death. For hours she'd listen to the moan of the wind, wonder if she'd ever see her home again. Her mum.

'This is what it is to feel truly alive,' Stu would tell her enthusiastically, clutching her gloved hand in his. 'We are *living*, Elena. And it's bloody wonderful.' Stu was always there with his open smile, his confidence, able to pull her out of any hole, no matter how deep.

And now he's gone.

Elena tugged off her soiled sock, blinking back tears, eyes so dry and sore she was surprised they had the capacity to weep at all any more.

So many times the two of them had skirted the gnarled clutches of the reaper. Side by side as they waited out deadly storms, together as they watched a distant avalanche, smoothly claiming a campsite where they had been only hours before. With Stu, she used to feel indestructible.

And it was me.

Every near miss, every almost slip, every lucky moment, Stu always came home unscathed from his exploring. He never feared the mountain, only respected it. The true danger had been beside him every night, in his bed, his arms, in his—

Elena was sobbing, clutching the kitchen island as the sound shook its way out of her.

Stop it.
Stop.
You have to get it together.
For Olive.
You need to be strong for Olive.

Finally, freshly bandaged and face red but dry, Elena returned to the lounge and the door creaked open and Nellie walked in, followed by Dalton. Elena anxiously searched both their faces for signs of anger, betrayal. Judgement.

'I think I've got all I need.' Dalton tapped the pocket of his suit jacket. 'For now.'

'We're happy to help.' Nellie gave him a nervous, eager smile.

'Catherine Roberts is most determined to find whoever killed her son.' He was looking at Elena. 'Normally, in these high-profile cases, the police will do their due diligence and the likes of me, well, we just aren't needed.'

'So why are you here?' Elena asked icily, too tired to feign politeness.

'Because you have a most interesting predicament.' His blue eyes pinned her.

Here we go; she told him.

As a reflex, Elena took a step closer to the Moses basket, to her baby. If only Olive would wake, then she'd have a reason to hold, to hide behind her.

'There are a lot of people who would like POP to be the instigators of this,' Dalton was explaining, hands folded against his chest. 'There's an awful lot of money floating around More You and it's no secret that they resent the presence of organisations like POP.'

'Right . . .' Elena said tightly, resting a hand on the Moses basket.

'However POP has publicly denied any link to your husband's murder. Most fervently, they look to assure people that this is a line they would never cross.'

'I'm not sure—'

'For the police, it would be awfully *convenient* for it to remain a POP-motivated attack. A lot of pockets would be lined if things stayed as they are.'

'Meaning?'

'Meaning, they won't be looking at this as carefully as they should. As carefully as *I* will be.' Dalton glanced back towards Nellie, who had paled behind him. 'Catherine did the right thing in hiring me. There's something afoot here.' He turned to look at Elena, smirking. 'No pun intended.'

Her face began to burn.

'But rest assured, ladies, I'll get to the bottom of this. There's a reason I'm regarded as the best.' He made to leave but Elena scurried across the lounge, ankle throbbing, to join him in the hallway.

'So who do you think killed my husband?' she demanded.

'I'm not sure,' Dalton admitted, glancing along the wall at the framed pictures of Elena and Stu on their wedding day, on a beach. 'No baby pictures?'

'Not yet,' Elena snapped. 'We've not had a chance to put any up.'

'Huh.' Dalton thrust his hands into his trouser pockets, nodded thoughtfully to himself. 'He seemed like a decent guy,' he offered, 'from all that I've heard. Strong too.' He nodded towards a picture of Stu atop K2. 'For someone to get a chance to take down a healthy, strong man like him, they'd have needed the element of surprise.'

'Well, they did come in through the window. That's not exactly expected,' Nellie told him sourly, stealing the words right out of Elena's mouth.

'Hmm.' He looked to the floor, rocked back on his heels. 'Well, ladies, I've taken up enough of your time. I'll be in touch.'

And then he was gone. No doubt caught by the paparazzi who had embedded themselves across the road.

'Are we okay?' Elena asked quietly, staring at the now closed front door.

'Of course.' Nellie leaned in close to hug her shoulders. 'We're together. Everything will be fine.'

From the lounge, Olive began to cry.

'Let me.' Nellie gave Elena a final squeeze. 'You need to be looking after yourself. Go and shower in the main bathroom, put on some clean clothes. You'll feel better, I swear.'

'What did you tell him?' Elena wondered as she peered up the stairs. 'In the bedroom, what did you say?'

'What I was supposed to.' Nellie fondly stroked Elena's greasy hair. 'I told him our truth. We're safe, Elena. You can trust me.'

Olive's crying rose in pitch.

At the foot of the stairs Elena felt numb.

You can trust me.

But *did* she trust herself? Because that had been Stu's mistake, hadn't it? Trusting her.

You had no choice.

You can trust me.

.43

People were shouting. Their voices barked beside Elena's ears as her arms were pulled back.

'That's her! That's the one!'

'Please!' she tried to call out, but her words felt raw. Broken. Blue light pulsed across her face.

'Cuff her and get her in the van.'

There was a slap of metal against her wrists, tight and restricting. Somewhere out of sight a baby was crying, their howl rising above the shouting. The commotion.

Olive.

Elena's guts twisted; she tried to break free of her restraints.

'Please!' she repeated. 'My baby. Don't take me from my baby.'

Blue in her eyes. Breaking up the dullness of the night.

Something pulled at her wrists, forcing her to stand to attention, the metal of the handcuffs digging into her skin. Leaving a mark.

'You did this.' A growl in her ear, breath hot. 'You killed him.'

With a gasp Elena awoke, pulse pounding in her ears. As her eyes adjusted to the dim light of the lounge she noticed Nellie looking down at her, frowning.

'Are you okay?'

Elena drew in a long breath, massaged her wrists, which still ached from her nightmare. 'I'm . . . I'm fine.'

'I didn't mean to wake you, but we have guests.'

Elena's stomach lurched.

Not the detective.

Bile crept up her throat.

But as Elena stood, raised up her arms and unknotted her spine, it was two women who entered the room. She instantly felt lighter.

Margot and Leanne both ran to her, wrapping her in their arms, holding her close as she wept.

'Oh, my sweet, it's okay, it's okay,' Leanne whispered over and over.

When Elena was finally able to catch her breath, she settled herself on the sofa, dragged her fingertips across her cheeks, gathering up the last of her tears.

'You didn't have to come,' she declared hoarsely to them, voice as broken as her spirit.

'Of course we did,' Leanne enthused, leaning forward and tucking a strand of hair behind Elena's ear. 'We would have come sooner, but—'

'But we wait,' Margot interrupted, 'we wait until we know it's okay.'

Both women glanced to the door through which Nellie was emerging with a tray, upon which rested several cups of tea.

'She called you?' Elena wondered, eyes sore.

'She did.' Leanne gave a gentle nod. 'She thought it might do you some good to see some friendly faces.'

'We have been so, so worried,' Margot declared as she nodded in gratitude at Nellie and claimed a mug for herself, her long nails tapping against the china.

'Beside ourselves with worry,' Leanne quickly expanded. 'When we heard what had happened, well . . . we couldn't believe it.'

Elena's smile dropped. She struggled to believe it herself. One moment Stu was there in her home, living, breathing.

Loving. And now he was just . . . gone. She could search every inch of the entire world and never find him, never see him again, never watch his eyes crinkle when he laughed, never taste his kiss. Never hold him. A spasm of grief rocked through her.

'Oh, you poor thing.' Leanne was embracing her, clutching her tight as she shook. 'I can't even begin to imagine how awful this all is. But we are here.'

Margot was perched upon the far end of the sofa, studying the door that led through to the kitchen, detached.

'If there's anything, anything at all I can do. That you need, you just say.' Leanne's kind face was staring at her, open and hopeful.

'Is she with Olive now?' Margot asked curtly.

Elena gave herself a shake, raked hands through her matted hair. 'Er . . . Nellie? Yeah, she is.'

'She found him?' Margot turned to look at her, eyes narrowed.

'Y-yeah. She . . . I was feeding Olive and she heard a bang upstairs and went to check on Stu.'

'So you did not find him? She did?' Margot pointed a long finger at her friend.

'Yes, it was Nellie.'

'There's no need to go over any of that,' Leanne tutted. 'We came here to be with you, to look after you.'

'He was hit with candlestick?'

'Margot!' Leanne said with a menacing flare of her nostrils. 'Enough!'

Elena squirmed on the sofa. Margot had clearly done her research. She expected they both had; how could they not? Stu's death had dominated the news cycle. Had they messaged each other theories? Doubts? Had they pored over the details and spotted holes in her story? Was that really why they were in her home? To expose her as a liar? As a killer?

'You think she did it?' Margot crept along the sofa, keeping a keen eye on the doorway, voice low. 'She found him. She could have done it.'

'Margot! Stop it!'

'She's not like you,' Margot implored, looking at Elena, pressing a hand to her chest. 'Like *us*.'

'Of course she is,' Leanne scolded, reaching for a tea. 'She's like Elena. Which means she's *good*.'

'No.' Margot wore a look of disgust as she shook her head. The pleather leggings she wore squeaked as she edged even closer to Elena, keen to make her point. 'You do not *make* people' – she clicked her fingers – 'it is not as easy as that. She' – her eyes flicked to the ceiling – 'she not you. Not *really*. Is there a chance she hurt Stu?'

No.

Because I did. It's me. She's protecting me.

Elena met her friend's severe gaze. 'I mean . . . I guess . . .'

'Really' – Leanne patted Elena's knee – 'there's no need for this talk. We can focus on—'

'He said there had been a moment between them. A few days before it happened . . .'

'A moment?' Margot's eyes were wide with interest.

'Stu . . . he . . .' Elena swallowed, she felt bone dry, like paper. Like every part of her was about to rip apart. 'He was in the kitchen and he . . .'

He thought she was me.

'He said she came onto him.'

A shocked intake of breath from both of her friends.

'There,' Margot was jabbing the air. 'There you go. I have heard of this, when the . . . the *other* you goes too far in the assimilation process. Thinks they are the main one.'

'But that's just a myth, right?' Elena fretted. She had heard the rumours along with everyone else; the trashier end of the tabloids loved to speculate about More Yous who went too far. Though nothing had ever been confirmed. Even Stu had told her as much when she presented him with stories of rogue units online.

'Just made-up crap,' he'd said dismissively. But then he'd attacked her when he'd thought she was Nellie. He'd tried to kill her.

'I think it can happen.' Leanne nodded, mouth forming a tight line. 'I think that's why the whole "rehabilitation" situation is in place. But they don't *hurt* people, least not that I know of. They just . . . try to take over someone's life. At least early models did.'

'But it's just speculation, right?' Elena looked anxiously between her friends.

'I mean, maybe.' Leanne gave a nervous smile. 'There have been videos online, blogs, people talking about it all. Why don't you check with Stu's mum?'

Elena was already shaking her head. 'No. She . . . I don't trust anything she says.'

'Mmm.' Leanne made a sound of agreement.

'This.' Margot was jabbing the air with her finger. 'This is happening *here*. Now. She must go.'

'I don't—'

'Hold fire, Margot,' Leanne said sternly. 'We don't know anything yet. If the unit was involved, the police will get to the bottom of it.'

'Catherine, Stu's mum, has hired a private investigator.'

Another intake of breath from her friends.

'Seriously?' Leanne frowned.

'See!' Margot was almost jubilant. 'Something wrong. Something off. Investigator . . . good. They will find truth.'

'I want them to find who did it but . . . it's not Nellie.' Elena held her head in her hands.

'You sure?' Margot prompted.

'*You* would never do anything awful' – Leanne glanced between the friends – 'but she isn't *you*, Elena. Don't lose sight of that.'

'Do you think maybe she hurt him?' Margot pressed.

Above them, a floorboard creaked and they all froze, heads quickly tipped towards the ceiling.

'What about the fail-safe?' Leanne wondered aloud. 'The do-no-harm imperative?'

'Yes, but she's a . . . newer model,' Elena admitted.

Leanne faltered for a moment and recovered. 'New or not she will still have the fail-safe, along with the location chip. She has to.'

'Even if she does' – Margot's expression turned dark – 'people are people. We hurt. We pain. We hurt each other. It part of what makes us . . . human. There no off switch for that.'

Elena rubbed a shaking hand across her eyes. No matter how much she slept she remained exhausted. What she wouldn't give for Stu to walk into the room and just make the world right again. Without him, everything felt more than wrong . . . it felt broken. Twisted.

'Have you been tracking her?' Leanne asked, scanning the room for Elena's phone. 'Make sure you keep doing it, give you some peace of mind.'

Elena plucked her phone from where it was wedged between the sofa cushions beside her. An endless stream of notifications was waiting for her but she ignored them all to open up the More You app. She tapped 'locate' and a spinning wheel appeared on the screen. 'Fucking thing,' Elena muttered.

'Well we know she here already,' Margot remarked, unimpressed. 'Don't need app for that.'

'She's here for now,' Leanne countered. 'I'd keep an eye on that, if I were you. Maybe the app just needs updating. Good job she has that chip in her ankle, so you can track her.'

'Yeah . . .' Elena agreed, feeling uneasy. 'Good job.'

Another creak above them. Then the sound of footsteps coming down the stairs. The door opened and Nellie walked in, cradling Olive in her arms and looking every inch the proud mother; glowing and radiant. Margot and Leanne instantly rose to their feet and went over to see the baby, making all the right oohing and ahhing sounds. From the sofa Elena watched, a tightness gathering in her chest.

This was her life.

Her baby.

Her grief.

How easily Nellie could resume normal life, could pretend that everything was fine. Because she hadn't known Stu. Hadn't loved him. Hadn't lost him.

Look how cold she is, how unfeeling over his death.

Did the rest of the world think like Margot, lay suspicion at her More You's feet?

Just let them see what they want to see.

Olive's eyes were open and she was looking at the different women, gummy mouth hanging open.

Nellie's protecting you. Keeping your secret.

Elena got up, walked across the room. 'Here, baby, Mummy's here.' She took Olive in her arms, the baby instantly fidgeting. Unsettled. 'Here, it's okay.' Elena pressed a kiss upon her daughter's tiny forehead even as she began to bleat and cry.

This is my world. My child.

'Here, let me help settle her,' Nellie offered.

'No.' Elena recoiled from her, stalked back to the sofa. 'She's my baby, Nellie. I've got it.'

She felt her friends watching her, understanding.

All I have to do is paint her as a killer, as wanting to take my life. People will do the rest themselves. I need only to provide the rope, let everyone else make the noose.

What else was Elena supposed to do? Let her nightmare become real and be taken away herself?

Olive needs me.

Nellie wants to help.

To help me.

'Are you sure you're all right?' Nellie wondered from across the room.

'Fine,' Elena snapped in response, Olive shrieking in her grip. 'I'm fine.'

.44

She dreamed of it. Of Stu's final moments. His blood warm on her hands. Slick. The thump of his body as it crumpled to the floor. Elena awoke, heart beating frantically in her chest, face glistening with sweat.

'Fuck.' She sagged against the pillows on the sofa, weary even before the day had begun. 'Fuck,' she repeated, awkwardly moving to sit up, cradling her head in her hands.

He's gone and it's all my fault.

Olive will grow up without a father. Because of me. Because I'm a fucking monster.

A solitary tear beat a path down her cheek. As Elena swiped it away she noticed the figure a few feet from her. Stationary. Staring.

'Christ.' With a start, she tugged her legs up beneath her, making herself as small as possible. 'How long have you been standing there?' she tersely demanded of Nellie, who wore a passive expression.

'You have a guest,' Nellie informed her simply.

'Have you been watching me *sleep*? I've told you *not* to do that.' Elena fired the accusation hotly, imagining Nellie standing there, hour upon hour, observing. Studying. Elena glanced at the Moses basket. 'Where is Olive?' she almost shrieked.

'Sleeping.' Nellie frowned at her as though it were an absurd question. 'She wouldn't settle down here so I've taken her to the cot upstairs.'

'No.' Elena got to her feet.

'I've been watching her on the monitor.' To prove her point, Nellie slid the device out from the pocket of her cream turtleneck.

'She shouldn't be in there.' Elena pushed past her, hurrying towards the hallway, then the staircase. She darted past Dalton, who was standing beside the door, hands in his pockets. Elena took the stairs two at a time.

She can't be in there.

Thinking only of her baby, she rushed into her bedroom and froze. Everything was as it had been. The bed, still neatly made. Her perfumes a rainbow of glass atop her dressing table. But the reminders of all that had changed were suddenly obvious: the wood against the broken window making the room darker than it usually was; the stain upon the floor. A whimper escaped Elena as she turned back towards the landing, hand clamped over her mouth.

I can't do this.

With a grunt of effort she stepped into the room again, eyes streaming.

Olive can't be in here. She can't be where he died. She can't.

The cot was on the side of the bed closest to the door and furthest from where Stu had fallen. It took a single step for Elena to be beside it, stooping down and plucking out the soft warmth of her daughter. Olive stirred as she was lifted by her mother and pressed against her chest. Breathless, Elena dashed onto the landing, stretching back to firmly slam the bedroom door behind her. With a gasp she leaned against the wall, waiting for her heart rate to slow.

Why would Nellie put Olive in there?

Was this a test? A test for me? Is she pushing me? Trying to make me crack?

A cough from the hallway. Dalton confirming his presence.

This fucking private eye.

Gathering herself, Elena held Olive and squared her shoulders.

'Everything all right?' Dalton asked as she descended the stairs towards him.

'Everything is fine.'

'Everything doesn't seem fine.' Dalton's blue eyes flicked over her. 'You ran up those stairs like you thought the house was on fire.'

'What do you want me to say?' Elena suddenly demanded of him, too tired and wrung out to entertain his questions. 'Of course everything isn't *all right*. My husband was fucking murdered. Here, in this house. And I'm doing my best to carry on, truly I am, but forgive me if I'm actually just falling apart. You try caring for a newborn in the wake of all—'

'Elena, let me.' Nellie appeared, hands extended. 'I'll go settle her in the lounge. There's fresh cups of tea in the kitchen, and some toast. You can go and talk to the detective in there.'

Elena wanted to object, to remind Nellie that Olive was *hers* and hers alone. But she felt Dalton watching, taking everything in, so she smiled falsely in agreement and handed over her daughter. 'Thanks.'

'Make sure you eat,' Nellie remarked as she drew Olive to her bosom and then left the hallway.

'Little early for lunch.' Dalton raised an eyebrow at Elena.

'It's breakfast,' she deadpanned, moving towards the kitchen and assuming he would follow.

'It's half eleven in the morning.'

'Hence it being too early for lunch.' Elena glowered at him when she reached the island and turned back. The detective raised his hands in deference.

'Sorry, sorry. I'm sensing some sensitivity today.'

'Wow, I can see why Catherine hired you.' Elena bit into her toast loudly, savouring the crunch. After a few seconds chewing it went the way all food did lately – becoming claggy and thick in her throat. Impossible to swallow. But she knew she had to force it down, consume something else she risked wasting away. With great effort she committed the churned-up toast to her stomach, washing it down with warm, sweet tea.

'I had a few follow-up questions.' Dalton removed his recording device from his pocket, placed it atop the island between them. It glowed green.

'Clearly.'

'I wanted to ask about your More You.'

Elena's eyebrows lifted in surprise. 'About Nellie?'

'You named it?'

'Doesn't everyone?'

'When did you first acquire the unit?'

'Umm . . .' Elena fought to find her timeline. Everything had ceased to make sense in the aftermath of losing Stu. It was like a grenade had been thrown into her life, destroying everything, including clocks and calendars. 'Five . . . maybe six weeks ago.'

'Wow. Okay.'

'What?'

'It's a reasonably new unit then.'

'Yes,' Elena agreed tightly.

'For such a new unit it's very . . . together.'

'She's a fast learner.'

'Evidently.' Dalton sipped his tea, looked at her over the rim of his mug. 'Could you describe a regular day to me? One involving yourself, the unit, your husband and daughter. I'm assuming it was acquired to help with childcare.'

'Yes.' Elena squirmed, hating the sensation that she was being judged. Who the fuck was Dalton anyway? What were his credentials? Elena was too tired, too out of it to do any kind of research. Was she really just going to trust Catherine's judgement on him? 'She helped with basic childcare. Changing nappies, night feeds, that sort of thing.'

'And you were around the unit for much of this time?'

'Yes.' Elena was losing patience.

'Sounds like it's had plenty of time to watch you, to assimilate.'

'So?'

'I'm sure you're aware of what can happen, when a unit believes itself to be the original.'

'I'm aware.' Elena glowered at him. 'But I'm not about to leave her alone with my child. The whole point of her is to help with my baby, I clearly need to be around too.' Elena's nostrils flared. 'I'm not just going to give my daughter over solely to some stranger.'

'But it's not a stranger, is it?' Dalton countered. 'It's *you*.'

'Look, Mr Dalton, I'm not really sure what you're doing here or why—'

'Do you know why she hired me? Catherine?' he interrupted, eyeing her coolly.

'Let me guess: because you're the best.' Elena snorted with a roll of her eyes. 'I don't need the sales spiel.'

The detective carried on, undeterred. 'She hired me because I specialise in More You crimes. They happen much more than you think. And of course the government doesn't want any of it to get out, too many people lined up to lose a lot of money.'

'What are you saying?'

'I'm saying' – he stepped closer to her and she could smell traces of lavender upon his clothes – 'while the police might be satisfied to pin this on POP, I'm not. It was your More You that found your husband.' He dropped his voice low. 'Can you be truly certain it wasn't your More You that killed him?'

For a moment Elena couldn't breathe. She felt like she was back with her friends, facing the same question.

You know she didn't do it.

'I . . .'

'If you don't feel safe in your own home' – he reached for her wrist – 'speak up. I'm here to help.'

Elena snatched back her hand, flustered.

He thinks it was Nellie.

'N-no, she found him and . . .'

Nellie knows the truth. Could expose everything.

'I know it's hard to accept' – Dalton gave her a pitying look – 'because you think it is *you*. But it is not. A carbon copy, yes. But beyond that, very much a person. With thoughts. Motivations. Capabilities.'

'You said this has happened before?' Elena stared into his eyes, questioning. 'That there have been other crimes committed by More You clones?'

'Many.' He gave a grim nod. 'There's a reason the decommissioning service is so . . . severe.'

'I don't—'

'Units don't get sent back to More You to take up some admin job.'

'Then what happens to them?' Elena's voice grew small.

'What do you think?' the detective held her in a steely gaze as Elena's mouth grew dry.

'You're not suggesting—' Her words caught in her throat.

'Look' – Dalton gave her a look of frustration – 'the newer the model, the higher the chance of it going too far in the assimilation process. It happens. Though of course More You never mention that in their fucking brochures. Which I guess is good for me else I'd be out of work.'

Elena stared at him, taking in his words.

'Being so close . . . sometimes memories can get interlinked. Confused. Lost.' He continued.

The cat.

The soil.

Elena closed her eyes.

'If nothing else, you must keep the baby safe, at least until we know for certain it wasn't your More You.'

'My baby *is* safe.'

Dalton looked at her. Elena hung her head, picturing Nellie in the other room cooing over Olive, holding her close. Feeding her. 'I told him I didn't want this,' Elena whispered, growing tearful. 'I told him it was a bad idea. But it was... her, Catherine. She *insisted*. Made it impossible to say no. She... she's connected to the company and...' With a sigh, her words fell away.

'We all make mistakes,' Dalton stated gravely. 'It looks like Catherine is trying to fix hers. Take the baby to her. Keep her safe.'

'Olive... Olive stays with *me*.'

'Then go too,' Dalton suggested. 'Go do your job, be a mother. And let me do mine.'

Elena bit her lip and looked towards the door to the lounge. 'Do memories really get interlinked?'

'Sometimes.' Dalton nodded. 'Especially in such close proximity. And in these newer models. What you need now is distance.'

Maybe it was never me after all. Maybe it was Nellie. Maybe she's not covering for me at all. It was her hands upon the candlestick, her skin stained with blood.

'If she did it, how will you prove it?'

'How does anyone prove anything?' Dalton asked, smirking. 'With cold, hard evidence. If it's there, I'll find it. This is what I do, Mrs Roberts.'

'Okay, great... well...'

The dream. Stu dropping to the floor at her feet.

Only what if it had never been her?

'Do what you have to do. Just find out who did this.'

The detective gave her a curt nod. 'I intend to.'

.45

Elena rarely went to Catherine's house. It was a place so like its owner: austere, stiff, unwelcoming. Over the years she would reel off various excuses to Stu whenever he suggested going.

I'm unwell.
I need to work.
Felix doesn't like me.

Felix was Catherine's ragdoll cat and, in truth, he liked everyone. He'd rub against Elena's leg with his rocket-ship purr the moment she set foot inside. But the moment she became pregnant, he was collateral damage in her desire to avoid Catherine.

I need to avoid all cats while I'm pregnant, Stu. It's best to be safe.

And Stu, of course, agreed. While he loved his mother and was a dutiful son, he adored his wife and the prospect of fatherhood growing within her.

Visiting Catherine had been a snap decision Elena had made that morning while feeding Olive as she watched Nellie butter toast. Nellie moved so effortlessly around the kitchen, seemingly unburdened by grief, fatigue. Elena felt anger twisting inside her, along with something sharper, colder. Along with fear.

'I just need a change of scenery,' she explained as she struggled to hoist the baby seat into the back of her car. Already she could feel eyes upon her, the neighbours, the press. 'I won't be there long.'

'I could come.' Nellie dashed down the front steps, carrying the changing bag, pretty face blanched with worry. 'I could be with you and—'

'I need you here,' Elena told her sternly. Baby seat clicked into place she turned, swept a hand across her brow. 'Dalton, or the police, could return at any moment with additional questions, with things they need to see at the house.'

'I suppose.' Nellie passed her the changing bag, which Elena accepted with a flat smile. 'But we don't like her.'

'Hmm?' Elena pretended to have misheard as she bundled the bag into the car.

'We don't like Catherine.' Nellie was almost upon her when she straightened, right upon the edge of the kerb.

'Oh . . . we . . .' Elena exhaled, glanced beyond her More You, down the street, certain she saw the telltale twitch of curtains in distant windows. 'She's Olive's *grandmother*. She's . . .' It was a battle to get the word out when every fibre of her wanted to spit and curse upon the ground before she said it. 'She's *family*.'

'I see.' Nellie eyed her coldly. Then, suddenly, her face brightened. 'I can get some cleaning done in the meantime. And I'll have dinner ready for you when you get back.'

'Th-thank you,' Elena replied, dubious at the whiplash change of tone.

'Have a great time.' Nellie leaned forward and kissed her cheek, lips damp and cold.

'Thanks.' Elena was grateful to climb into the car, hear the soft whisper of the electric engine. As she pulled away from her house Nellie remained in her rear-view mirror, waving enthusiastically. Smiling until she was out of sight.

Elena didn't *want* to visit Catherine. But where else could she go? While Margot and Leanne would welcome her with open arms, she knew she would be intruding upon their lives. They had children, husbands. Catherine was... alone. The only thing Elena would be intruding upon were the old woman's sensibilities. With each passing minute, each turn in the road, each crossing of a roundabout, her sense of dread rose. The previous night, as she'd curled upon the sofa and stared dead-eyed into the darkness, she'd thought about all Dalton had said. She'd listened for every creak and wince within her home, wondering where Nellie was, what she was doing.

The most important thing was for Olive to be safe. And while Catherine obviously had her numerous flaws, she did care for her granddaughter – especially now Olive was her sole remaining connection to Stu.

Elena blinked back tears as she bounced onto an A road. Behind her, Olive slept, pink face peaceful.

The first time Elena had visited Catherine's house had been towards the end of her second year of uni. Stu had taken her there for a family barbecue. Elena hadn't been entirely sure what to expect. She and Stu were from different worlds, that much was already evident. To her, a family barbecue consisted of burnt sausages, dry rolls and soggy salad. Plastic chairs people would fight over on her mother's scrap of lawn, navigating around the pole of the washing line. As soon as Stu had pulled into the driveway of his family home, she had known that things were going to be vastly different.

Elena braked at a pair of black iron gates, waiting for the circular camera wedged into the wall beside it to notice her. Recognise her. The minutes dragged by. Through the gate she could see the paved driveway leading up to the black-and-white house. A modern building, designed to appear much older and more interesting than it actually was.

'I always wanted to feel like the lady of the manor,' Catherine had boasted when she gave Elena that first tour of the house, pointing out random ceiling beams and mentioning how they'd been shipped in from somewhere hot and far-flung.

In the baby seat, Olive puckered her little mouth, eyes scrunching and preparing to open, the rumble of the engine no longer comforting her.

'Come on, you old cow,' Elena said through gritted teeth as she continued to smile up at the camera. Finally, with a loud wince, the gates began to part. 'Thank Christ.'

Elena eased the car forward, following the sweep of the paving. She parked in front of the triple garage in the space Stu had always occupied, back in the days he'd driven a sports car. Elena used to get nauseous every time she sat in the passenger seat; he'd raced along the country lanes like he thought he was at Silverstone.

'Oh, what a surprise this is!'

Elena had barely left the car when the front doors were thrust open and Catherine strutted out, a long chiffon blouse blowing out behind her.

'I'm sorry to intrude like this.' Elena was fumbling with the baby seat, face growing red. She hated how she sounded, how desperate, how reaching. She imagined the welcome she would have received from her own mother. The open arms. The warm embrace. Any day, any hour, home had always been home.

'Oh, come now.' She didn't realise she was crying until Catherine pressed a tissue against her cheeks. 'Let us not be common and cry on the driveway. In. In!'

Elena looped the baby seat over one arm, hoisted the changing bag onto another, while Catherine watched. She was so overburdened she had to kick her car door shut as she followed her mother-in-law up towards the grand home that had been built to the old woman's exacting specifications.

It *was* a beautiful home. With a vaulted hallway and a sweeping staircase. Seven bedrooms. Panelled walls, dark wood, beams shipped in from Norway. It managed to be both grand and beautiful. But so often it felt like Catherine was living in a museum. Everything had its place. Right down to the coasters and candles.

'I was not expecting company.' Catherine threw the remark over her shoulder as she led her visitors into the main lounge. Felix strutted out to greet her, pressing his soft body up against her legs. Elena was grateful to reach one of the floral upholstered sofas and drop the changing bag, letting it slump to the floor. Sweat gathered along her back.

'Like I said, I'm sorry, I was just—'

'How is my princess?' Catherine cut her off as she knelt down before the baby seat, faux lashes fluttering as she looked at Olive. 'Beautiful, beautiful girl.' She stroked a cherubic cheek with a long nail. 'I'm glad you're here.' She straightened just before Olive could begin to cry.

'You are?' Elena felt a wave of relief. Stu had always wanted them to go over and stay. The seven bedrooms crying out for the return of the beloved son. And before, Elena loathed the idea. Sleeping within Catherine's starched sheets, beneath her roof. Following her rules. But she needed a bolthole. Somewhere safe.

Somewhere away from Nellie.

'Dalton told me everything.' Catherine pursed her lips and gave her daughter-in-law a knowing look. 'Best you be here, my child. Best you keep precious Olive where she can be happy.'

'She was happy at home,' Elena objected.

Catherine waved the comment away with a sweep of her manicured hand. 'Tea?'

'Yes, please.'

'You know where the kitchen is.' Catherine smiled sweetly at her. 'While you do us a fresh pot I'll get in some Nanny cuddles.'

'Sure.' Elena had no fight within her, still very much in the flee part of her day. Feet squeaking against the polished floor, she wandered to the grand kitchen that overlooked the large garden.

What am I doing?

The kettle hissed and bubbled.

Nellie wouldn't truly hurt anyone. Would she? Could she? And now Catherine can get her claws into Olive.

'Fuck.' She wilted against the countertop, noticing a framed picture of Stu on a nearby windowsill, beside a bouquet of fresh lilies. 'I need you,' she told the man in the picture, who was tanned and smiling. She guessed it was taken around the time they first met. 'I need you,' she repeated, voice weak.

And he's gone. It's just you. You need to be strong for Olive.

Elena rubbed her wet cheeks, pulled in a long, shaky breath.

You can do this.

Carefully, she carried a tray bearing two cups and saucers and a teapot into the lounge, aware of how this was the very thing she'd been making Nellie do at her house.

Because it's not just you, is it?

'Here you go, Catherine. Did you want—'

The tray trembled in her hands.

Above the fireplace in the middle of the far wall was a television. Catherine was staring fixedly at it, Olive in her arms, forgotten.

The tray trembled again, porcelain chattering.

'What is this?' Catherine demanded haughtily. 'Did you speak with the reporters before coming here? Because in the corner, it says it's live, but it can't be.'

Elena couldn't speak. She stared at the television. There she was, standing atop the stone steps of her home. Face sombre.

'Thank you for all the kind words and support you've shown since I lost my husband.' The woman on the television blinked tearfully towards the cameras. 'I'm determined to be strong for my daughter, and to find who took him from us.'

The information running in a band along the base of the screen revealed *Elena Roberts addresses press outside her home*.

'But you're *here*,' Catherine insisted shrilly. 'It is most misleading to present old footage as live. I really don't—'

The tray crashed to the floor. Loudly. Tea spilling and spouting, plates cracking. Elena barely noticed.

'It's her,' she cried, one shaky finger pointing up at the television. 'It's *her.* It's Nellie. She's doing this.'

Olive began to cry.

Elena stood amid the broken crockery, the tea staining the floor, eyes never leaving Nellie's. She watched her give a solemn nod to the cameras and then disappear inside. Into Elena's home. Elena opened her mouth and started to scream.

.46

Catherine was doing her best to stay calm. To be in the moment. She reminded herself that Elena had *chosen* to come to her. Olive in tow. Yes, Dalton might have been prepped to nudge her in that direction, but still, Elena was there because she wanted to be.

As much as she wanted to enjoy her granddaughter in her home, Catherine felt shredded internally, her grief over Stuey still a gaping wound within her. A part of her knew that even if she discovered who had killed him, it wouldn't bring him back.

Would it?

She thought back on the fraught call she'd had with her contact at More You the previous afternoon. The way she had threatened to retire from the board (though she had long suspected this would be ideal for the company). Her husband had been so *sure* that it was the right thing, this new technology. Clones. That it would be a gold mine for them. And it had been.

But at what price?

With Stuey gone, what did Catherine care about money? She already had more than enough of it. What she cared about was her son. Her family.

She told her contact this repeatedly during the call.

'And what if it turns out this new unit *did* kill my Stuey?' she demanded. Silence on the other end. Catherine trotted the length of her vast hallway, phone in hand, Felix shadowing her, weaving through her legs. 'What then?' Catherine snapped.

Because that would change everything. How could it not? She had been open to allowing the newer unit into her Stuey's life, eager, even. She'd thought she was helping. Making things better.

A strangled sob left her as she suddenly ceased pacing.

'I'm going to find out what happened to him,' she told her contact threateningly.

'We can make this right,' he suddenly assured her. 'Trust us, Catherine. We are looking into this.'

'As am I,' Catherine thundered. When she'd met Dalton she sensed he was a man on a mission, determined to prove that More Yous were not safe, should not be in the domestic space. Or any space at all. His hatred for the clones radiated off him. She sensed he had experienced a loss that had changed him but knew better than to pry. She wanted his mind and his fury sharp, like a blade. Not blunted by grief. Men like him could be dangerous, but not when bent to your will. Catherine knew that if she exposed Nellie as Stuey's killer, she risked burning everything down. More You. Her place on the board. The money that kept rolling in. But what did she care? Losing her second son had fuelled her with a kamikaze fire. She'd burn the whole world down if she had to.

Olive.

The one thing that stilled her manic heartbeat. The tiny baby who would one day grow to become a girl, a woman. Who was part Stuey. A part of Catherine. When she thought of her granddaughter, Catherine's fury abated. Slightly.

'You need to make this right,' Catherine told her caller.

'Trust me, we will.'

When the spilled tea stretched across Catherine's carpet she wanted to be calm, composed. But again she was losing herself to anger, too many emotions burrowing far too close to the surface to be contained.

'Try to be nicer,' Stuey was always imploring her. 'Please, Mum.'

But nice was a language Catherine had never learned. Her own mother forever cold and distant.

'I try,' she'd told her son. 'I do.'

Yet it always proved too difficult. Whenever she looked at Elena she saw all that she had lost: the little boy who used to gaze at her adoringly now withholding those looks solely for his wife. A wife who lacked all that Catherine had fought to have.

No money.

No name.

A nobody.

And yet her son loved her.

Catherine had spent a lifetime searching for such love. How many times had it felt like Eric was looking through her? And even her beloved boys . . . Clive, taken. And now Stuey, taken too.

How much was one woman supposed to endure?

Catherine did not have the time to be *nice*. Nice was one of the few luxuries she didn't have.

.47

'Oh, gracious, my carpet! That was imported from Peru! How can you be so careless when . . .'

Elena could hear Catherine's laments but they seemed far away. Her pulse throbbed within her ears as she drew in harried breaths. Nellie was gone from the television screen, another story taking centre stage, but the image remained imprinted upon Elena's mind.

Nellie on her steps.

Nellie at her front door.

Nellie *being* her.

What the fuck was she thinking?

'. . . and tea is a stain that never comes out. Now the baby is crying and . . . Elena. Elena!'

Hands upon her shoulders, shaking her.

'Elena, the baby.'

Elena blinked, cast her gaze down to the debris around her. 'Catherine, I'm—'

'See to the baby,' Catherine chided her. 'I can't stand another second of someone screaming in my house.'

Elena, in a daze, moved over to Olive. She scooped her out of the car seat and held her to her chest.

'Hey, now, it's okay.'

Elena padded out of the lounge, away from Catherine's tuts and aggrieved stares, gently rocking the baby in her arms. 'Are you hungry? Okay, shh.' She found an armchair tucked away in what had once been a study and now served as a shrine to Catherine's late husband. It was all tartan and dark wood, yet another picture of Stu upon a large desk. This time in his cap and gown. Beaming.

Elena fumbled to prepare herself for feeding while Olive squirmed, impatient. Finally her breast was free and she pushed the baby against it. 'There you go.' But Olive continued to twist away from her, little face flushed with indignation. 'Hey . . . come on.' Elena was too fraught for a fresh challenge. 'Just . . . just eat. *Please.*' She bowed her head as little fists pummelled her cleavage.

She thought of Nellie at her door.

Olive doesn't want you.

Elena gave a slight whimper, then closed her eyes, forced herself to be strong.

She wants Nellie.

She tried to picture Stu at her side, the kind words he might offer, the glow of adoration she'd find in his blue eyes. She was so lost to the memory of him, to the ache in the pit of her soul that longed for him, that she didn't notice when Olive eventually latched and began to feed, the room falling into a blissful state of tranquillity.

It didn't last long.

Catherine stormed in less than ten minutes later, thrusting Elena's phone towards her.

'This just keeps ringing,' she exclaimed, dropping it onto Elena's lap, barely registering the baby feeding. 'I've already got a headache as it is.' Theatrically pressing a hand to her temple, Catherine swept out of the room again. As if on cue, Elena's phone pulsed to life with an incoming call. The screen glowed with the number of the More You office.

Shit.

Elena sucked in a long breath, adjusted herself in the chair, made sure Olive was settled. Then she answered.

'Hello?'

'Mrs Roberts?'

'Yes.'

'This is Hannah Carlson from More You. I've been trying to reach you.' The voice on the other end of the line was overly bright.

'Sorry, I didn't have my phone to hand.'

'I'm the customer liaison for your area and I really wanted to speak with you considering all that has happened.' Still that forced brightness in her tone.

'Look, I'm not—'

'It's important that all our customers are completely satisfied with their More You.'

Elena chewed her lip and studied Stu's picture atop the desk. She couldn't deny that it was strange to have this woman call now, after what Nellie had just pulled. Did they know? Could they track when a More You was stretching things too far? When they crossed a line?

'I wouldn't say I'm satisfied, no,' Elena declared, the sting of betrayal on her tongue.

Nellie has been protecting you.

The image from the news was fixed firmly in her mind.

'I'm so sorry to hear that.' Hannah Carlson didn't sound sorry. 'Let me come over right away, I'm in your area and—'

'I'm not home.'

'Not a problem,' Hannah declared. 'Just let me know where you are and I'll head straight there.'

Olive was sleeping in her baby seat when a silver Mini pulled into the driveway behind Elena's car. Catherine was beside her at the window, studying the new guest.

'I figured they'd send someone,' the old woman commented darkly. 'She can't come into the lounge.' Catherine wrinkled her nose. 'No one can until I've had the carpets professionally cleaned.'

'Sure.' The lounge was where Olive was asleep, curtains drawn, so the room was off limits anyway.

'She's coming to try to clean up her mess,' Catherine remarked as they watched a small, plump blonde woman climb out of the car, neat in a trouser suit almost the same shade as her car.

'You mean what Nellie did?' Elena studied her mother-in-law out of the corner of her eye.

'She said she was you.' Catherine continued to stare out of the window. 'I can't see how that isn't an issue. Can you?' The question hung in the air between them.

'Is there something strange about Nellie?' Elena stared into Catherine's eyes. 'Something . . . unusual? Different?'

The old woman bristled, puckered her lips.

'It's just that Stu mentioned—' The doorbell chimed, cutting her off.

'She's here.' Catherine moved quickly, seemingly grateful for the distraction.

'Beautiful home,' Hannah Carlson repeated at least four times as she was shown through to the large conservatory at the back of the house and instructed to sit upon a wicker sofa.

'I'll fetch some drinks,' Catherine stated icily. 'Can't have a repeat of last time.'

If Hannah was curious to what she was alluding to, she didn't say anything. She rapidly blinked her blue eyes as she forced a pained smile as she stared at Elena. 'So, how are you?'

Elena looked at her, almost laughed.

'How am I?' She frowned at the rep from More You, wondering if it was a serious question.

I'm a mess.
I'm a widow.
I'm a mother to a newborn.
I'm a murderer.
I'm broken.
I'm so fucking broken. And now your More You is trying to steal my life. How do you think I am?

Elena managed to feign a smile. 'I'm holding it together. Just about.'

'Obviously, everyone at More You is deeply, deeply upset over your husband.' Hannah gave a staged nod of her head. As if she gave a shit about Stu. 'I came here today to ensure your More You is doing everything she can to support you through this difficult time.' She peered around Elena. 'Is she here?'

'No.'

She's back at home pretending to be me.

'I see. So how has—'

The drinks arrived, a new set, teapot included. Catherine ensured everyone had a cup. Then she folded herself into a wicker armchair, clearly having no desire to miss the conversation.

Catherine eyed Hannah coldly. 'Tell me, how many times have More You models been caught up in murder investigations?'

Hannah burned the brightest red. 'Excuse me? I can't—'

'Because as the company well knows, I have a private investigator looking into my son's death and he claims that there is a possibility of foul play from your model.'

'That's . . .' Hannah was floundering, blue eyes misting. She reached into her bag and grabbed a tablet, began tapping on it furiously. 'All of our models are fitted with a do-no-harm failsafe. It is quite simply *impossible* for a More You product to hurt someone.'

'You can spare us the marketing spiel' – Catherine's tone was hard – 'or are you unaware of my position on the board?'

Hannah opened and closed her mouth, chin trembling, flailing.

'The issue here is that we both know what More You models can be capable of.'

Elena threw her mother-in-law a barbed look.

What can they be capable of?

If Catherine had been aware of potential dangers, why would she ever place one in Stu's home?

To replace me. To push me out.

The thought made her turn cold.

'P-please, I'm confident that no model has ever—' Hannah was fumbling for a response but Catherine snapped through her excuses.

'But they're human, are they not?' Catherine's gaze was like steel; cold and cutting. 'You advertise how they are just like their original. More You . . . only better. Isn't that the promise?'

'Look, I can assure you—'

'Earlier today, my More You claimed to be me.' Elena gripped the arms of her chair, scratching the hard wicker. 'She went on the news and she—'

'It's very common for More You models to mimic their originals.' Hannah furrowed overly plucked eyebrows at her. 'Often that is a core part of their responsibilities. To handle interviews. Press work.'

'But I didn't tell her to.'

Hannah tapped upon her screen some more. 'Mrs Roberts, your More You will only ever act in your best interests.' Her brow furrowed in frustration as her nails clacked upon the screen. 'The . . . the tracker seems to be experiencing some lag.' Sweat began to glisten upon her temple as she looked over at Elena with a nervously strained smile. 'If your More You claimed to be you, I'm certain she had good reason. After all' – Hannah gave a tilt of her head – 'she will think like you. The app must need updating,' she half muttered as the tablet was returned to her bag. 'I'm here as part of our care initiative.' Hannah turned up the wattage of her smile. 'More You cares about our customers beyond the adoption date.'

'Yet you don't care about who killed my son,' Catherine seethed. Hannah didn't even twist her head to glance in the old woman's direction. 'I asked for support and they sent a sales rep!'

'We care that you are still receiving ample support, and if not, given your husband's recent passing, perhaps a second model will enable you to—'

'So this *is* a sales pitch!' Catherine raged. 'Oh no!'

'I want my More You returned. Rehabilitated. Whatever it all means,' Elena blurted.

I want it to be just me and Olive.

Hannah paled. She swallowed, bulbous chin trembling.

'I never wanted the More You,' Elena explained. 'My husband did.' She shot Catherine a pained look. 'I'd be happier now without it.'

Hannah swallowed again. 'Well, the returns process is—'

'I don't care what it is,' Elena objected. 'I just care about getting it done.'

'Sure.' Hannah gathered her hands together in her lap. 'But you have to apply for a model to be rehabilitated. And then a committee has to approve the request.'

'That wasn't in the terms and conditions.' Elena snapped.

'The terms state that the process is ever-changing' – Hannah reapplied her saleswoman smile – 'and given recent . . . pressures . . . from certain groups, the returns process has been forced to slow. In an effort to be more . . . humane.'

'Then I want to put in a request.'

'Of course.'

'How long until . . . until a decision is made?'

'Around twelve months.'

'Christ.' Catherine whistled from her chair, shaking her head. 'That's a little excessive, don't you think? I'm sure I'll be able to expedite things.'

'We have to tread carefully, especially with so many groups campaigning for models to have additional rights.'

'What about our rights?' Catherine was on her feet, flushed with fury. 'What about what we want? What we paid for?'

'Please, all I can do is—'

'Try to sell us another one.' Catherine rolled her eyes and gestured to the door that led back into the kitchen. 'You've taken up enough of our time as it is. And my granddaughter has woken up.'

Beyond them the house was still and silent.

'Of course.' Hannah nodded at each woman in turn and got to her feet, drawing her bag up to her side. 'Thank you for your time today.'

Catherine and Elena followed her to the front door. Outside, it had started to rain.

'Tell me,' Elena asked as the door was pulled open, 'if a More You *was* found to have caused someone harm, would that expedite the returns process?'

'Of course.' Hannah smiled falsely. 'Though, of course, that would never happen.'

'Right,' Elena agreed tightly.

Standing beside Catherine, she watched the More You rep drive away from the house, rain pattering against the roof of her little car.

'You know, Frankenstein was never the monster in the story,' Catherine mused wistfully.

'Isn't Frankenstein the creator?'

'Exactly.' Catherine gave a self-satisfied nod and slammed the door shut. 'The company is more at fault here than they'd like to accept.' Catherine strode back into her house, towards the kitchen, leaving Elena alone in the hallway.

'Do you know something?' Elena called after her. 'Do you know something about More You?'

But technically I made Nellie. She's me.

Does that make me the monster?

She remembered how it felt to have Stu's blood upon her hands. The slickness. The warmth it still held.

Coming here was the right thing.

It was what Stu would have wanted.

'Family is so important,' he was always telling Elena.

And Catherine was downright intolerable. But she *was* family. Despite her often odious nature, the old woman loved Olive. Which meant that Olive was safe. Elena was filled with the maternal drive: to protect her daughter.

In the lounge, Olive awoke and began to cry, drawing Elena to her, demanding her to abandon all her dark thoughts. At least for now.

.48

Catherine knew what she was to More You. A seat-warmer. Filling the void Eric had left at the company. Poorly. Her job was to sit in on meetings when required, vote as needed. Just exist. Catherine liked to fool herself into believing she was important by proxy, that her association with the company made her special. Valuable. The visit from the plump sales rep had relieved her of such thoughts. Felix was in her lap as she stared at the hologram glowing atop Eric's desk.

Usually she opted for the phone. Trusted the phone. But now . . . now she needed to see his face. Look upon Christopher, the fellow board member who had been Eric's friend. Who now served as her confidant, her ally when she needed it. Or so she'd thought.

'It is unacceptable!' she told him stridently, taking care not to let her voice rise too much as it was dark outside, both Elena and Olive now sleeping.

'Look, Catherine—'

'I ask you to fix this situation, to help me out, and you . . . they send a *sales rep*. Really?' Her entire face crinkled with disgust. 'We do not need *another* Elena. She already wants to get rid of the one she has.'

Within the blue-tinged projection, Christopher nodded thoughtfully. He wore a shirt and cargo shorts, a large cocktail in his hand. Catherine was aware that she'd disturbed him while on holiday though she didn't care where he was. This was more important.

'There is only so much that the company can do.'

'My detective thinks she killed Stuey.'

Christopher's eyebrows lifted, just a fraction.

'The More You,' Catherine continued, voice low, conspiratorial.

'Catherine, you know that—'

'On the old models, yes,' she swiftly interrupted, leaning forward, causing Felix to raise his head and throw her a weary glance. 'The fail-safe. But we both know it doesn't always hold. We've sat in enough meetings where we have had to approve pay-offs, had to—'

'Perhaps this meeting might be better held in person,' Christopher blurted nervously, casting a glance over his shoulder.

'There's no time,' Catherine snapped. 'This . . . this newer model. What can it do?'

'Well.' Christopher massaged his jowls. She could sense he was withholding information from her. While Christopher didn't control the science, he held most of the purse strings. And, in the company, that made him powerful in a way that Eric never had been. A way Eric had always envied. Catherine needed that power now. That influence. 'I mean, you insisted we disable the chip so now we can't track it and—'

'Here.' Catherine picked up a tablet from the desk, proud of herself for finding the information she had sought. 'These are the minutes of our meeting six months ago: "The transition with newer models will be seamless. They will come with fully formed memories and believe they truly are the host."'

It was hard to tell thanks to the quality of the hologram and Christopher's gaudy tan but she was fairly certain he'd paled at her words.

'"Believe they truly are the host."' She slapped her hand upon her desk, victorious. 'At the meeting you all gave some spiel about this belief enabling them to do their job better. To feel more fulfilled. It's rubbish and we both know it. Today . . . today the unit was on television. Claiming to be my daughter-in-law. We cannot underestimate what it may be capable of.'

'Do you deem her to be dangerous?'

Catherine considered the question. 'My detective does.'

'What is it you're asking of me here, Catherine? You want the clone decommissioned? Done. I'll set things in place. You always knew it was going to be risky fixing your son up with a newer model in his home. You were aware—'

'My silence. My shares and my seat. What would you give me for it?' Catherine suddenly demanded, noting how Christopher's eyes grew wide. Hungry. Another seat on the board, more money in his pocket. More power. That was the problem with people who had it all; they always wanted more.

'What do you want? I can get rid of the model, that's no issue, so—'

'No.' Catherine began to stroke Felix's back, fur soft between her fingers, his purr loud and thunderous. 'I want more than that.'

'Name your terms.' Christopher paused to take a confident sip of his cocktail. 'As you know, I'm a very rich man. I'm sure we can come to some arrangement.'

'I want something money can't buy,' Catherine told him.

Now he appeared nervous.

'Give me what I want.' As she said the words she felt emboldened by them, imagined Eric at her shoulder, glowing with pride. When it came to business he was always a shark, so adept at negotiating the best deal for himself. 'And my seat is yours. And I'll keep the fact that Nellie is a newer model secret.'

'What is it that you want?'

Catherine took a steadying breath. She knew what she wanted, had known since Clive was taken from her. Catherine closed her eyes and then told her secret, her desire. All while Elena and Olive slept, the house still around her.

.49

Elena was restless. She had awoken from a nightmare, tangled within the sheets upon the large bed in one of Catherine's spare bedrooms. The room reeked of lavender and furniture polish. Damp with sweat, Elena perched on the edge of the bed, listening to the gentle breaths of her sleeping daughter to calm herself.

In the nightmare she had been back home, back in her own bedroom, back with Stu. This time his hands had not been around her neck as she reached for the candlestick, he had been cowering upon the floor, staring up at her, eyes wide. Fearful.

'No, please no,' he had rasped before Elena lowered her arm swiftly, with force, feeling the tremor along her bone as the candlestick smacked against her husband's skull, for ever silencing him.

That's not what happened.
It's a nightmare. Nothing more.

Elena rocked back and forth. Exhaustion gnawed upon the frayed edges of her sanity. How she longed to just fall back upon the bed, swaddle herself within the sheets and close her eyes. But she couldn't risk seeing him again, not like that. Just the thought of the panic in his gaze made her stomach roil.

Needing to keep herself occupied, Elena reached for her phone upon the bedside table. With a quick tap she opened up the app that located Nellie. Elena pictured her sleeping contentedly in the spare bedroom, mere metres from the place where the world had ended. Oblivious. Unconcerned. Elena ground her teeth as resentment rose within her.

It's all her fucking fault.

The app was open and Elena blinked to look down at the screen.

'What the—'

An error message was glowing above the usual image of her street.

> Unable to locate More You unit.

Elena was suddenly wide awake, every nerve, every muscle, on high alert. She closed and reopened the app.

Same message.

'Fuck,' she hissed as quietly as she could.

Close.

Reopen.

> Unable to locate More You unit.

Fuck. Fuck. Fuck. Fuck. Fuck.

Phone in hand, Elena jumped out the bed and scurried towards the door, the glowing light of the landing. Beside a family portrait of a teenage Stu and both his parents, Elena stared at her screen, at the app, trying to process what she was seeing.

'How can this be—' She tapped furiously, willing the app to work. Because Nellie *had* to be back at home. Where else could she be?

A creak. Downstairs.

On the landing, Elena froze.

Shit.

The slap of a door closing.

Elena squeezed her eyes shut in frustration.

Stu. Jesus, I need Stu.

275

Normally, he was the investigator of any strange sound. Elena would stretch out and nudge him in bed, whispering within the darkness, 'Stu, I heard something.' And without further prompting he'd groan but still remove himself from the plush comfort of the duvet, shove on his slippers, a nearby jumper, and trudge out the door.

But Stu was gone.

Elena glanced back at the bedroom, at the shape of the Moses basket containing her sleeping baby. Then she approached the stairs, emboldened.

If Nellie was downstairs, she could handle her, couldn't she? Overpower her?

Has she come for Olive?

Elena was almost at the foot of the stairs.

Or has she come for me?

Could Nellie have sensed that Elena was considering having her returned? And the interview earlier . . . Was she trying to replace Elena before she could be erased?

Because that's what I would do.

Elena swallowed, throat desert-dry.

Another slap of a door closing. A cupboard door. Now Elena could see the light from the kitchen seeping out into the darkness of the hallway. She quickened her steps. Filling her chest with a stabilising breath she pushed open the door, a spring ready to unleash.

'What the hell are you—'

She stopped mid-sentence when she saw the forlorn figure of Catherine perched at the kitchen island, a wine glass before her, an empty bottle beside it.

'Catherine.' All the fire left her voice as she slowly approached the old woman, who was almost unrecognisable in her white dressing gown, head bowed and devoid of make-up. Catherine's skin had a grey tinge to it, her eyes pale and watery, so small without their framing false lashes. Her lips, puckered and withdrawn. And so many lines. She appeared to have aged decades overnight.

'Oh, don't look at me.' Catherine curled into herself, shaking her head. 'I look absolutely awful, I know.'

'No, no, it's fine, you look—'

'Elena, don't. I have mirrors, I know how I appear without my usual face on.'

'What are you . . .' Elena glanced towards the digital clock atop the dual ovens. It was three in the morning. 'Why are you up?'

'Can't sleep.' Catherine gave a quick shrug of her bony shoulders. 'Every night it's the same thing. I go to bed, drop off, dream of him. And then I just . . . I feel so awful, I have to come down here and . . .' Her voice cracked and completely broke as tears washed down the canyons age and time had placed upon her face.

'It's okay.' Elena edged closer to the island. 'I . . . I get it. And same.'

'There's another bottle in the fridge if you want some.' Catherine lifted her head to nod in the direction of the sleek refrigerator behind Elena.

'Thanks, but I can't. Olive.'

'Sure.'

Thinking of her daughter, Elena quickly checked the baby monitor linked to her phone. All was peaceful within the spare bedroom.

'I wonder if we will ever sleep properly again?' Catherine mused drily.

'When Olive was born, all I wanted was to sleep again.' Elena raised herself up onto a stool opposite her mother-in-law. 'Now . . . it's the last thing I want. Because when I dream, he's there. And then I wake up . . .'

'And he's gone,' Catherine concluded in a shaky breath. 'I looked into it.' She drained the final dregs in her glass.

'Into what?'

'More You.' Catherine swallowed. 'I contacted them about Stuey. Thinking maybe they could . . . you know.'

'But they couldn't?'

Catherine gave a sorrowful shake of her head, hair so thin and grey, like burnt shrubbery without her usual adornment of a wig. 'The host has to be living.' She shot Elena a pained look and Elena felt it; the old woman's regret. Her hatred. Her pain.

She wishes we had cloned Stu, not me.

'What are you going to do about *her*?' Catherine dropped from her own stool and shuffled towards the refrigerator, returning with a fresh bottle of white wine which she proceeded to liberally pour into her glass. 'I'm afraid this is the last bottle. Normally I'd send Stuey down to the wine cellar to get another.'

A pained silence passed between them.

'I never did like it down there; it was Eric who insisted we have one. Who loved his merlot. But Stuey, he'd always go down there for me, help me out.'

Catherine drank deeply from her fresh glass, then stared at her daughter-in-law. 'Like I said, what will you do about her?'

'Nellie?'

'I spoke to my contact at More You, they said they'd consent to a swift return. Have her decommissioned quickly and quietly. Much faster than that insipid marketing girl told us it would be. But we need proof. You'd have to have proof she caused someone harm.' Holding Elena in a steady gaze, Catherine sipped her wine.

'When you say decommissioned . . .'

'They will kill her, Elena.' Catherine's voice was hard. 'It will be painless and quick.'

A shudder passed through Elena's body. The kind of feeling that made you wonder if someone had walked on your grave.

'If she's dangerous, she can't exactly hang around now, can she?'

Elena chewed on her lower lip.

Painless.

Quick.

'Can he . . . Dalton, can he find any? Is there proof?'

A gentle shrug from the old woman. 'He's searching.'

'I don't even know where she is,' Elena muttered wearily.

'Oh?' Catherine placed down her glass.

'Maybe the app is broken but . . .' She showed Catherine the error message on her phone.

'So she could be anywhere?'

'I mean . . . maybe. Or the app isn't working.'

Please let the app just be broken.

'First the news, then this . . .' Catherine tutted loudly. 'She's looking to expand her boundaries. Fill a gap.'

'Because Stu is gone?' Elena asked, worried.

'Perhaps.'

'I don't . . . I don't know what to do,' Elena admitted, dragging her hands through her hair, feeling the slickness of grease. When had she last showered?

'She needs to go,' Catherine stated flatly.

'Well, that's easier said than done,' Elena snapped. 'And you were the one who forced us to get her in the first place! This was all your doing!'

'I was just trying to help!' Catherine matched her angry pitch. 'I saw you *drowning*, Elena and I offered a life raft. You could be more grateful.'

'And now I'm supposed to just . . . what? Throw her away? Let them *kill her*? It doesn't work like that!'

'Doesn't it?' Catherine's eyes shone.

'Catherine, I can't—'

'You said the app is perhaps broken.' Catherine brought her glass to her lips, sipped delicately from it. 'So if she, say, went missing, who would know? She's human, yes? She needs things to survive. Only she lacks the awareness, the savvy, that comes from experience. Take her somewhere remote, a woodland. Disorientate her. Then leave her there.'

Elena considered this, a strange feeling within her chest.

She's still me.

We're connected.

She gestured to Catherine's glass. 'Actually, may I?'

The old woman slid the glass towards her. Elena took one single, deep drink from it. After months of abstinence from alcohol it tasted glorious.

Nellie killed Stu. It wasn't her hand that held the candlestick, but he thought I was her. If she'd never come into our home, he would never have made that mistake. She's guilty in this. She can't stay.

'I'm just . . . she's smart, Catherine. She'll find her way back.'

'And in that time, Dalton will have discovered his proof. I'm sure of it.' Catherine pursed her lips. 'We just need her away from the house, unable to meddle.'

'I don't . . .' Elena drummed her fingers against the stem of the glass. As she did, Catherine glanced down at the floor, frowning.

'First tea in my lounge and now you're dripping blood everywhere!'

'What?' With a jolt Elena realised her ankle was weeping again, the bandages she'd put on back at home now soiled and useless. 'Urgh, dammit.'

'Ankle still troubling you?' Catherine was watching her with interest, sipping on her wine.

'Yeah it's . . . still hurting.'

With a wince Elena peeled back the plasters, the wound as red and angry as it had ever been.

Why won't it fucking heal?

'Looks nasty,' Catherine commented.

'It's not as bad as it looks,' Elena lied. 'Have you got any plasters or anything I could use?'

'Third cupboard on the right.' Catherine nodded to the far corner of her kitchen. As Elena hobbled over to it she felt the old woman's eyes upon her.

'Such a deep cut,' Catherine remarked. 'Did you catch it on glass or something?'

Glass.

Or something.

Elena might have been mistaken but she was certain she felt the sharpness of an accusation within the comment. She kept her voice light as she replied. 'A plant pot, actually. Hence why I think it's gotten infected.'

'Hmm.'

'Does Dalton really think Nellie killed Stu?' She pivoted the conversation as she dabbed her ankle with a sterile wipe, sweating through the pain.

'He certainly has his suspicions,' Catherine confirmed. 'Don't you think she did it?'

'I think . . .' Elena applied fresh gauze. 'I think she was the one who found him so . . . I mean, she definitely *could* have. Especially since POP isn't claiming responsibility.'

Catherine nodded in approval.

'So I should, what? Abandon her somewhere?'

'She can't stay in your home, Elena.' Catherine's voice was factual, flat. 'You can't hide here while she's out in the world pretending to be you.'

'I'm not—'

'I'll take care of Olive, don't worry. You go and clean up your mess.'

'*My*—' Elena's face flushed with anger as she put a fresh plaster on her ankle, but she stopped short when she looked over at Catherine. She painted such a sorrowful scene with her fresh bottle of wine, her stooped posture, her blanched face. This was a woman broken. A woman grieving. A mother who had lost her son. Catherine Roberts was many things, but she had always adored her boy and been a loving mother to him. Elena snapped her mouth closed and gave a brisk nod.

'I'll do it, I'll take Nellie away from the house. Buy Dalton some time.'

'Good girl.'

'Are you sure you'll be all right with Olive?'

Catherine's face tilted up with thinly veiled fury at the question.

'It's just that—'

'You forget that I raised my Stuey. And his brother. I'm accustomed to *babies*, Elena. Once a mother, always a mother. Remember that.'

'No, no, I get that. I—'

'Stuey may be gone, but my love for him' – Catherine blinked away tears and tapped her chest – 'it stays. For ever. Until I am in the ground with him.'

Elena could only nod. Catherine was right. In this, their grief, they were linked. Together lost. Catherine would care for Olive because Olive was the daughter of Stu. And for the time being, that would have to be enough.

.50

Elena could barely remember driving home, her thoughts so frantic, so tangled together.

Nellie needs to be out of the house.
Returned.
She pretended to be me.
She's part of me.
Stu is gone.

Twice she almost ran a red light.

My fault. It's all my fault.

When she pulled up outside her house she half expected to see the pulsing of blue lights, the neon strip of a waiting police car, the reporters who watched her relentlessly salivating at the unfolding story of the More You who had gone wrong. But all was as she had left it: still. Calm.

Elena stole a moment to snap down her visor and check her reflection. It felt like looking at a ghost. Somewhere behind the shadows, the sallow skin, was her true self. With a sigh Elena left the car and steeled herself for what was to come.

'Nellie?' Her footsteps echoed in the hallway. 'Nellie?'

Was Nellie even here? Shoving a hand into her pocket Elena retrieved her phone, opened up the More You app to be confronted yet again with the error message.

'You're home.' Nellie appeared from the kitchen, a tea towel in her hands.

'Yes.'

Nellie peered around her. 'But where is Olive? Is she all right?' A look of panic appeared on her face.

'Olive is fine, she's just with Catherine.'

Even saying it didn't feel natural. But what choice did Elena have? For now, her baby needed to be with her mother-in-law. She would be back with her soon enough and by then Nellie would be lost in some far-flung scrap of woodland and they'd be one step closer to being just the two of them. To being okay.

'Your chip isn't working.' Elena held up her phone, tone accusatory.

'Oh?' Nellie took a tentative step towards the device, brow furrowing. 'I'm not sure why that would be. Perhaps my chip is malfunctioning?'

'Have you left the house at all?'

'No.'

'Not even to talk to the press?' Elena's free hand made a fist at her side.

Nellie stiffened. 'I did speak with reporters who called at the house, yes.'

'Why?' Elena raged. 'Why the hell would you do that?'

'I thought I was—'

'And why the hell would you pretend to be *me*?'

'Because I thought I was helping.' Nellie matched her heated stare. 'They kept calling, desperate to just hear from you. So I gave them what they wanted and they ceased bothering us. Did you look outside? They are gone. Satiated.'

Elena had to admit that the street was quieter than it had been in days.

'But you didn't need to say you were *me*.'

'Didn't I?' Nellie asked. She wore dark denim jeans, a cream turtleneck jumper, hair drawn back in a low plait. She was elegant, effortless. Everything Elena currently was not. 'Had I explained I was your More You, they would not have listened. And that is my role, is it not? To be you when I'm needed to be.'

'I didn't ask you to speak to the press!' Elena thundered, her words bouncing off the walls.

Nellie was staring at her, a look of concern on her pretty face. 'Did you express adequately for Olive? Why did you leave her with Catherine? How long will she be there?'

'Can you just . . .' Elena pushed past her, into the immaculate kitchen, every surface clean and clutter free.

'Answer me,' Nellie pressed, shadowing her every step. 'I'm worried about our daughter.'

'*My.*' Elena stopped and spun around, veins thick within her neck. 'You're worried about *my* daughter. You have no child. Because you have no life. Nothing. You're just my fucking clone.'

'You and more,' Nellie replied icily, reciting More You's motto.

'Olive is with Catherine as we have something to do.' Elena glared at her, then turned to continue striding towards the lounge. 'What the—' She froze on the edge of the room, taking in all the debris.

There were pictures everywhere. Albums strewn across sofas, photographs plucked free from wallets and fanned over the carpet. Framed images taken down from walls and shelves, stacked in unsteady piles.

'What the fuck!' Elena declared, her ankle beginning to throb, the pressure of using her foot to drive home catching up with her.

'I remember.' Nellie darted forward, grabbed a sterling silver frame within which Elena wore a lace bridal gown, Stu with an arm around her waist, so handsome in his suit, so young. Both of them smiling. 'I remember this.' Nellie poked the glass.

'What are you doing? Put these away! They're not yours to look at!'

Is this what had been happening while Elena was away? Nellie rooting through all her personal things? All her memories?

She's trying to become me.

'Give me that.' Elena snatched the picture.

'We were married at dusk, on a beach, with a steel drum playing. Later that night Stu got sick from the oysters at the wedding breakfast. Oysters Catherine had insisted we have because they're *classy*.' Nellie was speaking quickly, words tumbling together.

'No.' Elena kept her voice low and quiet. 'You do not remember that.'

Elena remembered that. How furious she had been at Catherine as Stu spent their wedding night retching into the honeymoon suite toilet, certain the old woman had spiked the food on purpose just to ruin things.

Elena clicked her fingers at the mess. 'Put these away. All of them. Now.'

'And here.' Nellie ignored her, darting towards an album filled with pictures from a holiday, Elena sun-kissed and golden in them, slim in a turquoise bikini, a shimmering ocean behind her. 'Our first holiday with Stu. We got drunk on cheap tequila and had sex near our cabin on the beach but were spooked by that other couple who came walking by.'

Elena remembered. Of course she did. She felt her face reddening.

'And this.' Nellie jumped to another picture, one taken upon a mountain peak. 'It was the hardest climb we'd ever done, legs felt like jelly. When the second storm hit we—'

'This is *my life*,' Elena screamed at her. 'Mine! None of this happened to you, none of it. Fucking put them away.'

Nellie continued to hold the framed picture, staring at her.

'Put it away,' Elena repeated more menacingly.

'If this isn't my life' – Nellie took a step towards her – 'then why do I remember it all so clearly? Why can I taste the salt from the sea, remember the caramel fondant from the wedding cake? Remember how it felt to be with Stu and—'

'You took him from me.' Elena's teeth were clenched, tears streaming down her cheeks. 'You took him from me, from Olive. Now he's gone and—'

'You killed him.' Nellie interrupted her flatly. 'That was you, remember? I came upstairs and found you candlestick in hand. Or have you forgotten?'

'That's not what happened.'

'You know it is.'

'Do I?' Elena pawed at her cheeks and pushed away the worst of her tears. 'Because I think you're going to make history, Nellie, as the first More You that fucking malfunctioned and murdered someone.'

Nellie gave her a sorrowful look and then extended the framed picture towards her. Elena snatched it into her possession, pressing it against her chest.

'I'm sorry you're struggling to remember things,' she said, edging back and beginning to stoop down and gather up photographs.

'I'm not . . .' Elena shook her head, wincing in frustration. 'I'm remembering things *just fine.*'

'I enjoyed it, you know.' Nellie glanced up, a stack of albums in her arms, and gave Elena a sad smile. 'Going through all these, experiencing it all.'

'You were never there.' Elena scowled at her. 'These moments were never yours.'

'And yet they feel like they were.' Nellie shrugged.

She's fucking with you. She's trying to take all that you have.

'Show me your chip?' Elena asked suddenly, thinking of the app.

'Sorry?'

'Your . . . your chip.' Elena gestured to Nellie's ankle. 'Show it to me.'

'Oh, okay.' Slowly Nellie straightened, putting down the photo albums, and then she carefully drew up the hem of her jeans and lowered the fabric of her sock, revealing the curve of her ankle. Like a flawless piece of pale porcelain. Elena frowned at it.

'There's no mark where they put it in?'

'I suppose not.' Nellie pouted with impatience. 'Satisfied?'

'Other foot,' Elena snapped. She was most definitely *not* satisfied.

The other ankle was exactly the same, blemish free.

'Have you taken it out?' Elena demanded hotly. 'Is that why the app no longer works? Because you removed it and crushed it somewhere?'

'Of course not!' Nellie replied, taken aback by the accusation. 'It is an issue within the app, nothing to do with me.'

'Did you take it out?' Elena asked again, voice shaky.

Because that's what I would have done.

'No, I've told you! I've not touched it!'

Within her pocket Elena's phone pulsed. Groaning, she pulled it free, looked at the new message from Catherine.

> Dalton is heading over to yours now. Be out of the house, let him look in peace for evidence.

The old woman was brisk even in her messages. Not like the adoring reams of compliments she used to send to Stu. Always concluded with numerous kisses.

'We're going for a drive,' Elena barked at Nellie, and began striding towards the hallway.

'Sorry? What?' Nellie hurried after her, wearing a look of bewilderment.

'I said we're going for a drive,' Elena repeated.

'I don't . . .' Nellie began to look afraid. 'Are we going to Catherine's? To get Olive?'

'Sure.' Elena gave a lazy shrug of her shoulders. 'Whatever.'

She just wanted it *done*. The avalanche of pictures in her lounge, the fact that Nellie had been *studying* them, was all too much. Elena needed distance from the house. From Nellie. From all of it.

'You're angry,' Nellie remarked, lingering in the hallway as Elena thrust open the front door.

'No shit.'

'I'm not sure you should be driving either of us anywhere when you're so angry.'

'I'm angry because you crossed the fucking line.' Elena was yelling at her, not caring if anyone out on the street heard them. 'You pretended to be me, Nellie. That's fucked up.'

'I *am* you.'

'And then you went through all my pictures. Those are private. Got it?'

'I know losing Stu has—'

'And my husband is fucking dead.' Elena's chin trembled as she spoke. Hearing it, holding the words upon her tongue, it left her feeling so woefully hollow. Like someone had taken a spoon to her soul and scooped out all the best bits, leaving her raw and empty.

Suddenly Nellie was holding her, pressing their bodies together as Elena shook. For a brief, blissful moment Elena thought she was being embraced by her mother. A feeling of calm washed over her.

'It will be all right,' Nellie whispered to her. 'Together we are going to figure this out. I promise.'

Her kindness. Her purity. Her fucking innocence. Elena envied that in Nellie. She also didn't trust it. Not any more.

Again.

That's what Stu had said. Right before he tried to kill her. Elena knew that Nellie was so very like her. Too like her.

Do you trust yourself?

Is that what this all came down to? If she didn't trust Nellie, what then? Did she not trust herself?

Elena choked back a sob and untangled herself from the embrace. Within her pocket, her phone pulsed anew, no doubt Catherine distantly spouting more demands.

'Get in the car,' Elena sniffed, turning to point towards her parked vehicle. 'There's something I want to show you.'

Nellie nodded and obliged, hurrying towards the car, sliding into the passenger seat and clicking her safety belt in place. Neither of them spoke as Elena manoeuvred out onto the street, the house growing smaller in the rear-view mirror until it was completely gone from sight.

.51

Christopher was as good as his word. He called Catherine back while she fretted over her granddaughter, hoping the little baby would continue to sleep while she tried to fix everything.

'Everything is in place,' he told her. Then, hesitantly, 'Can I trust you on this?'

'Yes.'

'You understand the terms?'

'Of course.'

She hung up quickly, abruptly. Then she called Dalton. He picked up right away.

'They're both out of the house,' she told him.

His reply was curt. 'Good.'

'Can you do this?'

'It's my job.'

Catherine drew in a feathery breath. 'I don't . . . we don't want a mess.'

'I'll get it done.'

'Thank you.' Glancing quickly at Olive, Catherine tapped her fingers nervously against her phone, imagining all that was due to unfold. 'Tell me, Mr Dalton, why do you dislike the More You models so much?'

He hung up without responding.

From: POP@outward.co.uk
To: Full Mailing List
Subject: Sorry

We must apologise for our silence over these past days. You must have seen the news – the murder of a man in his home, the press trying to pin it on us. Clearly, this is the work of More You. Yet another cover-up on their part. But we will not be collateral damage. There is chatter online that the model in his home was different. Newer. Smarter. We need to get our hands on it before More You do. This model could change everything – prove what we have been saying. That models no longer just exist to support us but to replace us. Imagine the damage that could do? The damage that has already been done.

We have always kept our protests peaceful, organised. Never have we hurt someone. This will not change. But More Yous are not people. In this war, we must remember that. If we wish to continue protecting the integrity of our humanity we must be willing to do anything.

Stay vigilant.

.52

Elena drove with no clear destination in mind. She just knew that she wanted greenery, fields. A world that slipped away towards the horizon.

'Are we going to Catherine's?' Nellie asked as they zoomed over a roundabout.

'Not exactly.' Elena gripped the wheel tightly, not daring to trust auto-drive. She needed to do this herself. Needed to feel each bump in the road, each turn.

Needed to feel alive.

'Look, I'm sorry if you think I've overstepped.' Nellie sagged against her chair, head dipped low. 'I was truly only trying to help, with the reporters.'

Elena turned briefly to look at her. Nellie had changed so much in the weeks since she'd been welcomed into their home. The way she held herself, the way she spoke. There was a naturalness to it all, an ease, which hadn't been there before.

'You've always been a quick learner.' Elena's mother would beam with pride whenever she spoke about her daughter as a little girl. 'Top of the class, every time. You'd read all the books on the shelf and then be asking for more. Always knew you'd go far. So smart, my girl.'

Some days grief was a shadow that snapped at her heels. Others it was a slab of concrete that pressed against her lungs, strangling every breath. This was a slab day. Elena blinked away tears and raised her chin, thundered through an amber light. She missed her mother so much that the feeling was palpable, like she could reach out and grab a handful of her sorrow. What would she say now if she could see her? Would she think Elena crazy, manically driving her clone out to some distant woodlands?

She'd just want to help.

Her mother had been forever kind, forever supportive. And oh, how she loved Stu.

Stu.

The slab upon her chest grew in weight and Elena sputtered behind the wheel.

'Are you all right?' Nellie asked quickly, a nervous urgency in her voice.

'Fine. I'm fine.'

Around them the town had thinned away, replaced by sweeping farmland. It felt refreshing to see a patchwork of green. Nourishing.

'Should we check on Olive?' Nellie fretted. 'She's been with Catherine quite some time.'

'She'll be fine.' Elena's hands grew ever tighter against the wheel.

Would Olive be fine? Was Catherine currently throwing up her manicured hands in despair as the baby screamed until she turned purple? Would the old woman be able to change nappies, give Olive a bottle? Burp her?

I'll be back with Olive soon enough.

Elena applied more pressure to the accelerator and the car bounced along a country lane.

'I wish you'd drive a bit slower,' Nellie objected, reaching a hand forward to steady herself against the dashboard.

'Why? Scared?' Elena taunted.

'It's just . . . a bit fast. That's all.'

'Do you think you could do it? Drive?' Elena challenged.

'I remember the test.' Nellie smiled wistfully as she spoke. 'How it wouldn't stop raining and Mum made me wear her favourite necklace for luck. The one with the silver shamrock.'

'No.' Elena slammed on the brakes so suddenly that both women lurched forward in their seats. 'No! That's *my* memory. Not yours! She was *my* mother!'

'But it's in here.' Nellie tapped her temple. 'All of it. Every moment, every heartbreak. Every Christmas morning, every kiss with Stu. So if they're not mine, why are they in here?' There was desperation in her voice. Frustration.

'Because you're me!' Elena lamented, smacking the wheel in anger. 'You have *my* memories because you basically have my brain. But they're not yours! For you, it's all a lie!'

'How can you know that?' Nellie was frowning at her. 'What if you're the lie?'

'This is fucking ridiculous.' Elena started up the car again, more determined than ever to leave Nellie to rot in some woodlands.

'Dangerous, to marry a smart woman,' Catherine had remarked one evening ahead of the wedding to Stu when she thought Elena had slipped out of the room, out of earshot.

'What are you talking about?' Stu objected. 'You're a smart woman.'

'Smart enough to know my place,' Catherine told him coolly. 'Women like Elena, they have *ideas*, sweetheart. They think they can have their cake and eat it too. She will likely give you children but insist on keeping a career.'

'And what's wrong with that?' Stu protested.

'It's not the natural order of things. Smart women tip the scales, and not in their favour. A woman belongs in the home, Stuey. Raising the children. Being a wife, a mother.'

'You realise the world stopped working like that a good fifty years ago, right?'

'She wants too much, Stuey. Thinks too much.'

'Mum, I love Elena and I'm marrying her. You need to get on board with this.'

'What I want for you, my boy, is to marry a woman who will always put you first.'

'Mum.' Elena could hear Stu swatting his mother away. 'What I love about Elena is that she's my equal. My best friend.'

'But she won't put you first. Trust me, Stuey. When it comes to it, she will always choose herself. Always. It's the curse of the smart woman.'

Listening, unseen, from the landing, Elena had felt the fire of resentment burning through her.

Now, in the car, the conversation came back to her and Elena recalled her final moments with Stu.

I had no choice.

Either I died or he did.

And I picked me. Of course I did. Anyone would have done the same.

'Where are we going?' Nellie demanded, pulling her out of her thoughts. 'Please, Elena, I'm tired of this. What is going on?'

'I'm . . .' Elena saw the stretch of woodland up ahead, a thicket of trees. 'There.' She nodded towards the windscreen. 'We're going there.'

Nellie leaned forward to scrutinise the vista. 'There's nothing there.'

'No, there's something in the woods. Something I need to show you.'

'Why not just tell me?'

'Where's your sense of adventure?' Elena chided as she parked in a lane just before the woods. 'We live for adventure, remember? Don't you have all my mountain-climbing memories tucked in up there?' She pointed at Nellie's head.

'So often I was afraid.' Nellie gave her a sorrowful look. 'That moment, existing on the edge of life and death. Stu was exhilarated by it, but me, I feared it.'

'Stop talking about it like it's you!' Elena raged, shoving open her door and climbing out. A light rain had started to fall.

'I don't like this.' Nellie copied her and came to stand beside the car, both of them facing the woodlands. 'Can't we just go back home?'

'No,' Elena snapped, pulling out her phone and checking the More You app. Again the error message flashed on the screen. 'Where is your chip?' She turned to stare at Nellie, standing eye to eye with her. 'Did you take it out?'

'If I'd done that, I'd have an ugly wound upon my ankle, would I not?' Nellie raised a single eyebrow at her. Elena fought the urge to punch her clean in the face.

'Considering you're me, you're very fucking annoying.'

'Maybe you just don't actually like yourself.'

'I know you've taken your chip out.' Elena began to trudge towards the trees, the rain gathering in strength. 'There's no point in lying about it.'

'I don't want to be here.'

'You've no choice,' Elena scowled at her. 'You're my More You and you do as I say. Let's go.'

'It's not meant to be like this,' Nellie called to her as Elena approached the edge of the woods, twigs snapping underfoot.

I fucking know that.
But this is what I've got.
This is what I need to fix.

.53

'Walk.'

The rain was coming down harder now. Elena fired off her orders like some jaded drill sergeant.

'Just . . . just fucking walk.'

Together she and Nellie trudged deeper into the woods, their hair wet and flat against their heads. Elena started to shiver.

I can't go back. Not yet. I'm so close.

Fingers around her wrist, tugging her back. Forcing her to stop.

'What is this?' Nellie asked pleadingly as rain dripped from the end of her nose. 'I don't understand what you are doing. Why we are here.'

'Yes you do.' Elena edged herself closer to the protection of an old oak tree. It provided little shelter, but enough for her to feel like she was no longer getting completely soaked.

'I don't know what you're—'

'The pictures. What were you doing with them?'

'I was—'

'Studying.' Elena blurted angrily. 'You were *studying* me. My life. My past. Because you want more than being chained to baby care. And I know that, because you're me.' Elena slapped a hand to the wet fabric of her top.

'Maybe that's how *you* feel,' Nellie objected, nose crinkled. 'But I actually care about Olive. *Love* her. I was looking at the pictures because I *remember* them. Because they're *my* life.'

Elena slapped Nellie. Hard and fast. The sound of palm hitting wet skin loud even against the falling rain. 'How dare you suggest I don't love my daughter.'

'You don't.'

'I'm here *because* I love my daughter. You . . . you only exist because of my love for her.'

'Then why leave her with Catherine?' Nellie demanded. 'A woman neither of us trusts or likes. Why even risk that?'

'You tried to sleep with Stu! He told me!'

'I didn't!' Nellie's voice matched hers in pitch. In fervour.

'He's dead because of *you*,' Elena screamed. She wanted to scratch Nellie's eyes out.

'I've only ever tried to help you!'

'Stop!' Elena grunted in frustration and drew her wet hair back, away from her face. She was getting sidetracked from the task at hand.

Too busy arguing with myself.

Focus.

'I need to go back to the car for something,' Elena told Nellie. 'Wait here.' She stepped away from the tree and the other woman was instantly on her, fingers on Elena's upper arm, digging in.

'No.' Nellie's voice was unusually forceful. 'Where you go, I go.'

'I said' – Elena pushed the hand away; it took some effort – 'wait here.' She hurried forward but this time Nellie grabbed her shoulder, drew her back with ease.

'And I said no.' Nellie was staring her down, both of them now soaked to the bone, starting to shiver. 'I'm not letting you leave me here.'

Elena's eyes widened with surprise. 'I . . . I wasn't—'

'We think the same.' Nellie wildly tapped her forehead. 'Remember?'

'Look, I'm not sure what you—'

'I didn't kill Stu. You did.'

Elena narrowed her gaze. 'I'm going to the car and you're going to wait here.'

'Please.' Nellie grabbed her hands, squeezed them tight. 'You know I've done nothing wrong. You made me, you brought me here. You wanted me. All I've done was do as you said, care for Olive, keep your secrets. I don't deserve this.'

Nellie was shaking, but whether it was from the cold or fear, Elena couldn't tell.

'I am *you* and you are me.' Nellie blinked away tears and raindrops that gathered together in her eyes. 'We are linked, Elena. I would never, ever hurt you.'

All around them the rain whispered, softening the ground.

'You know, there's a theory,' Stu had mused several nights before they were due to collect Nellie, who was at that point unnamed. He was sitting up in bed, tablet in hand, a trace of dark stubble shadowing his jawline.

'What theory?' Elena asked, yawning wide as she stumbled from the bathroom, already unsure if she had remembered to brush her teeth. How she longed for sleep. A clear, endless river of it she could drown in.

'The doppelgänger theory.'

Elena groaned as she rolled her eyes and crawled into bed, pausing briefly to check the cot and that Olive was still sleeping. Thankfully, she was. Which meant Elena had roughly forty minutes to drop into a fitful sleep before their baby woke, screaming and hungry. 'Mmm?' she mumbled in response to her husband, eyes already closed.

'In German it means double-goer.'

She could tell from his cadence that Stu was reading from his tablet. 'Uh-huh.'

'And there's a theory that everyone has one. They're not like . . . someone who just looks like you. They are an *exact* copy. Right down to how they walk, talk. The only difference is that one is the shadow self. The bad self.'

'Right.' Elena curled onto her side, an ocean opening up between them. She just needed to get carried away, to the blissful release of—

'So maybe she's already out there.' Stu was suddenly against her side, breath warm on her cheek as he leaned down to speak to her. 'Your other you.'

'Mmm.'

'So which would you be?'

'Mmm?'

Why won't he just go to bloody sleep?

'Are you the good one or the bad one?'

'Right now, definitely the bad one,' Elena grumbled into her pillow. 'Please Stu, let me *sleep*. She'll be up again soon and I'm fucking exhausted.'

'Okay, okay.' Her husband retreated to his side of the bed. 'But just think, this time next week, she will be here, helping. The good you.'

Elena was silent, eyes suddenly open.

'Night, honey.' Stu reached over and patted her back as Elena kept staring fixedly ahead.

The good you.

She knew he was just teasing her, but still. The comment was unintentionally barbed and it stuck in her side. When Olive woke just under an hour later, Elena was wrenched from a dream in which her whole home was underwater, her entire world had been sinking around her and she had been powerless to stop it.

'Dalton knows you did it,' Elena told Nellie as rain peppered the ground around them.

Nellie's face crinkled with dismay. 'What?'

'He knows you killed Stu because I would never hurt him. Everyone *knows* that. The . . . the POP stuff, no one is buying it.'

'Elena, I—'

'So I'm doing this for your own good,' Elena sniffed. She looked at her More You standing before her, soaked and shaking. 'If I take you home, they will decommission you. Do you know what that means?'

Nellie's chin quivered. She knew.

'And you . . . you don't deserve that. I know what you want – a world of exploration. Of seeing things. Experiencing things. I'm letting you *go*, Nellie. I'm setting you free. Giving you a chance to . . . to go find your own mountains. To go and see the world.'

'You're letting me *go*?' Nellie repeated in disbelief.

'Yes.' Elena nodded enthusiastically.

Because I'm the good one. Because this is the right thing to do.

'Here, in the middle of nowhere?' Nellie asked as rain dripped into her eyes.

'Yes!' Elena almost screamed at her. She was doing the *right* thing, setting Nellie free. Wasn't she?

Nellie looked around as though she expected to be ambushed by the stirring trees. 'Do you think I'd leave Olive?' Her voice was suddenly so low it was hard to hear her over the wind, the falling rain.

'I don't—'

'I'm not leaving Olive.' Nellie wiped her wet cheeks. 'And I'm not leaving *you*. I don't want freedom, Elena. I want my home. My life.'

'It's not—'

'I remember being six years old and winning a goldfish at the fair. We came home, back to the kitchen that had been freshly painted that soft shade of lavender and placed the fish in a bowl. He swam around and I watched him while I ate cheese on toast, my hair wet from the bath, my pyjamas soft and clean. I remember feeling so *happy*. So *loved*. Mum stroked my hair and asked if I'd had a good day.'

'I told her it had been the best day,' Elena whispered, tears streaking her cheeks. She remembered that moment, clung to it in dark times, crystallised and precious within her mind. The way the kitchen held the musk of paint, her mother's soft voice as she spoke, the way her body ached in that blissful way that meant she'd had a full day.

'We can give that to Olive.' Nellie gripped her shoulders, stared into her eyes. 'We can do that, Elena. Together. We can give her a life full of love, full of security. We can give her what we had.'

'Look, I just—'

Suddenly Nellie was holding her, clutching her tight. And Elena was back in that kitchen, watching the golden light of dusk fall across the floor, reflect upon the surface of the water in which her new fish swam.

'Let's call him Sunset,' she'd told her mother, who had smiled in approval.

'That's a wonderful name, my little flower.'

A kiss upon her cheek.

The best day.

'I'm real, I'm you,' Nellie was whispering into her ear. 'Please don't hurt me, please don't let them take me away.'

Elena's knees buckled, and it was Nellie's embrace that kept her on her feet. She was so cold, so tired.

'D-Dalton . . . he's been looking round the house. He will find something and—'

'Dalton will find nothing,' Nellie said soothingly, sounding almost like her mother. 'Because there is nothing to find. Everything will be okay, Elena. Trust me. Let's go home.'

Elena wanted to believe her. She did.

'We have to get back to Olive.' Nellie was leading her back through the woods now, towards the car, their feet sinking into the mud as they moved, leaving a dual set of prints. 'She's been with Catherine long enough.'

Elena winced as her foot knocked against a raised tree root. 'Fuck,' she gasped, leaning down, gripping her ankle. Always the same one, the wound that refused to heal.

'Let's get you home and get that cleaned up.'

'Th-thanks, I'm not sure I can . . .' She was going to say *walk* but already Nellie was boosting her up, lacing an arm around her back, beneath her shoulders. Together they awkwardly retraced their steps back to the car, the rain relentless around them.

'Let me drive.' Nellie was already placing Elena in the passenger seat.

'What? No, I can—'

'Not with that foot.' Nellie frowned at her and then slammed the door. Panting, Elena leaned into her chair, the rain hammering hard upon the car roof.

'You don't know how to drive,' Elena objected as Nellie settled herself behind the wheel, clicked her seat belt into place.

'The car will do most of the work,' she stated, starting the engine. She glanced at Elena's slumped form. 'Besides' – her eyes shone as she tapped her forehead – 'what you know, I know.'

'Sure.' Elena tried to sit up, her clothes squelching. Nellie instructed the car to return home and they were soon powering down country lanes as the windscreen wipers whipped back and forth in a frenzy. Twisting, Elena moved to look down at her ankle. It was hidden within her trainers but she could feel the blood pulsing out of it and sure enough, the tinge of crimson seeping over the rim of her shoe.

Shit.

'You really need to go to a doctor about that.' Nellie threw a sideways look at her, both hands neatly upon the wheel.

'I know,' Elena grumbled. She wanted to stay awake, she did. But her clothes were so wet and the heaters in the car were fired up as high as they could go. She tripped over into a light sleep, dreaming of freshly painted kitchens, of melted cheese. And of a goldfish turning round and round within his bowl, moving back and forth in a loop, never aware of all that existed beyond the glass, only mildly aware of the warped reflections he sensed through the water.

.54

Somewhere between the sprawl of the countryside and the twisting buildings of the town, the rain ceased. When the car turned into their street a jaundiced light was filtering in through the windscreen, pressing against Elena's eyes, waking her. Foggy, she tried to rub away her fatigue with the heel of her hands.

Had she slept the whole way home?

What time was it?

Blinking, she peered down the row of parked cars and felt her gut twist, as though someone had just skewered her with a knife. Something was wrong.

'What's going on?' The words fell from her as Nellie pulled the car up into a spare space, still some distance from the house. Outside Elena's front door the street was clogged with vehicles, impassable. Blue light pulsed from gathered police cars. She squinted against it all, turning to look at Nellie who had paled behind the steering wheel. 'Are the police at our house?'

Nellie was staring ahead, brow furrowed. 'You . . . you said that detective was coming by. Didn't you?'

Dalton. Shit. Shit!

He must have found something.

Elena looked down at her shaking hands, expecting to find them coated in blood.

'Look.' She managed to keep her voice firm. 'Let's just go and find out what's going on, okay?'

Nellie spun in her seat to look directly at her. 'I don't like this.'
'Me neither. But they must have found something.'
'We were so careful.' Nellie unclicked her belt.
Were we?

Elena scrambled to put her thoughts in order. Everything that happened with Stu now felt like it came from a dream. A nightmare. That it wasn't even truly her memory.

Because it wasn't.

She eyed Nellie warily as together they left the car, walked side by side up the street. They'd only managed a few paces when Elena fumbled, searing pain shooting up her ankle.

'Dammit,' she hissed as she buckled.

'Here, let me help.' Nellie hoisted her up, held her close to her side.

Elena remembered the first time she and Stu had walked past what would become their home. They were fresh from summiting Everest and riding on the wave of their achievement. Even though Elena's body ached she was keen to resume her training, plan her next climb. Hand in hand, she'd walked with Stu through Whitstable on an early summer's day. It had been warm enough for shorts, a T-shirt, her toned legs slowly turning golden.

'I like this street,' Stu told her, squeezing her hand. 'I've always thought it was really nice.'

Elena glanced around, studying her surroundings. She saw neat rows of immaculate terraced homes with long bay windows that looked out over a car-lined street, the occasional tree fenced along the pavement. It was definitely *nice*. Markedly nicer than their flat and its view of yet another brick building, but when she thought of her forever home she pictured a long garden, a rolling lawn, a sweeping oak tree her children would one day climb. A place for adventure.

'I could see us living here one day,' Stu told her with confidence.

'You could?'

'While we still need to be close to town,' he explained, leaning down to gently kiss the top of her head. 'And then, when the kids are a bit older, we'll leave the town, get a barn conversion somewhere, with a huge garden.'

'How many kids are we having?' Elena teased, thankful that they were on the same page. She'd tolerate living in town for as long as she had to, but her sense of adventure, her need for escape, was always within her, scratching to be released. There was only so long either of them would be happy in a home on a busy street.

'Five, six,' Stu laughed. 'As many as you'll let me put in you.'

'Let's start at one and see how we go.' Elena matched his laughter. They walked, bathed in glorious sunlight, studying the houses with a keen eye. Picturing the next stage of their lives together.

'He's coming towards us,' Nellie whispered into Elena's ear, dragging her up higher. Elena looked ahead and sure enough, there was Dalton, suit freshly pressed.

So Catherine was right, he did come round and snoop.

'Mr Dalton.' Elena was suddenly aware of how she must look – hunched beside her More You, both of them soaked and dirty.

'I'm going to make this as painless as I can.' He looked between Elena and Nellie, expression stern. 'We're here to arrest the unit.'

Nellie yelped.

'It would seem that additional evidence has been brought forward.'

Elena's pulse felt thick and heavy behind her ear. She looked over Dalton's shoulder, to the gathered officers and the crowd that had been drawn in to stare, currently being held back. Elena spotted familiar faces and her stomach hitched. Leanne and Margot were anxiously looking on.

Why are they here?

'My . . . my friends are here.' Elena blurted, pointing.

'As I said, new information placing the unit at the scene of the crime.'

'They spoke to you?' Elena was struggling to catch up with what was happening. 'What did they say?'

'Please.' Dalton was doing his best to usher them closer to the waiting officers. To the police van, back doors open wide, a cold, clinical interior on view. 'If you can just come with us and—'

'Are you arresting us?' Nellie demanded loudly, speaking to the police. But it was Dalton who answered.

'There's no us,' Dalton snapped at her. 'The police are here solely for the unit.' When he spoke he looked at Elena.

'You can't arrest More You units,' Nellie continued, arms still protectively around Elena who struggled to stand at her side.

Dalton gave a frustrated shake of his head. 'Perhaps not technically, no. Since they don't have rights like you or me. But the police can take them away. Hence . . .' He gestured to the van and several officers stepped forward.

'Mrs Roberts, I can assure you this is all standard protocol.' A heavy-set brunette officer with a young face was speaking loudly. 'The accused unit will be returned to More You pending further investigation.'

'Decommissioned,' Elena whispered frantically.

Because that's what was happening, wasn't it? They'd come for Nellie. Elena's friends had voiced their suspicions and Dalton had pushed for that to be evidence enough to have Nellie taken out of circulation. Destroyed.

Or did Catherine have a hand in this? Pulling strings from her armchair.

'Mrs Roberts, there is no cause for alarm, just let us take the unit and—'

'No!' Elena stared at the officer, noticing how she kept addressing Nellie when she spoke. 'You . . . you can't just take her and—'

'Mrs Roberts, please.' Again to Nellie.

'*I'm* Mrs Roberts!' Elena cried, hand pressed to her chest. 'I'm Elena Roberts.' She edged slightly away from Nellie, struggling on her feet, pointing back to her. 'This is my More You unit.'

Elena wilted, exhausted, and paused for the inevitable. She pictured Nellie being put in handcuffs and led towards the van, throwing her a final sorrowful glance. But what could Elena do? Better Nellie be taken away than her. And then she could return to Olive, start to look ahead to what would come next. She just needed to—

'I'm so sorry, my unit has been malfunctioning for quite some time now,' Nellie said in a crisp, confident voice. 'I'm Elena Roberts.'

.55

Elena felt like she was falling as the shock passed through her. Stumbling forward, she looked first at Dalton, then back at Nellie. 'Wh-what are you talking about? I'm clearly *me*. I'm Elena. This... this is my More You. Nellie.'

Nellie refused to meet her gaze, looking straight at the detective, the plump face of the brunette officer beside him. 'As I said, the unit has been malfunctioning ever since the... incident.'

'Incident?' Elena raged. 'You mean when my husband *died*.' She could feel the tears that gathered behind her eyes, the burn of betrayal in her chest.

Why is she fucking doing this?

'I'm Elena, this is my More You. Take her away.'

Elena wanted her gone. Destroyed. The moment she'd posed as her for the press had been one thing but this... this was different. This was personal. This was cruel.

She'll say anything to protect herself.

'Please, can you help?' Nellie looked at Dalton, eyes wide and fearful. 'I didn't even know they could do this... lie like this.'

Just like I would.

'Lie?' Elena balked at the word. 'Nellie.' She pushed her More You's shoulder hard, demanding her full attention. 'Stop this. Stop it right now.'

'I had my suspicions ever since she discovered Stu's body.' Nellie turned swiftly away, speaking to the officers. 'I never believed her about the intruder. And now this.' She gave a hapless shrug and Elena noticed the officer's expression darken.

'I've seen it before.' Dalton scratched at his sharp jawline, holding Elena in a cruel stare. 'They begin taking things too far, mimicking the original.'

'I am the original!' Elena seethed. 'Just take her and let me get on with my life!'

'There's a quick way to settle this.' The brunette officer stepped forward, a small chrome device in her hand. 'We'll just scan the chip.'

The corners of Elena's mouth dipped low. She thought of the error message in the app.

'Right.' The officer swept the length of Elena's body with the device and gave a sharp grunt of disapproval at the lack of response. 'No chip.'

'Of course there's no chip!' Elena snapped at her. 'I'm . . . I'm me.' Her temple was beginning to throb; she was so very tired.

'Feel free to check me.' Nellie smiled sweetly, offering herself to the officer. Another sweep of the device, another grunt.

No chip.

'I knew it.' Elena scolded. 'I knew you'd removed your chip.'

'Well, someone has removed a chip here.' Dalton looked between the women. 'You can't both be Elena Roberts. Can you . . .' He gestured to Elena's trouser leg, noticing the stain of red on her trainers.

'Let me.' Nellie quickly slid up the hem of her own damp clothes, pulling down her socks, revealing her unblemished alabaster ankles.

It's still in there, it has to be. It's just faulty.

'Check her again,' Elena demanded. 'Her chip has been offline the last few days. It's in there, just not picking up.'

'Look, can you please . . .' Dalton again gestured to her trousers.

'Show us the ankle,' the officer demanded curtly. Slowly Elena bent down, wincing. She tugged up her trousers and then peeled back her sock, hearing the collective inhalation from the gathered crowd as she did.

Fuck.

'I caught it a few weeks ago on a pot in the garden,' Elena told them all desperately. 'It . . . it got infected and—'

Dalton was beside her, crouched down, studying the wound, his hands suddenly gloved. 'Yeah, it's been yanked out.' He twisted to call back to the officer, not even glancing up at Elena.

'No!' Elena staggered back, away from him, face hot. 'This happened in the garden, it's merely an infected cut.'

'I suspected she'd done it.' Nellie was speaking to Dalton as though Elena was no longer even there. 'I'd been using the app but kept receiving an error message.'

'You didn't think to report the error to More You?' the brunette officer asked.

'I had a lot on my mind' – Nellie gave a theatrical sigh – 'with losing Stu and having to take care of my baby, it's been . . . it's been difficult.'

My baby.

Elena lurched forward, palms connecting with Nellie's chest, shoving her hard. It felt satisfying to see her stagger back, to see fear bloom across her face. But before Elena could lunge for her again her arms were being pinned behind her back, causing her to buckle to her knees. 'She's my baby!' she screamed at Nellie who had the audacity to cower from her, to raise her hands to protect her face. 'Olive is *my* fucking baby. You monster! You liar!'

'Please, keep her away from me.' Nellie scurried away, shielded by several officers as Elena fought against Dalton and the brunette who'd pinned her arms.

'This... this is ludicrous!' Elena cried, firing spittle into the air. 'I'm *me*. I'm *Elena*. This is...'

Chest aching she searched the crowd for Margot and Leanne.

'Tell them!' she screamed to them. 'Tell them it's me! We... we meet for coffee every other week. I was with you in the antenatal group... you helped me when I spilt orange juice all down my top during the first class. Margot... your... your nails were jet black that day. You *know* me.' But the faces looking back at her didn't seem to know her at all. Margot and Leanne turned away, glancing towards where Nellie was being comforted in a corner.

'You know me!' Elena cried, voice catching. 'You... you know me.'

'I hope you get to experience it one day.'

'Experience what?' Elena turned on the bed to look up at her mother. They were reading side by side in the haze of a late summer evening, the windows to her mother's bedroom thrown open, the sounds of crickets drifting in along with the scent of freshly cut grass. Intermittently, between turning the pages, her mother would stroke Elena's hair, which had grown long during her sixteenth summer, and release a contented sigh.

'Having a daughter,' her mother stated softly. 'There's really nothing like it. It's like all the best parts of me were taken out and bundled into something wonderful.'

'Stop.' Elena turned the page of her book, savouring the vampire romance she was reading. Once she was done with it, she'd pass the book on to her mother, as was their custom. Then, at the end of summer they'd watch the film adaptations together. A ritual they'd enacted ever since Elena discovered the books at twelve and became entranced by them. 'You're always extra nice because you're my mum and you have to be.'

'It's more than that.' Her mother tenderly stroked her head again. 'It's *knowing* someone. I know everything about you and you know everything about me. Throughout our life, people will come and go. But you and I . . . our bond, that stays for ever.'

'I'm close to finishing the book, you know.'

'I know.'

'You need to keep up.'

'I know.' Her mother was smiling. 'These summer days . . . every year I think I've had the best summer. And every year we manage to top it.'

'What will you do when I'm away at university? When I'm off seeing the world?'

Her mother shrugged and kept smiling. 'I'll still be here, still reading our books. Your job is to go off and live your life and I get to hear all about it when you come home.'

'Won't you miss me?'

'Of course I'll miss you, silly girl.' Her mother laughed, kissed the top of her head. 'But you deserve to see and do all that your heart desires.'

'Maybe I want to stay here.' Elena glanced up from her book. 'Maybe I want to spend all my summers doing this, reading the same stories over and over.'

'No, you don't.' Her mother ruefully shook her head. 'You want to see it all. And do it all. I know you, Elena.'

'Mmm.' Elena rolled onto her back and held the book above her, a gentle sunlight warming her legs.

'As much as you love reading stories, you want one of your own. And I love you so much for that.'

'You'd love me no matter what I wanted.'

'Of course,' her mother didn't hesitate to answer. 'I'd love you no matter what. But please, hush now, I've got some reading to do, someone pointed out that I'm lagging behind.'

Elena heard the peal of distant laughter, the grumble of a car engine. She turned the page in her book, contented.

*

'Load her into the van,' Dalton instructed, roughly hoisting Elena onto her feet.

'No!' she screamed, pushed against his grip. 'I'm . . . I'm me. Elena. *Me*. Check me, ask me anything.'

'The chip is the only test we have.' The brunette officer was speaking into her ear. 'And you plucked yours clean out.'

'No! I didn't!' Elena fought as they tried to jostle her towards the open doors of the van, the smooth, empty interior looking out at her. 'This . . .' She searched and found Nellie huddled behind some officers, face pinched and fearful. 'You're *lying*.' Elena called to her, tears slicing down her face. 'We *made* you in a goddamn clinic. Me and Stu. You know you're not real.'

'Enough of this.' Dalton was pushing her forward, ever closer to the van. Elena felt the eyes of the crowd upon her, judging.

Stu.

If only he was there, he'd run out and clear everything up. He'd take one look at Elena and *know* it was her.

No, he wouldn't.

Her head dipped to her chest as she recalled their final moments together. How he'd thought she was someone else. A stranger.

'Margot! Leanne! Please!' Elena shouted out to her friends. 'You know me! We . . . we met up *last week*. I told you what Nellie had done. *Please!*'

'Look.' Leanne pushed to the front of the crowd, addressing the brunette officer. 'This doesn't seem right. There has to be a clearer way to assess which one is the More You.'

'Like I said, the chip, but she's removed hers.'

'I didn't!'

'She says she didn't.' Leanne gave Elena a pitying look. 'And . . . and we did meet up last week. She's right. Isn't she?' She nudged Margot in the ribs. Margot who looked like she could have just glided off a catwalk in Paris.

'This . . . this not normal.' Margot pointed at Elena. 'She is *very* distressed.'

'I've seen it before,' Dalton grunted at her. 'They will say or do anything to protect themselves. Like rats when they're cornered.'

'That's why she's lying!' Elena blurted, tasting her own tears. 'That's why she's saying she's me! To save herself!' She felt emboldened by the uncertain gaze Margot and Leanne flicked in Nellie's direction. 'Don't . . . don't let them do this,' she implored her friends. 'Don't let them take me away from my baby.'

Leanne's face was flushed, eyes misting. 'I don't see . . . how is all this necessary?'

'Because a man was killed.' Dalton fired his response at her. 'Murdered in cold blood. Or does that not bother you?'

'It does, I just—'

'Please, please don't take me away from my baby,' Elena howled.

'We need to push the crowd back, we don't need a spectacle here,' Dalton told the brunette officer.

'Please!' Elena cried again. 'My baby!'

Margot and Leanne looked pained as they were edged back by a fleet of officers, pushed further down the street, blue lights pulsing across their anxious faces. Elena furiously blinked away tears to try to hold them in a steady gaze.

'Please . . .' she rasped. 'Please help me.'

She's lying. She's lying to you all. I'm the mother! I'm Olive's mother! She's mine! Fuck!

'Try to stay calm,' the brunette instructed.

'Just get her in the van,' Dalton snapped, roughly grabbing Elena's arms.

Elena looked towards the open doors, bucking against his grip. 'I'm real!' she cried. 'I'm fucking real!'

Olive had already lost her father, Elena wasn't about to let her lose her mother as well.

'Let . . . go . . . of . . . me.'

Over the sound of her struggle she heard Nellie talking with officers, selling them her story.

'This is how it's been . . . completely hysterical . . . saying she's me. It's madness. All of it.'

.56

Catherine held her granddaughter in her arms, searching her little scrunched-up face for glimpses of Stuey.

How she missed her son.

Him and Clive both.

When she'd found out she'd lost him, she hated how her heart betrayed her by continuing to beat. It wasn't natural, to lose a child. And for Catherine not one but two. It was almost more than she could bear.

'Hush, little one, Nana is here.' She gently rocked the bundle in her grasp, savouring the scent that babies carried – of milk and new beginnings. That's what Olive was. A new beginning. A chance to set things right.

As Catherine held the baby she kept looking to the front door, a tightness in her chest. Both Dalton and Christopher had warned her that removing the More You unit was going to be ugly.

'They lash out,' Dalton informed her clinically. 'The desire to live, to breathe. It's in all of us, even them.'

Christopher had been more nervous. 'As a newer model, there's no telling how stressed she may become. How erratic. We'll need to handle the situation swiftly. Return her to More You with as little fuss as possible.'

Catherine wondered how events were unfolding back at her son's house. Was the accused allowing herself to be quietly led away, or was she fighting? Catherine's grip against Olive grew tighter, causing the baby to squirm. She understood that desire to do *anything*. When Clive died she'd felt so helpless, so worthless. But she kept going. For Stuey. He became her entire world. Her purpose.

How many hours had she floated through her grand home with only a cat for company since Stuey got married? How many hours had she stared at her phone, wishing her single living son would reach out with a call. Hell, even a text. Catherine knew there was something profoundly painful about losing your worth. Being forgotten. Obsolete. But losing Stuey sharpened it all.

'Hush, now, Nana is here,' Catherine cooed to Olive. 'Everything is going to be all right.'

Holding the baby, Catherine felt alive again. She'd applied make-up, styled her hair, put on one of her nicer dresses. Felix twisted through her legs, brushing against her, as each prolonged minute ticked by. Catherine kept staring at her front door, fearing the intensity of her gaze might bore a hole in it. They'd told her he would arrive within the hour. Soon he would be there. Her heart sped up in anticipation.

.57

'Just get her in the van.' The brunette's voice again, tight with annoyance. 'We don't need to create a scene here. Let's go.'

'No.' Elena twisted as Dalton's fingers dug deeper against her flesh. 'Let . . . me . . . go.'

Fresh hands, on her shoulders, her back. Pinning her. Pushing her. Officers surrounded her, edging her ever closer to the van.

'This is the one, the More You,' Dalton panted to the others as he kept shoving Elena. 'See what it's done to the ankle.'

'No!' Elena could barely see through her tears. 'I cut it. An accident! In the . . . in the garden.' She tried to turn to look back at Nellie but she couldn't, there were too many strong arms holding her in place. 'You're wrong!' she screamed against them. 'You're wrong, I'm me!'

I'm real. I'm fucking real. I need to get to Olive.

Her knees buckled and she was carried forward by the momentum of the officers around her, the van now just inches away.

I'm real.

Her tears burned as they slid down her face, which was twisted with despair.

I'm me.

I'm Elena.

So many memories, moments. She held them all in her mind.

Reading beside her mother in the sunlight.

Crying over a boy at the train station.

Meeting Stu at university.

Holding Olive for the first time.

A life. Elena had lived it. It was *hers*.

She cried out as her shin connected with the back of the van. Then she was being pushed down, back bent, body hoisted upwards.

'You're wrong!' Elena kept yelling until her voice grew weak. Her hands were thrust into her lap and bound with plastic ties.

'You need to sit still and shut up,' Dalton snapped at her. 'They'll deal with you back at More You.'

Two officers slid onto the hard metal benches around her, flanking her. Dalton retreated and the doors were slammed shut, Elena felt the vibration deep in her bones.

'There was a case like this just last week,' one of the officers was saying to another as distantly the front door opened, an engine started.

'Happening more and more,' the other agreed.

'Please,' Elena rasped, woefully raising her head to look between them. 'You have to believe me, I'm real. I'm . . . I'm the original.'

A rough laugh from the slimmer officer. 'Yeah,' he remarked, 'that's what they all say.'

.58

Catherine Roberts was in her kitchen when the call came through from Dalton, Olive bundled in her arms, finally asleep.

'It's done,' he told her, tone sombre. 'We made the arrest.'

She released a long, slow breath, felt some of the tension she'd been carrying since her son's death leave her body.

It's done.

This was what Catherine had been campaigning for. Striving for. Justice. The moment the police appeared to turn cold on Stuey's case she'd made the call to Dalton.

'She killed my boy,' she told him, an icy certainty tight against her heart. 'I need you to prove it.'

She was walking laps around her kitchen island. Whenever she paused to idle over her thoughts, Olive would stir, threaten to wake. And so Catherine kept moving although her arms had long since started to go numb.

She should be here by now.

Catherine hoped it hadn't all been so very sordid, the arrest. That there had been nothing too *distasteful* about it all. The last thing she wanted was to later turn on the news and see her daughter-in-law's stricken face splashed all over it. Catherine kept moving, kept clutching the babe in her arms. Things needed to be kept quiet. More You had been quite clear about that.

'It's not my fault,' she said aloud, to herself more than to her granddaughter, 'none of it. I was only trying to help with the More You. Trying to . . . trying to look out for Stuey.' Catherine glanced down at Olive and for a moment there he was: her son. In the curve of her lips, the soft button of her nose. Coughing back a sob, Catherine straightened when she heard the doorbell chime.

Finally.

She scurried through the house as fast as she dared move while holding a young baby. A part of her was excited to see her daughter-in-law, to hear about all the unfolding events from a direct source.

Although a part of her thought of the unit, wherever she had gone to. What would become of her.

A sigh fell from her glossy ruby lips.

But what was there to do? She had to go. And then Dalton had charged a pretty penny for his services.

It was the right thing to do. The price to pay.

Her nails, long like talons, tightened around Olive. Over and over More You lamented that the new unit must be contained. Words like *unstable* were batted about. Catherine closed her eyes wearily, so very, very tired of waiting.

'I'm so glad I have you.' She drew the little baby up towards her, kissed her forehead, breathing in the sour tang of milk. 'For you, little one, I would do anything.' Olive's eyes slowly opened. 'And what a beauty you are.'

The doorbell rang again.

Catherine pulled open the front door, flashing a smile at her precious granddaughter who now wore a stain of lipstick above her barely there eyebrows. Branded.

'Elena.' Catherine stood aside to let the younger woman in. She had to admit that she appeared smarter than she had when she left. Tidier. Her blonde hair was sharply pulled back in a neat bun and she wore dark jeans and a flattering lime jumper. 'I heard from Dalton. How are you? It all sounds dreadfully stressful. Did she resist?'

The younger woman smiled placidly at her and held out her arms.

'Oh, of course.' Catherine passed her the baby, grateful to be relieved of the physical burden though she felt a pinch in her heart. 'She's been such a good girl.'

'Thank you so much for taking care of her,' Elena said softly, drawing Olive against her chest and gazing down at her, face glowing with adoration.

'How did it all go?' Catherine pressed. She wanted all the sordid details. To know if her son's killer had wept as she was hauled away.

'It was . . .' Elena gave a sad shake of her head. Beneath the bright light of the chandelier in Catherine's hallway she looked radiant, skin flawless and flushed. The removal of Nellie seemed to have rejuvenated her somehow. Catherine took this as further proof that she had done the right thing in soliciting Dalton's assistance. 'It was a lot,' Elena concluded, a look of sadness on her pretty features.

'Yes, yes, of course.' Catherine began leading them towards the lounge, hoping Elena wouldn't be in a great hurry to leave, that she might stay a while. Keep Olive close. At least for a bit.

'I so appreciate all your help in everything, Mum.' Elena drew up close and kissed Catherine on the cheek. 'Really, I couldn't have done it without you.' Then she glided past, elegant and refined, moving towards the sofa and neatly folding herself onto it. Olive had begun to fuss and so Elena was sliding one arm out of her jumper, preparing to nurse her. Catherine watched, mesmerised.

Mum.

In all her years as Stuey's wife, Elena had never once called her that before. There had always been a distance between them. A canyon neither woman was prepared to cross. But now...

Catherine's heart fluttered hopefully. She felt buoyant. Almost joyful.

So it was done. The switch had been made. Everything she'd hoped for ever since she first mentioned More You to Stuey, remarked on how it might improve things. For all of them.

Mum.

Catherine studied the woman feeding Olive and felt her smile widen.

Could it really be—

'Come sit with me,' she suddenly called, voice bright and welcoming. 'Let me tell you all about what happened.'

'Oh, oh yes.' Catherine was nodding and making her way to the sofa. 'Please, yes, I want to hear everything.'

'Of course.' Her daughter-in-law was smiling so warmly at her, eyes glowing. Catherine had never seen her look that way before. Not at her. 'I'm just so thankful to be back with her.' She stroked Olive's cheek as she fed. 'Back with my daughter. My Olive.'

'I'm sure you must have missed her terribly. You understand, don't you, how a mother would do anything for their child?'

She gave a gentle nod.

'Then, dear girl' – Catherine reached out and gave her guest's knee a squeeze – 'I hope you'll understand what I'm about to show you.'

When Catherine stood up she felt giddy. Dizzy. Like a child on Christmas morning.

.59

'Do you remember, when you visited the More You offices?' Catherine's eyes glowed as she spoke. 'I'm not sure how it happened, but when you were scanned, Stuey was too. Which was most fortunate.'

Turning, Catherine left the room with a flourish, disappearing towards the kitchen. When she returned she was not alone.

Proudly, Catherine guided Stuey into the room.

'Stuey, sweetheart, meet your wife, Elena. And your baby, Olive.'

She watched Elena's eyes widen with shock, Olive tight against her breast as she fed.

'H-hi.' Stuey waved a nervous hand at them.

'Go, go.' Catherine nudged him forwards, towards his family. Then, quickly, she glanced at the window, hurried towards it and closed the curtains. Not that anyone could see in, she lived in a grand, remote home. But still, you couldn't be too careful. Especially not in these early days.

'Are you sure you want this?' Christopher had fretted during their hologram call. 'This . . . it's unheard of, Catherine.'

'I know you can make it happen.'

'Catherine . . . he died.' There was pity in his voice.

'And you have the power to bring him back.' Her tone was as firm as her gaze.

Christopher sighed, sipped his cocktail nervously. 'I regret telling you he got scanned.'

'I regret losing him. So let's fix that.'

'Catherine—'

'Either bring me a More You of my son or I'll tell the world how one of our newer units killed him. You pick.'

'If you do this . . . there's no going back. No normal life. He will have to live in hiding, with you. People can't know about him.'

'I'll keep him safe.'

'This isn't right, Catherine. It's not . . . not natural.'

'None of this has ever been right or natural,' Catherine snapped at him. 'But I want my son returned to me. Can you do it or not?'

Christopher looked pained as he nodded. 'I mean . . . yeah, I can do it.'

'Has it been done before?'

He threw her a barbed glare.

'Your silence, Catherine. For the boy. That's the deal.'

'That's the deal.'

'No one can ever know that it was a newer unit malfunctioning.'

'And no one ever will,' Catherine assured him.

Curtains closed, Catherine clicked on a lamp and rushed back to her son, placing a hand protectively on his back as he edged closer to Elena and Olive. She'd wept when he'd arrived earlier that day. As the More You was being taken away, Stuey was being returned to her. How unsure he had looked, how lost.

But it was him.

Her son.

In time, he would return to being the Stuey she had known and loved. His memories would come back to him. She would show him old pictures, videos, let him discover who he had been. Who he was meant to be. The whole incident with having two Elenas would just be an unpleasant bump in the road. Her son was home.

Catherine pressed a hand to her chest, which felt like it was expanding at an alarming rate. Her heart was so full.

Stuey, her Stuey, he was home. And now he could never leave. He would always be hers.

.60

As the van bounced along Elena didn't dare think about where she was going. The officers beside her eyed her with open contempt. She had no voice left to defend who she was. *What* she was.

'I hear it's happening more and more,' the slimmer one noted, 'units believing they are real.'

I am real.

Elena's head throbbed with the certainty of it all.

Suddenly the van halted, thrusting her forwards.

'Hey, Mick, what the hell?' the officer beside her craned forward to yell towards the front cabin.

'There's someone in the road,' a voice yelled back to them, 'a group. They're armed.'

'Gear up,' the tallest officer snapped. She pressed a button on her helmet and the visor slid down. The other officer cocked his gun, muscles tensing.

'Let's go, Mick,' they yelled. 'Run through them.'

Beneath the frigid pressure of the bench Elena felt the van's engine rumble, build. Then they were surging forwards.

'Fucking protestors,' the tall officer complained. 'They must have gotten wind that we'd done a pickup. Happened to me last month, just before—'

She didn't get to finish her sentence. The van listed sharply to the side. Elena was thrown from her bench. And then she smacked against the side of the van, tasting copper.

'Shit!' The officers were scrambling to get up. 'Mick, what happened? Mick?'

From the front of the van there came no response.

Beyond the metal walls Elena could hear voices, raised and angry. Then the scrape of something cutting close by.

The back doors suddenly opened, golden sunlight pouring in. Elena and the officers squinted against it. Hands, so many hands, grabbing for her.

Gunshots. Sharp. Quick.

The hands fell away.

'Jesus Christ!' one of the officers cried, Elena didn't know who. Hands bound, she shuffled towards the light. Her knees connected with hard ground, breath harried. Behind her she could hear more voices. Struggling to her feet, Elena felt the whisper of something brush by her ear.

A bullet?

She swallowed, unable to focus on the sensation. In her peripheral vision she saw people running towards the overturned van, being met with gunfire, but not before getting in some shots of their own. They'd crashed in a cornfield, the high stalks just up ahead. Elena tucked her head to her chest, ran towards the corn with all she had.

'She's getting away!' a distant voice cried.

Stems and husks slapped her in the face as she moved but Elena didn't stop. She just kept running. This wasn't how she'd pictured it. Any of it.

.61

The nights came in quickly, the days growing short. Catherine knew she had to be extra vigilant. Exhaustion tugged on the edge of her existence. Every chime of the doorbell, every chirp of her phone, she feared her Stuey was about to be taken away from her.

But thus far, their bliss had been undisturbed. Within her grand home they all lived together, joyful day after joyful day. Olive was beginning to sit up, using pudgy little hands to shove pieces of banana into her mouth.

And Stuey. Oh, her Stuey.

He was different, yes. That light within him, the one that warmed everyone he met. It wasn't there yet. But it would be. In time. She understood it was harder for him, without the original to mimic. To watch.

Catherine hugged her son frequently, inhaling his scent, clinging to the realness of him. His breath, his muscles. He was *there*.

He and Elena cooed over their baby, took turns changing nappies, laughing over the impressive stench. They did not need to leave to go to work. To pursue a life beyond Catherine's home. They had everything they needed. It was perfect.

Autumn was about to twist into winter. Catherine was already envisioning where she would place the Christmas tree. What she would buy for her beloved family. Her mind was occupied with thoughts of twinkling lights and bulging stockings as she sipped her tea in the lounge, the only sign of all the previous chaos a stain at her feet which she now couldn't risk having outside cleaners come in and fix. A small price to pay for what she had, but a price, none the less.

'I was just thinking, Stuey.' She turned to her son, who was beside her, his little daughter in his lap as he gently bounced her and she giggled. 'With this being Olive's first Christmas, we should do something special.'

'Sure.' He beamed at her, eyes wide and expectant. 'We want to make it extra special, don't we?'

He delivered the question to his wife, who had drifted away from the sofas, from the warmth of the fire, over to the front window, where she now stood, curtains slightly parted as she peered out into the dwindling day.

'Elena!' Catherine stood so quickly her cup and saucer tumbled from her grip, falling to the carpet. 'Get away from there!' But Catherine didn't notice as the original stain deepened, so focused was she on crossing the room, grabbing her daughter-in-law's wrist and tugging her away from the window, her paranoia rampant. 'I've told you to *never* look out the windows. To *never* risk being seen.'

Elena flashed her a hard look that made Catherine's stomach clench. It was a look she'd previously been accustomed to receiving. But then it was gone and Elena was smiling apologetically at her. 'I'm sorry, Mum. I just wanted to catch some of the sunset.'

'You need to be careful.' Catherine embraced the young woman, breathed her in. 'We have our perfect little world here, we must protect it.'

'Of course.'

Elena padded over to the sofa, to her husband and daughter, leaving Catherine by the window. Perhaps it was paranoia that made Catherine part the curtain and peer out. It was already dark out, her driveway filled with long, deep shadows. But something moved. Catherine frowned, doubting her senses. A figure upon the driveway. A face. Pale and ghostly.

Catherine gasped as a hand clasped her shoulder.

'Mum, are you all right?'

She was still staring towards her driveway as the same face was now reflected in the glass. Slowly, feeling unstable, she turned to look at Elena. 'Are you . . .' Her mouth fluttered open, lips trembling. 'Did you . . .'

'Come on, we're about to start watching that film you were telling us about.' Elena's grip on her elbow was strong as she guided Catherine away from the window, back towards the sofa. 'Come sit with us.'

'Was she out there?' Catherine demanded shrilly, looking between her son and his wife. They both looked at her as though she were mad.

'Who?' Elena asked innocently.

'You know who!'

'That's impossible.' Elena gave a quick shake of her head, a condescending smile. 'You saw to that, remember?'

They'd taken her away. Catherine knew that much. But after that . . . she had no idea. Since Stuey had arrived, all ties with More You had been severed. She was completely cut out. Completely isolated from the outside world.

'Yes, yes of course.' Catherine's voice was shaky as she sat down.

'Why don't we send Stu out to check the driveway, if you're concerned?' There was a challenge in Elena's tone that Catherine didn't appreciate.

'No, no, it's fine. Stuey has to stay inside.'

'Of course.' Elena fondly leaned towards Stuey and kissed his cheek. Then, to her cherub-faced daughter, 'Who's my beautiful girl? Who?'

Catherine wanted to go back to the window but didn't dare.

'You're probably just seeing things,' Elena remarked quietly to her as the film began to play. 'Don't worry about it.'

But it was *how* she said it.

So like her.

.62

It felt like she was forever in darkness. Moving through shadows, at night, to cross rivers, roads. Each mile was etched into the cuts on her hands, her face. The matting of her hair. But still she walked, moved, low and quick, like an animal. Instinct guiding her. When she slept it was fitful. Days twisted together into an indiscernible knot. Still she moved.

How she ached.

How her bones throbbed.

How her feet burned.

But everything paled against the pain in her chest. With every beat of her tormented heart she thought of her.

Olive.

It was the thought of her that pulled her through her worst days. Her most arduous nights.

And now she was here. At the iron gates. Breathless. Waiting. Nothing stirred. No cars in. No cars out. Were they even in there?

They had to be.

Dirt thick under her fingernails, she scaled the wall, aware of the single camera that had been faulty for months. The blind spot.

As she hopped down onto the driveway twigs crunched underfoot and she held her breath until her chest burned.

No one could find her.

Not yet.

.63

The morning was dark, the garden a den of shadows within which Elena waited. She had seen the upstairs light click on, imagined movement inside the grand house. Had Olive woken, crying? How quickly had Nellie gone to her, soothed her? Elena pushed down her anger, let it gather as a weight in the pit of her stomach. It would serve her no good now. She needed to focus.

As the back door creaked open she rose up slowly, still held within the darkness, studying the figure that stepped out, nappy bag in hand, and made the short journey to the bin.

Elena drew in a breath and held it as she watched Nellie. How the More You moved quickly, with brisk, nervous steps. There was no time to waste.

Nellie was almost at the door when Elena pounced like a cat, grabbing at her shoulders to push her back against the wall, one hand firmly clasping against the More You's mouth. Silencing her.

'You saw me,' Elena hissed, drawing close, the tip of her nose almost touching Nellie's. 'Out on the drive, last night, you saw me, I know you did.'

She didn't want to look at this mirror of herself. Nellie in her soft pyjamas and fluffy pink slippers, shivering against the cold. Elena knew how she must appear; ragged and worn. It had been weeks since she had slept in a bed, showered. Eaten properly. She felt feral, alert. But more than anything she felt determined.

Pushing her hand tighter against Nellie's mouth she felt the other woman trying to scream.

'Shh,' Elena ordered. 'If you were going to tell on me you'd have done it already.'

She looked into Nellie's eyes, wide with fear. 'I know you saw me,' Elena said, keeping her voice low. 'I waited for the place to light up with police but it never did. Because you never told. Because you *are* me. And I'm' – she fought against the tight lump of emotion gathering in her throat – 'I'm a *good* person. Did you know they'd kill me, when they took me away?'

A look of sadness in Nellie's gaze.

'You did know.' Elena eased her grip, just slightly. 'But you didn't want it to be you. You just knew one of us had to be taken away.' With a grunt Elena fully dropped her hand, breathing quickly, watching Nellie, braced for the scream that never came. 'I don't care if you think you're me. I don't. I care about Olive.'

'As do I.' Nellie matched her tone, whispering against the brittle morning air.

'You must understand what Catherine did, how she tried to get rid of me. Tried to have me killed. She knew I'd hurt my ankle, set me up to be taken away. Maybe she truly believes I hurt Stu, but . . .' Elena anxiously scanned Nellie's face, still fearing a moment of betrayal. How easy it would be for the More You to scream, for Elena to be forced back into the shadows, reduced to living like a hunted animal yet again. 'Catherine is dangerous, I know you can see that. Stu . . . was an accident. He . . .' Elena lost her words to emotion.

'He's here.' Nellie threw a glance over her shoulder, towards the utility room and the house beyond it.

Elena frowned.

'She remade Stu.'

Stu.

For a moment Elena teetered on the edge of something; shock, remorse. Fear. She didn't know. But then she shuddered, resumed her plan with cool clarity. She had planned for this. All those long miles she'd walked, all those nights she'd skulked in shadows, afraid of being caught, she had planned. How she would get back to Olive. What she would do when she saw Catherine. And it all hinged on Nellie truly being like her.

She couldn't think about Stu. Not now. She needed to think about Catherine.

'I need your help,' she told her More You. Nellie looked at her expectantly. 'We need to make her pay.'

.64

'Catherine! I can't get the coffee maker to work!' Nellie called loudly from the centre of the kitchen. Then she glanced at the open door from behind which Elena peered out at her. 'Don't worry, Stu won't come,' she explained quietly. 'She lets him sleep in every morning in his old bedroom.'

Elena gave a roll of her tired eyes.

Of course she does.

She tried not to think of the routine of this new Stu. Back in his childhood home, with no original to mimic. A man caught in his mother's web.

'Catherine!' Nellie bellowed again.

Elena heard footsteps approaching through the hall, pressed herself back behind the door, holding her breath.

'I'm here, stop shouting!' The old woman arrived in a swish of satin, her dressing gown long and ornate. 'You'll wake Stuey!'

Elena moved with the powerful precision of someone hungry. Someone on the edge. She sprang out from behind the door and was upon Catherine before either one of them had the chance to breathe. She hooked an arm around Catherine's neck, clamped a hand against the old woman's mouth.

'I was always good enough,' she whispered hotly into Catherine's ear as she held her tight. Elena felt each mile of her arduous scramble back to her daughter in her muscles; how it tightened her, fused her resolve with steel.

'We need to be quick,' Nellie said as she hurried towards a door, thrusting it open.

'Move,' Elena ordered her mother-in-law, whose muffled protests died against her palm. She could feel the heat of Catherine's breath, the hummingbird flutter of her panicked heart. She ignored both, edging towards the doorway, to the stone steps it exposed which led downwards.

'Let me help.' Nellie offered, grabbing a tea towel.

'If you scream, we'll kill you.' Elena warned as she lowered her hand for just a moment. Nellie quickly thrust the towel between Catherine's teeth; Elena pinned it behind the woman's head.

Their descent was awkward and laboured. With each echoing footstep Elena paused, braced for Stu to appear from the kitchen, demanding to know what was going on. But they remained alone. Eventually she reached the flagstone floor. Nellie was dragging a chair into the centre of the room, its back a bunch of ornate spindles. It had probably been used for tasting sessions, conducted by Eric, where he would uncork a bottle and toast himself. Elena unceremoniously dumped Catherine in the chair, watched as her More You bound the old woman's hands behind the chair, using some tape they'd found by the back door. Later they'd need to figure out a more permanent solution but for now, this was enough.

Elena was silent. She didn't know if she wanted to scream, to cry, or just pass out. She took a moment to let her breathing even out, looked down at Catherine's mottled face, the fear and disgust in her gaze.

'I never came down here much.' She glanced about at the wooden racks pressed against stone walls like some man-made hive. Bottles of wine winked out at her. 'I seem to remember you didn't either. This was Eric's domain wasn't it?'

Catherine screamed into the tea towel she was being forced to taste. Elena imagined the stream of vitriol that would fly from her thin lips if she removed the piece of cloth.

'No one will come.' Nellie was standing across from Catherine but looking at Elena. The old woman bound between them. 'No one ever does.'

'How convenient for us.' Elena wiped sweat from her brow.

'Us?' Nellie looked over Catherine's head, at Elena.

'Us.' Elena repeated. 'I'm not about to turn you in. Where would that leave me? I'm a fugitive, remember?'

She could feel Catherine looking between them, taking them both in.

'What do we tell Stu?' Nellie nodded in the direction of the stairs that led up to the kitchen.

'The truth.' Elena offered. 'He's still a fresh model, right? No memories to bind him to her. At least, not yet. We can tell him all of it. Poison him against her.'

Catherine blinked away tears and Elena refused to feel an ounce of pity for the woman. She ground her teeth together, remembering how it felt to be yanked into that van, hauled away from her life. Her daughter.

'If she had her way I'd be gone. Destroyed at the fucking More You facility. I'm pretty sure that's been her intention all along.'

Catherine was silent, cheeks damp.

'So what now?' Nellie asked.

'I want to see my daughter.' Just thinking of her baby filled her aching body with warmth.

Olive. It had been for Olive. All of it.

'She's upstairs, sleeping. Go be with her. I'll sort things in here.'

Weary, Elena looked at her. This reflection of herself. Nellie smiled.

'Go be with her.'

Epilogue

Night and day lost all meaning. For Catherine there was just the wine cellar. Twice a day the door opened and food was brought down. They'd left her a bucket as a toilet. It was beyond awful, it was monstrous. Inhumane. She had no idea how many days had passed. She clung to the fragile hope that Stuey would soon come to his senses and rescue her, dash down the stairs, ever the hero, and remove the ropes that cut into her wrists. For hours they left her bound to the woeful chair and then they watched as she ate. As she defecated.

Catherine didn't dare consider how wretched she must look. This was all too awful to bear. This was her home. And here she was . . . a prisoner within it. Eating meagre meals beneath the glare of a bare light bulb while above her Elena played house. Cared for Olive. For Stuey. Just thinking about it made everything within her curdle and sour.

But she clung on. For Stuey. Her darling Stuey. For him she could endure this. She must. A mother's love, it was stronger than even the darkest of days. Catherine could do this. She could.

And all the while they slipped in and out; she could no longer tell them apart.

Elena and Nellie. Two sides of one hideous coin.

How foolish she had been to sever contact with the board. With the outside world. But someone would surely come. They had to.

And Stuey, her Stuey. He would save her.

Was he up there now, dealing with two wives? Getting to know his daughter? Was his second chance at life worth this sacrifice?

As Catherine stared at the walls, counting the cracks in the stone – because what else was she supposed to bloody do while living through this hell? – she considered that, yes, for her son she would give away anything. Everything. Even her freedom. Her life. That was the price you paid for being a mother.

Above her she heard the house creak and moan as they moved about.

Not one Elena, but two. Her greatest nightmare realised. This wasn't how she'd pictured it. Any of it.

Be You . . . but More!

At More You we promise more than just an organic clone of yourself. We promise you a better life!

Tired? Overworked? Wrung out?

Find out why thousands have already signed up for the More You programme. Our units are just as unique as you are – they come fully functional and ready to integrate into your life.

They say two hands are better than one; here at More You, we believe that two of you are better than one! Why not come by today for a consultation? See for yourself our outstanding work and bring this flyer for an introductory offer of 10 per cent off a base model.

Discover just how great you can be at More You.

Acknowledgements

I have so many wonderful people to thank for their help in the journey to making this book a reality.

Liza DeBlock, thank you for all your support and kindness.

Katie Ellis-Brown, I loved having you as my editor and wish you so much success on your own author journey.

Kate Fogg, it was such a pleasure to work together; thank you for shaping the story in its final stages.

Sania Riaz, thank you for always being so passionate; it's been wonderful to have you back!

To the wider team at Harvill – it has been amazing to work with you all again.

My writer friends: Sandra, Amy, Tess and Jenny. Thank you for always listening, for being there. I'd be lost without you!

My family, the people who are stuck with me. Mum, Dad, Sam. I owe you all so much.

Rose. You made me a mum. I do it all for you. Being a parent has left me strung out, exhausted, worn down. But it is always completely worth it.

Rollo, I still miss you every single day. I know I always will.

Pipkin, you're my handsome little man but if you could stop weeing up the curtains and chewing my laptop I'd be ever so grateful!

To all the other parents out there – well done on surviving, because it is tough. Some days I truly think I'd be tempted to clone myself if I could!

Credits

Vintage would like to thank everyone who worked on the publication of *The Other You*

Agent
Liza DeBlock

Editor
Kate Fogg

Editorial
Sania Riaz
Liz Foley

Copy-editor
Sam Matthews

Proofreader
Saxon Bullock

Managing Editorial
Graeme Hall

Contracts
Emma D'Cruz
Gemma Avery
Ceri Cooper
Rebecca Smith
Anne Porter
Rita Omoro

Humayra Ahmed
Kiran Halaith
Hayley Morgan

Design
Dan Mogford

Digital
Anna Baggaley
Claire Dolan
Brydie Scott
Charlotte Ridsdale
Zaheerah Khalik

Inventory
Rebecca Evans

Publicity
Mia Quibell-Smith
Amrit Bhullar

Finance
Ed Grande
Aya Daghem
Joe Thomas

Marketing
Sam Rees-Williams
Preetnoor Nagi

Production
Konrad Kirkham
Polly Dorner

Sales
Nathaniel Breakwell
Malissa Mistry
Nick Cordingly
Sarah Griffin
Ben Tapson
Elspeth Dougall
Amber Blundell
Amanda Dean
Andy Taylor
David Atkinson
David Devaney
Rachel Cram
Dan Higgins
Lewis Cain
Phoebe Edwards
Sophie Dwyer
Justin Ward-Turner

Caroline Newbury
Reanna Issacs

Rights
Catherine Wood
Lucie Deacon

Lucy Beresford-Knox
Beth Wood
Maddie Stephenson
Agnes Watters
Sophie Brownlow
Amy Moss

Olivia Diomedes
Jake Dickson

Audio
Nile Faure-Bryan

About the author

Carys Green is a thriller writer based in Shropshire, where she lives with her husband and daughter. When she's not writing she can often be found indulging two of her greatest passions – either walking round the local woodland or catching up on all things Disney related.